We were q... ... platform was one of th... ...llation of bridges and de... ...ace. Only a latticework of steel bones separated us from the sky.

The creature hung from the central pillar of the platform, just beneath the braided iron of the suspension cable. It looked like a cross between a crab and a spider, with angular plates covering its black body, and six spindly legs that clutched the cable. Dozens of spherical eyes roamed over the creature's back, seemingly unattached to the kymera's shiny exoskeleton. The kymera scuttled around the pillar, raising a knife-thin appendage in our direction, as though it were testing the air between us.

As it moved, the monster dragged a thick bundle of glistening tubes with it over the platform. From the end of each tube crawled an engorged sac. Dark shapes hung inside the sacs. And there, pressed against the thin membrane of the largest sac, was the missing girl. Her wide amber eyes stared sightlessly through the cloudy liquid that surrounded her. Dark veins sprouted from her head and back, feeding into the cable, pulsing silently.

"Broodmother," I spat. Unchecked, a broodmother could terrorize the countryside for years. "Vel, try to get to the other side of it. If we can cut those cords, we might be able to give the mayor his daughter back."

"More interested in keeping my neck intact," he muttered, but shifted carefully around the platform. The humming length of his godsteel blade flickered to life as he moved.

—from "A Murder of Knights"
by Tim Akers

BAEN BOOKS
edited by
CHRISTOPHER RUOCCHIO

Sword & Planet

WITH TONY DANIEL
Star Destroyers
World Breakers

WITH HANK DAVIS
Space Pioneers
Overruled!
Cosmic Corsairs
Time Troopers

WITH SEAN CW KORSGAARD
Worlds Long Lost (forthcoming)

SWORD & PLANET

+++

edited by
CHRISTOPHER RUOCCHIO

A Baen Books Original

Baen Publishing Enterprises
P.O. Box 1403
Riverdale, NY 10471
www.baen.com

ISBN: 978-1-9821-9214-3

Cover art by Kieran Yanner

First printing, December 2021
First mass market printing, September 2022

Distributed by Simon & Schuster
1230 Avenue of the Americas
New York, NY 10020

Library of Congress Control Number: 2021042478

Printed in the United States of America

10 9 8 7 6 5 4 3 2 1

CONTENTS

INTRODUCTION Christopher Ruocchio 3

A MURDER OF KNIGHTS Tim Akers 5

OPERATRIX TRIUMPHANS
Susan R. Matthews 35

POWER & PRESTIGE D.J. Butler 63

A BROKEN SWORD HELD HIGH
L.J. Hachmeister 87

THE FRUITS OF REPUTATION
Jody Lynn Nye 121

**A FUNNY THING HAPPENED ON THE
WAY TO NAKH-MARU** Jessica Cluess 147

SAVING THE EMPEROR Simon R. Green 179

A KNIGHT LUMINARY R.R. Virdi 203

**CHRONICLER OF
THE TITAN'S HEART** Anthony Martezi 235

BLEEDING FROM COLD SLEEP
Peter Fehervari 293

THE TEST T.C. McCarthy 325

QUEEN AMID ASHES Christopher Ruocchio 341

ABOUT THE AUTHORS 467

SWORD & PLANET

✠✠✠

INTRODUCTION

I'm going to make a pretty controversial statement for any writer or editor of science fiction to make: I'm not really interested in the science part. Don't get me wrong, I'm not allergic to technobabble, and the latest takes on quantum mechanics or marvels of aerospace engineering certainly enhance stories, especially when wielded by an author who knows his or her stuff to new and interesting effect, but the *fiction* part has always meant more to me. I don't care that hyperspace or psychokinesis might be scientifically impossible, nor do I care that Mars is—in reality—a barren (if possibly not completely lifeless) desert.

I just want to go on an adventure, even if it's to some pretty difficult places.

You and I might fractionate science fiction into all manner of subgenres and categories, but one such division lies between the camp that believes SF stories must be science-first (and even educational) and those who see science fiction as only another kind of fantasy. This first group comprises the descendants of Gernsback, of Campbell, and even of Verne. These are the people who seek legitimacy for our field in the hallowed halls of

3

universities, citing science fiction's power to explore not just the hard sciences of physics and engineering, but biology, medicine, even the softer sciences of anthropology, psychology, and sociology. (That the champions of these softer sciences deride the harder, technical science fiction while being essentially cut from the same cloth is an irony lost on them, but that is a topic for another time.)

The second group, those believers in science fiction as fantasy, count for their ancestors such writers as Edgar Rice Burroughs, Leigh Brackett, and Jack Vance, and while those in the first camp might dismiss such stories as "mere entertainments" or scoff about the lack of literary merit or scientific theory on their pages, nevertheless, I'm sure such fantastic stories have inspired untold thousands to pursue careers in the sciences, just as sure as any of the more technical stories have. Because stories don't have to be scientifically rigorous to be inspiring. They only have to be good.

Here then are stories from that second camp, stories that put the fantasy back in science fantasy, stories that honor (or lampoon) the legacy of John Carter and Dejah Thoris, of Eric John Stark, Paul Atreides, and Cugel the Clever. Some of these stories verge on space opera, for which reason I include Paul Atreides in my list, but all share in common the basic building blocks of that most venerable and overlooked subgenre of our tradition: sword & planet.

I hope you will enjoy them.

—Christopher Ruocchio, AD 2021

A MURDER OF KNIGHTS
Tim Akers

Slay the monster, save the girl—it's nearly the oldest story there is. Even at the end of history, when the sun's gone dark and the technology we created has become like gods to us, it's a story that rings true. Because even at the end of history, there are still monsters, and still knights whose sacred duty it is to slay them . . .

The dead hulk of the sun crawled across the starlit sky. I followed its path up from the horizon, eclipsing the dim lights of the eastern constellations, spreading like spilled ink. It would have been easier to wait until night, when the four moons gave some illumination, but our task was suited to darkness. When the sun's black disk cleared the horizon, I rose from my crouch and awoke my companion. Vel's wide amber eyes blinked up at me.

"Get the horses," I said. "It's time to go."

"They'll still be sleeping," he complained.

"Good men don't work during the day. If they're awake, we will know the oracle's words were true." I shrugged into my raven-feather cloak and hitched the black leather scabbard onto my belt. The sword was nearly weightless. "And if they are asleep, we will simply have faith, and do the duty we have been given."

"And what if some of them are asleep, and some of them are awake, eh?" Vel asked as he rose from the nest of blankets he had made beneath the bushes. His crooked form limped over to where the horses were tethered. "What do we do then?"

"Stop being an idiot," I answered. I watched as he unhooked the horses and throttled their souls awake. The beasts growled to life, the soot-stained vents of their lungs glowing red with fire. I didn't like the way Vel was moving. He was turning. One of the spirits in his flesh had bent inward, and was changing him. It wouldn't be long before my duty would turn to him. "Where is your cloak?" I asked.

"Patience, child," Vel said. "I had it watching over us while we slept." He snatched his cloak from a nearby tree and slung it over his shoulders. The feathers settled smoothly against the metal of his armor, steel plates fashioned to look like wings. His face was long and smooth, his head bald, though wrinkles lined the aperture of his eyes. He smiled at me. "Awake or asleep, they will be waiting for us. The oracle has spoken."

"The oracle has spoken," I repeated, then swung up on my saddle. It took longer for the old man to mount, but once Vel was settled, we departed camp and turned our steeds south. The little spirit in my head, placed there by our domaen at the start of this mission, sang its song of direction and distance. I pushed it to the back of my skull and tried to relax.

The stars flickered overhead, sometimes disappearing behind the sun. A few glimmered dimly, on the verge of going out. In the far distance to the west, much farther than we would be going tonight, the sky was empty. No stars, and the orbit of sun and moons never crossed that unseen terminator in the sky. There was just darkness. The land beyond the stars.

"You're awfully quiet this morning, Hanrick. What are you thinking about?" Vel asked. He sat slumped forward, his arms crossed over the godsteel broadsword in his lap.

"Nothing," I lied. "Nothing at all."

The village of Halfspire lay clustered around the base of a broken tower at the head of a shallow valley. The tower's exposed ribs climbed high into the sky, its heights bristling with turbine kites and the fluttering banners of the raven god. Rings of fertile soil surrounded the village, emanating from the tower in concentric circles, richer the closer they were to the broken spire's base. The village lay between the rings, linked by bridges and walkways that stretched over the fields, careful to avoid trammeling the ancient earth. There was no wall surrounding the village, by order of the raven god. Vel and I cantered down the main road toward the center of town. A nesting vulture dog dropped from the broken tower's shadow and slowly circled the village.

"Asleep, then," Vel noted. The houses we passed were closed tight, their windows shuttered and chimneys cold. "I don't know whether to be relieved or heartbroken."

"This isn't a cull," I said.

"Not yet. But they're hiding something." He shifted in

his saddle, leather creaking and feathers shifting. "Else we wouldn't be here."

"Aye." We entered the village round at the base of the tower. The building's wide gates lay open. The darkness beyond was silent, even to my ascended hearing. "Sound the bell. Let's see what we're dealing with."

Vel grunted and rode to the platform at the center of the round. The structure served as podium, gallows, notice board, and bell tower. The elderly raven knight unhooked the hammer from its place and struck the bell. The sound echoed off the tower and rolled down the surrounding streets. A wake of vulture dogs startled from the heights, flapping lazily for a minute before settling on the rooftops overlooking the clearing. The sound of their bone-white jaws scissoring open and closed accompanied the last peals from the bell.

The citizens of Halfspire opened their doors and came out. The mayor of the village ducked back inside when he saw our crooked forms waiting by the bell, emerging minutes later in full regalia. Everyone else made their way to the round, barely filling the perimeter. Either there were a lot of empty houses in this village, or some of the citizens decided they were safer behind locked doors than in the sight of their god's chosen messengers. Probably both. They avoided the arc of the round that led to the tower, I noticed.

Properly attired in the vestments of the oracle's cult, the mayor scrambled to our side, bowing as he approached. Vel giggled. I drew myself to my full height and waited patiently as the man made his apologies.

"My lords-raven, what an unexpected honor!" he

proclaimed, loudly enough for the gathered audience. "As representative of the people of Halfspire, and appointed clergy of the All Seeing, let me welcome you to our humble—"

"All Seeing," I interrupted. The mayor's voice cut off. He froze in mid-bow. I swept my gaze across the audience. "And yet you are hiding something."

"My . . . my lord, I don't know . . ." He swallowed hard. I signalled to Vel.

"By edict of the Raven, Oracle of Murdermont and Domaen of all he Sees, a message." Vel's voice changed into a faint static buzz. He cranked his mouth open, jaw slack as the recorded spirit of our god proclaimed. The voice that issued from Vel's throat was barely a whisper, and yet it rang off the tower's heights like a cannon-shot. "Something lurks in Halfspire. Clouds fall across the feed. I am blind to their works. Release them from their darkness."

I first heard those words last night, when the domaen summoned me to his altar and fixed me on this task. That I would carry out my duty was unquestioned. What atrocities I would have to commit to see that duty done depended on how the mayor reacted, and what he was hiding.

A moment of heavy silence followed the proclamation. I fixed the mayor in my gaze. His face was turned down, the gentle glow of his eyes hooded. At least he was still bowing.

"The oracle has spoken," I said, just loud enough for the mayor to hear. The villagers knew what I said, though, and answered.

"The oracle has spoken," they intoned. The words struck the mayor like a hammer blow. He looked up at me, then nodded.

"Where is it?" I asked, though I already knew. He motioned toward the open gates of the tower. Vel cursed under his breath. Corruption at the emanation point of a village like this could poison the entire valley. If it spread, we would have to rouse the entire murder to contain it. I brushed my fingers across the hilt of my godsteel blade. I should kill this man now. Something stayed my hand, though. "What are we dealing with?"

"None of us have seen it," he said. "Only a shape in the darkness. The vultures didn't seem bothered, and the crops still grow, so . . ." His eyes fell on my sword, and he flinched back. "We hoped . . . we hoped it would sort itself."

"Do you know who it is? Someone with knowledge of arms, or a criminal?" The spirit always bent the host, but if the body that was taken was already dangerous, the resulting kymera could be even worse.

"Just a child. A foolish girl, who should have stayed in the house, as she was told." The mayor's voice broke on the last word.

"Your daughter?" I asked. He nodded. "You have my condolences. Vel?"

"We'll try to give you something to bury," Vel said as he rode past the mayor. The man stood stock-still, tears wetting his cheeks.

"Get these people back in their homes," I said. "And don't open your doors for anything. Not the bell, or screaming, or anything."

The villagers did not require prompting. As I nudged

my horse away from the cowering figure of the mayor, they turned and melted back into their houses. A few moments after we arrived, the streets of Halfspire were once again empty. Empty, except for the vulture dogs. As soon as the last citizen was safely behind closed doors, the scavengers dropped from their rooftop perches and loped contentedly in our wake. Black nails clicked on the cobblestones, and the sound of their heavy breathing through the exposed bone of their skulls filled the air. Vel giggled again.

"The vulgs know when a feast is on," he said. "No matter how this goes, those bastards'll eat."

"Focus on the task ahead, Vel," I said. As we approached the yawning gate, I glanced back at the mayor. He stood in the middle of the round, surrounded by a tentative pack of vulture dogs. One sniffed at his hand, then nipped a finger. I turned back. "We'll have to deal with that man afterward."

"Give him back his girl, and all will be forgiven."

"I doubt he will be thankful for a body."

"No pleasing some people," Vel said. He spat on the cobbles. It sizzled against the stone. "Should be glad we're here."

"They rarely are."

We crossed some invisible barrier, and the vulgs stopped following us, though more of them circled high above, and a few perched among the spars of the broken tower. I glanced up at the choir of silent shadows, punctuated with glowing red eyes, and the distant stars beyond. The black gate swallowed us.

"We should leave the horses here," I said. "The vulgs

will leave them alone, and I don't want to risk exposing them to whatever corruption lies ahead."

"Sure, why not? Nothing I'd like more than traveling the width and breadth of this blasted tower on foot." Vel slid gracelessly from his mount, adjusting his godsteel sword across his back and tugging at his cloak, like a bird preening ruffled feathers. "Will be good exercise for my weary bones."

"If the kymera gets ahold of these beasts, you'll be walking all the way back to Murdermont."

"True enough, true enough," Vel said with a sigh. He led the horses to a nook just inside the gate and cycled them to idle. "Perhaps the monster will kill us both, and save us the trouble either way."

"We can always hope," I answered, then looked around.

The interior of the tower was a puzzle box. Half-built staircases crawled over one another like a nest of snakes, and walls stood and fell at seeming random. The floor was cracked and uneven, marble tiles pushed against each other, mixing with tracts of stone that looked like rushing rivers that had frozen in place. An age of madness consumed the spirits of these ancient places, before the domaens ascended to impose order once again, and the ruins left behind offered little clue to their original form. This tower was no exception. Though it still breathed life into the ground around it, and stood against storm and wind, no one was fool enough to shelter in its haunted corridors.

"This place is worse than that water temple in Dossing," Vel said. "We'll be wandering these halls for the rest of our lives."

"Perhaps not." I pointed to a series of flags just inside the wall. "Judging by the kite turbines on the heights, it seems clear the villagers venture in occasionally. At the very least they need to harness the kinetic batteries from those kites. Perhaps they have rituals to appease the spirits of the tower, as well."

"Those would be the mayor's duty."

"Yes. And the host is the mayor's daughter. The girl would likely know her way around the tower as well as anyone in the village. If we follow these paths, surely we'll find some sign of the kymera as well."

At first our task was simple enough. The flagged path picked across the terraced staircases, winding higher and higher until we reached a balcony that overlooked the entrance. It was true dark here. Vel and I both had our eyes cranked open as far as we could, drinking greedily of the limited light. The yipping songs of vulgs carried in from outside, but there was no sign of their filthy nests this deep in the tower. The path we followed was well maintained. Makeshift bridges and handrails of rope and dead metal spanned the gaps that the tower's madness left open. Clear flags signaled when the path split, or when the way forward wasn't clear. I paused at one of these turnings.

"It's hard to see how the child would get lost," I said.

"But easy to see how she could become adventuresome. Perhaps she was lured here by an orphaned domaen, looking for a body." Vel took a few steps down the unmarked fork. "This way looks clear. Even a half-mad spirit could manage an ambush in this place."

"We can't walk every hallway in this place," I said. "Besides, I'm still in communion with the oracle. The raven said there was a place in Halfspire he could not reach. That's where we'll find our monster."

"Perhaps, but—" Vel stopped, spitting and waving one hooked hand across his face. "Gah. Spiderwebs. Bloody things!"

A tangle of thin filaments came free in his hand. The webbing was nearly invisible in the darkness. I chuckled.

"So at least we know the girl didn't go down that path. Come on. There's more light up ahead. I think I can see the sky."

The mismatched hallways and broken rooms of the lower levels gave way to a vast open space spanned by hanging bridges and platforms that dangled like victims in a spider's web. These weren't the rough constructs of mortal hands, formed from dead steel and harvested wood. The ground under our feet sang with domaen energy, the walkways strung in living glass and flexible steel. Sight lines shifted, with vast distances opening up from one vantage point, while ten feet later we were plunged into a tangle of suspension cables and towering pilings whose bases stretched into impenetrable shadow. The outside walls of the tower splintered, allowing a view of the stars. The shadows of flying vulgs passed around the tower. The silence found us soon after.

I was just navigating a creaking bridge when the constant dirge that my domaen whispered into my skull went silent. The look on Vel's face told me he had lost communion as well. I stopped and looked around.

"This is a bad place to try to hold. Let's make for that

platform," I said, pointing to a bowl-shaped span that hung from a latticework of steel cabling thirty feet ahead. "The beast can't be far."

"Not to doubt you, but that's where I'd be waiting, if I meant to pounce on a pair of likely hosts," Vel said.

"We're here to get pounced upon," I answered. "Loose steel, and prepare yourself."

I drew my sword as we trotted toward the platform. The godsteel blade was nearly weightless, the only mass in the hilt and the kinetic generator in the pommel. She was fully wound, and when I popped the release on the handle, the blade spun to life with a slithering whir. The dull edge of the blade folded open like a card trick, growing razor sharp.

"Careful to not clip any of these supports," Vel warned. "Don't want to go spinning off into the dark just yet."

"Grow some wings, Vel," I snapped, then marched up the bridge.

The platform was hollowed out, so that the lip where we entered was about ten feet higher than the center. A series of concentric terraces led down to the middle, where a central pillar bore the weight of the platform, depending from a braided iron band that rose into the darkness. We were quite high up in the tower, and this platform was one of the higher structures in the constellation of bridges and decks that formed this vast interior space. Only a latticework of steel bones separated us from the sky.

The creature hung from the central pillar of the platform, just beneath the braided iron of the suspension cable. It looked like a cross between a crab and a spider, with angular plates covering its black body, and six spindly legs that clutched the cable. The limbs were multi-jointed and barbed, thick at the stalk and growing thin and sharp at the tip, with scissoring claws that snipped jerkily at the air. Dozens of spherical eyes roamed over the creature's back, seemingly unattached to the kymera's shiny exoskeleton. That exoskeleton was made of dozens of overlapping chitinous plates in a symmetrical geometric pattern. The plates shifted back and forth, leaking a small amount of blue light in the gaps. The kymera scuttled around the pillar, raising one of those knife-thin appendages in our direction, as though it was testing the air between us.

As it moved, the monster dragged a thick bundle of glistening tubes with it. The bundle ran from somewhere deep in its torso down to the floor of the platform. From the end of each tube crawled an engorged sac of fluid, dragging itself forward on hundreds of milky legs. Dark shapes hung inside the sacs. And there, pressed against the thin membrane of the largest sac, was the girl. Her wide amber eyes stared sightlessly through the cloudy liquid that surrounded her. Dark veins sprouted from her head and back, feeding into the cable, pulsing silently. The other sacs held different shapes, some as small as a razorhawk, but most contained vulture dogs in various stages of growth.

"Broodmother," I spat. Though every kymera was different, many of them fell into similar patterns. Broodmothers harvested material, both organic and not, and converted it into monstrous constructs. Unchecked, a broodmother could terrorize the countryside for years, overrunning villages and consuming the residents and buildings alike. "Vel, try to get to the other side of it. If we can cut those cords we might be able to give the mayor his daughter back."

"More interested in keeping my neck intact," he muttered, but shifted carefully around the platform. The humming length of his godsteel blade flickered to life as he moved. The kymera's bluish glow cast a thin webwork of shadows across Vel's face.

The kymera's eyes rolled like marbles across its back until they formed two large clusters, one following Vel, the other focused on me. Several of the trailing sacs burst, and the foetal shapes of half-formed vulture dogs slopped out. Still trailing glistening umbilical cords, the beasts hobbled to their feet and trotted in our direction. Their eyes glowed the same blue as the broodmother's shell. The umbilical cords pulled tight, then snapped with a wet popping sound.

"Kill them, but be careful of the child," I called across to Vel. "And don't get too close to the mother. Those claws are pretty long."

"Wasn't born yesterday, boy," Vel said. He shook his head, then rolled his shoulders and brought his sword to a guard position. "Let 'em come."

I turned my attention to the four foetal dogs loping toward me. Their bony heads were slick with amniotic fluid. Vulture dogs didn't scare me, but I wasn't sure what sort of spirits the broodmother had pumped into their flesh. They were just about in striking distance when a noise from the kymera startled me. It sounded like a horde of beetles taking flight, their shells buzzing against their wings.

I looked up just in time to see the broodmother's hundred eyes iris shut. I was still wondering why it would blind itself when the overlapping chitinous plates shuttered open. The dim light that outlined each plate suddenly flared into sapphire brilliance that momentarily washed out my ascended vision. Vel's sudden cry of pain matched my own. My eyes irised into pinpricks, but the glowing afterimage of the kymera hung in front of me, leaving me blind. I went to one knee, sheltering behind the blade of my godsteel weapon. The clatter of nails on steel was the only warning I had.

The first embryonic dog barreled into me, sliding across my sword and ramming its bony head into my shoulder. I spun around, catching myself with my other arm just as thick teeth closed around my bicep. Steel plate crumpled in the dog's jaws. Blindly, I swung my sword in that direction, feeling the satisfying thump of holy steel in flesh. The jaws fell away. I stood and took a step back, but stopped when my heel went over the edge of the platform. I was completely disoriented. Growling, snapping jaws surrounded me, left and right.

"Han?" Vel sounded confused and in pain, somewhere on the other side of the platform. "What's happening, Hanrick?"

"Sit tight, Vel. I'm on my way."

In truth, the broodmother doubtless lay between my raven-brother and I, and my sight was returning too slowly. My eyes burned as the spirits stitched the damaged tissue back together, but I needed to act now. I shuffled to the side, swinging my sword in a tight arc in the hopes of catching one of the vulgs, or perhaps driving back the kymera at the center of the platform. I had to stay to the platform's edge and out of reach of the broodmother's snapping claws, at least until I could see well enough to fight back. The whistling growl of vulture dogs followed my slow transit. Blurry shapes filled by vision. The branching form of the broodmother loomed overhead, and the smaller vulgs danced in front of me. Glancing over, I caught sight of Vel. He was facing the wrong direction, arms slack at his side as he stared out over the precipice.

"Vel, don't move! You're nearly to the edge. I'll—"

Three of the dogs leapt at me. I buried the forte of my sword in the skull of the lead vulg, splitting it from nose to neck. Black ichor sprayed across my helm and stained my gauntlets, the beast's living blood squirming like flat worms across the steel of my armor. I twisted the blade and sliced sideways, taking the top of its head off and driving the tip into the second dog. Godsteel pierced flesh, catching it just under the right forepaw. It twisted in midair, jaws biting at the thorn, muscular body trying to wriggle free of the shallow wound. I braced and thrust forward. The sword slid smoothly through its body, cutting straight through the spine. The vulg gave a final rattle and then died.

The third vulture dog slammed into my plant leg at full speed. Jagged molars crushed my armor and sliced through the soft meat of my calf. My greaves spared the bone, but bright blood splattered against the stained exo-bone of the vulg's skull. I screamed. The weight of the dead vulg impaled on my sword slowed my reaction, and as I swung the pitted corpse slid sluggishly down to the hilt. With my hands buried in the severed belly of the beast, I hacked at the neck of the vulg gripping my leg. Slick blood and twisting viscera loosened my grip, and it took three solid blows before the vulg released my leg. Bleeding profusely, the creature backed away and glowered at me. The broodmother skittered higher on her pillar, straining the dozen or so tendrils that still hung to various pods on the floor. I spotted the girl among them, her dead eyes watching us closely.

I took the respite to shake the dead vulg free of my blade and closed the distance with Vel. He hadn't moved throughout the fight. His godsteel sword hung loose in his hand, the blade dormant. Something was badly wrong. I grabbed his shoulder and shook him. Vel stumbled a few feet to the left, then drew himself up and turned to face me.

A spiderweb of black scars covered his bald head. The wounds near the top of his skull were blistering, or at least that's what I thought at first. But as my vision cleared, I saw that the milky lesions were connected to a thin veil of black thread that floated away from his skin, like the finest corona of hair. Vel stared at me with blank eyes.

"The...the spiderweb. Hanrick..." His mouth stopped moving, and a thin line of drool spilled out from his lip. Then he made a ratcheting sound deep in his throat. He clenched his jaw, muscles bunching across the ingrown valves of his ventilator. For a brief second, my friend's eyes focused. "Run!" he screamed through clamped teeth.

His sword flickered to life. Dull pewter scales clattered down the length of the blade, turning the blunt edge sharp, awakening the weapon's divine power. I stared at it in horror, my mind frozen in place. I barely lifted my sword in time to block the slice that would have cut me in half if it had landed. The force of the blow shoved me off my feet. The sound of godsteel striking godsteel shrieked across the chamber. I hit the ground and slid.

"Hanrick . . . Hanrick, it has me. Do something, man!" Vel's voice was strained, and his face was twisted with the effort of speaking. "Kill it before I can't . . . I can't . . ."

Vulg jaws clamped onto my shoulder. The beast shook me like a rag, clattering my helmet against the bony ridge of its skull. I shoved my free arm under its chest, then heaved, lifting it into the air and throwing the wriggling beast at Vel's stumbling form. Vel sliced it in half, like sun cutting through a bloody morning fog, then kicked the squirming halves aside. I struggled to my feet, left arm limp, right gripping my sword like a warding sigil between us.

"Vel, you have to fight it! Think of the Raven! Think of the blessings of the oracle! Fight it, Vel!"

Instead of answering, he lunged forward, whipping the sword back and forth. I parried, sliding our blades together until the hilts met. Vel had always been stronger than me, but the force behind the punch he landed on my chest was inhuman. The steel plate of my armor dimpled, and I heard the bones of his hand breaking like a bundle of twigs. It was enough to drive me back. I stared at him. Swollen fingers twitched from the pulped knuckles of his left hand, but his face showed no sign of pain. The corona of black threads that rose from his head connected to a narrow cord that floated, as light as a breeze, through the air. The other end of that cord sprouted from the broodmother's chest. I swore.

"Burn my body, Hanrick." His voice had a dreamlike quality to it, and his face was slack. "Do that much for me."

"I will bury you in Murdermont, an honored servant of the Raven," I answered. "But not for a long time, old friend." But I knew I was lying.

A sound like breaking glass came from Vel's throat, then he grabbed his sword with both hands and came at me. The broken fingers of his left hand burst, splinters of bone poking through callused skin, the hilt slick with blood. I caught the blow with the forte of my sword, deflecting rather than blocking. The force of the attack buried the tip of Vel's sword into the platform. I drove my elbow into his face. Teeth and valves broke, shredding his cheek and dislocating his jaw. He responded by planting his face in my shoulder. As I spun away he whipped his sword at my legs. It was only luck that put my blade in the path. I hit the deck once again, the breath driven from my lungs, my skull ringing from the impact.

Vel stood over me, and the broodmother hung behind him. The kymera watched with all of its hundred eyes. After the flash of light that initially blinded me, there hadn't been a glimmer from the creature's chitinous shell, but now there was the dimmest glow between the plates. It was drawing power from somewhere.

My thoughts were interrupted by Vel's renewed attack. He struck clumsily, with none of the smooth transitions and balanced blows typical of our days in the practice field. He thrashed the blade like it was a club, standing straight and narrow. But it was still a godsteel weapon that could cut steel like paper, wielded with whatever inhuman strength the kymera's possession had given him, and I was flat on my back, and stunned. I kept my sword between us, intercepting the vicious downward blows, my fingers soon numb from the effort, and then my forearms, my shoulders. I crawled to the edge of the platform. Vel paused as whatever connection enslaving him to the broodmother reached its limit. The kymera skittered down the platform to let out a little slack as I climbed awkwardly to my feet. Miraculously, I was at the bridge Vel and I had first taken to reach this platform. Holding on to the handrail that anchored the bridge to the platform, I backed onto the bridge. Vel approached, stiff-legged and slow.

I took one last look at him, at my friend. His body was a ruin, and his mind was struggling under the kymera's infection. If we had caught it immediately, I might have been able to save him. But not now. Now all I could do was try to stay alive. He took a step forward.

I turned and ran.

I gripped the ruined ledge in both hands and swung out into the open air. I paused to shake out my left arm. The muscles were still stiff, but the scar tissue that bubbled up in the wounds left by the vulg's bite was already melting away. Even my leg, nearly crushed in the attack, was nearly back to normal. I would have to spend some time in the restorative chambers at Murdermont, but for now I was fit enough for service to my god.

It had taken hours to climb the long way around the

tower, avoiding the areas that seemed to be infected by the broodmother. It was good to be in the open air once again. I paused and looked down. Night had risen. The steady light from the four moons shone across the pebbled roofs of the village below, turning them into jewels. Citizens went about their business, tending the fields and selling their wares, completely unaware of the doom that hung overhead. Small groups gathered in the round, carefully avoiding the entrance to the tower. I thought I could even make out the mayor, lingering beside the gallows-bell. *Not long now*, I thought. *One way or another, the mayor's wait for his daughter will be over soon.*

I heard the ruffle of feathers half a second before the creature landed on my shoulder. I drew my blade and whirled toward the sound, cycling up the godsteel even as I searched for my attacker. But it wasn't the enemy. It was my god, or a messenger at least.

The pearl-white shape of a raven perched on my outstretched sword. The godsteel transformed beneath him, edge dulling and tip blunting, like an icicle melting in the sun. The bird preened the feathers of its wing with its serrated beak, then fixed me with crimson eyes.

The corruption continues. The silence is spreading. Raven's voice vibrated at the base of my skull, like an echo through an empty canyon.

"Yes," I answered. "It has taken Vel. A broodmother. I don't think I can save him."

You will be lucky to save yourself. The raven hopped from my sword to a piling that stretched out from the facade.

"How did you know to be here?" I asked.

I am the oracle, it hummed. *I sensed your failure, and have summoned the rest of the murder. They are on their way here as we speak.*

"Excellent. I was worried I wouldn't be able to take Vel down on my own, much less the kymera. When will they get here?"

High night, it answered. *If you have not destroyed the kymera by the time they arrive, they will cull the town and tear this tower to the ground. Including you.*

"I hardly think that's—"

The oracle has spoken. It wiped the sharp edge of its beak against the stone pillar, then fluttered into the air and away, disappearing like a puff of fog.

"Well, that complicates things." Judging by the position of the moons, there couldn't be much more than an hour until high night. If I was going to get Vel away from this monster and save the village . . . and myself . . . I had to get a move on.

The platform that held the village generator hung just above me. A dozen thick ropes led to the turbine kites that dragged through the river of wind overhead. The winds above us were constant, as ordained by the gods. Raven tried to take credit, but even I knew the winds were outside his control. They bent the knee to another domaen.

Climbing the last ledge, I pulled myself up onto the platform. There were doubtless passages to this platform inside. After all, the villagers had to harvest the kinetic batteries, but those walkways must have been monitored by the kymera. In retrospect, it seemed obvious that the girl had been caught on her way here. She had done nothing wrong. None of us had. Just bad luck, and the predation of feral gods. I had crawled along the outside of the tower because I wanted to see what was here without drawing the broodmother's attention.

The generator was an ancient device. The air around it smelled like a lightning strike, and my hair tingled as I approached. The engine roared, its crying cycling loud and then louder, like a millstone biting into steel. The cables that led out to the kites were sheathed in blackened rubber, to keep them from tangling. A row of kinetics sprouted from the generator's base. They were cold to the touch. They weren't feeding off the turbines for some reason. Just as I thought.

I squeezed through the gap at the back of the generator to reach the rear panel. I had seen one of these machines in the wastes, among the ruins of the City After the Stars, before my service with Raven. Some tremendous force had broken that machine open, exposing its guts to the air, and stealing its magic.

Sure enough, the back panel of the generator had been forced open. Bright wheels whistled as they spun in the depths of the machine, connected by a tangle of wires. I knew nothing about how it functioned, but I still found what I was looking for. Black cords, mucous-slick and as thick as my arm, leached off of the machinery and trailed into the wall behind. Spasms ran down their length. They looked like vivisected throats, swallowing their fill. The kymera was tapped into the generator.

I raised my boot and stamped down. The feeder tendrils burst in a shower of sparks and burning blood. In the distance, I heard the broodmother scream from a dozen mouths. Now I had to hope the monster came looking before the murder descended on the village. I had a lot to do while I was waiting.

The walls began to sing. Steel cables woven into the fabric of the tower started to hum and vibrate, and the floor danced underfoot. The beast approached. I tucked the last cable into place, then snatched my sword from its sheath and hid myself away under a banner of the raven god. The platform wasn't very big, but there was enough wreckage at this level to provide at least temporary shelter.

The broodmother descended from the outside of the building. What had the villagers thought of that? Her weight set the ground shaking. For a second my hope surged, thinking that the kymera had come alone, that I would be able to kill it without harming Vel or the girl. But then a pouch along its belly burst, and Vel and the other embryos fell onto the stone platform. The broodmother picked its way carefully through the maze of cables and ropes that led to the turbine kites, its hundred eyes scattered across its body. I held my breath and kept my sword silent. Everything depended on the beast reaching the generator. It was halfway across the platform when it stopped. Its attention focused on the broken machine. I ground my teeth together in frustration.

At a twitch from the kymera, Vel unfolded from the pile and stood up. He was much changed. Feeder tendrils burrowed across his body, black and pulsing. Cysts rose from his chest, and more of his armor had melted into his flesh. Only the raven-feather cloak remained pure. The spirits inhabiting the cloak must be fighting a hell of a battle. Of his sword there was no sign.

Vel walked jerkily across the platform and approached the generator. He examined it with newly segmented eyes. His nostrils flared at the smell of kinetics. The broodmother chittered excitedly, her carapaced body arched toward the generator. The bundle of embryos dragged forward. I was able to make out the girl, curled tight on herself, blank eyes staring at nothing.

When I looked back at Vel, he was frozen in place. The kymera still moved through him, but his body was as still as stone. Glistening tendrils burst from his outstretched hands and strained toward the generator, their mouths gasping for power.

He turned and looked directly at me. Vel's eyes were glassy, his attention torn between the room and the pain wracking his body, but I swear that he saw me. Then he nodded, took a step forward, and gripped the generator firmly in both hands.

The front of the generator tore free, powered by the dozens of kinetic batteries that I had re-rigged and set along the floor. It slammed into Vel, flattening him to the ground. A second hissing explosion released the anchors of the turbine kites. The net of steel cables that covered the floor slithered loudly across the platform toward the open air, gathering up Vel as it went. The broodmother skittered to the side, watching her host plunge toward the void. The umbilical cords attaching my friend to his murderer drew tight, jerking the broodmother off balance and briefly dragging her across the floor. I pounced.

Throwing off the banner that covered me, I raced silently across the platform. The dragging net, the power arcing from the ruined generator, and the howl of whipping cables masked the sound of my godsteel shriek. The broodmother was busy trying to disentangle itself from Vel's limp form when I fell on it.

Godsteel could cut the sun. It broke stone, it felled iron, it severed bone and blood and flesh. Even domaens fear the edge of a godsteel blade. And the broodmother, for all its horror and its power, was less than a god.

My first blow sliced through two of the kymera's arms, sending them twitching to the ground, their claws still slashing at empty air. One hundred eyes scuttled across the beast's back to stare at me. It let out a scream, then opened the shutters of its soul. I never saw a glimmer of its burning heart, because I expected this trick. My eyes went black, irises hardening into shells. Even with that transformation, I could feel the heat of the light across my face. My skin cracked under the force of the blast, and the smell of burning feathers and singed steel filled my mouth. I drove my sword down, screaming through bloody lips.

The sound of godsteel striking whatever organ produced that light was titanic. I thought my soul would break at the crash. Shivers of power traveled up my arms, sending my muscles flickering and my bones to sing. My body went limp. I fell backward, slamming into the ground like a fallen tree. The only sound I could hear was the screech of blood in my ears and the hammering of my heart.

The shells of my eyes cracked open. I shook the chitin

away, then worked my way onto my elbows. The body of
the broodmother had collapsed, as though its insides had
dissolved, along with the light that powered it, leaving only
the exoskeleton and a flood of gritty fluid the color of
vomit. The desiccated corpse slid slowly across the floor,
tangled up in the net of cables that was being dragged into
the air by the half-dozen kites I had cut free. The hilt of
my sword lay on the ground. The blade was gone. Only a
smear of pewter scales remained, their lives given in the
broodmother's death. The winds roared outside the tower,
and the kites dragged the dead kymera toward oblivion.

Movement near the ledge caught my eye. One of the
gray sacks lurched forward, still attached by a glistening
bundle of cords to the dead kymera. Fingers pressed
against the thick membrane of the sac. I jumped to my
feet and ran, stumbling, dizzy, toward the motion.

The girl was awake. She stared in horror as Vel's body
tipped over the ledge. Vel spun free from the wreckage
of the generator, and tore away from his connection to the
kymera. He fell silently, arms flopping, striking the side
of the tower once before he cratered in the middle of the
village round. His corrupted body burst in red and steel
and bone.

"I'm here, I'm here!" I shouted. The girl's pale eyes
went to me. The kites had reached new heights, dragging
into the strongest winds. Free of Vel's weight, they pulled
faster and faster. The net flew into the air. The
broodmother, jumbled arms still trapped in the last cables
of the trap, followed.

The girl screamed as the broodmother scraped over
the ledge. It sounded like the burbling of a drowning man.

The kymera's drop wasn't sudden, but as more and more of it tumbled into the air, the umbilical cords that held the girl yanked her back. I grabbed at the membrane, but it was slick with fluids. Her hand closed around my wrist, separated by the sac's thick skin.

I grabbed the end of one of the broodmother's scything claws as it passed. Working the joints to press the talon against the bundle of umbilical cords, I started sawing. One of them burst, spilling cold fluids over my hands, making the work more difficult. We started sliding toward the precipice. I tried to pull against the drag, but the platform was slick with mucous and the spew from the death of the kymera. We left a trail in the ichor as we slid, slowly, painfully, toward the drop.

Another of the cords burst, and a third, but then the broodmother toppled over the edge. My cutting tool was torn from my hands, leaving a long gash in my palms as it went. The girl screamed again, a pathetic sound. The tear in the cords grew. I buried my hands in it and pulled, ripping out strips of rubbery flesh, digging closer and closer to the embryonic sac that held the girl. Wind blew across my face. I tried to not look at the stars, and the moon, and the drop that was closer by the second.

Suddenly, a flood of dark fluid burst from under my hands. The girl's hand thrust out of the tear and closed around my wrist in truth. My foot slipped out over the edge, then my knee. I shoved my arm into the wound, grabbed a bony elbow, and pulled.

We fell backward, arm in arm. The last of the broodmother's embryonic bundle slipped over the precipice. It dropped for a brief second, then launched into the air, dragged higher and higher by the fleet of turbine kites.

The girl lay against my chest, gasping for breath and screaming in equal measure. I wrapped her in the dark feathers of my cloak and whispered nothing into her head.

The mayor waited for us at the gate, bracketed by the remaining members of my murder. Attis led them. The tall, thin knight held the stained remnants of Vel's cloak in his hands. I swept my gaze across the murder. Swords sheathed, and the villagers were still alive. No cull. Thank the raven. I turned my attention back to the mayor.

The child slept in my arms. Her body had been dependent on the broodmother for so long that she had nothing in her, no energy, barely a heartbeat. Worse, she had changed. Her teeth were small and sharp, her eyes segmented, the shadow of darker things squirming under her pale skin. I limped from the shadows. I must have looked a fright, with my charred skin and the ash smeared across my armor. The mayor looked up at me and startled back. Then his eyes fell on his daughter, and his true terror showed.

"What have you done?" he asked quietly.

"Saved your daughter," I answered. When he didn't step forward, I held her out. The man flinched away. "What are you doing?"

"There's no mercy in this," he said. "Look at her. Look at . . ." His voice trailed off. The girl woke just enough to blink in slow sequence at her father, then nuzzled against the steel of my breast and fell back asleep. "You know what it will be like for her here. Among these people. What they'll say." He took another step back. "What they'll do to her."

"What would you have me do?"

"You're a knight. You keep us safe from such things." He ran thin fingers across his mouth and swallowed. "Do what you must."

The man ducked between Attis and the others, scurrying back to his burrow. Attis stepped forward, looking down at the girl, his face creased in a frown.

"Vel is dead," he said. It was neither question nor accusation.

"He died fighting. He died to save this child."

"He died doing the raven's will," Attis answered. He took the girl's chin in his fingers and turned her face. She woke up, confusion and pain in her eyes. Attis's frown deepened. "A deep corruption. It might be a mercy to let her die."

"It might," I said, but didn't move. Attis waited for a long moment, then looked up at me. He nodded.

"Very well," he said, then turned back to the rest of the murder, mounting smoothly. At a signal, they turned as one and rode out of the village of Halfspire.

I carried the child to Vel's mount and lay her thin body across the saddle. The horse woke up, shifting nervously under this new burden. I whispered into the beast's ear, then fired up his soul and started my own mount. We rode through the empty round, past the gallows, the shuttered homes of the main road. The village of Halfspire watched us go from behind curtains and cracked doors, turning aside whenever I glanced in their direction. I looked down at the girl curled up in the nest of my dead friend's saddle.

The murder needed a new knight. She needed a home. I would do what I must.

OPERATRIX TRIUMPHANS
Susan R. Matthews

Much has been forgotten. Little is understood. On the colony world of Eightend, all that is not crucial to the survival of the cartels has been cast aside. Necessity is the rule of law. But for the sword dancer Yusaravan, the lost knowledge of the ancients may be the only thing separating her people from annihilation. . . .

Yarbgardonry, Opterics, Delep Wartor. Ommastro, Obroniast, Eschapintor.

The chant had nothing directly to do with Yusaravan's presence in the transport cage that connected the huge underground cisterns beneath Sidarfels Station to the surface. Untold centuries those water-caves had survived, a natural reservoir of pure sweet water collected over an unknown span of time from the Sidarfels River—the largest in all of planet Eightend's largest continent—when it was in spate.

The chant was almost as old as the people of Eightend's presence here, though it was important now for reasons other than its listing of arcane sciences. Nobody cared about things that had no practical application. The ancient, almost incomprehensible, apparently irrelevant knowledge was buried in libraries in formats that few people knew how to read. There were too few teachers, for a start. The world of Eightend had never enjoyed a great material prosperity. No resources could be spared from practical applications to fund antiquarian studies until food crop productivity improved.

"Been down here before, Yusaravan?" Eversand asked, beside her. The transport cage creaked and shuddered, and made Yusaravan nervous. Eversand clearly knew that. Eversand was always watching for points of weakness of which she could take advantage. Yusaravan didn't think Eversand was a spiteful or malicious person; but Eversand was one of the most competitive people Yusaravan had ever met.

Yusaravan didn't like competitive people, and anyone surnamed Beach Dunes—like Eversand Beach Dunes— was almost always a member of one of the other cartels, all four of them, that governed their world. Each of them competing with the others for advantage. Eversand clearly knew that Exercitus, Beach Dunes's patron, had its best chance yet of taking Sidarfels away from the Granary Cartel into which Yusaravan had been born.

Eversand wasn't offensive about it, but she clearly felt that the transfer was as good as done. Yusaravan reluctantly agreed. "No, it's my first time."

Yusaravan was here in the lift going down to the cisterns because newly promoted fencing team captains went to the head of the roster. Eversand was here because she was the captain of Sidarfels' entire fencing program, recognized as formidable and dominant in the worldwide rankings. She probably expected to stay on at Sidarfels Station, in an expanded management role—with a juicy increase in salary. Yusaravan stated the obvious. "I think you know that, Eversand."

Eversand called Yusaravan by her personal name, rather than more formally by her family—Ringwall, upstream from the Sidarfels River in the mountains. Yusaravan was junior to Eversand. By rights Yusaravan should call Eversand "Beach Dunes," it was more polite, it was a daily affirmation of Eversand's rank; and because of all of those things Yusaravan had just violated protocol. For the first and last time.

"I'll never forget my first trip down," Eversand said, musingly. "The lift feels like it's going to shake right apart, doesn't it? Hasn't, though, fortunately. Yet."

That was either a bit of kindly reassurance or a subtle reminder of how long Eversand had had unlimited rights of access, because of how long she'd been the best fencer of one of the best teams. It could also easily have been both. Yusaravan didn't think she cared either way.

As the transport cage descended—how far below the surface were they, now?—the lights that illuminated the black rock shore, that traced the long pier across the water to the tally-pole, brightened to full gleaming globes of brilliant blue.

Svarteshavpurnam, Delboblurry. Pariemitics, Chaldroncury.

The shore was stunningly beautiful, the rocks glittering in answering shades of blue as the lights brightened, their increasingly intense shining seeming to spread out like ripples in an otherwise still pool of bioluminescence. Yusaravan couldn't help but wonder what purpose bioluminescence served life that never saw the light of day, here in these dark silent caverns. There'd been studies of Sidarfels' cisterns, once, but nothing new for many, many years. Generations. Maybe millennia.

"Yes, it's magical down here, isn't it?" Eversand said, though Yusaravan hadn't spoken. Eversand had to drop her voice; the official guests were talking, dignitaries from each cartel come to complete the formalities of transferring Sidarfels out of Granary resources and into Exercitus.

Yusaravan had paid little attention to the details. They were simple enough; most of the people would stay in place, but they'd become an instant underclass, enjoying less income, fewer consumer goods, lower wages. They'd find themselves guest workers on their own land, places where Sidarfels' people had worked with the river for the common good of all—including the river itself—for as long as there had been here people here, on Eightend. It was depressing.

"And look." Eversand pointed, her voice just loud enough to escape calling attention to itself the way a whisper would. "There's the column. You can see the problem from here."

The marker that had kept Granary firmly in possession of Sidarfels, the marker whose silent report had doomed them to be bereft of Sidarfels now, was a tall column of polished black rock rising from the waters to ascend into black obscurity above. The cave-lights caught against the incised bands of inlaid gold and made the awful evidence impossible to ignore.

Yusaravan could hear Sidarfels' senior administrator briefing the cartels' representatives, a part of the ritual. The cartels' reps were sure to have studied this before, it was so simple and so damning. It had saved Sidarfels for Granary, before. Now it was taking Sidarfels away, to the ruination of them all—including, as before, the river itself.

"Yes," Administrator Jaxon, Sidarfels' senior officer, was saying. "All in the records, as I think you'll find. We'd been maintaining a decent balance well enough until quite recently, but there's been increasing difficulties with illegal diversion."

Eversand, sublimely confident by the looks of things in the support of the cartel to which she belonged, gave not the slightest hint of a reaction. Eversand knew who it was that had been stealing from the Sidarfels watershed. Everybody did, though Sidarfels had been unable to prove it. It was all history now anyway. Who cared?

Yusaravan did. Every family in Sidarfels did. And more than that, how could it be their fault that the rains had failed, the snowpack had shrunk, that the glaciers were melting away more and more quickly every year? Had it ever happened before? Yet whether people cared was not material.

"So there's the place we like to be. It's called the reliable surplus marker," Station Administrator Jaxon said, pointing. The gold band that encircled the index pillar seemed fully a quarter of the way from the water to the darkness above. "We started falling from there almost two hundred years ago. Five years of drought did it to us, that time. You can read the rest as well as I can."

And Jaxon was too depressed to want to go on, Yusaravan knew, although Jaxon was still the professional administrator who'd fought to preserve Sidarfels' autonomy as few others could have done.

That was what they'd said to the more than five hundred people who made Sidarfels Station their home. Jaxon had done her best, which was better than most, but when everything Jaxon had tried had failed Jaxon had—reluctantly—accepted the inevitable, as they'd all been forced to do.

"Your records show the level below the mark at the last Great Reckoning, Administrator Jaxon? Sixty-four years ago?" That was the Neverice Cartel's representative, but she spoke for Exercitus by proxy. Cat's-paw. "And, furthermore, that the cistern depletion may even be speeding up. I don't think the facts are in question."

Neverice's representative spoke respectfully and truthfully. It didn't help, in Yusaravan's opinion. Not really. Administrator Jaxon lifted her hands with flattened palms off the old tubular passenger railings, then set them back down with so subtle an *and still you really should reconsider* or *I don't want to discuss it* gesture that Yusaravan wasn't sure she'd actually seen it.

"It is what it is, after all, Neverice," Jaxon said. *Svarte-shavpurnam, Delboblurry. Pariemitics, Chaldroncury.* "The standards must be consistently and equitably applied. That's all there is to it. The Board of Cartels has been generous. No complaints. But we're consistently down, and falling faster all the time. It'll take years to make up, even if the weather recovers. Longer, if it doesn't. We need fresh eyes with new solutions."

After a moment—during which Neverice made what was clear to Yusaravan was a show of struggling with herself, with the facts—Neverice nodded, her face turned down and away from Granary Cartel's representative. "We've seen enough, I think," Neverice's representative said. "Thank you, Administrator Jaxon. Yes. Let's go."

Granary Cartel had its own representative here, and she nodded her head as well, with obvious reluctance. It was the end of the world for Sidarfels. Nobody was expected to like it; even Exercitus stood solemn and silent, projecting sympathetic regret. Totally false, Yusaravan was sure. If Granary had been Exercitus, who was to say whether Granary wouldn't secretly exult, to have so rich a resource as Sidarfels come into their purview?

Worldwinds Cartel's representative chose to gaze into the darkness beyond the column—Worldwinds and Exercitus had never worked well together. Finally Ocean Cartel said, "Yes," and the ceremonial transfer was as good as done. There was a standard format for the details and the dates; it was already drawn up, waiting only to be countersigned to become official as accomplished fact.

"Thank you, Granary, for your tireless stewardship." It was up to Exercitus' representative to take the lead voice, now, as the acknowledged manager-in-fact of the Sidarfels watershed. "We hope to learn from your knowledge, and your experience. Nobody could have done better. This isn't your fault."

That it wasn't Granary's fault wouldn't save Sidarfels now.

The great tower of Sidarfels Station would continue to rest where it had landed, at the end—at last—of the Great Migration. Much more recently than that Granary had held Sidarfels for two hundred years, learning how to manage the gifts of rain and meltwater throughout Sidarfels' watershed communities, Lifespring, Wellershoal, Kazeraye, Grand Delta. In all of that time the mountains had yielded a rich harvest of winter ice, snowmelt, glaciation—but not anymore.

Exercitus' thefts were not the root cause of the problem. There just wasn't enough water coming down from the clouds and the treasure houses of the glacial ice. Who knew whether the water would come back in time to save the rich harvest of grain and fruit and all the good things that grew in Sidarfels' fertile soil?

The fact remained that it would be sixty-four years to the next Grand Reckoning. That was more than enough time for Exercitus to plunder Sidarfels, depriving Granary of a resource that was key to its prosperity.

With Exercitus Cartel in charge of the distribution of Sidarfels' water—at an increased price—the people of the watershed would have next to nothing left to sell but labor. And that at a bargain price, because they were by no means the only convention, reach, commons being pushed inexorably to the outskirts of rich and privileged and powerful polities.

It was unjust, it was unfair, it was just business. That was Exercitus. "Yes, thank you, Jaxon," Exercitus' representative said. "Let's go."

Yusaravan was as ready as any of them to return to the surface, glad as she was to have had the chance to see the unforgiving evidence for herself. Now she needed to get back to work on her fencing demonstration. The closing ceremonies for this review-and-decision procedure featured fencing demonstrations mounted by Sidarfels' famous program—probably the only thing, Yusaravan thought bitterly, that Exercitus would continue to nourish, as a prestige item.

Creatigenis, Peaternians. Lignihistria, Ackusicheros.

The cadence of her "free-form," the original performance she was to present as a final validation of her recent promotion within the program, was expected to put people irresistibly in mind of a commonly recognizable piece of music.

For her practice runs Yusaravan used out-of-the-way places such the greenbelt along the riverside on the station's expansive grounds and unused maintenance corridors, to work on her performance; because cheating for advantage, lying, stealing, and plagiarism were things as unchanging as the station-towers.

If a rival—Exercitus, for instance—could get an advance hint of what musical reference Yusaravan would be using, they could unpick the knots of the melody to harvest a great deal of information about the timing, the length, even what standard fencing sequences she was likely to bring into play. And then use their own free-form to invoke the same strain as if it had been their original idea all the time.

The tradition of fencing with its special sword, one that ended with a squared-off and unsharpened crown rather than coming to a point, had slowly developed over time. In contrast, people's interest and investment in some of the courses of study that they'd carried with them in the Great Migration had steadily deteriorated.

Over the years people lost interest in knowledge not of active use, since educational resources cost money and apparently obsolete technologies could always, it was argued, be recovered from obscure records as it was needed. Later.

Exactly what had powered the towers as spacecraft was no longer completely comprehended, but they weren't going anywhere, were they? The details on how the pioneers who'd come to Eightend had controlled those rockets had similarly faded into obscurity. Only a few persistent phrases remained, preserved in speculative literature. Plasma-core rocket. Asteroid-harvested water. Passenger-protective shielding. Colony ship.

Hotiseellery Joybuoyrady Zhobeproneas.

Even as fencing societies flourished in the open, however, secret societies sought the ancient learning for diversion as well as advantage, and Sidarfels had had members of the Thikologia society—water tables, aquifers, rivers, rain—above all others. Yusaravan hadn't gone Thikologian. Yusaravan had gone Operatrix, instead, because that was where some promising solutions to the last great unsolved puzzles were aggressively pursued.

The secret societies had been pursuing arcane inquiries for years, each answer leading to more questions after questions after questions. How did one start a tower into the sky? What had become of the structural elements that had surely been in place when the towers were brought down—stabilizer elements, external fuel tanks? Mass cargo containment? How could an object of such size, mass, and dimension have been brought down to the surface in an upright orientation at all?

Where had fuel been stored, or was it still hidden away within the towers somewhere like a still-compressed cloud of poisonous death; how did one interact with an immense engine more than two thousand years old?

Yusaravan had memorized each long-sleeping receptor in the fabric of the tower's uppermost reaches, the superstructure, where once long ago—so the ancient lore claimed—there'd been a beautiful, bright command center to monitor all systems as the immense structure settled, so slowly, so carefully, to earth and came to rest there.

If there was fuel, if it was poisoned and came to escape, Sidarfels would be of no use to anybody and no cartel would interfere with it ever again. If there was no fuel, Sidarfels Station might still hold other priceless treasure. To get at it, they had to ask the machine, so they had to use its language, and it wasn't listening to them. To get its attention they had to shake it awake.

And to do that they had to synthesize every scrap of information they could find on how to rouse a rocket that had come to land once in its life, never again, and gone to sleep forever after that.

No one had ever done that, because what would happen if they did? No one knew. But the tower of Sidarfels, like all of the rockets of all the other such stations on Eightend, had once come from some unimaginable distance and safely to ground. That meant power beyond imagining.

The lift rose through echoing chambers, through

tubelike columns of dead air that seemed to go on forever, past the long-sleeping bands of stone and sediment and silt compressed into stone with its knowledge silent and unsought until it came up into Sidarfels' maintenance tunnels with its familiar architecture and reassuring lights once more. Yusaravan was home; not really here for very much longer, but she would always know Sidarfels better than even Eversand, and that would have to do.

Eversand Beach Dunes's people from the Exercitus Cartel were so sure they would take Sidarfels that they were all but measuring the floor plans of the tower for reallocation of lodging. Not so unreasonable an action to take, perhaps, if a little premature; but it did encourage a daughter of Sidarfels to get away from Sidarfels Center while she could, and dance her fencing routine in the open air.

Yusaravan knew that the Exercitus Cartel might cut down the quick-springing Trevalyn tremblers for their silver-and-black bark. That would be a permanent loss: the tremblers were slowly dying back all along the banks of the Sidarfels River, new growth sparser and sparser year by year. Still the trees would live forever, in memory if not in fact.

"Ink galls setting up well," Yusaravan's friend Flander said, pointing. Her friend and her controller; the woman responsible for teaching her the Forbidden Sequence. "There'll be a good harvest. Plenty of ink for sale. So long as we can get to it before those Exercitus people push in."

Yes, there were oak galls, or near enough. No actual oaks grew in Sidarfels, not the ones from the ancient taxonomies. But when a tree looked like an oak, leafed out like an oak, smelled like an oak in the cold autumn rain, a person might as well call it an oak. The first settlers here on Eightend had done just that.

So. Oak galls, to which Flander was pointing. These particular oak galls were tiny receptor chips, distributed throughout the edges and outliers of the clearing, one among the 184 in total. The number of target sensors in the dome of Sidarfels' tower. Simulations, for Yusaravan to practice with.

Fencing meant shining a beam of light on a receptor embedded in the inner surface of the dome. To do that a fencer had to work in sequence to progress through a program that was only handed to the reviewers as the piece started. From there a fencer would describe an emotional state, or a poem or a song, by invoking a pattern that people would recognize in telltales from the receptors.

The bout was won when a fencer got through her entire program without making a single mistake in the disclosed map. It was more and more of a challenge as the program increased in complexity, because there were 184 sensors, each could be used more than once, and if a fencer hit one of them out of the disclosed order she had to go back to the beginning of her routine and start again.

"You are an arrogant piece of leaf-mold," Yusaravan hissed suddenly, her voice as full of venom as she could make it. She shoved Flander, hard, and nearly overset her; but—as all of Sidarfels Station would know—Flander was not a person to accept provocation.

Recovering her balance Flander came up from a beautifully dynamic crouch with her fencing sword in hand. They had to keep a degree of distance from each other. Otherwise Exercitus—and others—could easily guess there was an unspoken reason for two people with so many differences between to share an unstated common interest. Secret societies didn't stay secret without a good-faith effort.

Yusaravan wasn't meant to like Flander, and words spoken low-voiced could be made to present hostility, so that Yusaravan could keep the conversation going.

"Say that again and mean it," Flander snarled. "How dare you. You second-tier pretender. I outrank you, Yusaravan, and I'll have you on your knees or I'll report you to the team captain, then that'll be the end of that, won't it?"

"Are you quite sure they're all the correct positions, please, Flander?" Yusaravan sneered, covering her hopeful question with a poisonous overlay of contempt by way of camouflage. All of them camouflaged, all concealed, including those of the Forbidden Sequence. That was the set no one was supposed to know about, the set that could be taught but never written down, never documented. "I can come out tomorrow?"

The fencing swords were of an ancient pattern, something like the old pictures of executioners' swords that were missing the final third of their blade. Flander struck Yusaravan across the face with hers, drawing blood down the sharpened blade from Yusaravan's forehead at the slant the length of Yusaravan's cheek. Yusaravan yelped, her shout evolving from genuine pain and surprise into apparent fury as she reacted to Flander's assault.

"I'm in charge of that," Flander hissed. "Now listen. Some of Exercitus' people have been up in the dome, cleaning out the sensors. There's no hint why but take careful note, be alert. Come on, Yusaravan, make it look good, I think Eversand is spying on us."

Not spying, no, how could Eversand be spying on them? There was nothing to see, just teammates working off a little aggression under the stress of their important role to play in closing ceremonies. And yet Eversand was bright, and clever, and genuinely the best fencer on Sidarfels Station. It didn't do to underestimate her.

That meant Yusaravan's practice would have to be curtailed, that Yusaravan didn't dare risk a fully integrated rehearsal of her solo presentation. No chance flash of any reflected sunlight from the highly polished channel of Yusaravan's fencing sword could be allowed to catch Eversand's eye and start her thinking about anything but footwork.

Flander struck Yusaravan again, across her face, with the back of her gloved hand. Yusaravan wiped her mouth, glaring after Flander with resentment. Turning her back with transparent scorn, Yusaravan started to dance her practice sets.

Boddifrieze. Bellosculics Calchotriatrix.

Eversand seemed to lose interest, turning away to skirt the oak-tree clearing. *Problem narrowly averted*, Yusaravan told herself, and focused on seeing the map of the Forbidden Sequence in her mind as she danced her free-form presentation.

And now here they were: Yusaravan; Geoffin, who was Yusaravan's backup in case of accidents; and the dignitaries who represented all five cartels—including

Sidarfels' parent, Granary—sitting in the reviewing box beneath the open latticework floor of the dome above, where they could get a good view.

Yusaravan could feel Eversand's eyes on the back of her neck; taking her measure, perhaps, evaluating what progress Yusaravan might have made in her fencing since she'd been promoted to third form. *Let Eversand do her best to set me off balance*, Yusaravan told herself, sensing the building excitement within her, the joy of battle.

It was all over for Sidarfels as she knew it. She might be offered a place on the fencing team, maybe an increase in salary as an additional inducement to stay on; but she wasn't sure she could stomach it. Just this one final act as a Sidarfels team fencer, one last official performance, and she was done with it, done with it all.

The drummers struck the cadence, *come to the line*. Yusaravan stepped up to her mark. This was a demonstration fencing bout, not a formal contest, so the rules were a little relaxed.

Yusaravan bowed to the observers. Allenghin did the same, taking the second bow out of deference to Yusaravan's superior rank amongst the fencers in Sidarfels' fencing club. At a nod from Administrator Jaxon the drummers struck the next cadence. Yusaravan and Allenghin entered the fencing ground.

The early spring light came streaming through the dome's viewports, flooding the exercise floor with gold-tinted illumination and casting faint shadows of the open-grid ceiling above across the floor. The viewports had been cut into the fabric of the tower only just after the towers had arrived at Eightend. The technology—

both of cutting through the tower's skin, and the manufacture of clear viewports harder by far than silicon glass—was long since lost, or hibernating.

The *be on your guard* chimes rang; they were off, Yusaravan and Allenghin, two fencers demonstrating floor-exercise figures as carefully choreographed as any courting passage. Dancing with each other, bright sword ringing against bright sword to reach two separate sensors at once, working up to an invocation of their chosen tune for the observers to recognize and applaud.

Yarbgardonry, Opterics, Delep Wartor. Ommastro, Obroniast, Eschaptntor.

The program had been marked out with hidden sensors in the flooring, carefully noted on the steps-dance map displayed for the dignitaries in front of their reviewing box. The cheerful little bell that marked each successful contact according to the plan was so familiar to Yusaravan—as to all of Sidarfels' fencers—that she hardly even heard it anymore.

Allenghin got her marks perfectly, *nine, ten, eleven.* Then she paused in place, well balanced on one foot, waiting for Yusaravan's answering move. That was eleven down; 173 to go, once Yusaravan had paired up three steps' reaction to her partner. *Beautiful*, Yusaravan thought. She'd be sure to tell Allenghin so. Moving her foot to match Allenghin's nine, Yusaravan shifted her weight to the next position, careful to show no hesitation in the passage.

There was no confirmation tone.

Yusaravan had missed the target.

Her eyes on Allenghin—following every minute shift

of expression, to demonstrate her attention to what Allenghin was going to do next—Yusaravan still almost missed the tiny narrowing of Allenghin's eyes, quickly recovered, quickly concealed. No information there, Yusaravan realized, frustrated.

What had happened? She'd clearly let her touch-point drop good and proper, a significant error. A significant humiliation for a fencer of her rank, and against one junior to her as well. How could she have made such an error?

She could see the expressions on the faces of the dignitaries in the observers' box, little flickers of commiseration, some scornful. These were closing ceremonies. The piece was designed to give Allenghin space to show her progress, and Yusaravan was supposed to help Allenghin along. Allenghin had recovered the beat. *Good job, Allenghin.* Yusaravan was grateful.

But it didn't stop there.

When an error howsoever obvious had been made, the fencer's job was to note the fault against herself and then continue without pause as though no mistake had been made. It demonstrated that the fencer was solidly in her program, clearly focused on the correct sequence; that she was truly aware of what she was doing, though she'd had a slip.

Yusaravan put the jarring misstep to the back of her mind for later analysis. Though she'd erred in her mind-map of where the next touch-point was, the correct hit was almost always short and left-oblique by one floor-tile's thickness. She corrected her step with a double toe-tap to indicate that she recognized her error, which meant she was momentarily distracted but not lost.

Then there was nothing to do but go on. Any point reduction in the technical evaluation would be assessed against Yusaravan, not Allenghin—and not Sidarfels, though Yusaravan's error wouldn't reflect well on the fencing program as a whole. She would complete the demonstration, ensure that Allenghin's standing in the team would rise rather than fall. Yusaravan knew that she'd have more than enough time to meditate on how she had made such a beginner's error—later.

She finished her supporting phrase, thankful that she made no further errors. It had been a momentary lapse, and no more. Allenghin challenged her, standard procedure, the structure of the exhibition bout so often repeated at every step of a fencer's progression up through the ratings that a person was heartily sick of it within months of their first entry.

By then it was something that any fencer could do in her sleep. Could do with her eyes closed. Yusaravan's body knew the program, perfect in placement, flawless in transition from stance to stance—

But Yusaravan tripped.

Her foot caught against some minute bit of the resin used to give new shoes their traction. It should not have been there, but that didn't matter now. The sabotage was too cunningly done, and Yusaravan tripped over her own two feet, a raw beginner's error, a fatal mistake. An immediate disqualification, categorically denying Allenghin's chance to demonstrate her abilities in front of the highest-ranking dignitaries of every cartel in Eightend. All attention was focused on Yusaravan.

Yusaravan hadn't just ruined her own reputation. She'd

damaged Allenghin's demonstration so badly that it would take Allenghin two years to claw her way back to her current standing, if not more. Allenghin didn't look at Yusaravan, even as closely as she had to pass to leave the fencing floor. Yusaravan couldn't blame her.

Yusaravan stood in the middle of the dueling floor, confused and perplexed, until one of the team coaches put an arm around her, took her hand, kindly escorted her away from all of the people there who wouldn't meet her eyes, their expressions confused and angry and disgusted.

Tripping. Actually stumbling, in front of senior cartel representatives, especially in front of the representative from Exercitus, which was to become Sidarfels' new manager and guardian, master over all. What had happened to her? What?

The team coach found her a place on a high bench at the side of the room. Yusaravan could see everything, from one side of the fencing ground to the other. There was Eversand, right enough, suited up, calm, collected, walking with self-respecting dignity into the center of the floor.

Yusaravan could hear murmurs around her. The dignitaries in their viewing box put their heads together, smiling a little; she could almost hear the words, *Now we'll see something you'll really like*. She wanted to sink into the cool metal walls of the tower structure and disappear.

She would not disappear. She was Yusaravan of Ringwall, and she belonged to Sidarfels. She would own her errors, though she didn't understand how they had happened, and she would hold her head erect and look people in the eye until they turned their faces away. She wasn't going to let it end like this.

When a fencer left the floor the first thing she was expected to do was to set her gear in order. Yusaravan still held her sword, gripping the hilt so tightly that she wasn't sure she'd even be able to set it down for hours yet to come. She wiped its broad blade, squared at the tip, sharpened along the edges. A few passes of her polish-cloth and the shine came up along the length of the sword.

She could have run her program without the sun; all the artificial lights remaining in the tower were shining, for events such as this. Even though she had nothing left—her final error had been an absolute disqualification, a twelve-day suspension—she couldn't help but note the sun's position, regardless. It was still short of the vernal equinox, four hours and some minutes after sunrise. She'd meditated long and deeply on the effects of the sun's rays coming through the upper windows of the tower dome. She knew just where it shone.

At the same time, she couldn't take her eyes off Eversand.

First passes, stations one through five of the 184-item sequence that would—at least hypothetically—activate the sensor grid in the dome's ceiling. Perfect. Beautiful. No errors.

And yet Yusaravan—watching from the sidelines—realized that there *should* have been errors. Eversand's steps were correct in sequence, but her feet were in the wrong places. Too short, or too far. Not by much, nothing to call itself to the attention of people whose familiarity with the sensors in the dome above and those in the flooring below piece was merely casual; but if the coaches were watching they'd be a little confused, as Yusaravan was.

Eversand's steps were off track. Incorrect target points. Yusaravan had years of practice visualizing the fencing floor of Sidarfels' tower; she could see it in her dreams. She could tell, and she was certain. There was no way in which the points Eversand was hitting with her foot were the genuine touch-points. The grid had been altered. The sensors had been moved. It was rigged.

That wouldn't be so much of a problem; but Yusaravan recognized the steps, the phrase. Eversand was dancing her free-form, and the routine she was presenting was far more complex and sophisticated than anything Yusaravan could have created. It was a tease, a provocation, a challenge. The Forbidden Sequence.

And Eversand wasn't hesitating. Wasn't breaking the phrase by stepping into another pattern, which would have halted the sequence. *This is crazy*, Yusaravan told herself. Eversand couldn't mean to run the entire sequence.

There were no records, no verifiable historical information, but as a matter of common and consistent understanding to complete the Forbidden Sequence was to initiate the catastrophic destruction of the tower and everyone in it. Eversand knew that. Nobody at Eversand's level of skill and mastery could *not* know that. There was something Yusaravan wasn't seeing, not grasping. Something was even more wrong with her—Yusaravan guessed—than her failure in the fencing match. What Eversand seemed to be doing was unthinkable.

Whether Eversand had seen Yusaravan watching her or not, Eversand's very next steps carried her into safe territory. Deep within the 184 base sequentials, and the danger zone left behind. Where was Eversand? Running from point 113 to 134.

Yusaravan frowned. Something was still wrong. Eversand had made a confident transition from 126 to 127, but she stepped to the same contact point as the one that Yusaravan had meant to hit when she'd made her first error. And yet the chime sounded clear and true; there was no alarm. The control sequence in the dome did not flag the touch.

Yusaravan stared in horror, masked just in time before the fencing coach who'd escorted her away from the fencing floor shot a swift glance at her face. The coach had seen it too. The same contact point, the same discrepancy, and yet the confirmation tone marked the touch as true. Yusaravan had caught the key to Eversand's program, now, an old folk song of vengeance and betrayal. She knew where Eversand would go next, and Eversand committed no errors.

The contact had been compromised. The sequence had been rerouted. Eversand had returned to the Forbidden Sequence.

Yusaravan had never taken Eversand for a fanatic, but if Eversand was going to dance the Forbidden Sequence—if Eversand meant to destroy the tower of Sidarfels and everybody in it—then Eversand was insane. To be willing to sacrifice herself to win some obscure point of advantage for Exercitus, Eversand had to be. Nobody had survived any of those unexplained explosions, the earlier incidents at the other stations. Had it been done the same way?

First contact in the Forbidden Sequence: it started out innocently enough, just a few points of light at a few ceiling sensors. But after five, after eight in sequence, a faint answering—warning—light started to glow point by point, and Yusaravan had to do something.

Taking up her fencing sword, Yusaravan started for the dueling floor. She could do this. She'd spent months memorizing the dome map until she could almost complete the routine with her eyes closed. All she needed to do was interrupt Eversand's Forbidden Sequence, force an error in the sequence somehow, delay the progression for long enough, and it would all stop. Theoretically. Then Eversand would have to restart the sequence from the beginning.

The coach had seen that there was something wrong; somebody would step in, help her, take charge. But first Yusaravan had to stop this. She didn't have time to explain.

Eversand only barely glanced her way, moving inexorably to the next point in the sequence. That was 129. This was going too fast for Yusaravan. How was she to find a reset? The contacts had been compromised. The grid had been sabotaged. She didn't know where the crucial points of contact were. Eversand looked at Yusaravan over her shoulder, sneering; no pretense of politeness left; raw, naked triumph, nothing else. No hatred. No contempt. Only the certainty that she'd won. There were no hints in Eversand's face that she considered the loss of her own life as anything of importance in the pursuit of some greater goal; or even remembered that critical detail.

What could Yusaravan do, how could she do it, where could she find the key to saving Sidarfels? There had to be a way, some hint, some critical detail, some secret knowledge....

Secret.

Secret societies. When they'd been in their advanced education years at school together, Eversand had joined Thikologia—water, weather systems, monsoons, wind events, ice, water currents. But Yusaravan had pledged to Operatrix.

She'd loved it. She'd eagerly clutched every scrap of information, knowledge, instruction she'd been able to find. Dual paths of transmission. Interference; signals that could bend around corners. Diffusion. The behavior of light, waveforms, particle streams. Optics.

Yusaravan knew the placement of the sensors in the dome. She knew the pattern of the open-work grid that lay between the ceiling of the central atrium containing the fencing floor and the fabric of the great dome itself. She knew more than that. She knew that it was springtime, that it was two thirds of the master clock from the tenth hour after sunrise. She didn't need to know where the sensors Eversand was activating were, passionately as she wished she did. All she needed to do was intercept the flash from Eversand's fencing sword with one of her own, split the beam, scatter the light.

All I need to do, Yusaravan said to herself, scornfully. *Right*. She measured the angle of Eversand's sword, its horizontal channel catching the bright white lights that shone down on the dueling-floor. The reflected beam of light from Eversand's sword just missed reflecting back from one of the elements of the open grid above, but that was all right with Yusaravan, it gave her a moment to steady her resolve and gather her pretended confidence.

Eversand tried again. She *had* to try again, because she still hadn't made contact with the correct sensor, the ray of brilliant light from her sword blocked yet again by a beam in the open-grid flooring above. Yusaravan's invasion had disrupted Eversand's concentration, clearly, and won Yusaravan precious extra moments to calculate.

Once again Eversand lined up her target, adjusted her grip on her sword, moved it into position to catch a beam of the dome's artificial lights in its central channel.

Yusaravan had no time to adjust her own sword, but she knew things Eversand didn't. She knew the sun of Sidarfels throughout the year, its position in the sky, the refraction of its light through the uniquely composed fabric of the dome's windows. She didn't try to hit Eversand's beam. She tagged the spark on Eversand's sword where it came to life, and if one ray of the starburst of scattered light Yusaravan achieved reached the target sensor—whichever one it was—as it splintered, it clearly had insufficient energy to get the sensor's attention.

There were other sensor points nearer to the scatter-point than the Forbidden Sequence sensor Eversand was trying to activate. Yusaravan knew that by the lights in the dome that Eversand had apparently activated thus far: lights that faded quickly to silent sleeping non-reactivity.

That meant that the dome's sensor net had registered an activation beam out of place within the Forbidden Sequence's progression steps.

Eversand was angry now. Yusaravan was glad to see it; that meant Eversand would be that much easier to keep off balance. Eversand raised her sword again, but Yusaravan could see Eversand glance toward the uppermost reaches of the dome, as if looking for a reference point, looking to restart the Forbidden Sequence by going back to the beginning.

Yusaravan didn't want to give Eversand any chances, any chance at all. She directed her beam of sunlight into Eversand's face. Eversand recoiled, reflexively, raising her sword hand to shield her eyes, turning her face away too immediately and dramatically for her reaction to have been calculated to deceive.

Yusaravan had Eversand on the run, and Sidarfels' on-site police had caught up. Station security people surrounded Eversand, locking her arms behind her back with arm-and-wrist restraints. The finish on the restraints was a matte black finish, light diffracted, not reflected. No chance of a last-minute deployment, and no danger if there was.

Yusaravan collapsed to her knees on the fencing floor, suddenly exhausted; but why not? Was it every day that she faced her death, faced the deaths of everybody at Sidarfels Station, and averted it within the space of a mere bushel of breaths?

In the dignitaries' viewing box, Administrator Jaxon had stood. Bowing her head, she spoke, loudly enough for everybody to hear. "Representatives one and all," she said.

"Let's adjourn, please. Private meeting room. I think we should talk."

And Sidarfels stays with Granary Cartel, Yusaravan thought. If Exercitus had been wittingly involved in a deep plot to gain paramount power by destroying infrastructure, Exercitus would be paying the price for generations yet to come. Yusaravan wasn't sure that was the case: the representative from Exercitus looked sick. It wasn't Yusaravan's concern. She didn't have to worry about it.

Centuries, millennia, of knowledge gradually laid aside, outprioritized always. *Yarbgardonry, Operatrix, Delep Wartor. Ommastro, Obroniast, Eschapintor. Ommastro, Obroniast, Eschapintor; Boddifrieze, Calchotriatrix. Zhobeproneas.*

Operatrix, Operatrix, Operatrix.

The value of the old learning had been demonstrated, here, convincingly. Powerfully. Now Yusaravan would make it her life's work to see that Operatrix would be honored at Sidarfels Station forever, and forever, and forever after that, a threshold into the future that would be ready to reclaim its sciences at last.

POWER & PRESTIGE
D.J. Butler

The city of Kish is ancient, built on the bones of thousands of civilizations that came before. There is power in those ruins, for those with the skill to dig it up. But power corrupts, or so they say, and Indrajit and Fix are about to learn that some powers are better left buried. . . .

✤ ✤ ✤

"I feel I should warn you," the man with the doglike face said. "There's a possibility I may eat my feces."

"That's it," Indrajit said to his partner. "We're not hiring this guy."

Fix frowned. "Why do you say there's a 'possibility'? Remind me your name . . . Munahim?"

The three men sat at a table in the common room of the nameless inn where Indrajit and Fix rented a room to serve as both their sleeping chamber and the headquarters of their two-man jobber company, the Protagonists. The barkeep, a broad-shouldered Kishi with a black topknot and tattoos of snakes across his shoulders, was polishing his counter. A messenger stood in the doorway, shifting from one foot to the other. The sounds of camels and gulls drifted in through the windows.

Given the heat, all five men wore simple kilts.

Munahim nodded, the motion making his long ears bounce and his eyes fill with liquid. "I've done it before. I'm not proud of it, but you know, there it is. If it's going to happen, I want you to know about it in advance."

"You make it sound like an impersonal phenomenon," Indrajit said, "like rain. It might rain, so you should be warned. I might munch on my own waste, so don't be surprised. How about you just choose not to eat your feces?"

"I get caught up in the moment." Munahim hung his head.

"Speaking of the moment," Indrajit said to Fix, "we don't have any moments left. We need to get over to the Hall of Guesses and look at that hole in the basement, now. We don't have time for this guy."

"Wrong," Fix said mildly. He was shorter than Indrajit and stocky, with a high-pitched, womanlike voice. "We don't have time for any other jobber. But since we're already interviewing Munahim, and he happens to be a tracker, he's the one person we have time for right now. It's just a bit of good luck that we happened to be interviewing Munahim when a job offer came through."

"We really must go." The messenger from the Hall of Guesses nodded anxiously in the doorway.

Indrajit scowled at Munahim, who was nearly as tall as he was, and similarly rangy. "Can you track by smell?"

Munahim nodded.

"But I mean . . . really well? Are you good at it?" Indrajit pressed.

"I'm the best," Munahim said.

Indrajit sighed. "Okay, here's the offer. If we get this lecturer back, you get one share. Fix and I each get two. No promises that we retain you any longer term than that, but consider this a trial period. Does that work for both of you?"

Fix nodded.

Munahim held out a hand to Indrajit. Indrajit hesitated, uncertain exactly how this dog-headed man might eat his own excrement and whether his fingers were really clean, but then clasped his hand around Munahim's forearm.

"If I see you eating your own waste," Indrajit growled, "or anybody else's, you will not get paid, and this will, by every frozen hell, be a onetime engagement."

The messenger from the Hall of Guesses was a very ordinary-looking Kishi, skin coppery brown and hair cut short like an upside-down bowl. Indrajit might have lost him in the crowd, but for the vermilion color of the messenger's kilt. Indrajit loped ahead of his partner, Fix, keeping an eye on both Fix and Munahim with his excellent peripheral vision. All three men were armed: Indrajit had his leaf-bladed sword, Vacho; Fix had an ax and a falchion at his belt; and Munahim had a long, straight sword slung across his back.

"Have you worked in a jobber company before?" Fix asked, continuing the interview.

"I was a mercenary," Munahim said. "We fought in Ildarion for two years."

"And then gave up?" Indrajit asked over his shoulder. "Didn't like the life of living and dying for contracts, eh?"

"I didn't think I was really fulfilling my potential," Munahim said. His voice had a mournful quality, consonant with the melting look of his face. The fur covering his muzzle and forehead and running in a tapering diamond down his shoulders and back was black, as were his nails, and his skin was a grayish-blue. His eyes were golden brown. "I'm a tracker, really, and all the Ildarion barons wanted from me was to swing a sword."

"We definitely want to use all the skills of all our team members," Fix said.

Indrajit grumbled without words.

"Did you read that we were looking for men in one of our posted notices?" Fix asked.

"I can't read," Munahim said.

"Ah, excellent," Indrajit said. "Finally, a point in his favor."

"I wouldn't mind learning," Munahim said. "It seems very useful."

"That's interesting," Fix mused. "I suppose I could teach you. I could teach everyone we eventually hire into the Protagonists. You never know when reading might come in handy."

Indrajit grumbled wordlessly again.

The climbed from the alley off the Crooked Mile up through the Spill, through clouds of spice and smoke that smelled of fish. Alleys and side streets shot off in all directions like the strands of a spider's web, but the messenger picked the shortest route upward. The walk was steep and Indrajit worked up a sweat.

They passed through the gate, held by jobbers in yellow tunics, and into the Crown. Here the merchants were fewer, the buildings were larger, and the plazas were pleasant with green amalaki trees, ketakas, and aloes. A troupe of actors on a corner recited famous dramatic speeches, jugglers on another leaped upon each other's shoulders and wrestled flaming torches up and down into the afternoon sky. As they approached the solid block of buildings that comprised the Hall of Guesses, walled off within its own stone curtain, complete with battlements and arrow loops, Indrajit found himself grinding his teeth. He wasn't quite sure why. He didn't object to the scholars of the Hall of Guesses cutting open dead bodies and pressing plants between panes of glass and whatever else they did.

He did find it somewhat silly and effeminate that they felt the need to write it all down, and to take it all so seriously.

The messenger took them through the front gate of the Hall of Guesses. The men on guard here weren't jobbers, but warriors on the payroll of the Hall itself. They wore vermilion kilts and tunics and leaned on long spears. They glared at Indrajit and his colleagues, but when the messenger shouted a few words of authorization at them, they stepped aside.

Indrajit had imagined that the interior of the Hall of Guesses would be a single large courtyard, with tall buildings standing around the outside, against the wall. Instead, the center of the fenced-in area was filled with numerous buildings, the height of the outer wall or shorter, and a maze of lanes and alleys winding among them. Women and men paced deep in thought, conversed with one another beneath arched porticos, yelled over coffee mugs, or lay sleeping on the ground.

"One thing that is immediately apparent," he said to Fix, "is that these reading-scholars have no dignity. Look at that fellow over there, he's lying beneath a bench like any public drunk! All of them together don't have the respectability of a single Recital Thane."

"So you have doubled their respectability by merely entering," Fix said.

"What's a Recital Thane?" Munahim asked.

"Indrajit is the epic poet of his people," Fix explained. "He can recite their epic from memory. A hundred thousand lines about fish-headed warriors."

"Thirty thousand," Indrajit said, "give or take." He let the jibe about his resembling a fish pass.

"Perhaps some of these people might be interested in studying at your feet," Fix suggested. His expression looked serious. "You're looking for apprentices."

Indrajit scanned the area. "I would prefer people of my own kind, if possible. And in any case, committing the art of the Blaatshi Epic to memory is a serious undertaking that requires real discipline, hard work, and self-sacrifice. No one I see here seems capable of any of that."

"A few times a year, the Hall of Guesses puts on its formal robes," Fix said, "when they award each other degrees, and for major cult processions. Then they look impressive. The rest of the time, they mostly care about what's inside. Thoughts and ideas. That should appeal to you, no?"

"No thought is so noble that it matters a whit," Indrajit said, "unless it is matched to noble deeds."

The messenger stopped. They were somewhere in the center of the maze—within the larger warren of the Crown, and again within the still larger labyrinth of Kish—beside a small brick building. Next to the building's open door hung a bronze sign stamped with letters, and in front of the sign stood a man.

He was shaped like a cone, with the narrow tip pointing up. The wide base of the cone sagged on all sides, and the gray toga hanging over everything nearly obscured tree trunk-like legs that terminated with nails but no apparent feet, like elephant's legs. A whiskered tail swished quickly back and forth, agitating the lower folds of the toga. Long, muscular arms hung at his side, and his head was thick and boxy, with a prominent, bulging forehead and four yellowing tusks. His skin was pale white, callused, and speckled here and there with thick stands of black bristles.

Indrajit cocked his head to one side. "What race of man are you?"

It was not entirely a polite question.

"I'm an Olifar." The man's voice sounded like an iron sheet dragged over gravel. "Jat Bighra is my name. First Lecturer in Druvash Technologies. And you are Blaatshi. We see few of you in Kish."

"Few, or none?"

"You're the first I've seen, I admit."

The messenger bowed and retreated.

"Why did you send for us?" Fix asked.

"I wouldn't have sent for anyone." Bighra shrugged. "We have our own men. But the lord chamberlain was here, meeting with the prime magister, and apparently he felt strongly that you might be able to help. He insisted. We are grateful for the help, of course."

"And what are you paying?" Fix asked.

"The prime magister has authorized ten Imperials for the investigation, and fifty Imperials if you bring her back."

"Show us the hole," Indrajit said. "And tell us who the 'she' in question is. The messenger said a group of your scholars went down a hole in the basement and didn't come back up."

Munahim sniffed.

Bighra led them into the building. Through open doorways, Indrajit saw large rooms, each with a low stage at one end. The narrow halls connecting the rooms were decorated with drawings on the walls, but Indrajit couldn't figure out any of the images. They seemed to be of objects, but the illustrations were cunningly conceived to reveal both the insides and the outsides of the objects at the same time. Universally, the insides were much more complicated, consisting of wires and tubes and nodes that resembled gemstones and plates. The outsides mostly looked like rounded stones or boxes.

"What is this place?" Indrajit asked. "What are these drawings?"

Jat Bighra led them down stairs. "Ironically, one of the subjects studied in this building is Druvash Technologies."

"Of which you are First Lecturer," Fix said.

Bighra nodded. "And Sari was Second Lecturer. Her work was promising, if a little radical."

"I don't care about her work in Druvash Sorceries," Indrajit said. "Tell me about how she disappeared."

Bighra nodded, leading them down a second flight of stairs. The light down here came from oil lamps, set into niches in the walls. Kish was an ancient city, with multiple levels of previous occupation hidden beneath its streets in the form of mazelike underground ruins. The Hall of Guesses, or at least this building, seemed to have been constructed by sinking several levels of basement down into those ruins. That meant that beyond the walls surrounding Indrajit now, there might be flowing sewers, rapeworm nests, and worse.

It also meant that the Hall of Guesses was bigger than it appeared, and potentially *much* bigger.

"I care," Fix said. "What was the Second Lecturer studying?"

"Power," Bighra said. "Power generation. She had a theory about what powers Druvash artifacts that had managed to garner a few influential adherents."

"You don't agree with her theory?" Fix suggested.

Munahim sniffed.

Bighra shrugged. "From my work in Druvash weaponry, I can't see how her theory explains half of what it would need to explain, even to be taken seriously as a hypothesis. I encouraged her to continue to think boldly, but . . . no, I don't think she was ever going to prove anything."

"Druvash weaponry?" Indrajit asked. "I don't suppose that's available for purchase, say, to employees of the lord chamberlain?"

Bighra laughed. "Oh, heavens, no, it's far too destructive. Also, we have precious few pieces, so they have to stay available to us for study."

"Did Sari have an office in this building?" Munahim asked. "Or can you show me where her personal effects are?"

"Er . . . yes, hold on, we have to go back up one flight." Jat Bighra turned and led them up stairs and down a hallway to a narrow rectangular room with a desk at one end.

"May I have a moment alone in here?" Munahim asked.

Bighra shrugged and Munahim shut the door.

"Frozen hells," Indrajit said. "He's defecating."

"What?" Bighra blinked. "Why would he do that in Sari's office?"

"So we can't see him eat it," Indrajit grumbled.

"First of all," Fix said, "you don't know that's what he's doing. This is just your grumpy side coming out. And second, if that is what he's up to, then he's having the decency not to do it in front of you."

"Ah," Jat Bighra said. "He's a Kyone. I've read about their coprophagy."

"I don't know what the word means," Indrajit said, "and I think I'd rather not find out."

"Eating excrement is far from the most bizarre or repellent eating habit of the thousand races of man," Jat Bighra said. "Anthropophagy and cannibalism, surely, must rate at the top. I've read of a race of man whose members eat their own flesh as a means of suicide, when they become too old, and a burden on their communities."

"It isn't a competition," Indrajit said. "That's all disgusting."

"There are different hypotheses about why the Kyones

do it." Bighra scrabbed the thick, scabby skin of his jaw reflectively. "Some say it aids in digestion. Others think they do it when their diet is lacking some important nutrient."

"This is what's wrong with the Hall of Guesses," Indrajit said. "You sit around thinking about things like this."

"He said he gets caught up in the moment," Fix said.

"Which sounds like compulsion or madness." Bighra nodded. "But you see, that only raises more questions. Why would a race of man be constituted so as to feel compelled to eat feces? And why do some of them prefer their own, and some prefer the excrement of others?"

"Shut up right now," Indrajit said, "or I'll draw my sword and attack you both."

The door opened and Munahim emerged, his face mournful.

"I'm not going to ask what you were doing in there," Indrajit said, "and I'd prefer you not tell me."

Munahim's shoulders slumped, and he nodded.

"Right." Jat Bighra cleared his throat. "Just back down one level, and we're there." He turned and walked, and they followed him. "It was renovations, you see. The Hall had a jobber crew in here, fixing some corroded heat ducts behind the walls, and they accidentally broke through the floor."

He stopped in front of a door with a lock, and took a ring of keys from inside his toga. Indrajit guessed they must be in the corner of the floor, several levels down from the street . . . maybe five levels? If he exited the building horizontally, and could keep moving until he saw daylight, he'd come out in the Spill or the Lee or the Dregs.

Welcome to Kish; it's as hollow as its people's hearts.

"Beyond that door," Indrajit said, "are we still in the building?"

Bighra shrugged. "I think you would say no, we will have left the building, and be underneath the city. But the pipes and ducts and crawlspaces that serve the building pass through that space, so I'm not so sure. Where does the building really end?"

Indrajit took the oil lamp from the nearest niche. He held it in his left hand and drew his sword. "I really meant, will I need a light?"

Jat Bighra opened the door. Beyond lay a packed dirt floor, crumbling brick columns and arches, and bronze ducts. Indrajit's light proved to be unnecessary, because the space was lit. A few paces from the door, two brick arches came together, and where a column should have stood, there was only a crumbling orange stalactite, and beneath it, a hole in the floor. A splinter of green light came up through the hole; it wasn't much, but it was enough to see by.

"You might get along fine without a light," the First Lecturer said. "The workmen accidentally broke through the floor, with the result that you see."

Indrajit held on to his lamp anyway.

"And Sari went down in there?" Fix said.

"Yes," Bighra said.

Munahim sniffed.

"Something to do with her research?" Fix suggested.

Bighra shrugged. "I suppose. She got excited, and she

took two of the most experienced students who were reading with her and went right in."

"Not you?" Indrajit asked.

"I stayed up here," Bighra said. "I had work to do."

"What, this morning?" Fix asked.

"Yesterday," Jat Bighra said. "We shut the door to keep anyone else from getting hurt, or wandering off into the maze, of course. But she never came back."

"You didn't post a guard or anything?" Indrajit asked.

Bighra shook his head. "This door is always here. It's locked, and nothing has ever come through, other than our own people."

Fix rubbed his chin. "So Sari hoped to find a Druvash power source."

"Or perhaps she was finally ready to give up on that idea," Bighra suggested, "and hoped to find something new to study. Or perhaps she was just curious. It takes a lot of natural curiosity to make someone a good lecturer at the Hall of Guesses. Just because something is glowing green down there, that doesn't mean it's Druvash."

"It might not even be sorcery," Indrajit said. "It could be some creature that glows in the dark."

Bighra nodded.

"Why don't you give us the key?" Fix suggested. "You can stay here. We'll come back and report what we find."

"I'll come." Bighra smiled nervously. "She was my colleague, and I'd like to know what happened. And I'll have to make my report to the prime magister, so it's best if I'm actually a witness."

They all stepped into the crumbling brick maze and Jat Bighra locked the door behind them. Indrajit kept his sword in his hand. The air smelled sour, with a hint of charnel and ash, and it wasn't moving at all.

Fix and Munahim went first. Bighra gestured politely to Indrajit to go next, and Indrajit shook his head. "You're the client," Indrajit said. "You go in the middle, and I'll bring up the rear. In case anything tries to ambush us, you get the maximum protection."

"I'm quite capable," the Olifar grunted.

"Yes, you're a Druvash sorcerer." Indrajit pointed with the tip of Vacho. "You really look the part, in that toga. Now get moving, or else give me the keys and go back."

The hole in the floor opened at the top of a scree-cluttered slope. The source of the light was not visible as Indrajit stooped to avoid banging his forehead, and entered. Ahead, along the slope below him, he saw Munahim close behind Fix. The Kyone walked bent over, as if bringing his nose close to the ground. Was he really able to track by scent? And, if so, was he following Sari and her two readers now?

Readers. Indrajit snorted.

A hundred cubits or more separated the two in the lead from Indrajit and the scholar. With his peripheral vision, Indrajit watched for exits on the left and right sides of the slope of rubble, and saw none. About halfway down the slope, a long black scorch mark blighted one wall. Because he saw better to the sides than immediately in front of him, when he needed to be extra careful about his footing, he turned his head slightly to one side.

"What do your Druvash weapons do, then?" he asked.

"Some of them, we don't yet know." Bighra stumbled, but caught himself. "Indeed, some of my papers have presented arguments that unidentified objects may, in fact, be weapons that we do not yet understand."

Papers. Indrajit snorted.

"But surely you must know how some of them work," Indrajit said. "Or you couldn't be certain there were any Druvash weapons at all. Maybe someone would present the theory that the Druvash were entirely peaceful."

"That theory *has* been argued," Bighra said. "It was vigorously maintained by a Pelthite scholar named Umram Sog, about a century ago. But the blasted quality of Druvash ruins told against him; there's simply no way that the Druvash succumbed to a disease, or economic depression, or existential malaise."

"I don't know," Indrajit said. "Never underestimate the deadliness of existential malaise."

"And once we finally started to be able to use some of the Druvash artifacts and learned that they were efficient killing machines, his theory imploded."

"So you know how they work."

"That's not quite right. We can *operate* some of them. We're a long way from knowing how they *work*."

Indrajit nodded. Fix and Munahim had reached a flat space below the stones. Ahead of them stretched a featureless stone wall, through which were bored perfectly circular holes. The green light shone from the hole on the left-hand side.

Indrajit and Jat Bighra were nearing the bottom of the slope, too. The air here still felt stale and motionless, but the smell of ash was gone.

"And you say they don't kill by inflicting existential malaise."

"Some throw projectiles. Like Thûlian black powder weapons, only the projectile is packed in metal."

Indrajit grunted. "No pouring in the fabled powder, eh?"

"No. Other weapons fire heat rays."

"Heat rays?"

"Imagine a ray of the sun, but greatly intensified, so that it burned flesh to ash upon contact."

Something tickled at the back of Indrajit's consciousness.

"Have you ever seen the body of a Druvash?" he asked. "Or the skeleton, or the mummy, or whatever? Even an image, say a sculpture or an old mosaic?"

"No one has," Bighra said. "The discovery of an intact Druvash body would be a world-shaking step forward in learning about them. Scattered bones have been recovered to date, but not enough even to be certain how big they were."

"Is that because of the nature of their weapons?" Indrajit asked. "A ray of heat, if it was hot enough, might incinerate bone as well as flesh."

"*I* think some of the artifacts we haven't yet figured out are explosives," Jat Bighra said. "Others seem to be airborne poisons. One is said by a very old source to cause transformation of its targets, whatever that might mean. I've read an account of a mobile, controllable cloud of acid. Other weapons attack by *sound*."

"Fearsome, indeed," Indrajit said. "Do the lords of the great families know about all this? I would think they would be interested in controlling these weapons. Especially if it came to a war. If Ukeling pirates sailed up to the West Flats, I bet Orem Thrush would love to be able to sink their ships by hitting them with Druvash sunbeams."

"The Lords of Kish are aware of my work." There was pride in Bighra's voice. "It may be that Orem Thrush was meeting with the prime magister this morning to be updated on my researches."

"And this is how he heard about a missing second lecturer," Indrajit said. "And this is why he cares."

"I suppose." Bighra sniffed. "It's not every lecturer whose work is noticed by the powerful."

"What's the difference between being first lecturer and being second?" Indrajit asked. "Better pay?"

"People in my position can hardly be bothered about such things as pay," Jat Bighra said. "We get paid enough, and there is a pension, and living quarters within the walls of the Hall. All the food I want, of the best kind. Girls, if we want them. I suppose the first lecturer in any department has more honor."

Fix and Munahim were well along the length of the left-hand passage, appearing now as mere shadows. Indrajit and Bighra approached the tunnel mouth. Not only was the opening of the tunnel perfectly circular, but the passage beyond maintained the same shape all along its length, its walls completely smooth.

"Better job security?" Indrajit suggested.

"We're all pretty secure, as long as the wealthy of Kish are willing to pay to send their useless children here to be educated." Bighra laughed, a short, sharp bark. "And as long as we are patronized by the Lords of Kish."

"But you get to go first in the parades, as First Lecturer," Indrajit said. "Your name is read from the roll before anyone else's. You stand foremost in the . . . I don't know, the ceremonies. You get the better seating at the opera. You get prestige."

"All of that, yes," the First Lecturer said. "Prestige, yes."

"Prestige is worth a lot to some people," Indrajit suggested. "Many would envy you."

"Well, hum-ho," Bighra said.

"When would Sari have become first lecturer?" Indrajit asked. "Only if you died or retired, I guess?"

"Based on how her research was going, yes," Bighra said. "She was chasing a dead end, though I don't think she would ever admit it. I suppose if I had moved into administration, somehow, she might have become first. But I'm not the type."

The First Lecturer was nearing the end of the tunnel. His step was becoming slower, more hesitant. The silhouettes of Munahim and Fix had disappeared from view. A bass hum rolled into Indrajit's hearing and made his bones tremble.

"Did you go down this far?" Indrajit asked.

Bighra shook his head. "I stayed above, as I said."

"Should we be calling for them?" Indrajit said. "I mean, we don't want to attract the attention of anything nasty that lives down here, but, on the other hand, that's why we're armed. And Sari and her readers might be lying injured somewhere."

He adjusted his grip on his sword and raised it, resting the blade on his shoulder.

"Sari!" Jat Bighra called. "Chumble! Tom Tom!"

The names echoed up and down the circular stone tunnel, and there was no response.

Bighra exited the tunnel at the far end and his body seemed to acquire a green halo, surrounding the scholar entirely, for just a moment. Indrajit moved slowly into the next chamber, casting his eyes around while still keeping his attention fixed on Bighra.

To the right, a stone wall was incised with deep grooves in complex patterns. Was that some kind of writing? Bronze spheres sat poised atop those grooves, which might be the handles on levers, which might then . . . ride within the grooves? Indrajit shook his head. At a quick glance, there were maybe a hundred of the balls, and enough groove-cut wall to make a decent Rûphat court, if it were laid horizontal.

To the left, a handrail marked the edge of the flat shelf on which they all stood. Behind the rail, the floor dropped away and the ceiling rose, and the walls on the far side were smooth, without railing, walkway, or grooves. In the center of the resulting space, a green fire burned. It was the size of a large bonfire, or a small, one-room hut. Indrajit blinked and his eyes watered, but he couldn't tell whether the fire was contained within some kind of glass, or whether instead the fire was simply so glossy and iridescent that it gave the impression of being bottled. Indrajit could see no bottom of the fire, and no fuel. The green flame seemed simply to exist, floating in the air.

It gave off no heat.

Fix turned to face Indrajit and Bighra. "Sari came down here with her readers because she thought the green light might teach her something about Druvash power. It looks like she was probably right."

"I suppose so," Bighra said slowly. "Have you seen any sign of her?"

"One thing did strike me as strange," Fix said. "Why would she come down here with just a couple of students? Why not some of your Hall of Guesses guardsmen, or a jobber company? Indrajit and I are tough, armed men, and we avoid coming down into the ruins whenever we can, because there are dangerous things down here. Why would a second lecturer rush down here with so little protection?"

"Oh, that's obvious," Indrajit said. "You just have to stop imagining that the scholars in the Hall of Guesses have some kind of magical selflessness. These aren't the adepts of Salish-Bozar the White, Fix, these are ordinary, petty, ambitious men."

"Hey," Bighra objected.

"And how do men get power in this world?" Indrajit asked. "By controlling access to a resource. By controlling the contracts, in the case of the Lords of Kish. By controlling access to, what do you call it, in the case of the Paper Sook."

"Capital," Fix said.

"Capital. And by controlling access to knowledge, if you're a lecturer in the Hall of Guesses. Sari wanted the information for herself and her best students, and no one else. She wanted to prove she was right, after all, or get new information for her theory, whatever it was. She wanted work for her students to control and carry out, and this was a golden opportunity to have that. Bringing along anyone who might steal the information, or accidentally pass it on to someone on the outside, jeopardized that opportunity. And look, it was so close. What did it take us to climb down here, a mere twenty minutes?"

"Too bad she got lost," Jat Bighra said. "Wandered off and got eaten by some unknown beast."

Indrajit nodded. "She made one mistake."

"What do we do now?" Bighra said.

"Now," Fix said, "we have to go tell the prime magister that his First Lecturer of Druvash Technologies committed three murders."

Jat Bighra pulled something from inside his toga. It looked like a flat white disk, smooth and small enough to fit in the palm of his hand. One end was truncated and flat, and rimmed with black. He pointed it at Fix—

Munahim leaped, dragging Fix to the floor—

A white sheet of flame burst from the disk for a split second, melting a section of the railing ten cubits wide—

And then Indrajit brought his sword, Vacho, down in an overhand motion. He meant to strike with the flat of his blade, knocking the strange weapon from the scholar's hand, but in the excitement of the moment, he struck with the blade instead. Vacho sliced through skin and bone and bit deep into the disk.

A blinding flash of light and a wall of force hurled Indrajit backward. He struck the stone wall headfirst, and for a time he lost track of his surroundings.

"Indrajit," he heard. "Can you hear me?"

"I can hear you," he said, his voice slurring. Blinking, he climbed to his feet with the help of the wall. Fix and Munahim helped him up—Fix's eyebrows and the hair on the Kyone's muzzle were singed nearly bare, but otherwise they seemed unharmed.

Jat Bighra, on the other hand, was dead. His nose was smashed flat and his eyes jellied, probably by the same blast that had hurled Indrajit off his feet. His windpipe was also smashed flat, which was likely what had killed him.

"You could have just knocked him down," Fix said.

"I got caught up in the moment." Indrajit shrugged. "Be grateful that you're alive, after you called him out like that."

Indrajit found Vacho lying on the floor and picked the sword up, returning it to his belt. The oil lamp lay shattered and he left it in its puddle of fuel.

"How did you figure it out?" Fix asked Indrajit.

"It seemed pretty clear that he wanted Sari to fail," Indrajit said. "And there are flame marks on the wall back up there. And I couldn't figure out why he was accompanying us down here, unless it was to make certain we failed, too. I think he followed Sari and her readers down here and burned them to ash with that flame weapon before she even saw this thing. Frozen hells, maybe she was on the path to overtaking him as first lecturer, and he had no other way to stop her. How about you?"

Munahim shrugged. "I could smell from the trail that Bighra had been down here before. He was lying to us."

Indrajit almost shot back that the Kyone's sense of smell had been redundant, that he, Indrajit, had divined Bighra's guilt with no help. But he decided not to, and instead, he clapped the Kyone on the shoulder.

Munahim grinned, tongue lolling from his mouth.

"Do we tell the prime magister about this?" Fix pointed at the green flame.

"If we tell him," Indrajit said, "he can block off the passages around it, and stop anyone else from getting to the flame and, I don't know, causing an explosion. Lighting Kish on fire."

"But if we tell him," Fix said, "then his scholars will have access to this energy, which looks like it could be really dangerous."

"Hard choices." Munahim shook his head.

"On the plus side," Indrajit said, "the two leading scholars studying Druvash sorcery are now both dead. That probably sets the field back twenty years."

"Maybe more," Fix said, "depending on how jealously they guarded their knowledge from each other. So maybe the Hall of Guesses will come down here and fence in this green flame, but there will be no one who can do anything with it. Not for years. Maybe decades."

Indrajit sighed. "I guess that's the solution, then. Why does it feel like, no matter how hard we try to do the right thing, the powers that be always remain the powers that be?"

"The powers that be are not necessarily evil," Fix said.

"And the powers that be have cash to pay," Munahim said.

"That," Indrajit said, "is a really good point. And today, the powers that be owe us ten Imperials. I assume your math is good enough to know how many Imperials you get, Munahim?"

"One of five shares means that I get two," the Kyone said.

"Yes," Indrajit agreed. "As long as you don't slip up and eat feces between here and the prime magister's office."

Munahim grinned, somehow still managing to look mournful in his eyes. "I'll try."

A BROKEN SWORD HELD HIGH
L.J. Hachmeister

Generations have passed since the colonists on Terra Pax severed their connection to Earth and the wider universe. Though dragons stalk the wilderness, all violence—even when done in defense—is forbidden by holy law. But when the only guarantee of peace is surrender, Kira must learn not to lay down arms, but to hold the sword high....

✢ ✢ ✢

My father does not draw his sword, even as the Red Dragon circles around in the darkened sky for another attack.

"Kira!" he shouts at me as thunder booms overhead. "Run!"

But I can't. The flying beast spreads its wings, casting a great shadow upon the gathering party. As the other men flee from the riverside to the cover of the forest, I stand transfixed by its glowing crimson scales and fire-born eyes.

"Kira!"

My father runs to me as lightning cracks open the congested gray sky. As it dives for me, a bolt strikes its tail. Blue fire erupts across its spine and ignites its eyes.

I reach out, heart thumping in my chest, even as it bares its jagged silver teeth and—

A large body slams into me, knocking the breath from my lungs. I can't tell dirt from sky as I tumble down the grassy slope into the river. The shock of the cold water drives me to panic and I flail, gulping and snorting in the turbulence.

"Get her out of here!"

Strong arms scoop me out of the water and toss me to the grassy bank on the opposite side of the river. Ezra, the leader of our colony, lifts me up and helps me toward the safety forest as I cough and stagger.

Father—

I dig in my heels and turn around to see the Red lunging at my father, swiping at him with its armored forelegs. *Draw your sword!*

My father dives back into the icy waters as the dragon swoops down, slicing into the river with its spiked belly.

Ezra yanks on my arm, but I twist free and run back to my father. Behind me, our leader shouts to the men in the forest: "Deploy countermeasures!"

The beast roars and snaps its armored tail, twisting around for another attack. I reach my father as he throws an arm onto the bank, digging his fingers into the mud and grasses to pull himself up. Grabbing one of his sleeves, I try to help he gasps for breath. Blood gushes from the cut along his forehead.

"Kira," he wheezes, losing his grip on one side. He

doesn't finish his reprimand as I lose my grip on his sleeve, and he slips back into the rushing river.

But not before I grasp the hilt of his sword.

I meant to grab his baldric, as if I, a thirteen-year-old, gangly kid could somehow haul a full-grown man out of a raging river. Instead, I stumble back with sword in hand, struggling to lift and aim it at the incoming dragon.

"Kira, no!" my father shouts, clinging to a tree root jutting out of the mud. "Put down the sword!"

I hear him but can't comprehend the command. Not as the beast swoops in, bellowing, teeth and talons bared. I swing the sword from left to right in wild, uncoordinated movements, and it jerks back at the last second. The sheer mass of its body cutting through the air strikes me down, but I scramble back and use both hands to hold the sword up.

"Don't fight it!" Ezra screams from the cover of the forest.

Thunders boom across the valley, lightning splashes across the sky. Though my hair is tied back, the loose strands stand up, as do the hairs on my arm. The beast attracts the lightning, feeds off it, as if the storm and the predator of the skies are one. Even if the Red doesn't eat me on this next pass, I'm holding a 110-centimeter lightning rod.

Fireworks blaze up to the sky and explode in a sparkling burst of orange, yellow, and green. The beast shrieks and shoots up to the clouds, disoriented by the dazzling colors.

The smell of gunpowder hits my nose with the stunning reality of what I've done, and the rules I've broken. I drop the sword in the grass and return to my father, but Ezra's there with two other men, lifting my father out of the river.

Lightning zigzags through the tortured clouds. The beast electrifies, radiating blue, writhing. Its scream harkens my blood and chills my bone, making me feel more alive than ever.

And yet, I know the punishment that is coming.

What have I done?

The men deploy smoke grenades to hide our position as we flee to the sanctuary of the trees. I try to catch up to my father, but even injured and exhausted, he is faster than me. When we reach the white cliffs, he and the others pause long enough at the rope bridge for me to catch up.

One of the men hands the sword back to my father, and he accepts the burden with the penitence expected of all Terrans.

"Our youngest has strayed," Ezra says, nursing his injured shoulder. "This is a troubling sign."

My father looks back at me, face bloodied, blue eyes racked with guilt and disappointment. "Forgive me, Ezra. I misjudged my daughter's readiness. Please, may she live to see the morrow."

Ezra looks at me, eyes narrowing, as the beast roars in the distance. "You're lucky she's just a girl."

Just a girl.

Ezra's scorn burns hotter than the fever that sets in that evening. My mom tends to me as I toss and turn in bed, whispering forbidden words in her ancestral language as she reapplies the healing brown paste of mashed-up flowers and roots to my forehead and neck.

"Be strong, Kira," she says, switching to our common tongue so I can understand her through the fog. "This will pass."

"She fell into the river, probably caught a chill," my father explains, limping into my bedroom. I can only make out his silhouette in the flickering candlelight. I hate the pity in his voice. "Maybe she didn't take to this world."

My mother presses the back of her hand against my cheek. "She's stronger than you think."

Sweat drips down my body, soaking through the plant-fiber bedsheets. I can't stand the way my father sees me, shivering and shaking, weak.

"I—I'm ready to go g—gathering again."

My mom tries to keep me from rising, but I throw over the blankets and get to my feet. My father's gaze hardens as I stand there, covered in brown paste, a wisp of a creature compared to his looming presence.

"Always a fight in you," my father says, stepping into the candlelight so I can see his face. My mother's stitched up the gash quite nicely. It will fade like the rest of his scars. "But you're not nearly as powerful as you think."

I notice his Sword of Burden is once again strapped to his back. With whatever he did to his leg, I'm sure the extra weight of the weapon isn't good for healing, but he would never spare himself. Nor will my mother, until death—or worse.

"Wash up," my father commands.

He and my mother exchange glances as I shuffle to the bathroom.

I lean against the sink as I scrub off the paste, letting the cool water run down my neck and chest. I scrutinize myself in the mirror, knowing that if I leave a single dirty spot, my father will just send me back in.

I sigh at the reflection in the mirror. I look thinner and bonier than usual, my black hair barely contained in a ponytail. Most northern colonists have honey-brown irises, but I was born with eyes the color of a gray winter sky. My mom says they're beautiful. Ezra convinced my father that the unusual color, along with my stillborn twin brother, was an omen. Right now, they just look drained, much like how I feel.

"Kira?"

I drag myself back out to my bedroom. My mother is standing by my father, head bowed. She lost an argument, but her reddened cheeks say she's got more to say when they step out.

"You unsheathed my sword in the valley," my father states.

"I'm sorry, Father," I say, sensing this lecture was coming. Swords of Burden are a reminder of our violent past, of why our terraforming forefathers left Earth, and never to be used for violence. Only those deemed worthy to carry the heavy sword are allowed to speak in community circles and weigh in on colony matters. I could argue it was a mistake, that I meant to grab his baldric, but as much as I want to believe that, it isn't entirely true. If it were, I would have never used it to defend against the Red.

"Violence is *never* the answer," my father says, baritone voice rising. His meaty hands curl into fists that could knock out a stone pillar. "We are never to draw our swords, even if it means our life. Violence only begets violence."

"Even in defense?" I say, staggering forward. I catch myself, eyes closing for just a second to keep the mud bricks and thatch roof from swirling together. "I saved your life!"

My father guffaws. "And what's next? Defense turns to aggression, aggression to bloodlust, bloodlust to war. A path of the Sword Mage. If you were a boy, I'd offer your hide to Ezra."

I grind my teeth together to keep from shouting. My twin brother and I were born premature under the feared hundred-year cycle of the fifth "blood" moon. Legend says that the blood moon awakens the violent spirits, creating the Sword Mage, a being who can effect storms and draw out the Red Dragons.

But that's the mystical side of things, and it confounds me. How can the descendants of star travelers and terraformers believe in such things? If the colonists had allowed themselves to keep all the technology that brought them from Earth to Terra Pax, I'm sure there would be another explanation. My mom says to be thankful they let us keep indoor plumbing.

If it were Rorin in my place, I think, conjuring the imaginary image of my dead brother, *he'd have been killed on the spot.*

A strange hypocrisy in the Peacekeeper tenets, but my father claims that Sword Mages are dangerous enough to warrant such extremism.

A wave of nausea washes over me. I eye the bed,

wanting to lie back down, but don't want him to take that as a sign.

"How can defense be wrong?" I say, tears forming in my eyes. I swear it's the fever, not my anger. "I couldn't just stand there and watch you die."

My father wrinkles his nose, his forehead knotting, as if caught between a cry and a shout. Instead, he rummages through his gray-and-green tunic and tosses me a weathered baldric.

"You are not ready for your Burden, but you need to understand the consequences of violence."

He limps out of the room and comes back with another sword in hand. From my limited angle, it looks just like the ones my parents carry, forged from unique Terra Pax metals into a blend of Dao and Spartan design. The sharp blade glints in the candlelight. My heart thuds in my chest as he approaches me, hilt first, only to reveal the ugly truth at the very last second.

The broken sword. The one that was to be given to Rorin when he came of age. The one my father shattered against the mountainside when my brother would not wake.

"Peace is the only thing that matters," he says, tossing it at my feet. It clatters on the clay tiles. "We are nothing with violence."

Sweat dripping off my forehead, I bend down and pick up the sword. Even broken in half, the weight is onerous. I hold the ruined sword in both hands, wobbling. Feverish heat creeps up my neck, but I will myself to keep upright.

"I won't let you down, Father," I say, eyes drooping.

"No, you won't," he says, breaking apart my mother's

clasped hands. She glances at me, brown eyes lit by internal fires as they place their fists over their hearts. "Or you'll soon join your brother."

Snippets of reality drift through my fever dreams: My mother, weeping at my bedside. The crackling fire in the hearth. Birdsong drifting in through open windows, and the smell of rain from the afternoon showers. But anything real is tainted by the Reds, scoring my nightmares with their sharp talons and electrifying screams. Calling them dragons is a misnomer, especially with their reptilian bodies and feline faces, but the early colonists didn't have a better name for the native beasts.

"Stay away!" I shout in my dreams as they fly toward me. Their eyes light up like torches, lightning shooting from their mouths.

"Kira, raise your sword."

I jerk awake to Ezra's heavy bootsteps resounding in the entryway.

"Of course, she's fine," my father laughs.

I lay back down and pretend to sleep, but keep my eyes cracked. I can't see much, only the fireplace and the edge of the dining table. Ezra's come in, but doesn't seem interested in making himself comfortable.

"Has she shown *any* manifestations of a Mage?"

Pans knock over. My mother shuffles out of the kitchen. I see her gray skirt twirl just outside my bedroom.

"No, no," my father bumbles. "Besides, she's a girl, Ezra. There's nothing to worry about."

Ezra sighs. "The Red appearing this close to town is a concern, Dragen. Is she still sick? It could be a sign—"

"She's got the flu," my mom states, sounding more firm than usual. "And you two better mind the situation. Take it outside, gentlemen."

The front door creaks open, and their gruff conversation fades in the distance. I strain to listen, but my mom glides inside my bedroom with a steaming cup.

"I know you're awake," she says, pulling up a stool to sit by my bedside. "It's time for your medicine."

I scoot up on my elbow and wrinkle my nose. Whatever murky concoction my mother's offering me smells like swamp water with a dash of cinnamon.

"Yes, you're drinking it," she says, bringing it to my lips before I can even refuse.

It's better not to argue with her. My mom's a lithe woman with a pioneer's fortitude. I've never heard her complain about anything, even when the Peacekeepers impose another one of their ridiculous rules like segregating the colonies or destroying another relic of our ancestors' technology. Women aren't required to shoulder the same burden as a man, but she chose her father's sword as an homage to her family's struggles to survive on the alien world.

"Blech," I say, wiping off my lips. The inside of my mouth tastes like pond scum. "That doesn't taste like your flu recipe."

My mom sucks in her lips and touches the folds of her uniform top, something she's taken to doing when she's about to say something difficult to me. "You promised me you'd stay out of trouble if I let you go gathering with the others."

I lean against the cool bricks, not wanting to fight with her, too. "I did . . . until the Red showed up."

She purses her lips and takes back the teacup. "I'm sure Ezra will meet with the other Peacekeepers about this. There will be more rules."

I bunch up the bedsheets in my hand and mutter, "What now? More praying? Burn down the Spires?"

Tears brim my mother's eyes, but she wipes them away before I process the gravity of her reaction. "Let's hope not," she whispers.

I tilt my head, unsure if she means the Spires, the last remaining evidence of our ancestors' terraforming efforts and technology, or the praying.

She smooths out my bedsheets, pulling them from my clenched fists. "Your father is more supportive of Ezra's peacekeeping measures, but I remember a different time—one where technology wasn't feared. We even kept up the communications systems, just in case."

"Just in case?"

My mom lowers her voice. "In case we ever heard from Earth."

I gasp. From the stories Ezra and the other Peacekeepers tell, our forefathers left Earth to avoid the brewing world war after overpopulation, political unrest, and climate change devastated the few remaining resources of the planet. The last transmission from Earth was received not long after their starship cleared the solar system. There were only three letters: SOS. After that, our ancestors vowed to create a better world.

"Nobody knows Earth's fate," my mom says.

"But there weren't any more transmissions. Ezra says

humans destroyed themselves in the Last Great War and—"

"Ezra and the others believe in peace at all cost," she says, resting her hand on my arm. "Even if it means imposing laws that keeps our colonies apart—and truly harmonizing with nature."

"Harmonizing with nature? You mean 'harmonic restoration'?" I ask, referring to the fancy term for how the Peacekeepers handle dissidents. The last person to speak out was Traci Kitahama, a scientist of the *old ways,* who pushed for the reintegration of technology into our minimalist culture when her husband died from an accident five years ago. She claimed he could have been healed if the Peacekeepers let her use one of the old surgical suites aboard the original starship. Instead, Ezra had her tossed into the middle of the forest, naked and toolless, in the name of "harmonic restoration," so she could learn to love nature and appreciate her place in the world.

She hasn't been seen since.

My mother shakes her head, her eyes flitting to the doorway, then back to me. "No. That's Ezra's idea of harmony. I'm talking about becoming one with nature."

I hear my father laugh through the window, a deep baritone rumble that makes us pause. My mom resumes, her voice quieter, secretive: "Nature is violent. All living things fight to survive, from plants to animals to insects. Violence should be avoided, but there is a place and time to fight."

"Mom..." I whisper, scared of what she's implying. "That sounds a lot like...the preachings of a Sword Mage."

She nods, confirming my fears. "I wouldn't be here if it weren't for the last Sword Mage, Reznor. He struck down the emerald anaconda that killed my brother and tried to eat me."

"He *killed* it?"

"Yes."

I shudder. The emerald anacondas—though not really a snake but named as such because of its slithering body and serpentine mouth—are native predators to Terra Pax. With our terraforming efforts, they grew from small nuisances to twenty-meter-long killers with a taste for human blood. The Peacekeepers set up shields over the colonies, one of the few relics from the past we're allowed to use, but thousand-year-old technology isn't fail-safe. Still, to kill something, even out of self-defense, is forbidden, even if it meant a life of the colonist—or the colony itself.

"One day you will understand, Kira, how peace is different from penitence, just as fighting does not mean brutality. And when you do, I believe you'll be the one to bring true peace to all Terrans."

"Me? Why?" I exclaim, glancing down at my sunken belly under my sweaty T-shirt.

The front door creaks open. My father proclaims the traditional Peacekeeper mantras as Ezra's heavy footsteps sound just outside my bedroom. "Peace, my friend! Tomorrow will be our day of reconciliation."

Ezra pauses outside my window as my mother takes my hand, eyes glistening. "Because not all legends are true."

✦ ✦ ✦

The next day, my mother's satisfied enough with my improvement—or through with my whining—so she allows me to gather the medicinal lavendera flower close by the house. Our colony, one of five, focuses on gathering food and medicine from the forests, and every four months, we trade with the other colonies for tools, clothing, electrical pods, and other resources. It's the only time we get to see any of the other colonists, and seeing the red, blue, gray, green, and yellow uniforms mixing makes me happy. Ezra and the Peacekeepers from the other colonies monitor our interactions, and if there's any dispute, it's quickly snuffed with threats of harmonic restoration.

But while the Peacekeepers worry about even the slightest provocation, my attention goes to Noz, a boy from the "blue" colony of clothing makers who reside near the Unreachable Mountains. They weave plant fibers and genetically modified spider silk to make our weather-resistant clothing. Other girls think he's weird because he's quiet and usually has a prickly spider tucked away in his front pocket. I like that he's oddly handsome and pays about as much attention to Ezra's prayers to subdue the human heart as I do.

I think he likes me too. He once brought me a shell of a Dire seed, a rare specimen that grows only at the oxygen-starved, unreachable tops of the Unreachable Mountains. The hardened seeds are relics of the world before terraforming, a place no human could survive. Noz didn't say a thing, blushing as he handed me the seed, then running away. I'm pretty sure it was a marriage proposal, but I won't get too ahead of myself.

I'll see him in two days, I think, running my hand over huge, gnarled tree roots and tall grasses in search of the purple flower. *As long as I don't get sick again . . .*

I don't know why I've come down with high fevers in the last few months. My father thinks it's because I'm weak, that I'm one of the unlucky ones that can't handle the genetic modifications made by the first colonists to survive the new planet. My mother just insists I keep drinking her awful teas.

Gripping my new baldric, I shift the weight of the broken sword on my back. *I'm not weak.*

As I walk along the dirt path, the tight canopy of trees breaks up the sun's rays into long shafts that turn the grasses from yellow to gold. Even though my great-great-great-grandparents' generation finalized the terraforming for human habitation, everything feels young and fresh. Schoolteachers tell of a cold desert planet with low oxygen levels and hardy plant and animal life. But I can't imagine Terra Pax as such a hardscrabble place with the humidity that hangs in the warm air, iridescent butterflies that dance through the sunlight, or the sparkling lake a hundred meters down the rolling hill.

I love it here, I think, my fingertips finding the textured leaf of the purple flower amongst a ring of button-top mushrooms. A horned mouse, reputed for their shyness, scampers up to me. I extend my fingers and allow him to sniff my hand. His whiskers tickle my fingers. *This is home.*

An old song, one that my mother sung to me in her forbidden ancestral tongue, grazes my mind. I've never understood the words, but she translated them to me on one summer day, making me promise to never tell my father:

"Brilliant sapphire, open my eyes.
May my veins become the tree roots and rushing rivers.
May my pulse be by the beat of dragon wings
And my blood bear their fires.
May shining stars and sighing winds whisper
    their secrets
And doleful howl of the lion-wolf makes my heart ache.
May my lungs fill with the scent of heavy rains
    and blooming flowers
May I one day find my home."

As I pluck the soft lavendera, something rumbles overhead. I look to the cloudless blue sky, confused by the thunderous sound.

Boom. The ground shakes as the blast tears through the forest. Birds screech and fly out of the trees. I freeze, and the forest hushes.

Not thunder. An explosion—

But not like a misfired firework or an overheated electrical pod.

I place my hand on the ground, feeling, listening. In the distance, shouts and cries come from the colony.

Mother, Father. Dropping the lavendera, I run as fast as I can toward the smell of smoke—and the rising gray plumes from my house.

"Mother!" I scream, coming to a halt at the wall of heat. Roaring flames shoot out of the wreckage of my bombed-out house. Black ash and burning leaves rain down from above. Everything inside the blast radius of shattered trees is broken and on fire. "Father!"

I shield my eyes and try to find a way into the house, boots crunching over glass shards. The sky rumbles. A black starship streaks across the sky and the shock wave knocks me off my feet. In the tumble, I take in a mouthful of dirt and grass, and my head smacks against a tree.

Ears ringing, head throbbing, I crawl on my hands and knees. I struggle between breathing and coughing out dirt. I can't find a way through the smoke.

Mom—?

Shouting in the distance morphs into an inhuman shriek as the sky cracks open with thunder.

Mom—

A flaming tree limb breaks off and crashes next to me, embers singeing my face and left hand. Fire surrounds me on all sides. I unsheathe my sword and hack and slash at the limb, trying to cut a path through the inferno, but another branch lands behind it, reinforcing the fiery barrier.

Recoiling back, I hold my sword out in front of me in vain. "Help me!"

Lightning, white and hot, streaks down from above. It pierces the tip of the sword, shooting down my arms and igniting my body.

I'm dead, I think, but my body dissolves into infinitesimal points of light that rush to the sky. Whatever is left of me spins and flips, then slams back down.

I snap back together, breathing in sharply as if I'd held my breath for ages. The air is clean and aromatic with fresh flowers. Instead of embers and dirt, I find myself lying atop a feather bush surrounded by giant redwood trees, still clutching my sword. My entire body tingles as if blood is rushing back in.

Though sluggish, I'm back on my feet and brushing the leaves out of my hair. *My boots—*

I'm barefoot. My boots, blackened and smoldering, are lying meters apart from me and each other, like they've been blasted off my body.

What happened? My clothing is also singed, exposing patches of skin on my arms, stomach, and legs. Even stranger, my sword—and the arm holding the sword—is vibrating, as if supercharged by an electrical current.

But I'm alive.

And still close to the colony. The smoke in the air is subtle, but the booming noises persist to the west.

I shelve my concerns and do my best with a broken sword to hack my way through the dense foliage toward the colony. The slope guides me to a reflective white building overgrown with vines and mosses, and *DO NOT ENTER* painted on the exterior panels. It's a forbidden place, a reminder—and connection—to our unspeakable past. But when I spot a dozen colonists running into the building, I forget the rules.

"Father!" I yelp, seeing him carrying my mother. Her face is covered in black soot and—

Blood.

I sheath my sword and bound through the bush. When he sees me, I don't understand his surprise. "You're alive? I saw the branches fall—I thought you'd been killed. I barely got your mother out . . ."

"I'm okay," I say, unsure if he's angry or disappointed.

A black starship, trailed by two fighters, scuds across the sky toward the colony.

"Help me with your mother."

I follow him and the other colonists inside. The Communications and Surveillance Center, built decades ago, was meant to develop new tech to contact Earth, or at least get answers about her demise. Ezra's grandfather, Sahad, the first Peacekeeper, shut it down, preaching we shouldn't try to reconnect with our fallen brethren. The metal beams look intact, but the dust on the machinery and the plant roots breaking through the walls lend doubt that anything works.

I just hope it protects us from whatever is falling from the sky.

"Who are they?" one of the colony men shouts as my father and I lay my mother down away from the windows, on the tile floor by some shelving. Everyone who isn't wounded crowds around Ezra as he stares at the relay station. Thunder—bombs—continue to strike.

"You have to open a channel!" someone else shouts.

My focus is on my mom. Her breathing is ragged, gasping. I don't know what's worse—the burns around her face or the puncture wound to her chest.

"Apply pressure here," my father directs as he ransacks the office for supplies.

I press my hands over the wound. Warm blood squishes between my fingers and my mother moans.

"I'm sorry," I whisper, tears sliding from my eyes.

The other colonists continue to shout.

"Someone turn on the generator—"

"It's too old."

"Dragen!" Ezra yells over the commotion. "Didn't your father teach you advanced mechanics?"

My father stops his search in the shelves and looks to

me, cheeks reddening. "Y-yes. He did. But this place has no power—it's been shut down for decades."

Ezra's jaw tightens. "There have been a few caretakers."

The colonists gasp and talk amongst themselves in hushed tones. The forbidden communications post *wasn't* disassembled like Sahad vowed?

My father mumbles to himself, then runs over and barks orders at the other colonists. He sends two people to the power station, and another to check the wiring in the ansibles. A few minutes later, after another blast rocks the building, lights and computer monitors flicker to life.

Sweat lines my father's brow, and he looks to Ezra nervously, his hands poised over the keyboard. "Are you sure, Ezra? This is against—"

Ezra raises a hand. "It's okay, Dragen. We just need to know what they want. Peace may be possible."

A thousand questions try to leap off my tongue, but my mother's hand touches mine. "Soon, Kira . . ."

Confused, I smooth back her hair and squeeze her hand back. "It'll be okay, Mom. Ezra will find peace."

Eyes half-open, she stares at me, a smile creeping around her mouth. "Your eyes are so beautiful . . ."

What? I look up, eager to find my reflection in one of the smooth white surfaces of the office, but find none.

All chatter in the room dies as a man in a hardened exoskeleton appears in a holographic projection over the relay. His face is human, but his voice is not. ". . . *Do not resist . . .*" he says with an insect hiss. *"Our worlds will be one."*

"Who are they?" one of the colonists whispers. "Where are they from?"

All eyes turn to Ezra. He inhales sharply as distant sirens wail: "Earth."

The soldiers come next, spilling out of the dropships decked out in scaly black armor and bearing lighted plasma guns.

"Everyone, stay calm!" Ezra shouts, pushing down my father, and several other colonists, to take cover. "I'll handle this."

With what?! I want to scream. We have no weapons, no means of self-defense—except for some weighted swords that pain our backs.

My mother grasps my hand and holds me close. "Play dead," she whispers, smearing some of her blood on my face.

"But—"

She brings my head down to her chest, next to the wound. Warm blood trickles across my face and I squirm, but she pinches my arm as the soldiers blast down the front door, guns blazing with plasma charges.

"Please, you do not need to attack," Ezra says, holding up his hands and stepping out from behind the communications relay. "We are a peaceful people."

But they're *not,* I think, peeking one eye open.

"May we not discuss your intent?" Ezra continues, still vying for a conversation. A soldier fires at one of the colonists creeping toward a broken window, vaporizing him into a crackling red mist.

"Val!" his wife screams, going into hysterics. Two soldiers silence her with cuffs and a shock collar.

A soldier bearing a gold stripe across his helmet analyzes our pitiful group. "Drop your weapons."

"These are artifacts of a different era," Ezra tries to explain, removing his sword and signaling for the others to do the same. "We do not use them for violence."

Everyone surrenders, tossing their burdens to the floor and raising their hands.

Seeing no other option, I close my eyes and lie as still as a corpse, hoping my mother's blood hides my reddened cheeks.

"Single file," the soldier shouts.

Instead of calling for us to resist—to flee—Ezra softens his voice for prayer. "As the sun shall rise to meet the night, so will we bring peace to troubled hearts—"

Colonists scream as plasma discharges flash behind my closed eyelids. I don't move, not when a body falls on top of my leg and burnt flesh singes my nose. I remain still, even after all the footsteps, and the roaring engines of the dropships, have faded.

"Kira . . ." my mother rasps.

I don't want to move now, fearing what I'll see. She rests her hand on my head and rustles my hair. "Look at me."

I rise, tears spilling over my cheeks as I take in her pale face. "Run as fast as you can," she says, pulling out an envelope, stained with her blood, from the folds of her uniform top.

"What's this?"

Her eyes lose focus, drifting off to the side, then refocus back on me as I kick my way out from underneath the fallen colonist. "Answers."

I rip open the envelope to find a faded sketch of an area of land not too far from here. There are notes in my mother's secret language, and a circled location.

"Ezra isn't wrong," my mom says, her voice just above a whisper. "Peace is important—but to live in accordance with nature, we must be in active cooperation with the world and with fate, which means knowing when to submit and when to fight. That is the wisdom of a Sword Mage, something you must draw from within yourself."

"What?" I say, shaking her shoulders to keep her awake. "I don't understand."

She coughs, then inhales sharply to gather the strength for her voice: "You are more powerful than you know."

"This is what I am," I say, unsheathing my broken sword and staring at the useless weapon.

My mother smiles, something I didn't expect. "When the time comes, hold it high."

I scoff. "And what? Make everyone laugh?"

As the light in her eyes fade, she whispers: "Make them see."

I know the area circled on the map. The Reds reclaimed it about a century ago, circling high above the deep valley like sentries. Even if the sapphire flower grew there in bushels, nobody would ever dare venture there.

Numb and fueled by adrenaline, I sprint through the forest, my broken sword bouncing on my back, sketch in hand. I should wash the dried blood from my face or slow down through the thicket, but I don't want to stop. Not when I can still feel my mother's hand lose its grip on mine.

A Red shrieks in the skies as I break through a bush and come to a halt.

A starship?

Not like the ones I just saw streaking across the skies. This one is sheltered in a huge, modified cavern, surrounded by old terraforming equipment. A lighted generator whirs behind a support column, and the wavy distortion at the mouth of the cave indicates an activated shield. When I step out from the bush, my feet touch down on a hard gray-and-black surface.

A launch pad—

The pieces click in place. *A terraforming station!*

One of the early staging points.

I look up to the sky as the Reds circle in the gathering clouds. *They probably feed off all the geomatter,* I think, remembering my early lessons in terraforming. The stations housed protomatter and weather manipulators, and the organic by-products nourished the nascent Reds to become the behemoths they are today. The stations were eventually abandoned for the more advanced Spires, but the Reds remained.

And someone else.

Somebody hiding inside a yellow biosuit, pointing an ancient rifle in my direction. "Stop right there."

I skid to a stop and hold up my hands. I forget about the map until it's too late. When I try to hide it, the suited person yells, "What's that?"

I consider lying, but a Red breaks off from the swarm and swoops lower to inspect our interaction. As lightning dances across the sky, I shout, "A map from my mom!"

The suited person cocks their head to the side and takes a step back inside the shelter of the cavern, out of the line of sight of the Red. "Who's your mom?"

"Laela Northfall."

The Red screeches and dives down, heading straight for me. Other Reds, hearing its cry, rear around in the skies, joining the plunge.

"Come on!" the person shouts, shutting off the shield and waving me inside. I run as fast as I can, the wind howling as the incoming beast closes in.

I won't make it—

Lightning strikes at my feet. I propel forward, past the cavern of the mouth, and smack into one of the tail cones of the ancient starship.

As I lie dazed and confused on the concrete, the shield zaps back on. The Reds roar and snap their tails but can't penetrate the protective field. As the biosuited person helps me up, the Reds launch back up into the storm.

The person in the biosuit takes off the translucent helmet, revealing a beautiful woman about my mom's age, with silver-streaked black hair and warm brown eyes. "Are you alright, Kira?"

I rub the back of my head, already feeling a lump forming. "You know me?"

"Yes. I've been friends with your mom for a long time." She holds out a gloved hand. "Dr. Traci Kitahama."

I don't hide my shock. "The Peacekeepers said you died!"

She laughs and gestures to the starship. "It's better that they believed that than the fact I've been restoring the *Venture* and running experiments on the flora and fauna."

As I follow her onto the ship, she inspects my map. "Your mom really loved writing and speaking Armenian, even if it risked banishment."

"Armenian?"

"Yes, it's one of the many languages from Earth, before the Peacekeepers forced us to speak only one. I bet she sang you 'The Mage's Song' in Armenian, right? It's the one that starts, *'Brilliant Sapphire, open my eyes'*?"

"Yeah . . ." I whisper, unsure of how to feel.

Dr. Kitahama chuckles. "Her conviction is inspiring."

The starship panels and floor markings light up as we walk the hallways. I don't have time to inspect the living quarters behind each door, the empty mess hall, or the darkened classrooms.

This was one of the original transports! I realize.

Dr. Kitahama stops at a locked door and scans her retinas at the panel. A beep and click later and we're stepping inside a white-walled lab unlike anything I've seen in books. Bulky overhead scanners project readouts of recent diagnostics. Hundreds of plant and seed samples sit in transparent stasis cylinders across from a vast collection of animal claws, bones, skins.

"I saw the warships," Dr. Kitahama says, waving her hands over a console to bring up the holographic images of the alien vessels attacking the colony. With a flick of her wrist, she shows me other images of the other colonies under attack, bombing the buildings first, then rounding up the survivors onto dropships. "Did anyone else survive?"

"They got my mom." My shoulders tense and I can't keep the quaver from my voice. "They took everyone else."

"I'm so sorry, Kira. She was very brave—and so are you."

"She said I'd find answers here."

"Yes," Dr. Kitahama says, pulling up other images alongside the warships. "To protect each other, your mother and I would communicate once a year. It was too dangerous otherwise; Ezra watched her very closely. The last time was a few weeks ago. I warned her that when I fixed the communications network on the *Venture,* I'd picked up signals from Earth. I worried that something—someone—was headed our way."

"Who are they?" I ask, touching the projection of the warship. The hologram responds, zooming in on the writing on the hull. I recognize the letters, but not the language.

"Humans from Earth. There were survivors of the Last Great War, but during the recovery, there was an invasion."

Dr. Kitahama brings up an image of a sickened human with pale skin and sunken eyes. She then extracts a second image, one of an arthropod with a multi-jointed tail and an undulating maw. "I don't know where these things came from, but they occupy human hosts."

I wince. "Are there any humans left?"

"Someone sent distress signals to all the starships that fled Earth, including the *Venture*, decades ago calling for help against 'the bugs.'"

"Wait—decades?"

"Yes, around the time Ezra's grandfather, Sahad, started the Peacekeepers and restricted our tech. Eventually, they eliminated everything they considered a threat, which meant executing the Sword Mages. Do you see the connection?"

My jaw tightens. *Why would the Peacekeepers want to*

control our tech and keep our colonies apart? Why would
they keep us constantly burdened with our swords?

A voice deeper inside me answers: *Because they were*
afraid of reconnecting with Earth.

"I think so . . . But why kill the Sword Mages?"

"Sword Mages are masters of nature. They can unleash
her powers, both violent and healing, to keep balance in
the world. And the last Sword Mage, Reznor, wasn't afraid
of a fight. He advocated for reestablishing a link to Earth
to restore our connection with our brothers and sisters—
but Sahad and the other Peacekeepers knew what that
meant."

"War," I whisper.

"Exactly."

"We should help them," I whisper, touching the image
of the occupied human.

Traci smiles. "I think you can."

"Me?!"

"Yes. You were born under the blood moon. You are a
Sword Mage."

"Impossible," I say, stuffing my hands under my
armpits. "I'm a girl."

Traci chuckles. "Science says otherwise," she says,
calling up a hologram of an ancient Red.

"Much of it has to do with how we changed the planet,"
she explains, showing the rapid rate of evolution for the
species. "The *draco panthera*—the Reds—adapted to all
the lightning storms in the early stages of terraforming,
developing the ability to change biomatter into electrical
current and vice versa."

I stare at the rotating images of Reds disappearing and

reappearing in lightning strikes. "They travel in and out of lightning."

"Yes. It allowed them to expand their territory and grow at exponential rates. Most importantly, it allowed them to aid in the life cycle of the sapphire flower."

She pulls up a diagram that expands into several smaller pictures. "Reds prey on birds and animals that eat the Dire seed in the Unreachable Mountains. The Reds can't digest the pits, and when they travel in lightning, it alters the distribution of charged molecules across its membranes—"

Glancing at my knotted brow, she says, "Basically, it creates an electrical linkage that amplifies consciousness and connectivity to all living things. When the seeds are deposited into the lower valleys, the soil and the added light of the fifth moon cause them to blossom."

"Noz once gave me a Dire seed shell," I think out loud.

"Ah," the doctor says. "Noz's father is aligned with your mother's beliefs. It was probably a token of faith."

"Faith? Wait—I don't understand how any of this makes me a Sword Mage."

"If an expecting mother eats the sapphire petals, she risks fetal toxicity, especially in the presence of female hormones. However, in your case, having a twin meant greater distribution . . ."

I shrivel inside myself. *Rorin*.

Thinking I'm still confused, she explains: "By eating that petal, your mother connected you to all the flora and fauna on Terra Pax."

"Flora and fauna . . ." I repeat. I think of how I

transported out of the ring of fire in a flash of lightning. *Like a Red?*

Like a Sword Mage.

"But . . . I should have shown signs earlier."

"You can thank your mother's terrible teas for that. She suppressed your abilities with herbs until you'd come of age to make your choice."

My fevers, I realize.

I regard my hands—the dirty nails, the rough calluses. I'm not special, and I don't look like I could shoot lightning across the skies or call upon a legion of Reds.

Anger reddens my cheeks. *Why did she do this to me?*

Dr. Kitahama places a hand on my shoulder. "There are a few of us who believe like your mother. We desire balance, not suppression. Ezra and the Peacekeepers fear dominating nature because that led to the destruction of Earth, so they keep us burdened. But there is another way to live. Mages are connected to this world in the most intimate ways. They can guide us to become one with the world as stewards and caretakers, while continuing to evolve our knowledge of the universe. We need you, Kira, to guide us into a new era."

An explosion thunders through the ship. The doctor and I lurch, falling into the display. Lights flicker, then dim.

"Stay here," Dr. Kitahama says, inputting commands into the ship console. "I'm going to reinforce the hangar shield."

As she takes off toward the ramp, I hold a hand and arm over my ringing ears and brace the display.

I can't be a Sword Mage.

("Brilliant sapphire, open my eyes.")

I'm not strong enough.

("May my veins become the tree roots and rushing rivers.")

I look at the collection of seeds on the wall and grit my teeth.

I'm not connected to anything.

("May my lungs fill with the scent of heavy rains and blooming flowers.")

Another explosion, this one closer to the hangar, sends me careening into a display of terrestrial plants. Seeds, dirt, and other organic material fling across the white interior of a starship.

("May I one day find my home.")

I run out of the ship, to the hangar. Rocks and debris rain down from the cavern ceiling. Through the dust, there is no mirage from the shield, only harsh, saffron lights and the stink of engine exhaust.

I scramble up to the entrance, finding Dr. Kitahama buried under bits of rock and dust machinery. "Doctor!"

As a dropship's ramp crashes down just meters ahead, I dig out Dr. Kitahama and remove her shattered helmet. Blood trickles down her forehead and her chest is still. "Doctor!" I shout, shaking her shoulders. "Wake up— they're here—we have to go—"

Her eyes crack open. She holds the same confident gaze as my mother. "No. It's time to fight."

I give her arm a tug, but she pulls back with a wince.

Too hard to move her—

The whine of charging guns and shouts of soldiers rise over the crashing thunder.

No time to run.

I walk out of the cavern and plumes of dust, into the searching blue sightlines. Storm wind and the dropship engines whip my hair up into a frenzy. Lightning flashes in rapid succession as the Reds howl and shriek.

"Hold right there!" one of the soldiers shouts. Sightlines converge to my heart. Another group breaks off, firing above us at the agitated Reds. The giant beasts flash in and out of the lightning, igniting the skies in a blur of red and white furry.

("May my pulse be by the beat of dragon wings.")

"Drop your weapons and put your hands up!"

("And my blood bear their fires.")

I unsheathe my sword and crouch down, laying it on the platform. The ground quakes with gunfire, but I sense beyond that; down into the plant roots, through the lengths of grasses, up into the tree branches that touch the skies. To the world interconnected by life, by the pulse of all living things.

("May I one day find my home.")

In the broken sword I see my reflection. My dull gray eyes liven in the color of the blood moon.

"Put your hands up!"

I won't let you down, Father.

I grab the hilt of the broken sword and hold it high, to the electric skies. Lightning from all reaches converges and strikes down, through my sword, through me. The beat of a thousand wings shakes me to the bone, but I hold fast.

"Fall back!"

Reds blast through me, knocking over soldiers. Gunfire

sprays the side of the dropship, taking out an engine. Sirens wail. Still, I hold strong, pointing my glowing sword at the ship as it takes off. Lightning charges out of me, zapping the secondary engine. The dropship crashes into the trees, lights sputtering.

"Retreat!"

I disregard the fleeing attackers. The Reds, supercharged and radiant, corral around me as I approach the dropship. Colonists in all color of uniform, dazed and shaken, emerge from the wreckage.

"Kira..."

My father shoulders his way to the front of the prisoners. Tears in his eyes, he regards me, then my luminescent, broken sword, and the Reds at my side.

"They'll be back, Father," I say as the main warship takes off near the Unreachable Mountains, followed by a legion of dropships.

A hand rests on my shoulder. Dr. Kitahama, clutching her side, smiles at me. "All of humanity is at risk, Kira. Our brothers and sisters back home need our help."

I look back at the old starship, then to my reflection in my sword. My eyes, and the sword, are gray and dull again. "I can't do this alone."

Kitahama quirks an eyebrow. "You've got my science."

My father is the only one standing as the rest of the colonists take a knee, singing "The Mage's Song" in ancestral tongues. He approaches me, lips quivering, as all the Reds fly back up to the skies. "And you've got my sword."

THE FRUITS OF REPUTATION
Jody Lynn Nye

The Flarns have never fought a war . . . and they're not very good at diplomacy. So when a hostile invader moves into their planet, what's a species of fun-loving pacifists to do? Why . . . kidnap a warrior queen for help, that's what!

Her Serenity, the Empress Tromisia of Blarkenstar, shook the pale green nets enveloping her with furious hands.

"What are you doing? Who are you? Return me at once to my palace!"

The tall Flarn at the controls of the very small ship held up one manipulative digit to still her outcry.

Incandescent with indignation, Tromisia drew her slim body up to her full height of a blarken and a quarter. No one with any sense would dare to invade Blarkenstar! She had been raised a warrior and the daughter and many times granddaughter of warriors. Her cloth-of-silver raiment, as elegant as it looked, with swathes of shining fabric draping from jeweled pins at her shoulders, was made to repel radiation and laser blasts. The crown on her head—on the floor, now, where it had fallen after her captors thrust her into this undignified nest—bore jewels from fifty nation-states that looked to her as their liege. Each of those jewels had a history and a purpose that had been schooled into her by her weapons masters. Her platinum sandals, bound with ties up the length of her calves, concealed their own secrets. The swathes of silver at the temples of her thick turquoise hair had emerged in the decades since she had been an officer in her imperial father's military forces, but she had kept up with the punishing physical training befitting her station. She could kill every one of the creatures in the ship, once she saw the controls and was convinced she understood them well enough to pilot it back to safety.

The irony was that Tromisia had known an attack on Blarkenstar *was* imminent. She had been on the verge of addressing her assembled army about the sudden silence overcoming their towns to the east. A ragged embassy from what had been a prosperous seaport managed to float ashore in Blarkenholm with a tale of ships that blackened the sky, and cold winds that blighted the trees just weeks from bearing fruit. She never suspected that the Flarn were behind the onslaught. Flarns had never been known to be a threat to anyone. She never dreamed that they had such technology that would permit them to breach Blarken airspace without being detected, nor to blast through the ceiling of her palace, the Pearl Citadel, that had stood unbroken for four centuries.

In fact, Blarkenstar had not been attacked by anyone in twenty years, a long hiatus. The newest soldiers in her command had not yet been born when Blarkenstar had won the final battle against the Gloon Dominion and secured the western border between their realms. Trade had resumed between Blarkenstar and Gloon, and both nations prospered over the following decades. Neither realm on the vast continent of Torena had much interaction with the smallest landmass on the other side of the planet where the Flarn resided except to exchange goods through their fleets of trading ships.

She had been about to instruct the vast and colorful brigade of soldiers, seafarers, and airship pilots assembled that they needed to depart to defend Blarkenstar's borders, when the entire ceiling of the audience chamber collapsed, and a swarm of tiny, dome-topped ships had poured in through the falling debris. While the rest of the little craft had distracted her soldiers, one of them had landed on the very dais where she had been standing, bundled her inside, and taken off at speed that would have thrown her into the bulkhead if not for the elastic nets that had closed tightly around her.

"My soldiers will follow me!" she snarled, writhing to try and break free. "All of Blarkenstar will take mighty vengeance upon you for abducting me, or rather what is left of you when I finish rending you limb from rubbery limb!"

The small ship banked and made a barrel roll to the left. Tromisia tumbled up toward the top bulkhead. She braced herself, but the green nets kept her from impacting. The ship leveled out, arrowing through the night sky, and Tromisia climbed to her feet and shook the bonds surrounding her.

"Take me back at once!" she shrieked. "I know you can

understand me. You have translator bracelets on your arms! Why have you kidnapped me?"

The Flarn pilot, a being two full blarkens tall, with huge red eyes and flat, square, yellow teeth that looked startling in its dark blue face, turned at last to face her. It spoke, but words in Blarken issued from the glowing silver, toroid loop around its upper extremity.

"Forgive us, lady empress. Our nation is in crisis, and only you can help us."

The other three Flarns, stuffed into crash benches that ought to have held only one or two of their lanky bodies, waggled their heads from side to side, their race's way of showing agreement. Tromisia was taken aback.

Long hours of having listened to the droning of her ministers and ambassadors to the other nations of the planet Vintrix made her bite her tongue as she studied the strange faces. These Flarns weren't threatening. They were frightened.

Despite her undignified surroundings and the disarray of her hair and her person, she regained the sensibility of her office. She pulled out the flat metal jumpseat attached to the wall in the small enclosure and sat down, pulling a fold of the net over her legs.

"Tell me about it," she said.

"We are being invaded by Magdinos," the pilot said, guiding his craft expertly with only one of his tentacle-like manipulative digits. Tromisia knew them well. Magdinos were giant, yellow-scaled lizard people who inhabited the planet Dino, one orbit out from Ahser, the great white giant star at the heart of their system. How did they get to her planet without being spotted on Telemetry's scopes? Tromisia felt her heart sink, but she nodded for the Flarn to continue. "Our outer cities had stopped communicating with us one by one. We hadn't received word from the states to the east in flarnpassages, either by living messenger or automated flitter. We escaped from Flarnholm by the outermost surface of our dental incisors! You know us to be a peaceful people; we do not have battleships, or weapons. We are not trained to wage a war."

Tromisia frowned. *They* had been attacked?

"Then, what are these fighter craft?" she asked. "They seem to move at tremendous speed, and you destroyed the roof of my palace with a single blast!"

"They're fairground ride capsules," the Flarn captain admitted at last, his red eyes brightening in embarrassment. "It's all we could find at short notice. We blew up the roof with a charge we use for clearing sewer obstructions."

"Three, really," the smaller Flarn to his left said. "I wired them together."

Tromisia began to ask, but decided she didn't want to know why they needed so powerful an explosive to deal with underground waste. She shook off the thought with a shudder.

"Why are you taking me into the heart of danger? Why not come to us and *ask* for our help?"

This question caused all four Flarns to exchange nervous glances. Tromisia reached for the bracelet surrounding her left bicep. It contained a small but powerful thermite grenade.

At last, the captain replied.

"We are not good at diplomacy," he admitted. "Er, my

name is Zizzik. My companions are Elik, Waskio, and Dizpat."

Tromisia bowed her head gravely. "I am pleased to make your acquaintance."

"Uh, right. I should have said that, too. I told you we're not that good at fancy interactions. Apart from trade, and making games and amusements, we're not very good at anything. We thought it would make more sense to let you see our peril. Then you would be able to order a response from your army."

"It's world famous," Waskio interjected. "You ought to be proud of it. Um, you probably are." Dizpat shot a fold of its upper extremity into the speaker's midsection. Waskio emitted an "oof!" that was translated by the ring-shaped device.

Tromisia frowned. "But, why us? Surely the Enkafa are closer to your realm. They are menaced by the same threat as you. You are capable of mustering a fleet and creating weapons. Why do you need us?"

Zizzik dipped his chin.

"General, there's a big jump between commanding avatars in a screen tank and actually wielding weapons of our own—which we didn't have anyhow. We had to search far and wide to find a culture that had not only expertise in making war, but also the ethics to know when to *stop*. You here in Blarkenstar made war, then you achieved your goal and withdrew forces. Among nations, that makes you close to unique. We don't want to trade one conqueror for another. We just want help throwing out the invaders we have. You were the best prospect that we saw."

It was a compliment of sorts. Tromisia considered it

seriously, although it was couched in crude and blunt terms.

In the past, Magdinos had sent envoys to Blarkenstar and other realms on the world of Vintrix. According to the chronicles that Tromisia had read in her schoolwork, the hulking ambassadors had arrived in ships the size of cities and made a great show of courtesy. They had not stayed long, because the climate was too warm for them, but had flown over much of the country and the surrounding oceans, as though sizing them up like house-hunters. That had been in the days of Tromisia's grandmother or great-grandmother. No fool, her ancestress had made a point of guiding them to view the huge military outposts and defense systems—the ones that could be seen from above. *They* had been full of princely courtesies, treating the Blarkens with the respect of equal to equal. Thereafter, once in a while, gifts would arrive by rocket drone from that outer planet, mostly works of art and recordings of music. The presents had tapered off since Tromisia had become empress. She had not thought much about that decline, but she should have. It was an error, one she would not make again.

"So, they have built their strength to where they feel they can challenge us," Tromisia mused aloud. "They must still have weaknesses, though. We need to discover what they are."

The Flarn pilot brightened. "We were hoping you would say something like that."

"They are canny and patient," the empress warned them. "They have waited generations to move against us. I would not underestimate them."

"All we want you to do is observe," Dizpat said. "You will decide if your army will help us."

Beeping erupted from the console, and small red lights flashed a warning. The crew turned to their controls.

"We are approaching Flarnholm," Zizzik said. "Please brace yourself. The landing site is deep inside a maze of streets and buildings, concealed from the view of the Magdino invaders."

Tromisia wound her hands into the mesh of the green nets and hung on. The small vessel spun like a drill, descending rapidly among buildings whose outlines were picked out by bright, multicolored lights.

From what she could see through the capsule's transparent canopy in the light of broad beams sweeping back and forth across the landscape, Flarnholm wasn't that different from Blarkenholm. Tall, narrow towers blinking with red lamps, protruded upward among multistoried domiciles and commercial facilities.

"Security lights," Waskio explained. "They're constantly searching the skies for ships. But we've timed their beacons and know when they're not looking our way."

"Good observation," Tromisia said.

The Flarn shrugged. "Tactics. I design strategy games."

The lights vanished instantly when the small ship dipped into an alleyway.

"We set this up as a haven for the Rebellion, complete with communications and surveillance equipment," Zizzik said, slowing the craft gradually. He pointed to a tiny green beacon far ahead in the darkness. "Most of our coworkers are hiding out in a secure underground location. We ought to be safe there."

Red flambeaux burst around them, bathing everything in gory light. The ship shook fiercely, tossing the occupants around like beans in a jar. Tromisia had just enough time to recall what came of invoking the Curse of Hopeful Words before her consciousness faded away.

"Lady empress?" Zizzik's voice came from far away. "Are you all right?"

Tromisia tensed and sprang into a fighting stance even before her eyes were fully open. The Flarn crew, looking somewhat battered, huddled in a concerned cluster against a wall of a rather tiny room painted dark brown. She couldn't see any doors. Her head ached as though she had spent the night drinking the sacred liquors of the god Aitypruv.

"Where are we?"

Waskio sighed.

"It looks like while we were observing the Magdinos, they were also observing us," she said. "They locked us up. Our safehold is compromised."

"They took all our devices except the translators," Dizpat said, glumly.

"And your ship?"

Elik held up a small cube of metal and glass. "This is all that's left. They threatened to leave us in it when they squeezed it down."

Tromisia shivered, and not only at the thought of being compressed into nothingness alongside her erstwhile captors. The temperature had fallen at least twenty blarkdegrees. She wrapped folds of her silver gown around her shoulders. The captors had left her her jeweled crown. She wound her turquoise hair into a coil on her head and pinned the diadem in place.

"Why is it so cold?" she asked.

"The Magdinos are assembling a ring of frost generators around the perimeter of the continent," Zizzik said. "They have been emerging with pieces of equipment one by one from a gigantic bronze horn on the edge of Flarnholm. More of them come through it every day. They want to alter our climate so it resembles theirs. The temperature has been dropping several flarncrements a day since they started. When we all die of the cold, they will be able to move in and take over."

Tromisia's jaw set in a grim line. "They intend the same with us and all of Vintrix," she said. "They will *not* succeed."

With the Flarn dogging her like nervous house pets, she began a circuit of the room. Although it had seemed featureless at first glance, she observed irregularities in the walls.

"What is this place?" she asked.

"An escape room," Zizzik said. At her puzzled expression, he lowered his chin. "A place of entertainment. A group working together solves puzzles to learn clues to help them leave the room."

"So, there is a door?"

"Well, yes, but the problem isn't so much finding it as unlocking it."

"Is there any other way out?"

"Oh, yes," Waskio said. "My friend designs these. They always have a rapid exit, in case of emergency."

Tromisia considered that information. "It will be at

ground level, then, so medical personnel can evacuate a patient."

Waskio showed her flat yellow teeth. "Yes, that's true. But both exits go past a control center."

"Then they are observing us," Tromisia said, letting a wry smile purse her lips. "How many?"

"Well, we've only been able to count about twenty Magdinos altogether. They're really big, you know. At least four flarnlengths tall and at least that many long with their tails," Zizzik said.

"That means only one can fit in a control room built for your people," Tromisia said. She unwound a bracelet from her wrist. How fortunate that they had mistaken her accoutrements for ordinary jewelry.

"What should we do?"

"Find that second door and open it," the empress said, squelching her impatience. By the Tube Radio of Antikwity, any first-week recruit would have figured that out! "Then, we deal with the Magdino." She looked at their blank faces and sighed. It had been a long time since she had led troops, let alone ones as green as this. So much for merely observing. "Then, *I* deal with the Magdino."

The enemy in the control room would be a fool if they couldn't tell what the prisoners in the so-called "escape room" were doing. Tromisia tried not to fret as they felt along the walls and floor for the invisible join that would indicate the presence of an emergency hatch. Every blarksecond brought more enemies to their location.

Subtly, she checked the ruby bracelet of Majelen, an inheritance from her six-times great-grandfather, on her left wrist. It ought to be sending out a locator beacon to her people, informing them as to her whereabouts. The Blarken troops would take at least six times as long to reach her as the fleet craft of the Flarn had taken to arrive in their capital city, but they would arrive in force. If only this building was not blocking outgoing signals!

"Here it is," Elik crowed. She ran her floppy extremities over a portion of the wall. Until Tromisia got closer to it, she didn't see the lines of the hidden panel.

"Excellent," Tromisia said, prying one of the milky round gems out of her pectoral necklace and retreating to a safe distance. She flung the small gem so it landed at the base of the rectangle. "Stand back."

"But why?" Zizzik asked, moving forward out of curiosity. Tromisia grabbed him by the neck of his coveralls just before they were thrown backward by the force of the explosion. The empress landed painfully on her rump. The Flarn sprawled beside her. Tromisia clambered painfully to her feet and surveyed the damage.

The panel, no match for a Charge of Winslow gem, was blown outward into a brilliantly lit room. Noises of alarm and confusion came from the inhabitant of the chamber.

The room was too small for her sword. Instead, she drew a long gold pin from her hair and beckoned her companions forward.

"Come on!" Tromisia cried. "We have little time before reinforcements arrive!"

The Flarn rallied at her shout, and followed her. Wincing at the glare, Tromisia charged into the adjacent room.

As she guessed, the chamber had only one inhabitant, but a massive one, propped on a flat bench much too narrow for its yellow, scaly body and huge wide tail. She had only seen images of Magdinos preserved in the military archives. Clad in a bright red suit, the reptilian male dwarfed even the taller Flarn. It rose to its huge feet amid the debris from the shattered wall. As she bore down on the being, it scrabbled for a device on its bony chest, but Tromisia was quicker. She aimed the Firing Pin of Lanshester at it. The hot red light struck right in the center of the Magdino's body mass. It let out a bellow that shook the room, then collapsed over the control panel.

"Wow!" the Flarn chorused. Tromisia shook her head. She collected the objects in the chest pouch, which she recognized as a communications unit, an enormous brass-cased laser rifle, and a personal information device. Tossing the latter aside, she handed the weapon to Waskio. The Flarn sagged under its weight but held on.

"What do I do with this?" she asked.

"Point the open end at an enemy," Tromisia said, and pointed to the stock. "Press that blue button. Keep pressing it until the enemy falls down." No time for the finer points. Waskio wobbled her head.

The communications device in Tromisia's free hand burst into life. A small round, blue screen on its upper surface brightened to show another Magdino. At the sight of the Blarken's face, it emitted a string of what must have been expletives, and the screen went dark. All around them, sirens began to blare.

"They know we're free," the empress said, pulling the

nearest two Flarn to hurry them along the dim corridor. "They will try to capture us again. Perhaps they will kill us this time. Move faster."

Elik's eyes went huge with fear. "What can we do? We thought this location was secure!"

"Assume *everything* is compromised," Tromisia said, quoting from the *Strategy and Tactics Handbook* that was required reading for every young soldier in Blarkenstar. Still, her cardiac system pounded with dread. It had been a long time since she had led troops on the field, and longer still since she had been a new recruit. "You design maneuvering games. Surely you place obstacles in your players' way?"

"Yes, but we are in no danger when we play them." Waskio said, her voice trembling even through the translator. "This is real! I'm afraid!"

"So am I," the empress blurted out, though the words cost dearly to speak them. She hated to admit weakness. The Flarn all stared at her. "I'd be a fool not to fear overpowering enemies. That must not stop us! We have to find the nerve center of their operation, and shut it down. My people are many blarkensegments behind us. It's possible they will not be able to save us, but I will make my death meaningful!"

Brave words indeed, but they failed to convince either herself or her small party. No matter. The alarm had been raised. The enemy would surely send for reinforcements. She must stop any more Magdinos from arriving on Vintrix and defeat those she could. She gathered up the long skirts of her gown and tied them into a knot at her hip as she ran.

"Do you know the layout of this building?" the empress asked.

"Like the back of my manipulative digit," Zizzik said, his red eyes brightening. "The main entrance is this way."

To his credit, he led the small group without hesitation. Signs of conflict were everywhere in the labyrinth of strangely furnished rooms, all of it seemingly one-sided. Gashes in the walls matched the barrel width of the weapon in Waskio's grip. No other signs of holes from slugthrowers, slices from edged weapons, or other laser fire could she see. The Flarn really were without protection from assault. She feared for the safety of Zizzik's friends.

How she wished she could find out what the Blarkenstar Telemetry Office had detected in the skies above Vintrix! Unlike the tiny ships the Flarn had used to invade Blarkenstar, anything but one-being craft containing Magdinos would surely have set off proximity alarms. Therefore, she assumed little likelihood of a mothership orbiting the planet.

She thought, rather, that they had made one uncrewed landfall with the bronze horn to which the Flarn referred, and that had formed a portal for beings and equipment to pass through from their planet. One targeted strike, she decided grimly, would cut the Magdinos off from escape and end the invasion. Concentrate. Plan. Execute. She scanned her small force. Collaborate.

These Flarn viewed her as a hero who would free them from the invader. She wished she didn't feel so *rusty*. Blarkenstar prided itself on being a race of warriors who fought their enemies back behind well-established borders. They had been at peace because they were vigilant. But how much better were they than these non-warriors, when they had not practiced their craft in decades? Nor was she the young general that she had been over twenty years before. She must do her best. Their lives depended on her. The safety of Vintrix depended on her.

Zizzik emitted a hornlike beep, and wheeled to a halt.

"Uh-oh," the translator said.

Tromisia saw immediately what had caused his outcry. Beyond the transparent doors only blarkenlengths ahead, a squad of Magdinos on large, flat-panel craft was landing. Silhouetted as they were against the rising sun, she could discern only three of them clearly, but she was certain there were more.

"They're flying skid-loaders!" Elik shouted. "Another exit, quickly!"

"No," Tromisia said, an idea forming. "We need transportation. You identified those vehicles. Can you run one?"

"Oh, yes," Zizzik said. "They're simple cargo haulers."

"How fast can they move?"

Waskio's eyes brightened. "Faster than they can run."

"That's all that matters," Tromisia said. She pulled a hidden control in the temple of her golden crown. It reformed into a golden helmet, with a bridge that descended to protect her nose. "Stay close!"

It had been months since she had tested the repulsors in her rebounding sandals, but hoped that they had not had a chance to discharge their batteries.

"Cover your eyes!" she ordered. The Flarn ducked, their floppy limbs protecting their faces.

With the Firing Pin of Lanshester in one hand, she pried loose another opal and heaved it at the glass doors.

Crash!

The portal shattered outward in a satisfying blast. The explosion was enough to throw the first row of Magdinos back into the second lot. Tromisia tapped her silver ankle straps together to activate her sandals, and charged forward.

Her every step was quadrupled in length by the tensile strength of the high-tech coils squeezing her lower legs. She bounded up onto the chest of the first fallen Magdino, and blasted it in the forehead with the laser pin. It dropped back, twitching under her feet. Another yellow alien lowered a brass-cased rifle like the one Waskio was carrying. Tromisia didn't have a hope of turning it aside with a parry. She leaped from body to body, hoping to draw the rifle fire at one of the Magdino's own colleagues.

A wild scream just behind her told her that she had accomplished that goal. The Magdinos scrambled to follow her, but clumsily and awkwardly. Their reactions were blunted by the climate. Though she found the morning cold, they were used to a far more frigid environment. It made them easy targets for her Firing Pin and gems she wrenched from the edges of her crown-turned-helm.

Zizzik and the others tried gamely to keep up with her.

"Fire the weapon!" Tromisia shouted at Waskio.

As if she had forgotten the dead weight in her arms, the Flarn peered down at the rifle. She turned the device toward their pursuers and pushed the button. A hot beam of red lanced out of its barrel.

The Magdinos leaped in every direction to get out of its path—all but one unlucky individual, who caught the blast square in its bony chest. Pieces of yellow flesh flew outward, obscuring what was left of the body. Dark ichor splattered the enemy forces.

"Ew," Elik said.

The Magdinos knew the capability of the captured weapon. But these were soldiers. One casualty wouldn't stop them. The moment the shock had passed, they reached for their own guns. Tromisia jumped onto the shoulder of the nearest brute. He swatted at her, all the while grunting at his fellows not to shoot at him. She leaped to the next and signaled to the Flarn to move to the flat sled nearest the door. Zizzik rushed to the controls.

"Keep firing!" Tromisia ordered. Waskio obeyed, pushing the blue button over and over. Her first shot had been lucky. She didn't connect again, but she did provide a useful distraction. Tromisia peppered them with exploding gemstones and her small laser pin. The six Magdinos who remained standing ducked behind every obstacle they could find to avoid the crossfire: ground vehicles, planters, even the big sign in front of the building.

His mouth open in what passed for a Flarn smile, Zizzik swooped the sled close to the platform where Tromisia now stood alone and triumphant. The empress leaped aboard the loader. She tucked the gold pin into her bodice and took the rifle from Waskio. With deft shots, she blasted the power pods of each of the remaining sleds. Then, Zizzik veered upward and away from the damaged building. The batteries exploded with deafening bangs, peppering the cowering Magdinos with shrapnel.

"That will slow them chasing us," Tromisia said, hanging onto a cleat to keep from being thrown off. "Head for their transport device. I have to destroy it."

"That was amazing!" Elik said. "We didn't need an army, just you!"

Tromisia shook her head as the skid loader flitted eastward into the sun. "We're not safe yet. They have radios, and they're not stupid. Their command already knows we have escaped. Our obvious destination will be their weak point."

Their quicker movements had given them a head start on the slower-moving Magdinos. Tromisia fretted as Zizzik steered them over cropland and small towns. They had just left behind eight Magdinos—nine, including the one she had shot in the control room. That meant a minimum of eleven aliens who could potentially be waiting for her at the portal. Depending on how long it took to transfer from Dino to Vintrix, a greater force could be amassing.

Like the Flarn, Tromisia had been stripped of anything that the Magdinos could identify as technological devices. She particularly missed her forearm communicator. That silver metal bracer would allow her to speak to any of her ministries, ships, or brigades. The skid-loader possessed only a rudimentary radio with limited range. She had to trust that her army was closing in on her location. At least one of the Flarn ships had been downed by her defenders. The generals must know where she was.

In the meantime, she was on her own, with four

untrained recruits, one heavy firearm, and her jewelry. She checked the Firing Pin of Lanshester. Only three charges left, too few for the battle ahead. She put it through the bun at the back of her head, and drew the begemmed gold dagger pin from the left shoulder of her gown.

"What is that?" Waskio asked.

"My personal weapon," Tromisia said. "The Imperial Sword, Snik."

She pressed the stud hidden beneath the sapphire that served the tiny weapon as a pommel. Instantly, the brooch grew half a blarkenlength and broadened so the hilt fit comfortably into her grip. The others gasped. She gave them the smile of a warrior who did not know whether she would return safely home, but cared for nothing but the battle to come.

"Now, I am ready."

She needed all the preparation possible. As Zizzik steered them up over a rise toward the eastern coast of the small continent, she could see the gigantic bronze horn situated on a promontory jutting out into the ocean already rimed with ice. It glowed as a Magdino emerged from it. She had to stop the invasion. But, in between her and her target hovered a half dozen hovering platforms like her own, carrying Magdinos brandishing laser rifles.

As her makeshift craft appeared, beams of bright red light lanced from the heavy rifles in the aliens' yellow claws. One of the blasts hit the corner of the sled. The metal slagged and bubbled. The Flarn screamed. Zizzik began to zigzag, trying to avoid being hit again.

"Calm down!" Tromisia shouted. "Climb above them!"

"They'll shoot us full of holes!" Elik shrieked.

"Do it!" Tromisia said. "They will be too busy with me in a moment."

Wobbling his head from side to side, Zizzik hauled back on the controls. The sled tilted upward.

Checking to make certain her skirts were tied up out of her way and her helm was solidly attached to her head, she braced herself on the edge of the platform. Two beams of red pierced the deck from different angles. One of them hit Dizpat, who collapsed, moaning. The sled juddered wildly.

"See to her!" Tromisia shouted. One of the enemy zoomed into line, almost beneath them. She saw her opportunity, clicked her sandal straps, and leaped over the rail.

The Magdino below her clearly did not believe that she was close enough to jump onto its craft. She landed behind him, sword out. He swerved wildly, then abandoned the controls to defend himself.

That moment's delay was all Tromisia needed to plunge Snik into his back. The Magdino wailed in pain. Dark ichor bubbled out of the wound. The alien fell to his knees, then keeled over sideways. Tromisia climbed over him to take the controls and steer the sled toward the next nearest foe. Her ankles hurt from the heavy landing, but she couldn't take the time to nurse them now. She sheathed her sword and went looking for her next target.

Her actions had not gone unheeded. Four of the remaining five craft circled around, doing everything they could to stay out of reach. At last, Tromisia had to repeat the tactic of swooping in from above. She slew two more

Magdinos in this fashion, feeling more and more of her
age with every leap and one-sided duel. The three
remaining foes scooted out of reach and peppered her
with their beam weapons. A hot blast hit her squarely in
the back. She staggered, desperate to hold onto the
steering panel. Her laser-proof gown had saved her life,
but had not absorbed the intense heat. Resolutely, she
clung to the controls and took evasive action, veering,
diving, turning on a blarkencoin, all the while aware of the
inadequate maneuverability of her craft.

A little at a time, the sled was being melted away
underneath her feet. She dodged her enemies with more
and more desperate tactics, hoping none of the shots
would hit the drive mechanism.

Red laser fire erupted into the skies from the zone near
the horn. Tromisia glanced over. Multiple barrels from a
single central source tracked her companions'
conveyance. She saw Zizzik clinging to the control panel,
one upper limb dripping dark blue blood. Waskio
returned fire, until her weapon was knocked out of her
grasp by a lucky blast. The skid-loader finally lost power
and careened crazily to land on the ground. A handful of
massive Magdinos picked them out of the wreckage and
dragged them toward the gigantic brass device.

Ignoring her own peril, Tromisia turned what was left
of her craft toward them. She must interpose herself
between her hapless allies and the enemy, and take out
that gun emplacement.

The temperature dropped significantly as she came
closer. Frost swirled in the air. She shivered, wishing she
were in decent battle armor.

As she approached the promontory, the laser fire shifted toward her. With one hand, she undid the knot at her hip and swathed her body in the silvery material of her gown. Beams lanced off it in every direction. She ignored the heat of each impact, though the red blasts nearly blinded her.

At the very last minute, she activated her sandals and leaped off the damaged skid-loader sideways. The craft continued on its way. It crashed into the cannon. The gigantic weapon went up with a blazing explosion that sent scorching waves out for blarkenlengths. Tromisia gasped at the heat, hoping it had not burned off her eyebrows.

A Magdino, larger than the others by half, stood gaping at the ruin of his weapon. Tromisia bounded toward him, drawing Snik. He spun, bringing a blade to bear on her that was twice as long as hers. She dodged it, though more and more wearily. He was good with a sword, though he could not match the training that her instructors had instilled in her. She parried every thrust, beating down his blade. His growing anger made him careless. Tromisia watched until he lowered his guard. With a quick upward slice, she cut the underside of his wrist. The huge blade crashed to the ground. Tromisia sprang forward and landed on his shoulders, Snik at his throat. He spun, trying to dislodge her. She pulled the blade tighter until he came to a halt. His remaining troops barreled forward, dragging the Flarn with them, then stopped as they saw their leader's peril.

"Lower your weapons, or he dies!" she snarled. They made as if to break the Flarns' necks. She repositioned the sharp sword slightly, and ichor ran along its length. They loosened their grasp, but she didn't let go of hers.

"Who are you?" the leader bellowed.

"I am Empress Tromisia of Blarkenstar," she said. "I am here on a diplomatic mission on behalf of our beloved allies, the Flarn." The eyes of her erstwhile captors brightened at her words. "You have invaded this world, which has previously welcomed you as guests. You will stop your heinous plan to freeze this planet to make it like your own. My army is on its way, a force of thousands of brave soldiers! They will *destroy* you."

"Thousands?" the leader choked, not only because she had his neck in her grip. "Thousands like *you*?"

"Why, yes," Tromisia said, amused. "Only younger and stronger, and with *many* more weapons. I am older, and out of practice in making war."

At her words, the Magdinos let go of their weapons and dropped to their knees. More slowly and cautiously, the leader followed suit.

"Empress," he said, turning his head carefully to meet her eyes, "we've monitored you from the time you left the building in the city. If one warrior—older and out of practice—is capable of single-handedly overcoming my troops, we wish to have no conflict with you. We will withdraw immediately. Please, let us go! We will be good neighbors!"

Tromisia kicked off the huge being's back and landed on her feet. She straightened her gown and transformed her helm back into a crown. The Flarn, released by their captors, rushed to greet her. Her limbs ached, and her eyes burned from the glare of the lasers. She dreaded having her physicians examine the burn marks under her gown. But she had done enough. By the time it arrived, her army might have nothing left to do but destroy the frost-making equipment.

"That is good," she said, with a sigh. "Never let it be said that Blarkenstar waged war one moment longer than they had to." She smiled at the Flarn. "We have a reputation to maintain."

A FUNNY THING HAPPENED ON THE WAY TO NAKH-MARU
Jessica Cluess

Marooned on a far-flung world, the only survivor of his expedition, Jeff's taken up the life of an adventurer. But when he saves a girl from a group of bandits out in the desert passes, Jeff learns that, sometimes, rescuing the princess is more trouble than it's worth....

The vermillion sun had reached its zenith when Jeff of Ut-Maru realized his khefer was dying. The beast made erratic loops back and forth, its claws digging furrows in the desert sand. With a curse, he yanked on the reins and slid down from the saddle. Jeff stood before the creature, its antennae waving like flags of surrender.

Poor guy.

In his log, Jeff had described khefer as *mantis/ anteater/???* The beast regarded him with its honeybee eyes and made a mournful glugging sound. Jeff patted its

147

fuzzy, chartreuse-colored head. When a tongue escaped its cylindrical snout and tried to lick him, Jeff backed off. The tongues were acidic. He'd learned that the hard way.

"Sorry, pal." He gestured to his traveling companion. "Okay, lady. We need to walk."

The woman crossed her arms and spoke in a Marunian dialect Jeff hadn't mastered yet. She was high class. If the sarong of river pearls and platinum mesh hadn't hinted at it, the haughty line of her mouth would've done the trick. In Jeff's line of so-called work, running into the high society of Ut-Maru was inevitable. Above his own sarong hung a sword belt. To his left was a koh-pash blade of fine adamantine, gifted from the Nashwa of Sukh-Maru after Jeff rescued his infant son. On his right he wore a lead scabbard with a large X marked off in masking tape. He'd written VOID! BAD NEWS! on the tape. He didn't draw that sword unless he'd exhausted all other options.

The woman leapt down as the khefer slumped over and died. Jeff collected the woven saddle and bridle in a hurry.

She made a disgusted noise when the body began to pulsate and seven babies that looked like fat, green caterpillars chewed their way through the parent's corpse.

"We'd better go before they start spitting." Jeff ushered her away. "They're pretty venomous as newborns."

He'd learned that the hard way, too.

So now Jeff of Ut-Maru walked beside a high-class woman who looked like she wanted to complain to the desert's manager. He'd tried getting her name, but with the language barrier all they'd managed was a few rude gestures. He'd at least told her his name: Joffah. Marunians couldn't master the "Jeff" sound.

She stalked the sands like she commanded them. Like most born on Ut-Maru, she wore as little clothing as possible to allow the healing rays of the vermillion sun access to her flesh. She was small and curving, her skin the rose-gold color peculiar to her people, her hair a forest of copper ringlets. She wore a top of platinum weave, pearl, and crystal that revealed her stomach and the majority of her chest. Jeff couldn't give lessons in modesty. His muscular torso was always exposed to the vermillion sun. The rays didn't just give him good health and perpetual youth like they did the native Marunians. Jeff received added benefits, like running a mile in fifty seconds, or bench-pressing a house.

Reynolds said before the crash that human physiology might react to the peculiar radiation in a different way. She'd been right.

His skin had a reddish tint these days, and he wondered if he'd wind up a giant ball of melanoma. But the perks made up for it.

The lady began to wilt after twenty minutes of climbing up and down the iridescent dunes. Her sandaled feet turned in on themselves.

"Here." Jeff scooped her into his arms and trudged on.

The woman screeched and belted him across the face. He accidentally dumped her onto a dune and watched her roll downhill. At the bottom she dusted herself off, shook her fists, and shouted at him.

"Last time I do anything nice for you!" Jeff rubbed his jaw. Damn. The woman climbed the dune and started a colorful game of charades.

She grabbed Jeff's shoulders and forced him to kneel.

Her head was above his. She smiled. She made him stand, and measured her head to his chest. She scowled.

"I gotta keep your head above mine if I carry you?" Maybe saving her from that pack of raiders had been a stupid idea. He'd been headed across the Bowl of Sisi when he came upon a group of hooded men on khefer-back as they struggled with the kicking, furious woman. Jeff wasn't the type to ride past something like that, so he'd dispatched the bastards quick and helped the girl. Plus, judging by the fancy look of her he figured she'd fetch a good rescue price at Nakh-Maru. That'd been the one word she said that he understood: Nakh-Maru. The northern desert's capital kingdom, or nashwafiet. Jeff envisioned a reward for returning some aristocrat's daughter. Or concubine. Or both. Hopefully not both.

So Jeff of Ut-Maru trudged across the desert, giving the lady a piggyback ride. She couldn't be much younger than his thirty-four years, but she seemed to take juvenile delight in the whole thing.

"Joffah?" She tugged his hair.

"Yes, your exquisite pain-in-the-assness?"

She began speaking rapidly, even though she knew he couldn't understand. Jeff tried to parse it; he had always been good with languages. That and his military training had made him the prime candidate for this expedition six years ago. He'd set out with three others.

Now, three metal ID tags hung around his neck.

"I can't understand you! I. Cannot. Understand." He did the tourist thing of speaking slower and louder. She whapped him with her fist. "Ow! Lady, you wanna walk?"

But then he noticed a plume of rose-colored dust on

the horizon. Someone was headed their way. Jeff jogged to meet the figure. First a black speck appeared, and then came the whisper of scales upon sand. An Akh-Thoth crossed the dunes, slithering merrily into the deep desert. As was typical of his kind, the Akh-Thoth had a human torso and serpent bottom. His skin glittered with scales, and around his neck hung a red, fleshy frill that Jeff knew would fan open if he got mad. Fortunately, Akh-Thoths tended to be pretty agreeable, so long as you weren't some large variety of rodent. The lady spoke in a smug-sounding way and whacked Jeff's ear. He "accidentally" dropped her. She rolled down another dune. Such a shame.

"Excuse me." Jeff used the low-Maru dialect, which almost everyone (except the noble pain in the ass) spoke.

"Greetings, well-traveled one." The Akh-Thoth appeared surprised as the lady climbed up the dune and gazed murder at Jeff, dusting sand from her shoulders. "Is it not unwell to be about in the Bowl of Sisi without a mount?"

"She, uh, mounts me." Jeff realized how that sounded. "I mean, is, in this place of death, there come to be a khefer-farmer?"

Jeff wasn't as good with low-Maru as high-Maru, but those speakers mostly remained in the capitals.

"Yes." The creature pointed back the way he'd come. "Thirty leagues. I doubt you will make it, though."

"I'll be fine." He'd walk until the vermillion sun gave way to the crimson moons, then he'd rest. No use trying to journey after dark.

The woman spoke rapid-fire. The Akh-Thoth appeared surprised.

"Can you understand her?" Thank God.

"She speaks a very antiquated sek-Maru." He answered the woman, who threw up her hands in gratitude.

"Tell her to stop punching my head."

The creature conveyed Jeff's message. The woman spoke for forty-five seconds without drawing a single breath. The Akh-Thoth wrapped two of his four arms around his torso and laughed.

"What'd she say?"

The Akh-Thoth wiped a tear. "She says no."

Jeff stared at the woman. She regarded him with narrowed eyes.

"That's all?"

The creature shrugged. "It was the way she said it."

He slithered off in a cloud of pink dust.

The afternoon passed as the vermillion sun lowered in the sky. Jeff was careful with their water, but they would have to find a new source pretty soon. He didn't think they had enough to get them all the way to this farm, let alone to Nakh-Maru.

"I hear Nakh-Maru's a city of pearl." Jeff discovered that you could have a wonderful dialogue with somebody when neither of you knew what the other was saying. Now that she didn't have to deal with Jeff shouting "Do. Not. Understand," the lady was all right. When she poked at the hilt of his Void sword, Jeff stepped away. "No, no. You pull this when you can't control it, things get bad."

She seemed to understand by his tone what he meant.

Eventually, they came to a pair of red-salt ruins. The ancient Marunians had used the hard, layered stone, or "red salt," to form their wonders and temples. Unfortunately, sediment didn't last the way adamantine and titanium did, so all the old-world stuff had crumbled. Jeff and the woman found a pair of sandaled feet nearly four stories tall. Jeff couldn't imagine what it'd looked like finished.

At the base of the statue, they discovered an oasis. He and the woman hurried down to drink. The water on Ut-Maru was clear as glass, cool even in the desert. Back home, a satellite system on the fifth colony of Earth's long-distant descendants, the water was tepid and a little cloudy unless you lived in a high-end high-rise.

They drank, refilled their water skin. The woman shook off her sandals, then reached around to unwrap her sarong.

Jeff turned his back and waited until she'd finished her bath. Not that he wasn't interested; pain in the ass though she was, she was a damn fine woman. But he liked to think he was a gentleman.

He heard splashing, then dripping as she got out of the pool. The woman stomped around to face him.

She wore a furious look, and nothing else.

"Whoa, lady! I'm trying to do the decent thing." He turned his back again, heard her growl. She marched around and planted her nakedness in front of him, arms rigid at her sides. When Jeff started to look away, she let out a string of blistering curses. "Fine. *Fine*. You win." He glared at her.

The glare softened to a gaze. Clothed, she'd been comely. Unclothed, she defied description, all rosy, tapering curves. Not a sharp angle to be seen. His eyes went out of focus while she stood with her hands on her hips. Then she gave a brisk nod, like concluding a business meeting, before nabbing her clothes and getting dressed.

"Good job," he croaked, and winced. Smooth.

The sound of multiple thumping feet allowed some blood flow back to his brain. A herd of wild khefer had come to refresh themselves. Quick, Jeff opened his satchel and took out the bridle.

"Hold on." He sprinted around the edge of the pool, kicking up sand and dust as he went. The khefer scattered, thumping up the hill on their weird padded feet. They had six legs, born to scurry over the sands. Even a souped-up guy couldn't compete long with a wild khefer in the deep desert.

Jeff caught up to a small, strawberry-colored one. He wrapped his arms around the thing's middle and hefted it into the air. Khefer on average weighed almost a thousand pounds.

It was a mild workout.

The creature screeched, flicking its venomous tongue and scrabbling with its six feet. The rest of the herd ran on. Khefer had no loyalty to one another. Their short life spans meant they wanted to eat, procreate, and get devoured by the next generation. Jeff knew a lot of people like that back home.

He carried the squealing khefer until it calmed. "You're gonna do as I say? Huh?"

Khefer were naturally compliant. If something bested them, they submitted. He set the creature down, put the bridle on. Took a couple of tries, and he had to stay away from the tongue, but he finished and hoisted himself onto its back. When he tugged, it stopped. When he slackened his hold, the khefer went forward.

What a pain in the ass this day had been. "Wish I could just walk away for once," Jeff muttered as he rode back to the oasis.

But that was the best and worst part of him: he never walked away.

Jeff did feel pretty smug when he rode up to the astonished woman. She sat behind him, and they headed north.

When the vermillion sun had almost disappeared, Jeff located a good place to camp for the night. He tied up the khefer, found some spiny desert-milk pods for it to eat, then gathered sagebrush and built a fire. The second moon joined the third and first at different points in the sky. Jeff had never seen more stars anywhere else, even up in the dense black of space.

"Joffah?" The lady frowned. He passed her some dried khefer meat, took a bite for himself, and rummaged through his satchel.

"In a minute. Gotta record the day's log." Jeff pulled out a dog-eared notebook and increasingly tiny pencil. It'd been four years and he had to make the space last, so he wrote small and short.

Him, Reynolds, Takahashi, and Petrov had come here on an information-gathering mission. Reports had called this planet Second Mars, based on the fuzzy satellite feed. The Syndicate didn't think humanity needed another arid backwater, but they sent a small team to map the terrain, investigate the local flora and fauna, and do otherwise scientific stuff. Jeff had been the backup muscle.

As such, he wasn't the best person to record the official log. But Reynolds, dying, had asked him to continue their work.

Unfortunately, his entries looked a lot like:

Day 226

Found three more lakes. One is purple. Algae??

Or

Day 679

Many interesting rocks.

Jeff had included some useful shit, like differences between the low and high languages of Maru, and the names of certain types of animals and birds. Ut-Maru was a low-tech planet with some stuff that he wished Reynolds, the resident biologist, could've got a chance to record. She might've developed a theory for why the human body reacted to the vermillion sun as it did. For his part, Jeff had only written *The sun makes me STRONGER??* Beside it, he'd drawn a stick figure version of himself with three wavy lines coming out of his head. He'd also drawn the sun, smiling.

Day 1,572

Rescued a woman from high desert raiders. Taking her to Nakh-Maru. She speaks some antiquated dialect. Will start up vocabulary list later. She is a pain in the ass.

Satisfied, he put away his stuff and refocused on the woman as she chewed her dinner with disdain.

"It's got that briny taste, I know. If you choke it down fast, it's not too bad."

She swigged from the water skin. Afterward she

pointed at him, then gestured at the sky with a quizzical expression.

"Yeah. I come from up there." He gazed at the star-speckled heavens. "Place called Exodus-5. It's a satellite colony on Rhea, the second moon around Crius. Atmosphere isn't naturally hospitable to humans. Even with terraforming, you can't go outside the city confines too much." Jeff rested his head against the tanned leather of his satchel. "The city's like everywhere else in the satellite worlds. High tech. Instant dinners. Late-night porn. People are still boys at thirty-five and shit. I like it better out here."

At least on a planet like Ut-Maru, you saw action. Besides, there hadn't been anyone back home. Jeff didn't remember his dad, his mom was long dead, and his older brother traded in cryogenic bonds or whatever. He'd left for college and never returned.

That's what'd been nice about the expedition, and Reynolds and Takahashi and Petrov. Jeff gripped the tags around his neck.

"Hmm?" The lady pointed at his hand.

"These were my three friends." He showed them one by one. "Reynolds, Patricia. Takahashi, Hideo. Petrov, Konstantin. We came here together." Firelight winked on the tags. "The ship crashed. They died."

She made a sad noise. Seemed she could tell what he meant. In repose, just eating dinner before the fire, she seemed nice. Jeff sat up.

"Joffah." He placed a hand on his breast, extended toward her. "You?"

"Klionthe." A slight shrug. "Klio."

It was such a damn human gesture that he laughed, which got her high and mighty again. Klio nabbed the satchel that'd served as Jeff's pillow and rummaged through it while his head hit the ground.

"Come on," he groaned as she took out his lightweight blanket and wrapped it around herself, even though the night was warm. Jeff sensed that trying to argue with Klio would get a lot of angry gesticulations and maybe an attempted ball strike or two, and he just wasn't in the mood. "Join the service, they said. See new and exciting planets, they said. Observe wonderful new cultures, they said," Jeff grumbled. As Klio curled into an angry ball, he listened to the flames crackling in the otherwise silent desert night. Back home, he'd fall asleep to the ceaseless murmur of traffic outside his window and the low reverberations of some frat party down the hall.

Yeah. This was way better.

The dream was always the same. Him, Reynolds, Takahashi, and Petrov wearing stupid paper party hats and blowing plastic horns, laughing as the lunar clock rolled over for a new cycle. They'd spent two years traveling to Ut-Maru. The Syndicate hadn't valued the mission, and it showed in how second-rate their ship was. The cryo-pods quit working four months into the trip, meaning they had to spend all that time together. Birthdays. Holidays. Game nights, drinking powdered beer and shouting at a rerun of some classic sitcom.

Best days of Jeff's life. He dreamed of Reynolds playing cards and laughing. Him and Takahashi whipping up what they could in the kitchen. Petrov never understanding what was funny about the old sitcoms, which itself became hilarious.

Then Jeff and the others were running down the hall amid clouds of smoke and ozone. Their shitty spaceship had no pilot, only an AI program to land the thing. Turned out the AI program wasn't much of a substitute.

Jeff jumped into his escape pod. When he hit the button to close the shield and jettison himself, he noticed that the lights above the other three pods, the ones that should've been green, remained an angry red.

Reynolds was trapped across from him. He screamed, trying to break open the shield to get to her before he was launched into space. Jeff hurtled toward the planet alongside the ship, watching in horror as it hit the desert sands.

And then he was pulling Reynolds out of her pod. She was the only one who'd survived the initial impact, but she'd been broken. It took her hours to die. When she was fading, she whispered, "Please. Do the work. Don't let it have been for nothing. Please, Jeff. Please—"

Jeff awoke with a gasp.

"Joffah?" Klio perched by his side, looking concerned. He sat up.

"Sorry. Bad dream." He rubbed his eye, felt instinctively for the Void blade. He always kept it against his back as he slept. Still there. Good. "Guess I woke you."

He could see her anxious face in the triple moons' light. She swept the blanket over him. Jeff protested, but it was nice to feel her settle it around him.

"Shhh." She stroked fingers through his hair a few

times. Then she lay down not too far from him and began to sing. Jeff almost laughed. It was a Marunian lullaby people used on their fussy children.

"I don't normally have nightmares," he said, which wasn't strictly true.

"Shh." As her voice lilted and fell, Jeff drifted back into the cocoon of sleep. This time there was no crash.

Just Klio.

When Jeff woke again, the first blush of dawn was warming the sky. He hadn't slept so good in years.

"Klio?" He sat up beside the dead fire pit, pushed off the blanket. Jeff was alone. Klio had vanished.

Worse, she'd taken the khefer. Worst of all, the Void sword was missing, too.

Oh. That little . . .

"*Daimoh*," Jeff growled, the unflattering low-Maru word for an animal's withered ballsack. He got up, snatched his stuff, and followed the khefer's tracks, impatient for the sun to rise. Loss of sunlight sapped his strength and speed. He was still strong, but humanly so. He bounded up one dune, down another, and saw the woman galloping far ahead.

Unfortunately for Klio, the vermillion sun peered over the ridge of the desert, bathing Jeff in its light.

"No you don't!" he shouted, bounding toward her ever faster. Klio glanced over her shoulder and sneered, guiding the khefer over the waves of sand with a natural grace. Jeff put on a final burst of speed and snagged the creature's hindquarters. The momentum sent Klio flying. Fortunately, the desert made for soft landing.

"You insipid, arrogant pest!" she yelled while rolling down a dune. She seemed to make a habit of doing that.

Jeff found the Void blade tied up behind the khefer's saddle. Then he frowned. "Wait a minute. You speak high Marunian?"

"Of course I do!" Klio clambered back up, shaking sand from her sarong. "How could I survive in the day-to-day without it?"

"I dunno. You seemed to get by pretty good just punching my head and screaming."

Jeff took the Void sword, then cursed as the blade began to slide out of its leaden sheath. Fast, he managed to keep the weapon from exiting into the world.

Unfortunately, that gave Klio time to snatch the koh-pash's hilt.

"I can't believe I saved your ass." Jeff ducked and dodged as the woman swung his sword a couple of times. She was pretty good, too. Attractive quality, if only she hadn't been trying to kill him. All he needed to do was draw his Void blade and she was gone, but he wouldn't. While she was good, she wasn't *that* good.

"Give me the Worldeater and you can go."

The Worldwhater? Jeff snatched her around the waist, lifted her above his head. She dropped his sword, and her legs pedaled helplessly. "How *dare* you!"

"Feeling's mutual." Jeff tucked her under his arm like a piece of luggage, nabbed his weapons, and belted them above his sarong. Klio kicked and swore worse than anyone he'd ever met, and he'd been in the damn military. "Look, lady. We can either chat, or I can tie you up and drag you to Nakh-Maru. One is gonna be much more pleasant."

She seethed in that old-timey dialect. Finally, she grunted. Jeff set her down. Her rose-gold face had turned a mottled amethyst with fury. The khefer, meanwhile, drank from a desert-milk pod and ignored them.

"Let's start easy. Who are you? Why do you want my sword? And why'd you act like you couldn't speak my language?"

She lifted her chin.

"I am Klionthe Sioda aht-Larsa, Nashwatith of Nakh-Maru."

"You're royalty. Naturally." Jeff took a swig from the water skin. "Only royalty would get their ass kicked and act like they won."

She sniffed. "If you don't care to hear my woeful tale, I won't burden you."

Jeff tossed her the water skin. "Woe away."

"My father's throne has long been coveted by Efrekit, my many-times-removed cousin. I was traveling across the Bowl of Sisi with an armed guard to my aunt's palace in Yath-Maru. Efrekit hired raiders to kill my entourage and take me hostage in order to pressure my father to step down. They were spiriting me away when you came upon us."

"So far, pretty standard stuff. Not sure where my sword comes into all this."

"When you rescued me, I noted the Worldeater hanging upon your belt and knew I had to claim it."

"To steal my stuff."

She looked affronted. "To seize a weapon that would enable me to crush my enemy and grind their bones into dust!"

She was a woman with a plan. Kinda hot.

"Why do you keep calling this a Worldeater, anyway?" Jeff patted the sword.

"Do you even know what you possess?" Klio looked like he was some kind of dumbass. Hell, she might've been onto something. "Where did you find it?"

"Couple years ago, I got into a little altercation with some thieves. They cleared out of their den on short notice and left some stuff behind, including this. I call it the Void."

"Why?"

"Because it sounds badass. So what *is* it?"

"Look." Klio touched the scabbard. Her fingertips danced across a scrawled collection of runes. "Ut-Maru has known many gods, some so ancient they were forgotten even before our red-salt temples were built. These gods were merciless, and worshipped with blood rites conducted in caverns beneath the earth. Almost no concrete record of them exists."

"You a student of this stuff?"

She looked primly pleased. "I have achieved high ranks in classical studies and philology." College girl. Nice.

"So the sword belongs to a god?"

"Specifically to Tesu, the war god."

War god? Yeah, that tracked. "So this was stolen from a temple?"

"Undoubtedly. Most wouldn't know it on sight, but I recognized Tesu's sigil." She pointed out a spiral bisected by lightning. "Its capacity for destruction is rumored to be limitless in the correct hands. Now, I will wield it for my father and our nashwafiet."

"Lady. Klio. *I* can barely handle the thing. How were you planning to manage?"

"I'm adaptable."

Jeff wasn't going to argue with her. It got him nowhere. "I get it. You wanted my sword to protect your people. Why didn't you just tell me that? Why'd you pretend you couldn't understand me?"

"First, because a language barrier would make me appear more reliant upon you and lower your guard." Jeff frowned. College girl was smart. "And then, because it was funny." She laughed. "You were so exasperated."

"Think I liked you better when I couldn't understand you."

She glowered. "Give me the Worldeater."

"No. I wouldn't give it to anybody. I only keep it because I know I can handle it and won't abuse it. I can't trust anyone else to do either."

"Then wield it in defense of the Nashwa of Nakh-Maru!"

"I'm a simple man. I take jobs where there's a right side and a wrong one. Politics muddies the water. Always has."

"Then why did you even rescue me from those raiders?"

"Because you were in trouble."

Her thin eyebrows lifted. The expression in her blue eyes softened.

"Besides." Jeff cleared his throat. "You looked rich. Figured I'd get a decent reward for saving you."

She turned her face away with a *hmph*.

"I won't pay you." Klio folded her arms. "If you choose to leave me to perish, so be it."

He fought the urge to roll his eyes.

"I'll take you home, and protect you until we get there."

"Why?" She seemed genuinely puzzled.

"Because it's what I do." Jeff snagged the khefer's reins. "Hop on."

But Klio stared the way they'd come, a look of frozen horror on her face. Didn't take long to discover the problem.

A great dust cloud rose into the air. Shit. A storm? But this wasn't the season for them.

Klio plucked some shiny bauble from her sarong and peered through it. She swore, then passed it to Jeff. Hell, this thing operated like a telescope. Fashion and function, as his ex used to say.

Jeff saw almost one hundred men on khefer-back charging toward them. Green silk standards flapped in the wind. Some of the men looked like the desert raiders he'd rescued Klio from, but the others bore an insignia of three crossed swords on their breastplates. Wild calls and ululations rose into the air as they raced forward.

"So. My cousin appears to have found us." Klio cleared her throat. "He has brought a few reinforcements, as well."

"Reinforcements?" Jeff tossed her the jewel. "That's an army, lady. If you'd told me what this was about, I would've done a better job at covering our tracks."

"Shouldn't track covering be standard in your profession?" She winced, though. She was nervous. Good. "We must ride."

Jeff picked her up and tossed her on the saddle. She made a bewildered noise.

"I'll catch up," he said.

"You can't face them alone!" She sounded mad, of all things.

"Worried about me?" He slapped the khefer's rump. "Go!"

Klio raced away as Jeff faced the oncoming mob by himself. The dust rose, blocking out the sky. He sneered as he drew the Void and prepared a two-handed swing.

At first glance, the Void, or Worldeater, looked like a normal sword, with one exception: the blade was obsidian black. Then there was the weird purple glow that outlined the edges, curling into the air like steam. Weirdest of all, the blade seemed to have a mind of its own. When exposed to the air, it tugged the wielder this way or that. If you weren't strong enough, it'd control you instead of the other way around. Jeff's arms trembled. The sword tried pulling him forward, but he resisted. Sweat poured down his face. Running ten miles was easy. Wrestling the Void took effort.

The enemy approached. The sun glinted on adamantine helmets.

"Assholes," he whispered, and struck.

Jeff didn't kill them so much as explode them in a shower of gore. Chunks of smoking armor rained from the sky. Jeff grimaced at the splat of entrails as blood misted upon his face. The enemies' khefer began bolting in every direction. Jeff had taken at least ten lives with the first stroke. He charged headlong into the melee with a scream.

The Worldeater grew hot in his hands as he sliced. They fought back, but between the sword and his strength there was no competition. Thirty seconds later he stood alone amid the splashes of brackish red upon pink sands, at least thirty dead in pieces around him. Jeff sneered at the blade, which seemed to brighten with glee at the slaughter.

"Joffah!"

Klio called to him. Jeff turned.

Her wrists were bound. She was seated upon a strange khefer, with a large man riding behind her. This guy had rose-gold flesh, and green eyes so bright they seemed to glow. His head was shaved, his muscles gargantuan. He wore a breastplate with the three crossed swords upon it. Dozens more raiders and soldiers flanked him.

The shaved-head guy spoke in the same antiquated language Klio had used earlier. She wincingly translated.

"My cousin Efrekit demands that you sheath the Worldeater and surrender yourself. Or he will kill me."

To make his point, Efrekit held a dagger to her throat. Klio didn't cry or beg. She accepted her fate. After all, Jeff had told her he wouldn't give this thing to anyone. Now she'd seen why.

But high-and-mighty though she might be, he had to save her. Like an idiot, he couldn't walk away.

Jeff sheathed the sword and flung it to the ground. Klio's mouth fell open in shock.

Something walloped Jeff across the back of his head. They meant to knock him out with one blow, but he was a little too strong for that. He couldn't fight back for Klio's sake, and had to wait patiently until they succeeded after three or four more tries.

What a stupid day.

✦ ✦ ✦

"Joffah. Awaken."

Jeff opened his eyes. Took a few minutes for his vision to quit sloshing around. Already the back of his skull felt better, if a little tenderized. The vermillion sun's rays hadn't touched his skin in some time; he could feel his diminishment. Damn it. The air was clammy and smelled almost fungal. They were underground. He touched his right arm, and wrinkled his nose. They'd smeared some kind of sickly-sweet treacle-y crap on him. He sat up and noticed the ring of scowling soldiers. Wall torches provided dim lighting.

The chamber was circular, with pillars upholding a domed roof. The ceiling yawned away into darkness, probably thirty or so feet high. To the right, a massive statue stood upon a platform and extended its arm. The leering thing's face was demonic, with a crown of curling horns all around its head. The eye sockets were hollow.

Jeff glanced behind, and saw several men protecting a stone doorway. No exit. Before Jeff, a large cave mouth was the gateway to utter blackness. Before that opening was a stone dais, atop which stood Klio.

And Efrekit.

"We may be in some trouble," she said.

"I see you're fluent in understatement, too."

"They plan to feed you to a worm as tribute and take the Worldeater." She winced. "It is also my cousin's intention to marry me to every man in this room as payment." Jeff looked at all the burly, well-furred scumbags. That was a lot of marriage. "I wouldn't mind being killed by a monster instead."

"Sorry, I'm not trading."

Jeff looked up again. The very top of the chamber had a ring of boarded-up windows.

Windows . . .

"Can they understand us?" Jeff asked.

"That ancient dialect I used is considered the only appropriate language in the more fundamentalist sects. The soldiers here were raised according to the old customs."

"Come on. Everyone knows low-Maru," Jeff said.

Casually, Klio spoke. "Everyone in this room sleeps with their mother and urinates uncontrollably." No one batted an eye. Huh.

Efrekit talked, and Klio translated. "He would like you to grovel."

"Groveling's not my thing." Jeff crossed his arms while Klio translated. Efrekit grinned and spoke.

"He asks if your 'thing' is rotting in the intestines of a beast."

"If I have to choose."

Klio spoke. Efrekit did as well. "He says you seem stupid."

"Tell him he's not wrong." She did. The commander laughed, as did the men. At least Jeff was funny. "Actually, *he's* the idiot. He could've cut my head off, instead he brings me to an underground temple to fight some worm as 'tribute.' Tell him he's a backward, superstitious mouth-breather."

Klio glared. "*I* asked for death by combat. It was the only way to keep you alive long enough to escape."

Ah. "Well, then it's a good plan."

"I am a 'mouth-breather,' am I?"

"Don't take this personally."

"I take everything personally!"

"I noticed!"

Efrekit spoke. "He asks if we are like this always."

"Let's focus on getting out of here." He looked all around the room. Friezes littered the walls, images of horned monsters spearing men and women with delight. Great. There was also a carving at the front of that dais.

A spiral bisected by lightning.

Jeff looked at the sigil, then the statue. Its outstretched hand appeared awful empty. Oh man, what were the odds?

"Klio. Where's the Void?" He didn't use the term Worldeater. Didn't want anyone to catch on.

"Directly behind me. Efrekit wears your koh-pash on his belt."

Jeff's nostrils flared. Son of a bitch.

"Why do you ask?"

"I don't think these guys know where we are. When I give the signal, you need to get me the Void."

Before she could speak, the room trembled as an echoing cry sounded in the distance. The call came from within the cave, approaching the chamber. The cry changed to a muffled roar, drawing closer with every passing second. The men bellowed and beat their chests to welcome their worm.

Then Jeff heard the papery glide of massive wings. He glared at Klio.

"That doesn't sound like a worm."

"No translation is flawless!" she snapped.

A giant, pale moth swooped into the temple. Efrekit bellowed in joy, as did the rest of his soldiers.

The moth flapped high into the air, hovering directly overhead. At least, it looked like a moth. It had the bulbous eyes, the dusty wings, and the furred limbs. But the mouth was different, cavernous and filled with razor-sharp teeth. The thing screamed, the noise reverberating off every dank stone in this underworld.

Well. Shit.

The moth-thing swooped. Jeff threw himself to the ground, shuddering as a dusty, papery wing slid across his back. He coughed, the noxious dust filling his lungs, and ran to the other side of the circle. He wondered why the monster only went for him, then remembered the stickiness they'd painted on him. Probably monster barbecue sauce. The moth flew higher, ready to dive-bomb and swallow Jeff in one delicious gulp. But even without his superlative strength, Jeff was a tough son of a bitch. He raced over to the statue, climbed up its foot. Men roared their approval as the moth swooped again. Jeff crouched and waited. When the moth came for him, he jumped to the side. The thing almost bashed into the statue, but recovered.

That gave Jeff enough time to leap on its furred back. It smelled like dust and ass; he coughed and clung to the demon as it screamed, pulling him high into the air.

"Kick a window!" Klio shouted as the moth fluttered back and forth, flapping crazily through the air. Jeff almost tumbled off twice. "Don't fall!"

"Great strategy!" he shouted.

He cursed as the monster sped toward the top of the chamber, aiming to crush him against the ceiling. Jeff threw himself off in time, clutching the window ledge as he dangled above the three-story drop. The bastards shouted as he pulled himself up and kicked out one of the shuttered windows.

He saw they were deep underground. The broken window was half a foot or so off the desert floor. If only he could've got the hell out right then, but Klio and the sword were down below. A shaft of vermillion sun hit Jeff's leg. He crouched, letting the rays soak into his back. It wasn't much of a boost, but it was all he needed as the moth swung around to nab him. When it approached, Jeff jumped high and landed on its back. He grabbed the left wing and ripped it off like so much tissue paper. The moth shrieked in agony. As it fell, Jeff forced its head down so as to pile-drive it into the floor, kamikaze style. It worked; the moth splattered nicely. The sunlight still pouring down upon him, Jeff crushed the beast's head with two stamps of his feet.

"Klio! Now!"

As Efrekit watched in stupefied silence, Klio grabbed the koh-pash blade from its sheath and sliced her cousin's head off with a warrior's cry.

Damn.

She nabbed the Worldeater and leapt off the dais. Using the element of surprise, she raced through the soldiers and threw the blade. She threw well. Jeff caught and unsheathed it. The sword vibrated in his hand as Klio ran into the light. He held the weapon high over his head. "Tesu! Look what I brought!"

Nothing happened. Seconds ticked by. The room of cutthroats snarled and began to approach. Klio tensed.

The sound of stone grinding on stone froze everyone.

The immense statue's hollow eyes flared to red, fiery life. A bestial growl echoed throughout the chamber as the stone arm began to lower. Jeff felt the blade tug harder than ever. This time he let go.

The sword spun through the air, arcing upward until the statue clasped it. The living statue, god, or whatever it was surveyed the men who'd disturbed its temple and gotten giant moth guts all over its floor. He had to be pissed.

Then Tesu swung his returned blade. The first stroke wiped out fifteen men in a shower of blood. Jeff doubted that Tesu would be nice enough to give the mortal who'd returned his blade a pass.

Time to go.

"Get ready." He grabbed Klio and tossed her high into the air. She gripped the ledge and scrambled up it, heading out the window.

"Joffah! Come on!"

But as Jeff prepared to jump, he remembered the satchel.

It was on the dais, beside Efrekit's headless corpse. His log was inside. All the work he'd done for Reynolds and the others would be lost forever.

Cursing, he took his koh-pash and pushed past a throng of men. Some tried getting through the doorway, and Tesu murdered them. Others stampeded into the cave. He heard echoing screams as they ran, and then the high, unnatural cries of unknown beasts.

"Joffah!"

"The log!" He couldn't leave it behind. Not his one promise to Reynolds.

"You're going to die!" He could barely hear Klio over the cacophony. Jeff turned back and saw that she'd vanished. Probably nabbed a khefer and was hightailing it across the desert like a sane person. Good luck to her. But he couldn't leave.

He'd promised Reynolds. *Please. Do the work. Please, Jeff.*

Except that wasn't all she'd said.

Please live. Live a good, long time. Be happy. Please do that for me.

He could grab the log, or he could live. There was no third option. Jeff stared at the satchel as he gripped the tags around his neck, felt their names press into his hand.

He raced for the sunlight and the window. Out the corner of his eye, he saw Tesu prep another big swing in his direction. The blade had quadrupled in size after regaining its master's hand.

Jeff felt the sun on his skin. He crouched, and leapt just as the blade whiffed beneath his feet.

He clung to the ledge. Shit. He was still a little weak. As he tried to pull himself up, he heard the war god's cry.

A rose-gold hand reached in and nabbed his wrist.

"Hurry!" Klio pulled with all her might, and Jeff used the last of his strength to haul himself up and out of the window. He rolled into the sand.

The god's bellows died down. Maybe it had gone back to sleep in its temple of blood and death, sated, its power restored.

"Shit." Jeff closed his eyes, grateful to feel the sunlight. Then he looked down at the woman. "Klio. Thank you."

"Why?" She seemed a little embarrassed.

"For being good with a sword. And for not leaving me."

"Well. You *did* destroy my enemy. It's only fair."

She smiled. So did he.

Nakh-Maru was more than a city of pearl. It was titanium and adamantine, sapphire and emerald. Children played in amethyst gardens, and the gates yawned wide to welcome home their Nashwatith.

The palace resembled some spun-sugar concoction of silver filigree and glass. When the travelers arrived, servants outfitted in the purple silk livery of aht-Larsa descended, offering bowls of hot water for washing and candied flowers as a treat. Klio paraded along the halls of marble with Jeff at her side, his mouth agape. The northern capital was by far the richest he'd seen on this planet.

"I recall insisting that I wouldn't pay for your services," Klio said.

"Yeah." Jeff noticed a settee made of solid gold. "I can see money's tight at the moment."

"But I've amended my decision. You shall indeed have a reward." The woman gave a sly smile as they entered the throne room. A flight of twenty platinum steps led to a chair so resplendent with diamonds it almost hurt to look at.

"Thanks. What is it?"

Klio climbed two steps and stood before him. She spread her arms in a grand gesture. "I have chosen you, Joffah, to sit at my side in my father's palace and rule with me when his time has passed."

Jeff blinked. "Uh. What?"

"We shall be united in flesh, knit by ties indissoluble."

"Like . . . marriage."

"Every lavish delight shall be yours, as I shall be. You shall have days of power and nights of pleasure. Amongst our people, you shall be hailed as a god. Splendid shall be your raiment, and sacred oil shall anoint your brow. No creature that dwells upon our planet—nay, no creature that dwells within the boundaries of our universe—shall know such ecstasy. Your life shall be a paradise. Come and take your seat upon the diamond throne, and take me in your arms." She looked at him with those sapphire eyes, her coral mouth quirking. The most gorgeous woman he'd ever seen.

Jeff thought about it.

"No thanks."

"What?" Her smile vanished.

"Nice of you to offer, but I'm not the settling-down type. Plus we've only known each other, like, a day, and we fought the whole time."

"Not the whole time," she argued.

"If you don't mind, I'll take that khefer we rode up on and go. Though if you've got some water and dried goods that'll last me to the next nashwafiet, I'd be obliged."

Klio looked like he'd urinated in front of her as Jeff strolled away.

"How *dare* you take your leave when I have not dismissed you!"

"See? It's like we're married already." Jeff fought laughter as Klio threw herself in his path.

"You would give up a throne? You would give up *me*?" She sounded like the second one was more incredible. She didn't lack for confidence.

"I go where I want, do what I want. It'd take a lot to make me give it up."

"Do you suggest there is no desire between us?" She narrowed her eyes. "Perhaps that's why I had to force you to look upon my undraped form."

"At the oasis? That insulted you, didn't it?"

"It is a matter of etiquette! To avert one's gaze from the naked flesh of another is to shame that person. I could have you whipped for such insolence!"

"Sorry. Not into whipping." Jeff caught her up in his arms and lifted her so that their eyes met and their heads were perfectly even, height wise. "So if I saw you naked, you'd be happy?"

She sniffed. "Entirely. But only if you reciprocated." She wound her arms about his neck. "I believe in having all things equal between a husband and wife."

"Maybe you can convince me to stay," he said, bringing his mouth down on hers.

She convinced him. Twice.

SAVING THE EMPEROR
Simon R. Green

A man on the run. A woman on a mission. A renegade esper ... and the Emperor's life hanging in the balance. Time is running short, and to save an empire, an outcast must rise from the bowels of the Imperial City of Virimonde and become—and begin—a legend ...

The young bravo known as Hadrian Steel was stalking a saber-toothed tiger through the Garden of Death.

In the Imperial City of Virimonde, there were worlds within worlds. Special areas set aside, where everyone could pursue their heart's desire. The Garden of Death used to be a rookery, back in the day; a haven for thieves and rogues and political opportunists. The kind of place where the local law never entered, because they knew they'd never come out again. But eventually the rookery's villains went too far, perhaps because there was nowhere else left for them to go, and the Emperor Ethur sent in his personal troops, the Praetorian Guard ... And by the time they were finished, there wasn't enough left of the area to be worth salvaging.

The maze of dark and gloomy streets was left to rot and ruin, and strangling vines and hungry mosses crawled all over the crumbling buildings—until finally, someone saw a business opportunity. And so the Garden of Death became a sporting arena, for anyone who wished to enjoy the thrills of the hunt. The shadowy streets and squares were stocked with dangerous beasts and aliens from a hundred worlds, and anyone who could pay the price was free to test their courage and their skill in the most dangerous part of the most dangerous city on Heartworld.

The sign at the entrance said ENTER AT YOUR OWN RISK, though really it should have said ABANDON ALL HOPE, YE WHO ENTER HERE. Because while you were hunting the beasts and the aliens, there was a very real chance that something was hunting you.

Hadrian Steel moved silently down a shadowy back alley, his sword ready in his hand. He could hear the distant sounds of blasting energy weapons, the roars of ambushed animals, and the occasional scream from a hunter who'd underestimated his prey, but he kept his attention fixed on the massive beast ahead of him. He eased forward, step by step, being very careful where he set his feet so as not to make the slightest sound. The multicolored moss sprawling across most of one wall twitched and stirred as he passed, but it had already fed well that day, on a hunter who should have had eyes for something other than his prey, so the moss just went back to sleep again. And Hadrian took his left hand away from the energy gun holstered on his hip. He slowly closed in on the saber-toothed tiger as it padded calmly through the shadows of the alley, convinced it was lord of its domain.

The tiger was a magnificent creature, almost ten feet long, sleek and powerfully muscled. The silver stripes on its jet-black skin made it a part of the shadows, though light gleamed briefly on the huge curved fangs that gave the beast its name. It stopped abruptly, sensing some danger on the still air, and Hadrian froze where he was. And in the shadows behind him, Anastasia Charm stopped where she was too.

The tiger's great head came up as it sniffed the air carefully, and then its tail twitched as it took a cautious step forward. Hadrian took a step too, and his left hand snapped forward with vicious strength as he threw a knife into a dark opening in the wall ahead of him. There was a brief startled sound, and then a dead man fell forward into the alley with the knife in his throat. He hit the ground with a solid thud, and the saber-toothed tiger was off and running before the echoes had died away. Hadrian didn't even glance after it. He knelt beside the dead man, retrieved his knife and stood up again, casually stropping the blood-smeared blade against his legging. And then he looked back at the shadows where Anastasia was standing very still.

"You can come out now, if you want," said Hadrian.

Anastasia moved carefully forward into what little light there was, holding her hands out to show they were empty.

"I'm Anastasia Charm. Call me Anna. I already know who you are. How did you know I was following you?"

"The same way I knew he was there," said Hadrian, nodding at the dead man. "I pay attention."

"Who was he?"

"Just a bounty hunter, looking to collect the price on my head. I let him ambush me, so I could collect the price on his."

They studied each other carefully, taking their time. Hadrian Steel had the same look as the tiger he'd been hunting: a lean and muscular predator, with a handsome enough face, close-cropped dark hair and cool gray eyes. Barely into his twenties, he looked like he'd seen a lot of rough mileage. He wore simple leathers with no adornments, but the scabbard on his hip had all the elegant style of a family heirloom.

Anna was a tall, buxom woman, in a smart but practical outfit. Good-looking in a harsh kind of way, she had a mane of long blond hair and at least ten years on the young man standing before her. The body and the blood on the alley floor didn't seem to bother her at all. Hadrian nodded, acknowledging her composure. He didn't lower his sword.

"Why were you following me, Anastasia Charm? Assuming that really is your name?"

"No one uses their true name, in places like this. Or am I supposed to believe you're really Hadrian Steel?"

He smiled suddenly. "I haven't decided yet."

"Would you really have gone up against that tiger with just your sword?"

"That's why I came here. The sword is an honorable weapon."

"But are you an honorable man?"

"Depends on who you talk to."

Anna glanced at the dead man. "There's an unusually generous bounty on your head."

He shrugged. "My people aren't speaking to me anymore, just because I lifted a few family treasures when I left, to fund my new life. So . . . why are you here, Anna? Do you think you can collect the prize money, where the other gentleman failed?"

"I'm looking for a few brave and disreputable types, to help me save the Emperor."

Hadrian raised an eyebrow. "I wasn't aware the Emperor needed saving."

"Ethur is in danger," Anna said steadily. "A rogue esper has infiltrated his Court, and turned the people around him into puppets. Once she gets close enough to Ethur she'll put her thoughts in his head, and rule the Empire through him. We can't let that happen."

"Why not just alert his security people?" said Hadrian. "Let them handle it."

"Because the esper has already got to some of them, and I don't know who I can trust. We have to fight our way into the Imperial Court, and warn Ethur personally."

Hadrian smiled slowly. "So . . . you want to break into the Imperial Palace, the most heavily defended structure in the city. And then fight your way past the Emperor's Praetorian Guard, the finest warriors in the city. And finally, take on an esper who can dominate other people's minds?"

Anna beamed happily. "Exactly!"

"Why should I risk my life to save Ethur?" said Hadrian. "From everything I've heard, he's a hard-hearted son of a bitch."

"Comes with the job," said Anna. "He's as kind as he can be, to keep all the worlds safe and sound. But if the esper makes him her slave, the whole Empire could descend into chaos."

"How did you find out about this threat?" said Hadrian.

"I used to be part of Ethur's security force—until I noticed something was happening to the people around me. The next thing I know, someone was trying to get inside my head. Unfortunately for her, I'm part of the Vom Acht family. Gengineered long ago to be immune to psychic attacks."

Hadrian nodded slowly. "I've heard of them."

"When she realized she couldn't control my thoughts, the esper had her puppets denounce me to the Emperor, and I left the Palace one step ahead of the Imperial guards."

"How are we supposed to deal with this esper, once we get into the Court?"

"I used my security connections to make contact with an underground techsmith," said Anna. "And he built me a device powerful enough to shut down any esper's abilities."

She showed it to Hadrian, and he nodded slowly. "We're going to need some seriously powerful allies, to break into the Imperial Palace."

"I know where to find a couple of very special renegades," said Anna. "They're currently hiding out in the starport, trying to acquire passage offworld. I tracked you down first, so you could help me get to them."

"The starport is a very dangerous place," said Hadrian.

"But no one will mess with me, if you've got my back."

Hadrian looked at her thoughtfully. "Why choose me, out of all the bravos in Virimonde busy trying to make a name for themselves?"

Anna took a step closer to him. "Because you looked like someone I could trust to get the job done."

"There haven't been many people I could trust," said Hadrian.

"Everyone has to start somewhere," said Anna.

Hadrian smiled. "It would make a nice change, to have someone I could depend on."

"You can depend on me," said Anna.

Their eyes met, across a shadowed alleyway.

The saber-toothed tiger roared deafeningly as it burst out of the shadows behind them, launching itself at Hadrian. But he was already turning, his sword thrust out to meet the attack. The long blade slammed into the beast's chest, and the sheer impact from its leap forced the sword deep into the tiger's body. The oversized fangs strained for Hadrian's throat as the dying animal forced itself along the extended sword blade, until man and beast were staring into each other's eyes, its hot breath panting against his face . . . and then the light went out of the tiger's eyes. Hadrian lowered his sword, letting the huge body fall to the alley floor, and then he pulled the blade free and stepped back.

"I heard it circling around behind us," he said.

"You knew it was there, all the time we were talking?" said Anna.

"Of course," said Hadrian.

"And you let it attack?"

"I thought you'd want to be sure you had the right man

for the job." He grinned suddenly. "And the pelt should bring a good price in the markets."

"I'm not helping you carry it," said Anna.

Sometime later, they traveled to Virimonde's starport in a sedan chair levitated by an indentured esper. The comfortably padded conveyance floated serenely through the wide-open streets, wending its way through the bustling traffic of hover sleds, antigrav transports, and the occasional pack of aristos on stilts. Towering buildings blazed brightly as night fell, while uniformed guards gathered on every corner to keep a watchful eye on things. The esper driver out front of the chair chatted away cheerfully.

"At least I get to see the sights, in this job. More than I would from a prison cell, which is where I would be if they knew everything I'd done. Having a nice ride, are we? Good, good... Don't feel you have to join in the conversation. And don't forget to tip your driver. It's good karma."

He dropped them outside the starport's main gate, and Hadrian looked meaningfully at Anna until she dropped a few coins into the driver's outstretched hand. He stared at them for a moment and then sent the sedan chair shooting off down the street, in search of more generous passengers.

The security men at the gate were a scruffy bunch, but their weapons looked professional enough. A slightly more generous handful of coins persuaded them to glance the other way, and soon Hadrian and Anna were shouldering through tightly packed crowds with just enough arrogance to open up a path without starting a fight.

"Where should we look for these very special renegades?" said Hadrian.

"A bar called The Hawk's Wing."

"A cheap and nasty place, in a really bad location," said Hadrian. "I know it well. When we get there, stick close; they'll steal anything, including your shadow."

The actual starport was the great open space inside a circle of ancient buildings. Ships from all over the Empire teleported in, hung around long enough to pick up some cargo and the occasional passenger, and then blinked out again. Berths for people who wanted to get offworld in a hurry were always going to be at a premium, and the necessary transit papers that made it look like they were allowed to leave Heartworld were even scarcer. Such papers passed quickly from hand to hand, gaining value with every transaction, but most ended up being prized from the cold, dead fingers of the previous owner. Which was why starship captains always made a point of checking transit papers for bloodstains.

The buildings surrounding the starport started out as accommodation for support technicians, but down the years they'd been taken over by all kinds of small and suspect businesses, and people desperate for somewhere to live while they struggled to find a way offworld. The buildings had joined together into one great circular structure, supposedly because that made it easier for everyone to stab each other in the back at the same time.

The starport became yet another area cut off from Virimonde and its laws—a modern-day rookery. Once you'd made it inside, you could be sure no one would come in after you, because the starport protected its own. But the price of that security was that if you tried to leave, the city guards would shoot you on sight. On the grounds that you must have done something to deserve it.

All of which meant that some people had been living there for a very long time, scraping out a living by being useful. Hadrian and Anna passed rows of booths offering every delight or necessity you could think of, and a few that came as a definite surprise, while colorfully clad barkers shouted their wares and did their best to drown out everyone else. Here and there along the way, small groups of bullies and bravos with heavy face makeup and intimidating clan tattoos would take a thoughtful interest in Hadrian and Anna—until Hadrian turned his head to look at them, at which point even the biggest and best-armed would suddenly find a reason to become interested in something else.

"I didn't know you had such a reputation," said Anna.

"I don't," said Hadrian. "They just know the real thing when they see it."

"Then they should be looking at me," said Anna.

"They're probably too intimidated," said Hadrian.

Finally they came to The Hawk's Wing; a small disreputable backstreet bar with few charms and even less character. The bouncer in barbarian's furs nodded briefly to Hadrian, stepped aside to allow the two of them to enter, and then went back to scowling at the world. A heaving unwashed crowd—humans and aliens and every possible combination—packed the bar from wall to wall, drinking hard to forget the kind of day they'd had, because they had to do something to pass the time while they waited for a ship. Hadrian pressed steadily forward, and everyone seemed to just ease out of his way without even realizing they were doing it. Anna stuck close to Hadrian, peering around until she could point out the two very special people they'd come in search of, currently engaged in a shouting match with a local villain over by the long wooden bar.

"Ruby and Indigo," said Anna. "Almost certainly not their real names either."

"An Investigator and a Defender?" said Hadrian. "We might just pull this off after all."

Ruby was a tall, powerfully built woman, with the deep crimson skin that marked her as an Investigator, enforcer of the Emperor's justice. Just standing there, she looked dangerous as all hell. Indigo's skin was sky blue and covered in lines of silver circuitry, identifying him as a Defender of Humanity. A little shorter than average height, and lithely built, he stood easily at his partner's side as they faced down a local thug who clearly fancied himself a force to be reckoned with.

The oversized fellow in grubby silks was raising his voice to Ruby and Indigo in a way that suggested he wanted everyone in the bar to hear what he was saying. He was backed up by two glowering Hard Men: vat-grown clones from the local franchise. Mostly muscle, with just enough brains to follow orders, they waited patiently to be told to hurt someone.

"Who is that loud and obnoxious person?" said Anna.

"Stack! de Vere," said Hadrian. "A facilitator of surreptitious business. Also, an alien hybrid—which you probably guessed from his compact eyes and antennae."

"Is he important around here?"

"I think he's about to find out that he isn't."

Stack! thrust his face forward, almost apoplectic with rage that Ruby and Indigo weren't properly intimidated by his presence.

"The price for your transit papers just doubled! Pay up, or you'll never see them. Argue with me, and the price will double again!"

Ruby took a step forward and Stack! retreated in spite of himself, bumping up against his bodyguards.

"Nobody cheats us," said Ruby.

"What she said," said Indigo.

"It's bad for business," said Ruby. "And we really don't like being shouted at."

Stack! stared at them, shocked speechless at being so openly defied, and then he snapped his fingers at the two Hard Men.

"Kill them! Kill them both!"

Ruby blinked out of existence, and was immediately replaced by something else. A good foot taller, and only roughly humanoid, the new form was covered in seamless golden armor. The Investigator's battle form had a solid bullet head, four arms, and energy guns protruding from its barrel chest. They fired twice, and the two Hard Men were dead before they hit the floor, because they didn't have heads anymore.

Stack! dived for cover, screaming to be heard over the raised voices of the crowd.

"A hundred credits for each of their heads!"

And just like that, everyone in the bar had some kind of weapon in their hands. Indigo disappeared, replaced by something huge and blocky with metallic skin and razor-edged claws sprouting from its hands. And even the hardened denizens of The Hawk's Wing hesitated, faced with a Defender wrapped in his anger.

"Two hundred credits!" screamed Stack! from behind an overturned table.

The crowd surged forward, and the first rank died as Ruby's guns swept back and forth. Bodies crashed to the floor, and the bar's patrons jumped over them to get to their enemy. Indigo moved so quickly he was just a metallic blur, and wherever he went men fell screaming, cut open by blades moving too fast to be seen. The Investigator and the Defender took on the entire bar, hugely outnumbered but not seeming to give a damn. Hadrian considered the odds and then looked at Anna, raising his voice to be heard over the din of combat and the screams of the dying.

"Are you sure we need them?"

"They're the only ones who can get us into the Imperial Palace," said Anna.

Hadrian shrugged, drew his sword, and hacked his way through the fray with calm professionalism. Blood flew on the air as he cut down everyone who got in his way, because no one was good enough or fast enough to stop him. Soon he was standing behind Ruby and Indigo, guarding their backs so they could concentrate on the slaughter in front of them. The crowd quickly decided that the odds had turned against them, and that two hundred credits weren't nearly enough. In a few moments they were fighting one another in their eagerness to leave through the only door. The bar was suddenly very empty, and very quiet. Stack! peered out from behind his table, saw he was now on his own, and reluctantly stood up. He smiled weakly at the transformed Ruby and Indigo.

"I'm sure we can come to some agreement . . ."

Ruby shot his head off.

She resumed her human form, knelt down beside the headless body, and searched the pockets with unemotional thoroughness. She shook her head, got to her feet, and looked to Indigo, who was also human again.

"He didn't have the transit papers on him. We'll have to try somewhere else."

"Good fight, though," said Indigo.

They turned to Hadrian, who was calmly cleaning blood and gore off his blade with a piece of cloth.

"We didn't ask for your help," said Ruby.

"Didn't need it," said Indigo.

"You're welcome," said Hadrian. "Now, this lady has a proposition you might want to listen to."

"A guaranteed way to get you the transit papers you need," said Anna, stepping lightly over the dead bodies to join them. "Is there somewhere more private where we could talk?"

"Why not?" said Ruby.

"What she said," said Indigo.

The rogue Investigator and Defender occupied a single room above the bar. It was small and basic, with furniture that didn't even try to match. The barred window let in slices of light from the street, and the door had half a dozen locks on it. Something smelled really bad, but everyone was far too polite to mention it.

"It's not much, but it's nothing like home," said Ruby.

"Just as well," said Indigo.

"How much are they charging you, for a dump like this?" said Anna.

"Twenty credits a day," said Ruby. "I know—you wouldn't think they'd have the nerve to ask for it. But that's what it costs, when people like us are on the run."

"Still worth it," said Indigo.

"How did an Investigator and a Defender end up here?" said Hadrian. "Hiding from the law, instead of enforcing it?"

"The Emperor turned on us, for no good reason," said Ruby. "After everything we'd done for him, it turned out all our years of service meant nothing. And now we're stuck here."

"Looking for a ship," said Indigo.

"There's a lot of that going around," said Anna.

She explained about the Emperor and the rogue esper, and what needed to be done. Ruby and Indigo stared coldly at Anna.

"You expect us to save Ethur?" said Ruby.

"Why should we?" said Indigo.

"To have all your sins forgotten, and be reinstated," said Anna. "Or acquire the transit papers you need to get offworld. Getting past Imperial security and blasting our way into the Court is almost certainly going to be the most dangerous thing you'll ever do, but the odds have to be better than hanging around here, hoping to jump a ship before your chances run out. Save the Emperor, and he'll be grateful. Because that will encourage others to protect him in the future."

Indigo looked at Ruby. "She has a point."

"How, exactly, are we going to fight our way into the most heavily protected building in Virimonde, and gain access to Ethur's Court?" said Ruby.

"I'd be interested to hear that," said Hadrian.

"The Imperial Palace is being rebuilt again," said Anna. "Because Ethur gets bored so easily. Which means that, for a short period, security around the palace will be somewhat patchy. I have a small attack ship . . ."

"How did you get your hands on something like that?" said Hadrian.

"I won it in a card game," said Anna.

She glared at him, defying him to challenge her story. Hadrian just nodded, and she continued.

"I will pilot the ship," said Anna, "while you run the weapons systems. Ruby and Indigo, you will fly alongside in your most powerful battle forms, ready to take on the Imperial defenses. I will fly us into the palace and position the ship over the roof of the Court. We smash our way through, crash as painlessly as possible in front of Ethur's throne, and I will use my special device to take down the rogue esper."

"And then?" said Hadrian.

"We explain ourselves to Ethur, and allow everyone in the Court to applaud us," said Anna.

They all looked at each other for a long moment.

"Who knows?" said Hadrian. "It might happen that way."

"When do we go?" said Ruby.

"Now," said Anna.

"Right now?" said Indigo.

"Do you have anything better to do?" said Anna. "Those gaps in security won't be there for long."

Ruby smiled suddenly. "What the hell; it sounds like fun."

"Big time," said Indigo.

"I can't wait to see how this is going to play out," said Hadrian.

The attack ship turned out to be a sleek and stylish little number, with surprisingly sophisticated weapons systems and force shields. Hadrian refrained from saying *It must have been one hell of a card game*, but only just. He familiarized himself with the ship's gun controls, while Anna fired up the ship. She'd hidden it away on the edge of the starport, and had it up in the night sky and on its way to the Imperial Palace before anyone in authority could even think of objecting.

Ruby flew on the port side, in another of her golden armored bodies; something streamlined and vicious. Indigo took the starboard, in a bulky metallic battle form that looked like it could fly through a mountain if it felt like it. The crew shot across the gleaming city, scaring the hell out of all the air traffic they passed, and headed straight for the Imperial Palace.

Workmen were crawling all over the palace exterior, floating here and there in antigrav belts as they hammered new pieces into place, but they were all far too busy to pay attention to one small ship. Gun towers marked the perimeter at regular intervals, like massive steel sentinels that never slept, bristling with sensor arrays and row upon row of energy cannon. Anna steered her ship carefully between two of the towers, holding her breath for a challenge—and then both towers suddenly opened fire.

Dozens of energy cannon filled the night sky with flaring colors, as searing energy beams slammed into the attack ship. It rocked back and forth under the repeated impacts, its force shields failing. Warning sirens shrieked on the control deck, and somewhere something was on fire, but Anna just hunched down in the pilot's seat and aimed the ship right into the raging storm.

Hadrian's hands moved swiftly over the weapon controls, targeting Imperial attack ships as they lifted off the ground to intercept. His weapons were too much for their shields, and one by one he blew them apart like targets in a shooting gallery. But there seemed to be no end to their numbers, and he knew it was only a matter of time before some of them would get past him.

Ruby and Indigo streaked across the night sky, slipping past the stabbing energy beams, and flew straight at the two towers. Their armored bodies slammed through the force shields and hit the gun towers head-on. They punched through the massive structures and out the other side, swept around in a tight arc, and hit the towers again, surging back and forth inside them. Pieces of shattered energy cannon rained down on the streets below, while vicious explosions tore through the tower interiors. The Investigator and the Defender were having fun.

Suddenly the attack ship was past the towers and out of range, and Ruby and Indigo shot across the night sky like blazing comets to rejoin it. The ship was limping a little now, but Anna's hands darted over the controls, nursing it along. The Imperial Palace loomed up ahead, its brilliant lights sparkling against the dark like a crown of many jewels, but Anna only had eyes for the unfinished glass ceiling over Ethur's Court. She sent the attack ship howling down out of the night, with Ruby and Indigo diving in after her. The ship crashed into the Court, trailing glass and flames and smoke and discharging energies, and hit the ground so hard it bounced twice before finally screeching to a halt.

Anna hit the fire suppressor systems, shut down everything else, and then hurried out of the ship. Hadrian stuck close behind her, sword in hand. And as they emerged into the Imperial Court, Ruby and Indigo dropped lightly down beside them and took on human forms again.

A low ground fog of psychotropic pleasure drugs coiled sluggishly around the crew's ankles as they moved cautiously forward, passing through a forest of abstract sculptures fashioned from the living bodies of people who had displeased the Emperor. Lobotomized aliens lurched around the Court, looking cute and cuddly and endlessly confused. Politicians who were no longer in favor stood like statues, because their time sense had been slowed right down. To entertain the Court, and *encourager les autres*. Courtiers in wildly stylized gowns watched silently as the invaders made their way through the Court.

The Emperor Ethur sat on his Steel Throne, and watched them come to him. Over four hundred years old, his body was riddled with medical support systems and gengineered organs. He didn't rise from his throne because he couldn't. He was plugged into the medical machine that was the Steel Throne, while chemicals pulsed through a multitude of transparent cables. He had pale leathery skin, and his complexion changed constantly as chemical tides rose and fell. He wore no clothes, no robes of state, because he wanted everyone to see what he was; what he endured to remain their Emperor. His face was lean, with a beak of a nose and a straight line for a mouth. His eyes were as old as the world.

He gestured imperiously with a pale hand, and dozens of heavily armed Praetorian Guards came rushing forward to protect the throne. Ruby and Indigo took on sleek new enforcement bodies and neutralized all their energy weapons, so the guards abandoned their guns and drew their swords, because steel always works. Ruby and Indigo grew swords from their metal hands, Hadrian hefted his sword in a thoughtful way, and the two sides slammed together.

The Investigator and the Defender raged through the guards, untouchable and unstoppable in their altered forms, cutting down everyone who got in their way. Hadrian danced among the guards as though it was all just a game, hacking and cutting with elegant style as he carved out a path to the throne. Swords rose and fell, steel jarred against steel, and the finest guards in the Empire never stood a chance. Ruby and Indigo hit them like the wrath of gods, while Hadrian showed what one man with a sword could do, when he's spent his entire life training to do nothing else. The battle was soon over, and Hadrian cut down the last few men between him and the throne without ever taking his eyes off Ethur. Ruby and Indigo became human again and looked thoughtfully around the Court.

"There's no rogue esper here," said Ruby. "My battle form would have detected her presence."

"No controlling thoughts anywhere," said Indigo.

"I don't see any threat to the Emperor," said Ruby.

"Oh, there's a threat," said Anna, walking calmly forward through the carnage.

She pointed her special device at Ruby and Indigo, and they crashed unconscious to the floor. Anna smiled brightly at Hadrian.

"I just shut down their systems for a while. Nothing like having implanted tech, to make you vulnerable to outside control."

"That device isn't what you said it was," said Hadrian.

"It's more a sort of super remote control," said Anna. "Capable of overriding absolutely everything. It was created by Imperial Security, for situations in which they couldn't trust any tech. I stole it when I left the Court."

"You lied to me," said Hadrian.

"You wouldn't have come, if I'd told you the truth," said Anna.

"I might have," said Hadrian.

Anna shrugged. "I couldn't risk it."

She turned to face the Emperor on his Steel Throne, and he nodded slowly to her.

"Hello, Anna," he said, in a voice like a cemetery full of dust. "I see you've returned my private attack ship."

"Hello, Ethur," said Anna. "It's good to be back."

"What is going on?" said Hadrian.

"I was married to Ethur," said Anna. "One of his many wives; but he promised to make *me* Empress. All I had to do was give him a son. He's outlived all his previous children, or had them killed, but the throne needs an heir ... He's so old now it's impossible for him to father a child without extensive medical support, but he keeps trying."

"I'm guessing something went wrong on the heir front," said Hadrian.

"I found out just how much the Imperial surgeons would have to alter me, before my body could accept his ancient seed," said Anna. "You think Ethur looks bad; you should see what the medical techs had planned for me. So I said the hell with it, and disappeared into the shadows. Because I really did work for security, once upon a time. But I still thought I should be Empress. So I worked up a plan, recruited a few useful fools, and here we all are!"

"What happens now?" said Hadrian.

"Yes," said the Emperor. "I'd be interested in hearing that myself."

Anna pointed her device at him. "Back in my security days, I discovered this very useful little toy, buried away and forgotten. I can use it to shut down all the medical tech in your throne, and then ... I think I'll just stand here and watch you die. There are factions in the Court that will support me as Empress, rather than allow a power vacuum. And I will finally have what I was promised!"

Hadrian's left hand whipped forward impossibly quickly, and Anna cried out in shock as his throwing knife knocked the device out of her hand. It went skidding away across the floor, and Hadrian moved to stand between it and Anna. He smiled at her easily.

"I do admire ambition, but I think in this case it's definitely a case of better the devil you know."

"You'd defend Ethur?" said Anna. "You think you can trust him to be grateful?"

"More than I trust you," said Hadrian. "I knew all along you were up to something."

"How could you know?" said Anna.

"You claimed to be a Vom Acht," said Hadrian. "But they're the family I ran away from, and I didn't know you at all. And since I know all about psionic immunity, I could tell your little device had nothing to do with shutting down a rogue esper."

"You let me come all this way . . ." said Anna. "You killed all these people!"

Hadrian shrugged. "I was curious as to how this would play out. And I wanted to show what I could do."

"It's not too late," said Anna, holding his gaze with hers. "Let me do this, let me be Empress, and I will be very grateful."

"But how could I ever trust you, when all you've done is lie to me?"

"I had to!"

"No," said Hadrian. "You didn't. We could have been partners."

"I didn't want a partner," said Anna.

"I know," said Hadrian.

"You'll have to kill me to stop me," said Anna.

She was suddenly holding a concealed energy weapon, but he was already moving before she could bring in to bear on him. His sword leapt forward, to punch through her chest and out her back. She stared at him over the extended blade, and then the light went out of her eyes and she dropped to the floor. Hadrian pulled out his sword.

"You told me I could depend on you," he said quietly. "I could forgive anything except that."

Some time later, Hadrian and a revived Ruby and Indigo stood before the Emperor. He offered the Investigator and the Defender pardons for all past sins, and full reinstatement, but they politely declined, in favor of transit papers for offworld travel. Because the Emperor didn't seem to remember who they were, and what they'd been accused of, they thought it better to not still be around when someone reminded him. The Emperor turned to Hadrian.

"It appears I owe you my life. What can I offer you?"

"You need someone to protect you, who knows what he's doing," said Hadrian. "Someone you can trust."

"I do seem to be a little short on Praetorian Guards at the moment," said the Emperor. "Very well, you shall be my official bodyguard. Did I hear right, that you're a Vom Acht?"

"Not anymore," said Hadrian. "I think a new name would better suit my new life."

"Then what should I call you?"

"The name is Deathstalker. Giles Deathstalker."

Ethur smiled. "Welcome to my service, Sir Deathstalker. I'm sure you'll go far."

A KNIGHT LUMINARY
R.R. Virdi

In a universe at war with the Amalgam machine hive-mind, humanity's last, best line of defense are the Knights Luminary, warriors capable of channeling the divine power of Darklight. Novak is only a trainee: green, powerless, and out of his depth when a distant outpost goes dark and silent . . . .

✠ ✠ ✠

Novak would either rise to be one of the Luminaries in the next twenty-four hours . . . or dead. It all rested on how the mission went.

There was no sound in space, so they made their own.

Armored fists pounded against the dropship walls like the distant drum of thunder. Novak added his own beat to the tempo, finding the basso bangs bringing a steady calm to his nerves.

A hand fell on his shoulder and shook him lightly.

"Nervous?" The speaker's voice carried a mechanical warble, enhanced by the fact the noise carried through his comms as well as through the ship's interior.

Novak shook his head. "I've been training for this for years. I only thought when I'd get a chance to rise, I'd be back on the *Arbiter*—weighed and judged there for the next step."

"There's still time for that," Ilyus laughed and clapped Novak's back hard. His chasseur armor betrayed no movement as he shook, bringing an eerie stillness to his form even though Novak watched the man's shadow shift. The gray cloak and cowl, composed of interwoven mesh and more thin layers than he could count, billowed and sat with a leaden weight that masked motion.

The rest of Ilyus's armor would be sleek and form-fitting, easier to hide under the cloak. Its colors would be the typical blend and patchwork of gray to black with some hints of white. The only break from this was the gold-foil faceplates and visor common to all the Knights Luminary.

"You still haven't manifested your Darklight yet, right?"

Novak shook his head, not wanting to give voice to that fact. There was no embarrassment in the fact he hadn't triggered the divine light, it was a common enough thing. But it still sat uneasy in his stomach that he was so close to his rise and hadn't shown a speck of mystical potential.

Darklight had been discovered centuries ago when humanity met the *Arbiter*, an interstellar city-ship that had been abandoned. The first explorers settled it and became exposed to the *Arbiter*'s power source—Darklight, the ethereal energy that functioned somewhere between science and magic. It empowered the first knights to manifest celestial abilities that allowed them to channel the energy as a weapon and for defensive measures.

It gave humanity the edge they needed against the hostile forces of the galaxy, allowing them to compensate for the differences in tech advances with their Luminary powers.

They still didn't know how it all worked, only that humans could access the magical source after being exposed to traumatic situations—the Snap, as it was called.

After spending enough time on the *Arbiter*, a person could eventually reach out and tap into Darklight.

Except for Novak. He'd spent his life on the ship, surrounded by its magical energy. And he'd never showed a spark of potential all through the years of training and missions. This would be his last try, and it didn't look good. In truth, he'd given up the idea of manifesting his Darklight. Most people at least experienced a Flashing once before their Snap. They would have vivid images of manifesting abilities before they happened. Or a spark of Darklight would appear around them, too weak to do anything with, but it was enough of a sign. And he'd never seen any of it. There were rumors that some had still achieved rank among the Luminary without using the magical abilities of the *Arbiter*, and he held onto those dreams.

"Don't worry, kid. It'll turn up. Always does. Most of us don't show any flickers of it either until we have our Waking moment. Usually happens when things get really bad—out of control and then you've got nothing but your back to a wall." Ilyus sighed and slumped on the bench, crossing his legs. His head tilted back to lightly *thump* against the wall, letting Novak know the man sought a short rest before their drop.

Novak thought to do the same, but a short static buzz jarred him from the momentary reverie, sending his heart lurching.

"Listen up." The voice belonged to the OG (operation guardian), the one running charge of the mission. Parcis paced the length of the drop bay. He stood a head taller than most men, and the bulk of his armor exaggerated that greatly. His smooth and curved pauldrons flared at the ends into swooping arcs that reminded Novak of wings. Everything else about the man's armor fit that theme—arced, angular, and all the room for heavy curves that appeared more superficial than anything else. "We lost contact with Ipacrus Relay Station over thirty-six standard hours ago. All hails were ignored, no bounce backs, and a visual survey run by drones turned up nothing but wildlife movement."

"Nothing?" Zelkris leaned forward, resting his forearms against his knees. The deep plum of his bracers carried a glossy shine that seemed impractical to Novak. The coloring would be blasted off or fall to wear over the course of future missions. It would also draw unwanted attention to the man in the heat of battle, making him an easy target. Nothing in his flowing robes, all carrying varying shades of a similar color, brought the word _stealthy_ to mind. Add to that the fact the portions of his armor around the joints all boasted thin strips of glowing light somewhere between stark white and turquoise. The man would be a bright beacon to any hostiles, but then, every magus Novak had seen went for similarly gaudy aesthetics.

"Just wind and water, Zelkris, but we know that's never the case. They wouldn't send us in otherwise."

The magus nodded in agreement and even the almost dozing Ilyus tipped his head.

"We drop in ten. This is a recon assessment. Repeat: Recon. Scan and assess, keep on comms. Do not fire until told otherwise."

Zelkris grunted and Ilyus gave the OG a lazy thumbs-up.

"Yes, Guardian," said Novak.

Parcis turned his attention on the initiate, weighing him. "You'll do fine, son. First op with Luminaries?"

Novak nodded. "Yes, Guardian."

Parcis bent at the waist and rapped a heavy-armored fist against Novak's chest plate. "Eyes forward. Ears open. You do those two things and listen, you'll make it home a Luminary yourself, got it?"

"And if you don't, this backwater's a nice enough place as any for burial," said Zelkris.

Ilyus let out a light chuckle at that.

"Stow it." Parcis fixed both men with a long look before taking a seat himself.

The drumming resumed on silent cue, falling in measure with Novak's heartbeat.

"Dropping quick, knights. LZ clear." The pilot's voice cut off as quickly as it had come.

The drop door hissed open and air rushed to fill the void, buffeting Novak without reprieve.

"Ten and counting, knights!" the pilot's voice crackled.

"Novak, you're with me. Ilyus and Zelkris, lead the drop and take point from there."

The chasseur and magus both nodded and headed

toward the door. A handful of seconds later, they jumped.

"Alright, trainee. Let's go." Guardian Parcis grabbed Novak by the shoulder and they dropped together.

The world below raced into view.

Novak's HUD—heads-up display—brought it into better clarity.

An endless expanse of pale green greeted him with dull swaths of gray in the distance.

They dove toward a bright red marker that flared to life in his visor, indicating the relay.

Ipacrus Station looked like a three-story spire of once brilliant white, now dulled in its luster by weather and time. It lacked any glass or windows around it—at least any that were visible. A long section sprouted out from one side of the tower and ran along the side for the length of a few thousand feet.

"On the ground. No movement. Nothing on visuals. Over?" Ilyus's voice had come through clearer in comms than it had on the ship.

"Copy. Move into the station and keep hailing for a response. Remember, do not open fire until given the clear."

"Roger." Ilyus and Zelkris spoke in stereo.

The puck-sized boosters along Novak's calves, ribs, and back all fired at once, generating thrust to slow his descent. He hit the ground, letting his knees absorb the impact. The kinetic barrier around him, created by his armor, took the rest of the landing's brunt. Parcis landed by him.

"Let's go, trainee."

Novak nodded, shifting through his HUD to look at the world through infrared, then ultraviolet. Nothing. He finally returned to normal view and made his way toward the station, Guardian Parcis staying by his side.

They made it to the entry doors, but they refused to open.

Parcis keyed his comms. "Ilyus, Zelkris, anything?"

"Negative. Can't even find a way in. Wait, one of the automated shutters just opened. Still weapons silent, Guardian? I can blast a way in and open the main doors."

Parcis paused for a moment. "Do it. But don't train weapons on anyone alive in that station. I want any eyewitness accounts we can get on why Ipacrus Relay is down and not broadcasting."

"Roger."

A high-pitched blast echoed in the distance. Then quiet.

"What do you think we'll find, Guardian?" Novak looked at his ops leader, waiting for the answer.

"I'm not sure, trainee, but whatever it is, I have a feeling it's not good. Ipacrus is the telemetry station we need in the sector to keep an eye on Amalgam movement. If this place goes down, we'll be caught off guard if the Amalgam makes a move into the sector."

Unless they're already here. Novak quickly buried the dark thought as the main doors to the station vented and opened.

Darkness greeted him and Ops Guardian.

"Why aren't the automated lights on?" Novak's hand instinctively went to the heavy pistol at his side, drawing it. It held a reassuring weight even when gripping it in his

armor and with both hands. The machine pistol had a
frame nearly twice as large as his fist despite being only
as thin as his thumb in width. Sleek, angular, and with a
design like a skeletal frame measuring tool, it could still
fire hundreds of rounds per minute with deadly accuracy.

"Don't know, but that's enough of a reason to have
weapons up and heads on a swivel." Twin beams of light
flared along the top of Guardian Parcis's helmet,
illuminating the path ahead in a soft white. He raised his
own weapon a moment later—a long rifle the length of
his arm, all in black with a single core of neon blue
glowing through the whole of the frame.

"Got movement, Guardian. Two hundred meters from
your position. Moving in on them," said Ilyus.

Parcis didn't confirm, instead choosing to break into a
full sprint toward the location.

Novak fell into step a few paces behind the man.

They crossed the distance with ease, rounding through
a few corridors just as dark and without power as where
they'd entered from.

"I don't like this, sir." Novak's voice didn't break over
the sound of their footsteps hammering along the floor.

The ops guardian must have registered what he'd said,
but the man didn't bother replying.

They reached the rendezvous with Ilyus and Zelkris,
coming into a room with data towers standing feet taller
than any of them. All of the lights flickered through the
machines, indicating they still had some connection to
power.

Lights flickered intermittently through this hall,
snapping across their vision with stark white.

Ilyus came around the nearest bend, weapon drawn. The hand cannon trained on Novak's skull before the tip bobbed and lowered. "Sorry, kid."

Novak waved the man off. "It's fine. You caught movement?"

Ilyus gestured with his gun to a set of double doors ahead of them. "This section has power, running on backup. Backups aren't automatic on Ipacrus. They've got to be triggered manually." He turned to face Novak and the ops guardian before focusing his attention back on the doors.

That means someone or something is here and turned the backups on. Novak leveled his machine pistol on the doors, waiting for orders.

"One of the scientists?" Zelkris looked at each of them as he spoke, clearly wanting someone to answer.

"Could be. Whoever it is, they're the only lead we have as to what's happened there. We need them." Parcis pointed to the control panel beside the doors. "Get it open. Don't fire unless hostile. We go in, restrain whoever it is, ask questions. Understood?"

Everyone confirmed in unison.

Zelkris popped open the panel and tapped a few digital keys along one of his bracers. Lights strobed through a series of colors and the doors let out a low moan of protest. They slid open, pressurized gas venting out of the sides.

Parcis signaled the team in with a curt gesture of two fingers.

Everyone filtered in.

A series of screens dominated one side of the room, all

displaying camera footage of the areas surrounding the station perimeter. Some of the cams showcased the various darkened halls in a clear grayscale—night vision.

"Found her!" Ilyus came from around another section of data towers, hauling a young woman by the scruff of her collar.

She couldn't have been out of her early thirties. Lean, bronze, with dark hair falling to her shoulders. Her clothing marked her as one of the scientists on the station, all clad in canvas overalls with heavy work boots. She let out a string of obscenities as she flailed, trying to bat Ilyus's arm and break his grip.

She failed.

Parcis raised and extended a hand. "Easy. Easy. We're here to help. Who are you and what happened here? Why's the station dark?"

She muttered something unintelligible under her breath. Her eyes were wide and darting to each of them, then she focused on the open doors.

She's scared, realized Novak. *But of what? Not us.*

Parcis lowered his weapon, stowing it at his side. He raised both hands in a universal gesture of placation. "Hey, hey. Look at me. It's okay. But we need you to be clear here, yeah? What happened?"

Ilyus still held the woman firm in his grip.

"Let her go, chasseur."

The man obeyed, breaking his hold.

The woman shook herself and shot Ilyus a withering glare before turning her attention back on the ops guardian. "I don't know all of it." She spoke with a thick and heavy accent, stressing the consonants harder than the vowels. "Tauna." She placed a hand to her chest. "I work in the field—maintenance on telemetry posts we have across the local zone that ping data back to here. I was working two days ago when an alert came through communications. I heard screaming. Then everything went quiet. I couldn't hail anyone."

Parcis put his hands on the woman's shoulders reassuringly. "Easy. Breathe. Go on."

She nodded. "I waited for most of the first day, scared. I didn't know if I should come back so I stayed out low in the fields. Then . . . then I came back. Power was out, the whole place was dark. I couldn't get in so I went to the garage. It has a backup generator that runs on fuel. Enough power to work the motorized doors. I got in but then I couldn't find anyone—anything. Just blood on some of the walls. I stayed in the underground maintenance halls until now. They're heavily shielded and run off secondary power. Machines can't pick up life signs down there." Her eyes darted and speech came rapid fire as if still afraid and on edge.

"I saw your ship enter the atmosphere on the backup systems in the basement. When I knew people were coming, I came upstairs hoping for rescue. But *they're* still here. I haven't been able to hide for too long in one spot."

Zelkris stepped forward, his gaze slowly moving from the woman back to the cams. "Wait, what machines? What are you talking about? Who's still here?"

A high-pitched scream cut through the room, an odd metallic ring tingeing it.

Everyone turned toward the source coming from the other end of the room.

The creature stood half a foot taller than Novak with a body of bright silver. It was made of all swooping curves and glossy metal that looked at first glance to be polished plastic. A single lens served as an eye at the front of the thing's face. Most of its head was a flat and wide disc in shape.

The machine charged the group, battering Zelkris hard enough to send him into the commander.

Another two of the intruders followed close behind the first, lashing out with a hydraulic strength to slam Ilyus into a tower. They used the moment to grab the young woman and barrel through Novak, sending him crashing to the ground.

"Amalgam!" Parcis rolled onto his stomach, retrieving his rifle and firing on the last of the trio that had rushed by. The machine had already turned out of line of the doorway, dodging the shots. "On your feet. After them!"

Every one of the knights sprang back into action, breaking into full sprints.

Parcis keyed his comms. "Ground team checking in. We've got confirmed activity of Amalgam at Ipacrus Station."

Static buzzed through the line.

"Confirm again. Did you say Amalgam?"

"Roger."

"Oh . . . hell."

The group tore into the hall, spotting the trio that had kidnapped the scientist at the far right end.

"Run them down." Parcis took the lead just as more of the machines filtered in at the end of the hall. "Take cover!"

The machines knelt and opened fire, their arms splitting as white-hot bolts of plasma arced through the air.

Parcis spread his arms wide, a purple ethereal light pooling around the outline of his body. It coalesced into something like flames. The world flashed lavender before a translucent film spread wide before the guardian and the group. His entire body continued to strobe with the otherworldly light.

Every shot the Amalgam had taken struck the barrier, dissipating harmlessly against it.

"It won't hold for long. I didn't call on that much Darklight to summon it."

Ilyus stepped forward, leaning past the edge of the barrier to fire twin rounds in succession. His energy bolts struck one Amalgam twice through the machine's head. He fired another quick trio into the torso of another of the constructs.

Every single machine remaining twisted and rained fire on the spot Ilyus had been peeking past.

He spun back behind the barrier. "What the hell? Those freaks all focused on me at once."

Novak recalled something from his training research on the machines. "They have a unified mind—gestalt consciousness. They just registered you as the greatest threat."

Ilyus swore, then peeked back again. "I'll give them a threat." His body flared as a brilliant blue light, tinged with a tint of purple, flashed out of his core for several feet in each direction. The aura instantly collapsed into his core before spreading up his arm and into his hand cannon. The chasseur fired a single shot into the midst of the group.

The Darklight-empowered orb arced to the ground,

strobing once before detonating. The world flashed a violent streak of colors. Nothing remained in the aftermath of light other than charred surfaces.

Parcis dropped the barrier. "Nice shot. Let's get back after them. Zelkris, with me. Ilyus, take Novak and circle around the other end of the station. There are never as few Amalgam as we've just seen. If there's one, there's hundreds. And if they're in the system, then more are coming. We need to get that scientist back and call in a capital ship to dust the planet's surface."

Ilyus visibly froze. "We're scorching the whole world?"

"Tact Protocol is clear. Amalgam incursion on a planet without enough knights to destroy them in full warrants planetary dusting. Move." The guardian's tone was harder than any of their armor, leaving no room for argument.

Ilyus nodded, motioning for Novak to follow him.

Parcis and Zelkris tore off into a sprint in the direction the scientist had been taken.

Novak ran off with Ilyus in the opposite way, all the while realizing the mission was effectively over for him. He'd encountered the Amalgam, a perfect moment for him to Snap. And he hadn't.

Ilyus directed him down another hall, signaling to a set of closed shutters ahead.

"Shoot 'em open." The chasseur-class knight holstered his pistol, drawing a slender tube only as large as his forearm. It quickly expanded, a flat stock popping out of the back and a narrower barrel from the front. He leveled the shotgun and blasted one of the shutters.

Novak peppered the other with rounds from his machine pistol before driving an armored fist through the remains. They hopped through the openings, hitting the ground hard.

"We're going counterclockwise from Ops Guardian and Zelkris. We'll clear the other side and rendezvous back where they end. Got it?"

"Got it." Novak followed behind Ilyus as they ran along the station's immediate perimeter. They came to an open field of tall grass. The sky rumbled above. "I think we're in for crystal hail."

Ilyus grunted. "Kinetic barriers can handle that, but it'll be a pain to see through it, especially when pieces shatter and spray dust everywhere. We're going to need to end this—fast." He picked up his pace and Novak doubled up as well.

A chorus of shrieks pierced the air and more Amalgam filtered out of a part of the station.

Ilyus skidded to a halt, dropping to one knee. He slung the shotgun back into place and drew the hand cannon. A trio of shots rang out before he channeled another burst of Darklight. His body flared with the familiar light before he snapped his wrist in the direction of the Amalgam group. A net, conjured of violet and white flame, sailed overhead to tangle a pair of the machines. It bound them in place, the ethereal plasma burning through their metal with ease until only molten chunks of their bodies remained.

Novak released a set of slow controlled bursts from his machine pistol. Each of the superheated energy rounds peppered some of the Amalgam. None had fallen from his attack, however.

More of the machines came into view, quickly adapting their strategy. They broke into pairs, maintaining good distance between themselves so to keep from being easy targets for another net. They moved wide and around the duo of Novak and Ilyus, encircling them.

"This is bad." Ilyus drew his shotgun, spreading his arms out wide, a weapon in each hand.

Novak followed suit, pulling out the compact S-shaped submachine gun he had been outfitted with. "They aren't firing."

It happened as soon as he'd spoken.

"You had to open your mouth, kid?" Ilyus dove to the ground, avoiding a stream of steady plasma sailing overhead. He fired the shotgun, throwing an Amalgam to the ground with a hole larger than his head sprouting in its torso. His hand cannon punched a fist-sized crater into another.

Plasma pooled into Ilyus, battering his kinetic barrier. The unseen field finally shimmered to life in an electric blue static pulse, showing signs of failure. It crashed a second later and the remaining shots hammered into Ilyus. His armor charred and sections peeled away.

Novak howled, unleashing a torrent of fire in every direction before he succumbed to a similar fate. The barrage of fire staggered him, nearly knocking him concussed. His vision blurred as one of the Amalgam approached and clubbed him to the ground with a vicious hammer-handed blow.

Everything dimmed, and through his darkening vision, he made out two of the machines dragging Ilyus away.

The storm broke out overhead and his world fell to blackness.

✦ ✦ ✦

"Novak. Hey, son, do you hear me?" The voice felt familiar to him, but he couldn't peg it in the moment.

Dizzying pain swam through Novak's skull, muddying his thoughts until it felt like a static blur inside him. He groaned and tried to shake himself to his feet.

"Easy. You were out when we found you." The source of the voice clarified in his mind and he realized it as Guardian Parcis. "Any sign of Ilyus?"

Novak tried to answer but Zelkris cut him off. "None, Guardian. Picked up residual Amalgam particles, though. Can't make out anything in this crystal hail past that."

The steady susurrus of hailfall only worsened the pounding in Novak's head. His vision cleared and throbbing eased a bit. Enough for him to register the young scientist in their presence.

Parcis and Zelkris had succeeded in rescuing her, then.

"I think they took him, sir." Novak got to his feet, shaking away Parcis's supporting hold. "I'm not sure why. But they could have killed us. Last thing I saw was them dragging him away."

Zelkris swore under his breath. "Experiments? Been hearing reports back home of missing knights. All MIA. Few mentions of people figuring that the Amalgam have been trying to study our Darklight abilities. Technology they get. Divine abilities, less so. Don't think they can wrap their tin-can heads around them, so they've been trying to take our guys alive to find out how we tick."

The thought filled Novak's belly with molten iron, heat rising into his core. His hands balled into fists. "We've got to . . . find him." He staggered forward as the world spun under him. A hand steadied him but he brushed away.

"Can't do, trainee. Capital ship's en route. Ipacrus Station and the rest of the planet's about to be turned into hot glass. We can't let an Amalgam incursion spread off this world." Parcis moved away from the pair. "We're heading back to where we dropped in." He put two fingers to the side of his helm. "Four-oh-one Hardfang, this is Ops Guardian Parcis. Copy?"

"Hear you loud and clear."

"We need immediate exfil from drop location."

"Roger."

"Let's go, men."

Novak recovered his fallen weapons, giving them a quick visual inspection before holstering the pistol. "No."

Parcis stopped and Zelkris watched both men in silence. "What was that, trainee?"

Novak straightened up. "No, Guardian. I'm going after Chasseur Ilyus."

Parcis crossed the distance between them, placing a heavy hand on Novak's chest before pointing a finger at him. "You're turning around and heading back to the pickup with us, *trainee*. This is *not* up for discussion."

"Then don't discuss it. But I'm going after Ilyus. Otherwise why are we here? What's the point? Everything we're doing is to stop the Amalgam. If not outright, then their incursions, from spreading, from something— *anything*! And now that one of our knights is gone, we're going to write him off and just glass a planet?"

"Hold on. It's not like that." Parcis brought the finger up before Novak's visor, holding it there almost as if in accusation.

"How's it any different? Hell, how are *we*? Because

from where I'm standing, that's how the Amalgam think, Guardian. They're all cold numbers and math. Facts and figures. Maybe they're right to think like that. Maybe that's why they're so damn efficient. But me? I don't know, Guardian, but I think it's wrong. Because they would burn this planet if it meant losing it to us. They wouldn't go back for a hundred—a thousand of their own.

"But maybe that's what makes us humans. People are numbers. There's no math. No trading. No *calculations.* I don't need to know the odds. And I don't want to. I do know what I want to do and what I'm going to. Maybe it's dumb, but I know it's the human thing to do. And that might just make it the right thing to do, Guardian. Because if I'm dying, then it's as a human. Not like one of those things." Novak's chest heaved as he finished speaking. He gave his machine pistol one last look over, his HUD displaying it to be in perfect working order.

"I don't have any Darklight abilities. I haven't ascended, but I've got this"—he raised his gun—"and I've got this." Novak put a hand of his heart. "It'll be enough." *I hope.*

He pulled away from the guardian and began filtering his helmet to track the Amalgam particles through the crystal hail. It beat down against his kinetic barrier with a sound like splashing water.

"Hey, kid, this isn't a—" Zelkris started, but the guardian cut him off.

"Magus Zelkris, head back to the drop point with Tauna. Your orders are for immediate exfil with her and to relay everything you've heard back on the *Arbiter.* You get off this world whether Trainee Novak and I return or not, understood?"

Novak froze, realizing what the ops guardian had said.

Zelkris stayed silent for a ten count before nodding. "Yes, Guardian Parcis." He put a hand on the scientist's shoulder. "Come on. We've got to move fast." He broke into a jog, Tauna behind him.

Parcis clapped a hard hand to Novak's shoulder. "Come on, trainee, let's go find our man."

They tracked the particle trail to the mouth of a cave system.

"Picking up faint armor signature from inside, trainee. Ilyus is in there, and he's alive."

Novak exhaled in relief. "How many do you expect inside, Guardian?"

Parcis raised his rifle. "Enough. More than enough." He triggered the excessive charge system on his rifle. The glowing core intensified in its light, strobing violently. The change in function would force the rifle to overheat its core and dump every ounce of energy potential into a single and devastating blast.

Novak took that as a sign to make small adjustments to his own gear. He quickly tuned his machine pistol into a three-round burst instead of full automatic, minimizing the recoil of it.

They moved into the cave, their headlamps activating and bringing their surroundings to light.

A voice echoed down the hall, garbled—distorted.

"Think that's our boy?" Parcis hadn't lowered his rifle as he rounded a bend in the cave.

"I don't know who else would shout so much, Guardian. Amalgam just scream and chitter."

The ops guardian failed to properly stifle his laugh. He sobered a second later. "They'll charge us if they can. If they're taking Knights Luminary, then they'll try to grab me too. If this goes sideways, you are ordered to leave. There's no point staying. The planet's due to be glassed. Get out. Get off world. Get back to the *Arbiter*."

Novak said nothing, having no intention of doing that, but knowing this wasn't the place to argue. He'd meant what he said earlier: if he was to die here, he'd die as a Luminary, even one in training.

They came to an opening larger than the one they'd entered from.

Flashes of electric blue and green light filled the open room ahead.

Various Amalgam bodies had been reformed and shifted to create apparatuses Novak had no familiarity with. All manner of machines he could only guess were used to run diagnostics and collect data through. A makeshift table, all in the color and style of an Amalgam body, stood in the center of the room. Chasseur Ilyus lay bound to it by thick steel cabling.

He shook and thrashed what little he could. "Untie me and I'll blow a hole in each of your freaking heads, sentient trash cans."

Novak counted at least two dozen Amalgam standing idly around the other machines, a few watching Ilyus. Something about the stillness of them made him wonder if they were paying attention to anything other than whatever data filtered through them.

The machines shared a network mind, and while they could process near-infinite data, they were single-minded in their focus at times. A focus that left them blind to other things at times.

Parcis leveled the rifle on a group of Amalgam standing nearly in a perfect line. He fired. The rifle screamed and a lance of brilliant blue energy darted through the room. It slammed into the first of the line, disintegrating it before taking the rest with it.

The other Amalgam snapped alert, twisting and training their rifles on the pair.

Novak fired off a series of quick bursts, putting only a pair down. More filtered into the cave from other paths behind. "This isn't looking too good."

Two dozen Amalgam opened fire on them.

Parcis reached out, slamming the back of an armored fist against Novak to throw him to the ground. The ops guardian spread his arms wide again, channeling Darklight. The familiar barrier erupted into life, ethereal light and fire warding them.

Novak stayed on his back, firing blindly through the haze and light, knowing his shots connected from the sounds of damaged Amalgam filling his ears.

Ilyus cheered from where he lay fastened.

"I can't hold this for long, trainee. Not with this much firepower coming—" The barrier failed. A torrent of energy crashed into Parcis, throwing him to the ground.

Another hail hammered Novak down. His helm fritzed, static blurring parts of his vision. Bits of his armor cracked and he tasted salt and copper in his mouth. His ribs ached and breathing brought new pain to him.

One of the Amalgam lowered a hand toward his throat. The limb quickly reconfigured as if made of liquid instead of metal. The new claw grabbed Novak's neck and hauled him up with ease.

From his new vantage, he saw another Amalgam walk over to Parcis, grabbing him the same way. And a pair of the machines now moved to Ilyus, reshaping their arms into something like swords.

I guess they realized we're too much trouble to keep alive.

One of the Amalgam primed its arm to stab Chasseur Ilyus.

A scream built in Novak's chest, but it never left him. His vision exploded and something in his mind snapped. All thought left him and the heat from earlier resurged in his core. The world flashed a vibrant purple and he threw his arms wide. Ethereal fire burst from him, swallowing the Amalgam holding him whole.

He fell to his feet, quickly steadying himself. The fire ebbed and coalesced around him, coating his body in its protective glow. Something shone at the edges of his vision and he twisted to see a pair of wings, all made of the same flame, manifested behind him. An odd tingling weight filled his hand where his pistol had been. He now found a brilliant rod of fire, taking new shape before his eyes to resemble a sword.

The newfound energy buoyed him and washed away his fatigue. Novak screamed and lashed out in a horizontal cut with the blade. An arc of Darklight fire washed through the room, taking every standing Amalgam out from the chest up. Some of the machines still moved in their last functional throes, but they collapsed seconds later.

Parcis coughed and got to his feet. "Well . . . I'll be. Look at that. Been a long time since a knight's manifested as a seraph before. Knew you had it in you."

Seraphs were the class of knights who could manifest explosive amounts of Darklight energy and use it for both defensive and offensive purposes simultaneously. Their bodies manifested so much of the material that the excess power took form around them as wings most traditionally, lending to the old angelic reference of name.

"Yeah, I knew it too. Now get me out of here!" Ilyus thrashed again.

Parcis ran over to him, freeing the trapped man. "You okay enough to fight our way out?"

A familiar keen cut through the cavern halls.

"Yeah, and I'm itching to. By the sounds of it, looks like I'll get my wish." Ilyus ran over to another table, retrieving his gear. He trained the hand cannon on the table holding him and fired two rounds, slagging the construct instantly. "Don't want their pals to come by and reconfigure that particular trash can."

Amalgam poured into the room as soon as he finished speaking.

Novak swung again and again, cutting through swaths of them.

More continued to filter in, though, with no end in sight.

Parcis summoned his own Darklight, bringing the fire to pool around his fists. "Get down!"

Novak and Ilyus obeyed.

Parcis stepped forward, clapping both hands together with thunderous force. A concussive blast of Darklight took the room, shaking the cavern and reducing many of the Amalgam to dust. The ops guardian fell to one knee, breathing heavy. "I'm tapped. We need to get out—now!"

Ilyus came to Parcis's side, helping him up. He used his free arm to fire off a couple of blind shots down the halls behind them.

More Amalgam screamed.

"Go!" Novak gestured for the two to go ahead. "I'll hang back a bit and slow them as long as I can hold my Darklight!"

Ilyus didn't argue, helping their leader hobble forward.

Novak lashed out, taking parts of the cavern roof down. It collapsed to block some of the path. Then he turned on a heel and ran after his squad.

Energy blasts still sailed overhead as they ran, and Novak did all he could to hold the storm of power flowing through him and his mind. It threatened to rip away from him. The inner scream from earlier still rolled through him, pushing almost at his skin as if it wanted to burst free. He held to that feeling and, instead of reining it in, fed it.

His power surged and ebbed in that moment, caught between leaving him altogether and fanning into something greater.

Novak turned and pointed the tip of the ethereal blade down the tunnel behind him. The wordless scream finally found voice and left him. A gout of hellish fire burst from the blade and scorched the walls of the cavern, screaming through into the room they'd left behind.

Sharp Amalgam screams echoed back down the way, letting him know he'd turned a good portion of their numbers into molten slag.

The fire around him pulsed, losing a shade of its brightness. His last attack had taxed him severely. He knew from his studies that Darklight channeling didn't usually last this long; it was better saved for powerful and intermittent bursts when the knight needed it. But enough data suggested that during their first Snap, knights had shown far longer use of their abilities. It had something to do with their emotional states during that time and the adrenaline that went with it.

Some, however, never survived the first use. They burned out and succumbed to the new and hard-to-control surge of power.

Let's hope that's not me.

Novak felt the power fluctuate inside him.

The mouth of the cave sat ahead.

Not too much farther.

Ilyus and Parcis had made it out up ahead, the pair turning to signal him to run.

He did so, lowering his sword to his side and sprinting hard. The muscles in his legs protested and burned from the action. Acid seared him inside, but he fought through it. The duality of strain from his Darklight abilities and physical efforts stretched him in ways he had never been used to.

I can do this. He gritted his teeth and put the culminating pain to the side, knowing he'd pay for it later.

More Amalgam screams rolled through the cave behind him.

This time he refused to turn around and deliver another blow to them. Another expulsion of Darklight energy as hard as he'd been channeling would leave him drained beyond measure.

He broke through the mouth of the cave.

The world around him howled, more Amalgam keens filling the air.

He looked around to see hundreds of their shapes breaking into view through the fields, some storming down from the nearby mountains, their lights strobing through the crystal hailfall.

"Four-oh-one Hardfang, this is Ops Guardian Parcis. Confirm pickup of Magus Zelkris and our rescue."

"Can confirm, Ops Guardian. Still in the air. Need a ride?"

"Yes we do, and let the passengers know we've got Chasseur Ilyus with us."

"Will do. Glad to hear it."

"ETA on capital ship?"

"You don't want to know. It's better you move it and get to a clear LZ—*fast!*"

Parcis cut the comms and looked at Novak. "You heard him, Seraph. Let's move!"

Novak stared at the growing numbers of Amalgam sweeping over the area. *Yeah, sounds like a good plan.* He moved with Parcis, raising his submachine gun in his other hand. The steady stream of fire did little to deter the horde of machines, but he could see some succumb to the torrent of energy blasts.

Parcis followed suit, unleashing what looked like never-ending lances of fire. Ilyus joined in and sent heavy shot after shot when he could. Some of his carried the distinct flame and color of Darklight empowerment.

"Four-oh-one Hardfang inbound. It's gonna be hot!" The dropship roared in overhead. Its odd shape, something between a distended bulb and blunted triangle, broke through the obscuring sky and hail. Two heavy guns swiveled under the cockpit, training themselves on the largest mass of approaching Amalgam. They opened fire with a trilling scream that only rose in volume by the second.

Novak nearly deafened his helmet's audio sensors. He looked up to see the drop bay open and a figure standing on the ramp.

Magus Zelkris had his hands shoulder width apart, purple light and flame coalescing in the empty space between. Then the entirety of the mass morphed in shape and matter. The fire vanished and now resembled something like pure plasma streaked with bands of white lightning.

Matter and shape transformation of Darklight took great skill and twice as much energy investment. Some knights went decades before being able to even perform it much less master it.

Novak didn't know what the magus had in mind, but he knew it would be devastating and drain the man to the point of no longer channeling Darklight for the day at least.

The dropship lowered, still firing blasts to level a swath of the army.

Ilyus and Parcis still fired as they backpedaled to the landing zone.

The world exploded into a prismatic light show as a storm of Amalgam fire arced toward them, and radiant Darklight blasts of all manner soared back in response.

Ilyus fired fist-sized blasts empowered by his ethereal flame. He fell to one knee, channeling something larger than before. Twin streams poured out from his gun as it bucked. They danced around each other before striking the ground between a dozen Amalgam. The ground erupted into a line of horizontal fire that swallowed the group.

Parcis stowed his rifle, bringing Darklight to pulse around clenched fists. He raised them overhead then fell to the ground, slamming his hands down. The ground shattered and roared. Darklight fire surged through the earth, tearing it apart as it raced toward a second group of Amalgam. The length of fire sent the machines airborne, shattering their forms more from the strength of the explosion than the flames.

The dropship almost reached the ground, but the increasing numbers of Amalgam and their unending fire would tear through the ship's shields and leave them trapped.

"We can't keep this up. There are too many!" Parcis waved the ship off. "Abort. Get out. Copy?"

Static blurred the line.

Magus Zelkris sent the ball of lightning-charged plasma toward the closest chunk of Amalgam.

It detonated with the force of a bomb, filling the immediate area with a blinding light and the sounds of electricity.

A crater formed in the aftermath once Novak's HUD stopped dimming the world to protect his vision from the blast.

The single attack had taken nearly one hundred Amalgam out of existence.

The ship touched down. Zelkris collapsed on the ramp, the scientist coming to his aid and struggling to drag him back inside the bay proper.

Ilyus and Parcis ran, reaching the ramp.

But Novak knew lifting off would be impossible without another attack like Zelkris's to clear the area.

He stood in place, breathing heavy, thinking about what was left to do.

"Come on, Novak!" Parcis had used his proper name. No longer a trainee.

So he decided to no longer act like one. He looked to his sides, taking account of the burning wings at his back. *Let's hope they're not just for show.* He willed them and leapt. The ground grew farther away.

"Well . . . that's something." Iylus's voice cracked through the comms as he crossed into the bay.

"Liftoff! I'll meet you in the air!" *I hope.* Novak leveled the end of his blade at the encroaching horde of Amalgam. His body throbbed and he willed every ounce of Darklight he could into the next attack. Every bit of light left his shining outline but for his wings and the flaming sword. The weapon pulsed, taking in so much energy it no longer resembled a blade but a solid pillar of pure light, all without proper form. He screamed and the light bucked in his arm, sending rows of hot pain through the limb.

A comet of celestial fire burst from him, sailing toward the ground with one clear result to come.

The dropship lifted off, taking to the air with more speed than deemed safe for the small craft.

Electric violet washed with stark white took the whole horizon, blinding the world in a screen of light. When it cleared, the entire advancing front row of Amalgam had been turned to a lengthy puddle of slag. The burning remains streaked down from the mountains all across the field for as far as a person could see.

The Amalgam numbers hadn't been diminished enough to win the battle, but it bought them time.

Novak grinned, but the expression left him just as quick. His body failed him. The Darklight snapped out of existence and took his wings with him. The sky fell away from and he realized he tumbled in free fall.

Everything blurred.

"Hold out your hand, Novak. Novak!"

He did what little he could as he tumbled.

Something in his shoulder screamed as the ligaments nearly tore. His body snapped, then stopped in the air. He realized someone had caught him by the forearm, holding him in place. He looked up to see four hands clasping hard to the length of his arm.

Ilyus and Parcis both stood at the very edge of the landing ramp as the dropship soared higher. The two men had anchored themselves in place with cabling running from the ship bay ceiling.

"Good job, kid." Ilyus let out a little laugh. "I guess I should stop calling you that now."

Both men heaved, doubling the pain in Novak's shoulder, but he swallowed it. A small price to pay for what had been achieved. They brought him up onto the ramp, then helped him to his seat. The door closed.

"Good job, son." Parcis bumped a fist to Novak's chest

plate. "Can't wait to bring you back home to the *Arbiter* and introduce everyone to the newest Knight Luminary, Seraph Novak."

Ilyus thrust his chin up in an acknowledging nod. "Proud of you, kid."

Zelkris managed a shaky thumbs-up.

"Look out the window, Seraph, and enjoy the show." Parcis gestured to the wide length of clear metal running along Novak's back.

He turned as they broke atmosphere and quickly reached the dark of space.

A capital ship came into view, taking up nearly a kilometer of space. Orbs of energy formed all along its length and streaked toward the surface of the world.

"No Amalgam's escaping that. Job well done, Knights." Parcis had said it to everyone but he kept his stare on Novak.

The new Knight Luminary smiled.

CHRONICLER OF
THE TITAN'S HEART
Anthony Martezi

Petros is a humble fisherman, and for the crime of fishing in the sultan's protected waters, he is cast into an island prison whence no man escapes alive. But on the Isle of Shadow, nothing is as it seems—not the guards, not his cellmate, not even the prison itself. . . .

Ilo Issurio, the Isle of the Shadow-city, cast its shadowy loom upon the turbulent waves like a snare. It was darker than the night; the day had fled in fear of it. Even against the midnight storm clouds—tearing themselves ragged upon the spires of the prison-castle, with a backdrop of enshrouded stars and an empty, hidden moon—Issurio was blacker still. At times, the clouds might release a bolt of lightning, only for it to be smothered and its thunder muted. Issurio caught these flashing darts of fire and swallowed them whole, sound and all, as space silences and as a dead star eats its living brothers. It ate voraciously. Its loom caught fishermen, too, and the island prison-city gorged itself upon their spirits.

Poor Petros could not see any of this but sensed the cold terror of monstrous forms beyond his blindfold. He felt the chill rain seep into the rope fibers binding his wrists—felt, beneath his tattered soles, the warm hum of the mistico's wooden deck as its body thrummed against the sea's night-waters. Above all, he felt the misery of his shackled solitude. All he had for company or cheer was the scattered chatter of his itinerant guards.

One had the baritone voice of a rough storm, ragged with drink, or the lack of it.

"Not much farther to go. Flame on fire, what could this poor soul have done to merit all this? Just him alone?"

This first man was clearly speaking to someone else but their reply wasn't forthcoming until a breach of silence had been overcome.

The second man's tenor was light but firm, like cold sunlight in winter.

"He probably did nothing. Or at least, nothing so terrible. Winds send rain on the lamb and cool the serpent's belly."

"Seems flaming unjust to me," came the gruff protest of the first man.

"Ah, but surely the Kalitan is wise and merciful," came the second man's barely concealed jest. "And surely he would be mercy's sole measure, if the Winds never winnowed."

Petros noted the dim flash of a thunderless lightning bolt from behind his blindfold. The first guard grunted guttural again. "Might save some time and heartbreak if the Winds just struck the serpent dead with lightning and lifted up the poor lamb."

"*Anaphora*," came the second guard's reply.

"A-wha . . . ?" came the first guard's confounded grunt.

"Anaphora. It means to bear up. Some confuse it for carrying back. Same idea, in the end."

"Well I don't exactly need a fancy word for it."

"Savas, the word *is* the idea, as far as we can get at it."

"There you go again, Peri—"

A tumultuous rocking motion interrupted the guards' conversation. Concerned cries came from somewhere behind Petros as he fumbled to stay on his feet; he heard the boots of his guards clamber toward the cries. A great wave to his left crashed and threw him to the deck on his right. He was still conscious but figured this was the surest way to get any rest. So Petros lay there, still as stone, until his guards returned, lifting and bearing him to a prepared skiff.

"Time to leave, sorry sod," came Savas's deep grunt.

Petros had been rocked by the waves in his guards' skiff for a gulf of time too dreadful to estimate. A torrent of rain had begun falling on his shoulders as the crashing tide sunk into his tattered soles. He'd been forced to stand the whole voyage on the now-distant mistico. When his guards and he disembarked to this smaller vessel, and he'd been set aright on his feet, Petros found his knees had turned to rigid rock. Had he the mind to send himself over the side and attempt to kick to a distant shore, he would not have made it for the immobility of his legs. He pondered the dark purpose in that. One might almost see in that dead night the pallid fear siphoning color from his face as he considered his new fate. He glowed white as a ghost, though his skin was the swarthy bronze of fisher folk and his full beard was as dark as the night-shadows of evergreens.

Savas snapped out of his reverie of nose and fingernail picking once he saw the revenant face of Petros, staring out at his doom between the threads of his blindfold. The guard grinned in mischief and tried to get his fellow guard's attention, saying, "Ey, Peri, look at this one—"

"Who is this 'Peri' you speak of, Savas? I do not know him." The other guard gave an exasperated sigh. This second guard was at the fore of the ship, nervously tapping his foot, arms wound tightly upon his torso. He gazed out at Ilo Issurio, minding the great spires of twisting rock that sometimes wound their way to the shoreline. His brick-red cloak frenzied itself upon the unruly westerly wind that speeded their ship onward, so he removed, folded, and tucked it into a crate adjacent the small foreship mainmast.

"Ey," came the frustrated interjection of Savas. "Eyvah, you. Quit being a stickler about your name. Per—i—o—dos." He strained each syllable to obscene lengths so Periodos had no choice but to grant him his attention. "Get a look at our friend. He's got the Look."

Periodos stole a quick glance at the prisoner. He then burned a gaze upon Savas, branding him of falsehood. Savas reflexed, puzzled by the gaze.

"What? Look at him. Paler than the First Moon."

Periodos stood quiet for a moment. Then he stepped swiftly to the prisoner, looking him up and down in estimation of his spirit's quality. The prisoner's tan and brown rags had their mute nobility about them, the kind of quiet solemnity all workers of the sea have when tested against their chosen elemental foe. As though to confirm his suspicion, Periodos tore the blindfold from Petros's face and grinned in sure confirmation. There in those stern, still eyes, brown as an age-old tree root—though Petros knew nothing of it consciously and would deny it were he accused of it—was rooted the firm fealty of a good man.

"This is not the Look," Periodos said in proud, quiet awe.

"You're touched," came the irreverent tone of Savas. Petros himself nearly agreed, though not so brazenly; this "Look" likely betrayed his fear, which he felt to be real. "His knees are about to give. We needn't trouble ourselves with watching him. At best he'd sink like a dead log if he tried escaping. More likely as a stone."

With his eyes freed, Petros examined the skiff and his overseers. Periodos had looked at him with gray austere eyes and a face young, aquiline, and pocked with light stubble. Though he walked away with long, sure strides, he continued to tap his booted foot uneasily once planted at the ship's fore. He wore the helm of the Karituk well; its high, smooth form, like his jawline, tapered to a centered point, at which height it was adorned with a spherical stud. Through interlocking plates of gold, his stately crimson garb peaked rather than flared, muted in the midnight, while silver steel pauldrons and chained mail flashed in the white fire of lightning.

Savas, on the other hand, had none of Periodos's sobriety nor his bearing, though he wore the same armor and garb. His wrinkled cloak was cast over him like a makeshift blanket and his helmet was tossed to a distant corner. He splayed himself upon the ship's various supply crates and casks. The only orderly thing about him was his person; his robust chin was shaved to prim excess and nearly glistened in the darkness, much like his blue eyes. Golden waves of hair were oiled and fastidiously coiffed, high and tight. The man kept a keen, observant eye for himself and was clearly irreverent of all else, and all others.

Wait, the crates! And casks to keep sobriety away for many moons. Petros estimated nine months' worth of supplies for three persons, if they were packed as tight as his fishing catches. He came to a somber realization. These two were more than his guard: They were his keep. But for how long? And where would they keep him, exactly?

Petros looked ahead to their dark doom once more. *Issurio.* Its name held the correct portent: a city filled with shades. But even that seemed inadequate. From its deepness, Petros felt something more than his own quaking heart. He felt himself being appraised, like a slave at auction. Savas's irreverence could not bear the weight of malice this feeling held over him, threatening as a bludgeoning mace. It was ancient and sharply intelligent, moved to its rendering purpose as a knife to fat.

And there! Along the shore. He felt their look.

Eyes. Dozens of them, glazing over in fear and warning: *Leave! Go back! Die if you must!* Their whites seemed to scream and shine like diabolic stars in the black rock of the island.

Triadis abbasis, elupatheri namani! Petros's lungs were crushed within Issurio's clawing purpose and could not sound his plea, so he mouthed it in less than a whisper.

He felt beneath his shirt and clutched the red pendant that hung from his neck.

And at that moment—cresting the black clouds in a crimson dawn and silencing the storm—came the Third Moon. All the visible world was now cast in a subtle, ruddy glow from its peeking crown. Wine-red waters lapped gently against the ship. Rain had abated to a ruby mist. Profound stillness held sway upon the softened sea. Peace came with the red midnight.

Savas spat. "Bloody early Blood Moon." Petros, however, hid the smile that glowed in his heart. Softly on the seawind, he imagined he heard his daughter and wife singing the simple verse of the nightwatchers, one learned by every village child nearly from infancy:

> *Midnight silver—fishermen shiver;*
> *Dawning sapphire—ocean's ire;*
> *Red evening light—seafarer's flight;*
> *And the Winnowind's Sea is porphyry.*

Petros's thoughts quavered hopefully at the word "flight." The uninitiate had misinterpreted that lyric for ages, reading it as *take flight before the Blood Moon*. But Petros, like any good fisherman, knew its real significance. Uillo, the Seafarer's Moon, rising early in the middle of night was an omen of good winds, upon which the seafarer would fly far and to his heart's goal, and it came not long before "the Winnowind's Sea," which was an intense, rare calm that soothed the sea and sky alike.

Bless the Triune, he spoke in his heart. He clutched the red stone at his breast once more. Seafarer's Sign. A sign for his deliverance. He would not do as the Issurian Eyes pleaded. He would not die. He would live. Petros promised himself he would live—for his daughter, for his wife. At any cost, he would fly.

At their disembarking, grumbling Savas felt about in the dark for the skiff's landline rope. Periodos had furloughed the sail long ago and now readied himself at the fore to catch the small wharf's bollard. The red wash of midnight still clung about their eyes, but the black island rock reflected none of its light. It was an ominous, titanic shadow, edged and piercing the skyline with jutting obelisks of spiraling igneous rock.

Out of that shadow, two human forms emerged, dressed in unkempt martial garb such as Savas wore. They were haggard, they were harried; they were like two members of a lifeless, living corpse still flitting back and forth after the spirit's memory had fled. At first they stepped tentatively into the dim red moonlight cast about the pier. With each step, their pace quickened and gait lengthened, until finally they were a pair of flitting, hurried ghosts taking hold of the mooring from Savas. They <u>fastened</u> it to the bollard as though their lives were bound up in the knot.

Savas reeled back in complete bewilderment while Periodos's eyes softened and widened in a look that mingled curiosity with confusion. They looked at each other and shrugged. "Huh," was all Savas could manage to say.

"Hail . . . Karitaruk?" Periodos greeted them. It was less a hail than a question.

No response.

The two had sunken eye sockets, skin sagging and

encircling their bright eyes as folds of dust in quicksand. Beneath their haggard beards, their mouths didn't dare rustle, though the taut line of their lips stretched across their faces like knotted rope. Their hands worked quickly, and soon, they had exchanged places with the newcomers in thankless silence.

As the skiff departed, speeding the two mute Karitaruk away to the far-off anchored mainship—Periodos, Savas, and Petros left dumbfounded on the pier among their spare belongings and crates—Savas finally managed to ask the burning question.

"What spooked those two?"

Periodos continued his fathomless stare at their diminishing dot of a ship making swift into the night.

"No idea," came his whisper.

With Savas on point and Periodos leading the prisoner from behind—satchels and sacks bound to Petros's back as though he were a loaded mule—the three made their way into the pitch black of the island.

The road leading from the wharf was packed with black sand and small pebbles. They shone like ruby dust in the Third Moon's light. But in the distance, Petros could still spy the Issurian Eyes, glittering amidst the deep dark far from their path. The road eventually sped up a smooth incline for some ways, winding off to the left of the travelers between rising cliffs. They went along this path for some time.

With strange suddenness, the three travelers found themselves beneath a torchlit standard, flickering softly in the still wind. Its light had not shone far. In fact, the three hadn't noticed the firelight until they saw their own shadows traipse across it beneath their cautious steps.

They stopped. Petros dared a look at the torch from below his mound of fastened sacks and satchels. The torch was clasped atop a standard wrought of the same spiraling rock that twisted itself over the whole island. Contorted edges and sharp pricks rose to meet the night in mute agony. Petros felt the fear rise in him again. *Does any light escape this desolate place?*

He tore away his gaze, looked to his company, and gasped. His guards were just at the edge of the torchlight's circle of light, utterly transfixed by the sight before them.

A stone figure of human proportion and scale stood just within view, frozen in space and time, with small, scattered flecks of light sliding across its icy black surface. Petros might have thought it some unnaturally placed statue, but for its uncanny sense of motion. Its arms were outstretched, legs folded midair in a running spring. It was motionless, yet seemed to move in place, perhaps caused by some trick of perspective.

His face—*He's alive!* Every angle of that face was bespoke terror. He seemed to have been caught, turning about mid-stride as though to glance behind momentarily. Petros looked where the statuary had tried to look, just behind it. Complete blackness. Flecked about the man's legs and back were sharp edges of rock, like impurities in hewn artwork. The island's rock seemed to climb up to meet the human statue, not to suggest it was carved from the rock, but that the rock had . . . caught him. Caught in some great, terrible claw.

✛ ✛ ✛

The three had trudged along, silent in the darkness. Savas kept asking questions in sharp anxiety. Periodos kept ignoring them, or seemed to. Petros felt that Periodos was hiding his fear, and well. Here was his chance: *Now, bridge the divide*. Petros spoke softly for the first time.

"Sorry to cause you both such hardship. This can't be the best job you've ever taken."

Savas grunted a laugh from ahead. "The mute speaks!"

Periodos tripped, kicked a stray black stone ahead, and grumbled from behind, "Now if only we could get some sight for these blind."

Petros chuckled at that and shuffled his load of satchels. "I'd offer my services, but I'm a bit tied up at the moment."

"What makes you think you could help with this blasted darkness?" Savas turned in the dark ahead to face the prisoner.

"Well," Petros started, "in truth, I have this pendant around my neck..."

As swiftly as he'd said it, Savas had reached his hand beneath Petros's shirt and yanked the rope necklace through his beard. Petros had anticipated such a move and hadn't made any protest.

At the rope's midpoint hung the small red jewel. Savas lifted it to his face for closer inspection, but as he did so, a bright beam of light emanated from the gem directly into his eyes. Savas stumbled backward, cursing between his teeth. "What in the blood-blasted moon is that?"

"Well," Petros stifled a smirk, "I suppose it *was* in the blood-blasted moon at one time. It's Uillo's Eye. Seafarer stone. Moonstone." He pointed up into the night at the red moon dancing. "That moon's stone, to be precise."

Savas opened his eyes and held the pendant up and away from him. The bright beam continued to flash into the dark, spinning about as the rope twisted in Savas's hand.

"How does it reflect so much light in this dusk?" came Periodos's interested query.

Petros answered, "It catches Uillo's light, however small, and concentrates it like a prism. Depending on how you hold it, it redirects the light differently. Say, if you were to hold it face up to the sky..."

Savas looked dumbfounded for a moment, slowly realizing he was being asked to do so. He raised the stone well above his head, so as not to blind himself unwittingly again. As Savas turned the moonstone about in his hand, Petros looked out into the black unknown, preparing himself.

A soft red blanket of light spread outward from the moon crystal. All about the trio, the world seemed to come into newlit focus—blurred and misty, yet clearer than they'd ever hoped possible. But as soon as their hopes had risen, they'd plummeted back to the depths of their hearts.

Petros had feared such a thing was true, but the reality of this new vision was more than he could prepare for. He heard his guards draw swords from sheathes, panic rattling their voices. "Back off!" came Savas's crackled cry. Periodos held a surer control of his tenor, but it still warbled with muffled fear. "Hail! State your allegiance and intent!"

Encircling them in a wide berth across a length of open terrain were numberless forms like the stone figure under the torchlit standard. With unnatural stillness, they looked out from faces frozen in a displaced moment. Their eyes glimmered as stars in a blank night. Petros realized that these were the Issurian Eyes he had seen from the island's bay. Instead of their previous pallid shine, they now reflected the light red luminescence of Uillo's Eye.

They too were held captive by the black rock. Periodos and Savas, once they realized the figures couldn't move, stepped cautiously toward them. Savas drew his hand up to one graven form and indecorously rapped his knuckle against its cheek. A thudding sound of dense rock met their ears. Savas's laugh was strained and exasperated, relief and release more than joy, as he repeated the act. Periodos was unamused and motioned for him to stop.

Above them, above even the high skyline where distant cliff faces met the sky's starlight, Tol Issul, the Dome of Shadow, loomed as if bending over to watch. Periodos looked up at its broad-bellied hall and many twisting spires. He was both determined and obstinate, as if to deny the fortification any dominance over his spirit. "Come on," he spoke quietly. He took point. Petros lumbered behind him. Savas distanced himself in the rear, turning about intermittently to verify the Issurian statues weren't following. He couldn't be sure they weren't.

Their road led to a narrow split in the cliffs. The sky above, now clear of storm clouds, radiated the light of silver star and crimson moon, but the trio's path only saw bare traces of that light. Uillo's Eye was their only guide in the shadowy abyss. As they navigated the gorge, the prisoner tried his best to rekindle conversation with his captors. Most of his words fell on deaf ears—or they were more intent on discerning other sounds in the deepness. Finally, one question provoked a response.

"Did either of you know about this island?" Petros asked.

"Old wives' tales, mostly," Periodos responded from ahead. "Some of it, confirmed nonsense. Some of it—less so, it seems."

"My old lady tells the stories often enough. Told me not to come." Savas gulped. "I told her to bite a stiff wind because the job would net me a new rank, quickly. Now, I'm biting my tongue."

Periodos reconsidered his previous sentiment. "However, there is one story I quite enjoy. The tale of Tol Issul is manifold and changes with the teller. The Shadow-city existed long before the Kalitanate, before even the Inmeriate that preceded it, in the Age of the Aions. Tanis, the Titan of the Underworld Mount, fell here, on this very spot, his skull shorn by the blade of Ismir. Some versions of the story relate that, though his body rescinded to the depths and became whalefood, the head floated aloft and became the island. Still another story says"—and Periodos paused to consider his next phrase—"that the heart of Tanis, black and terrible as a sun-starved cliff, remained after the body passed, heaving its blackened blood over the island. That heart is Tol Issul, the Dome of Shadow."

Petros stared up at the great dome, awestruck and shivering. "Why'd *you* come here, Periodos?" he asked.

"Duty."

Petros whistled at that and smiled.

"Don't laugh," Periodos responded. "If I hadn't been volunteered, you'd be getting much rougher treatment, I'd warrant."

Petros did laugh at that. "You have me stand for a whole day on a miserable wet voyage, saddle me like a dead donkey with all this"—he shuffled the numerous packs on his back—"and, to beat all else, land me on a veritable isle of the dead. Ah yes, quite the spa treatment. I feel like I'm being pampered at a hot spring."

"Comparatively, you are," Periodos returned. "What did you do to land yourself here and ruin our year, anyway?"

"Naturally, nothing at all."

"Naturally."

"Well . . ." Petros trailed off as though to quit hedging. "If you consider night-netting in the Kalitan's quay to be criminal, criminal am I."

Savas whistled at that. "Surprised he isn't night-netting your neck from a tree this very moment. Though, all things considered, I suppose you got a rougher end of the branch. What'd you go and do a foolish thing like that for?"

"By accident, actually."

"Accident, my foot," Savas spat.

"Really, though," Petros assured him. "The night wasn't as black as all this, but it was unusually stark. I'd been sailing inland and was navigating blind. Found my way into the quay and, rather than ascertain where I was, found the fishing unusually good. I should have made something of that . . . Eventually, when the Kalitan's guard came rolling out on the water with a mainship and fire arrows ablaze, I did make something of it."

Savas turned about in the darkness to maintain awareness of his flank, then turned back to speak. "Here you are, mute for a day and night, then reveal all you've been nesting on for a week of being a prisoner. Blind me, you're strange."

"I have good company," Petros lilted irreverently. "So how about you, Periodos? You said you'd 'been volunteered.' What exactly does that mean?"

"Between present good company only," Periodos began pointedly, "I'm not keen on torturous prison sentences and overseeing prisoners, alone, for an entire deployment."

"Surely it's not your first time," Petros stated.

"Surely it isn't. But more surely still, I never asked to be Karitaruk."

Petros stopped in his tracks and stared at the hazy figure ahead of him. *Paedocast. Child-collected.*

Periodos grinned to himself and spoke as though he guessed the prisoner's thought. "Yes, you've got it right. I am Helian. But don't think for a second that means you've got yourself a way out. You don't. I am no traitor."

Savas spat a laugh. "Pah! This man's got more duty-bound bite in him than the Vicar, and all the bit heels at Kalighast would marvel at that!"

Petros did marvel, and fell silent.

In other realms and cities, in other times, Tol Issul was a dread name but held no fixed significance. For some, it was the portcullis marking entry to the underworld. For

others, it was the dark mark left by a monster from beyond
the firmament. The Kalitanate knew as much, or as little,
or indeed perhaps less of this place than any midwife or
oracle. All the Kalitan knew in truth was that the dread of
Tol Issul could be used as armor to protect his dynasty's
rule. His ambitious Karitaruk could feed on the dangling
carrot that was the promise of riches and social status for
a year of service on the island; his subjects were held in
the vise grip of being sent to this hell upon Nüun, should
they offend their ruler. None questioned his motive.

Tol Issul was a great-bellied beast of a prison—a titanic,
cavernous heart with twin chambers. One chamber
functioned as a general mess and atrium while the other
served as the communal cell for its prisoners. Spiralling
tunnels encircled the main chamber like aortae,
blossoming forth myriad tunnels that spun into webwork-
like arterioles that draped over the secondary chamber.
All the prison was blacker than night and polished smooth
by unnatural nature, but for the craggy spires that fled to
the sky in twining climbers of black coral honeysuckle.

Its doorway was the least natural feature of all. It was
a mandorla-shaped fissure, a gateway that looked as
though a great sword blade had descended from above to
carve out a cross-section of the atrium. There was no door
in its side.

The guards prompted Petros to relieve himself of his
burdens inside the cavernous atrium, then led him down
through it into a tiny hall that could barely hold two
abreast, so the prisoner was prodded along in front. For
the hundredth time, he considered smashing himself
backward into the guards and running, but he knew he

had no strength for it and hadn't since he first stepped off the mistico. He barely had the strength to clamber through the darkness, even without his burdens. He would need to build up his fortitude, in time. In due time.

Their path climbed forward until it ended at a tiny, gated portcullis, which opened to an abyss of shadow: the second chamber. Adjacent walls and the floor were made of the same smooth-polished black rock, but for some impurities and fragments where fissures had been carved long ago. Several of these fissures showed mounds of black rock like snowdrifts at their bases, as though the rifts had been blasted up and in by fire rather than carved by the steady erosion of time and the slow motion of the earth.

The fissures in the walls rose, rose . . . disappeared into the haze of shadow above, where echoes of the trio's footfalls only now began to reverberate.

Not a soul in any corner of this yawning chamber. Not a sound. Bare gray light could be discerned on the wall closest to Petros, but misty darkness fell over everything else. The guards led and left Petros to this frightening darkness. Crying metal announced that the gate had been shut.

Petros fell to the ground, numb to his new surroundings. He wept and slept the sleep of the dreaming dead.

Abba! Cast illiti!

Petros had to catch the kite. Little Nami had prayed so fervently for it. The funds for its craft had come by way of a miracle. Never had he caught so very many fish in the Atelian Sea. Every time he had pulled away the net, more had come, almost of their own free will. And now the gift they had bought was flying away on the wind!

"Ya ya, Mama! Casten tu!"

Petros had run so hard and blindly that he didn't notice Melia had already caught the kite by the handle, just outside their home's doorstep, as it whisked across her field of vision. She seemed confused by her discovery at first, but then turned a faux-malevolent grin on Petros that made him retreat his head into his shoulders. "Husband stranger! You certainly have a way with watching Nami. And with where you're going." He had run straight past her in his hurry.

"Nami! Little daughter stranger, never let go of this! It is a gift of great worth!" Melia bent down and handed the kitestring off to Nami, who had begun to pull at her mother's white peplos in anxious anticipation. The child popped up on her toes with a smile as she grabbed the kite. Just as quickly, her face turned dreadfully serious, and she walked with intent purpose down the whitewashed sandstone street back to the pier, kite firmly in tow and tied around her arm.

Melia turned about and faced her husband with mock severity. "Now, were you about to let Nami's kite get away after having paid Satiri a windswept fortune?"

Petros's neck retreated into his torso.

"Come back here," Melia said, strutting to his side and yanking his head toward hers. Her pillowy waterfall of midnight-black hair enshrouded them.

Petros assumed his normal stature and wrapped his arms around her waist.

"Now," he said, "hadn't you warned me about watching Nami?"

"Mm, duty can wait."

"My overseer is quite stringent, you know."

"I'm sure all she needs is a firm kiss on the mouth."

"Are you telling me to fraternize with my boss?!"

"No, I'm ordering you to."

"This conversation has taken a turn for the strange. I don't think Drachma will take kindly to me landing a large, wet kiss on his lips."

"That big old fishmonger doesn't know what he's missing."

"You *are* strange."

"That's why you married me. Don't complain."

"That's true. It's your most endearing feature."

"A blessing and a curse, I'm told."

"I'm blessed."

"Not yet you're not . . ."

They embraced in a whorl of Melia's dark waves.

Petros returned to his senses. "You know, were one to espy our little romances from near or far, they might call them gratuitous—"

"—ly adorable. Yes, I know."

"I love you."

"Yes, I know."

Petros pulled away from her for a moment. His look bespoke a serious turn, as one looks when attempting to hear a distant bell toll, or when hearing the crackle of fire or smelling its smoke but seeing no flame. He looked about him: at the sky hung delicate and pure blue, framed in whispers of cloud; at the full growth of distant olive trees on the cliff summits, their branches swirling like broad brushstrokes of some master painter. He smelled the high earth rising from the shore, distant grasses catching the sky, and the salt of the sea breeze flavoring the air. Beneath his sandals, the crunch of powderlike white sand against sandstone left his impression with texture. Silver sparks of sunlight pocked the ever-roaming sea. Nami stood proudly leaning against the small mast of Petros's fishing boat, moored and gently dipping in the small wharf. And the rounded lines of their tiny home, white-plastered and humbly domed, eased the edges of his vision. He wept in his heart for such beauty.

Who had netted him such treasures? From what ocean's depth had they been won?

"Love, what is it? What are you doing?" came the velvet tones of Melia.

"Remembering this," he said. "Forever. I can never let this pass away."

"I love you."

"I know."

He fell deep into Melia's raven whorl once more.

And there! Suddenly Petros was back in the bright sunshine, kicking his feet freely from the edge of the dock, watching Nami tie her kite to his ship's small mast. She paraded about the ship with a wooden sword in hand, politely giving orders to an invisible crew.

Petros lifted himself and came to oversee his daughter's play. "Nami, I'm surprised. Most ship captains yell their orders quite fiercely at their crew."

"Mm, yes, but I don't do that."

"And why not?"

"It doesn't seem very nice. And you never yell."

He laughed a bit at that. "Oh, I can yell pretty loud if you give your mother trouble!"

"Yeah, but that's only because I should know better. My crew is pretty new. They just need to know what to do, so I tell them: nice and gentle!"

Petros smiled. "Daughter stranger, that is very wise."

She smiled a big toothy grin from under her overlarge captain's cap. "Thanks! Want to know where we're going?"

"Oh yes, very much I do!"

"We've gone to seek the lost island of At . . . Atala. . ."

Petros gasped. "Atalatea! From what direction are you making for it?"

Nami considered that question. She hadn't thought through the particulars of her odyssey just yet. "Mm, well from here, I guess."

"From Tellio?"

She nodded agreement.

"Ah!" Petros jumped up on the ship and unrolled his map across a wooden rail. "See here: This is the Atelian Sea just around Tellio. Atalatea is . . . well, very far south! You can't even see it on this map; it's close to the Windveil where you see these clouds, here. You'd need a secret, hidden treasure map for that."

Nami's eyes shone with awe as she looked up from the map at her father, then turned back to it with rapt attention. "The Windveil . . . is that where the Zephyrim live?"

"No! Very good guess, my daughter stranger. However, they guard the Worldrender Gale that severs the nations, and they contain it, so none of its terrible Wraiths leave and haunt us.

"Now," he continued, "there is a great whorlrift that surrounds the island, so you need to be very careful when navigating. A narrow pass leads into the whorl from the west, but you want to keep on the east bank because the rift turns about in circles"—he drew a whirling pattern on the map in just the right shape—"clockwise on this centerpoint"—he jabbed the spot in the middle of his pattern—"and that is where you find Atalatea. But be careful! You'll be coming on it from the south; beneath the waves, in a great whirlpool to its south, there waits a gaping Maw! It would swallow you and ten other ships whole in one go! So you need to make your way 'round it on the west, keep away from the western and northern rocky escarpments, then come to it from the east side. And there." He made a chiasmus with his finger on the map. "You've made it."

As they talked, the knot of the kitestring loosened ever so slightly from the mast.

"Abba, did you ever sail far away like that? Looking for old treasures?"

Petros nodded sternly. "I did. Long ago."

The kitestring loosened further.

"Why'd you stop?"

"I stopped needing treasures."

"Why's that?"

The kite was nearly unraveled from its mooring.

"Well, you were born."

A great westerly stormwind whipped across the ship's deck, and with it, the kite was yanked and finally loosed.

Abba!

Petros spared not a second. He leaped to the ship's forward, jumped on the rail along the bow and balanced himself, then sprung high and far to snag the kitestring's handle as it bobbed and swung over the bay waters.

Cast illiti!

A great darkness like a thunderhead descended over all. The world became a dark blue, descending into near-black purple. Finally, all his vision faded as Petros motioned to snag the string and came up empty. He expected to hit the water hard and fast, but no impact came. He fell. Heavens know how long he seemed to fall. Petros cried aloud and, in his frustration, struck at the limitless air in desperation. Swipe. Swipe. Thud.

He struck at earth. Again and again he struck it. He continued doing so until the skin on his forearm became raw. He wept and wept for fear and frustration. He had been shunted from his dream; stark reality blinded him. He was caught again in the Issurian deepness of his prison chamber.

It had taken Petros some time before he realized he had struck earth, soft and almost tilled, rather than the igneous rock that even now shadowed his waking vision.

He lay there upon the soil, curled in a piteous ball, catching his breath and trying his best not to weep. To weep would be to admit he had no faith in Seafarer's Sign.

"Tears are signs of good faith."

Petros leaped to his feet from the dirt. He looked to the black abyss of the wide chamber, to its eastern awning. Around its bend, bare glimpses of moonlight still shafted into view from beyond prison bars. Yet he could not discern anything in this darkness. And certainly he could not see the person who had just spoken to him.

"Who are you? *Where* are you?" His words echoed into the spacious expanse. The words he'd heard had none of

Petros's strength. They were ragged and gnarled, whispers as of breath across a wine bottle's mouth.

"Again: Who and where are you?"

As if in response, a circlet of faint gray light began to glow a foot or so from the ground adjacent to the bend in the eastern awning. A trick of refracting light?

Rustling sounds emanated from where the circlet of light had shone. That same ragged air of speech came forth, this time clearer and with newfound force. Still, it was weak, as though the sinew and muscle of a long-dormant throat were remembering the function of speech.

"*A sign, I hope. Here I am.*"

A faint motion of light, like one sees when a bright-colored object moves through a room just before dawn, beckoned Petros down to the spot beside the awning. He could not ignore it.

Carefully, and with the caution of a fox in midwinter, Petros walked with his back to the perimeter of the chamber. He discovered that, as he moved along the curved walls, they too were not solid rock as he had supposed before his slumber, but seemed to have the verdant growth of thatching. Fingering blades of grass swept across his back like fields of wheat. The floor, too, was nothing but sod, dry in many spots but turned, tilled, and even somewhat moist in others. When Petros had come close to the intended spot, his feet alighted on a cool, springy patch of fresh verdure.

"*Careful, please. Careful of my garden.*"

An old man's face came through the darkness. The gray light fell within him and vanished. That face: It was the visage of long, slow life being drowned in darkness. Pale skin, folded over in manifold wrinkles, gave way to great billowing wisps of eyebrow and a beard left to weed in overgrowth. It trailed to the old man's knees and was tucked in at his sash. All about him was a torn and tattered garment that must have been a gray tunic at one time. He wore a gray cloak about him too and its hood was thrown back to show a moderately kempt head of cloudwhite hair, windswept and tied at his back below the cloak. Every inch of him bespoke a new, seemingly starved aspect of a piteous soul left to die, alone and forgotten. Yet the old man smiled. Twin orbs of moonsilver, his eyes, glowed with that smile.

"How can you smile, old man? You're nothing but bone and ash." Petros came close to tears again. Just the mere outline of such a creature would stun anyone to sorrow. Had he been forgotten in this chamber? How long had he been here? And why was he here?

Again, the whispered wind of a strained voice quavered in the air. *"My first words."*

Petros's face, if it could be seen in that darkness, knotted itself into a look of puzzlement. " 'Tears are signs of good faith.' What did you mean by that?"

A lilting cough struggled to make its way out between the old man's lips. It must have been the closest he could get to a real laugh. *"Only that I can trust you."* The old man rustled once more and seemed to swell up with some unheralded new strength. Drawing up his shoulders, he adjusted himself against the wall he'd been nesting against, sitting more upright. Full moonlight rippled past the awning beyond him. His voice too gained volume and depth. "Tears pour out the heart's knowledge: knowledge of what is, what ought to be, and that the two are not the same."

"Wise words, but there's not much good they do for you here."

The old man seemed to bristle at that. "They do very well for me, here, thank you. In point of fact, they are the best words for such a place. They remind me: This, too"— he raised his withered right arm half a foot and stretched out his pointer finger, as though to gesture at the darkened chamber—"will be made right."

"Is there anyone else here?" Petros wondered aloud.

The old man shook his head. The faint gray light created a kind of afterimage in the wake of that gesture.

"Utterly bizarre. An entire prison for two people?"

"*One.*"

The realization struck Petros. One.

"They don't know you're here?"

Another shake of the head. No.

"*No?*" Petros's eyes rounded themselves. Such strength, even in utter destitution. Where did it come from? "Who are you? How long have you been here? How did you get here? Where are you from?"

"Careful now. I have little strength as is. But maybe enough for that first question."

"Great apologies, abba."

Petros's eyes fell to the man's left arm, and for the first time he noticed the book it cradled. He could make out the barest gilded scratches of a title on its cover: *Ankhios Aïo Mnimi Tou Chronikou.*

"I've been gifted many names in many tongues: Niram.

Aram. Raqib. Pravuil. But one name I keep wherever I've gone, and it is truer than all the others: Chronicler."

Petros nodded. A historian of some sort.

"Now please, leave me to some feeble rest. I imagine you still need some, too."

The abba was right. Petros felt his fatigue settle again. He couldn't have had more than an hour's worth of sleep, judging by the Seafarer's light. However, Uillo's strength also seemed to be fading, and the night deepened. Having no more ability to stand or even search the room for anything resembling a bed, he settled down in the spot along the sodded wall next to Chronicler, and his was finally a restful sleep.

The two prisoners had only recently awakened but the barest snatches of sky visible past the prison bars indicated a soft, misted afternoon.

The old man gestured his right hand toward the window apse. The day was gray and a bare curtain of light edged into the circular chamber, but the expansive hall still seemed dark, as though this were the twilit shore of evening.

"You came from . . . that part of the room?" Petros said.

The old abba grunted, dissatisfied. He was still splayed on the ground, just as the night before, but he did not look so pale as he did in the pitch of night. Some bronze color had returned to him. From what source, Petros could not discern, just as he could not discern the abba's puzzle of an answer.

"The North? No, wait, the window is in the eastern face. The East?"

The abba's hand lightly struck his forehead in bewilderment. He rolled his eyes, then considered what he'd just done. He inclined his head upward.

Petros looked up at the ceiling, too. "The . . . ceiling?" For a few moments he just stared at it, as though willing the vaulted heights to reveal their secrets. They too were thatched with grasses and dirt, much the same as the walls and floor, covering over that terrible pitch rock.

With a thought like thunder, Petros suddenly stood up, backed away, and looked at Chronicler as if he would burst into wind and flame all at once.

"From the sky. *Zephyrim*." The word burst from Petros's mouth as though it held the power to upturn the whole prison-castle—indeed, the island—and send it to the sea depths.

The old man coughed a laugh. All his aged features suddenly struck Petros with greater impact than before. No, this was no Zephyr. Kindly, strange, and deeply surprising, yes, but not one of them.

Chronicler leaned toward him, upturned hand gesturing him closer, and Petros knelt to bend his ear near the abba's frail head. The words, despite their frayed texture passing in a quiet hush, came like a thunderbolt:

"I am from a distant star."

Petros looked into the old abba's eyes and saw how bright, round, and childlike they were, how genuine the claim was. And he pondered that in his heart while his reason utterly refused to entertain the notion.

As though bidden that moment by those very words, Periodos the Karitaruk rattled his gauntlet against the barred portcullis at the far end of the chamber. Petros kept quiet but moved adroitly to the gate along the prison chamber's walls, once more like a winter fox. He couldn't be sure of the darkness at the hall's epicenter. It hovered over the deep floor like a shroud over a hunter's trap, dug into the earth.

Clearly the old abba has lost his senses, Petros thought as he tread carefully. *Strange. He seemed so clear-spoken.*

Periodos said nothing to him but passed a meager tray beneath a low bar. A large clay vessel half filled with water; a torn scrap of bread; half of a slice of cheese. One tomato, no larger than a fingertip, tumbled across the tray as it exchanged hands. And well, well! A lemon wedge for flavoring the food; far likelier for digestion.

"All for the day?" Petros asked.

Periodos stood with his face in profile, downturned to face the black floor.

Petros frowned. "I see." He didn't know whether to mention the abba to the guard, so he kept the strange old man's presence to himself.

"Presumably the next guard rotation will come bearing more rations. They gave us enough to 'keep you alive' for the length of our station here. One year."

Petros looked over the meager scraps. If that was true, and he had no reason to doubt it, then the best he could hope for in mentioning the abba's presence would be an execution. If they had no food for a mouth, the mouth was removed. He didn't know what was worse: starvation in this terrible place, or an old man pleading in fear for his last moments before the sword descended.

"Enough for me to die. One meal of this for a year will leave me in a crate at sea, if I can hope for something approximating a seafarer's burial. Any chance begging for more, or at least my moonstone, would net me anything?"

Periodos smiled and closed his eyes, head still hung. "Maybe an earful from Savas and a slug in the eye."

Petros sighed in relief. "He still has the pendant, then. Who put a slug in his shorts?"

"I don't know. He's been . . . well, he's taken charge, as was his rank-given right, though he never exuded much authority on the voyage here."

That was an understatement. Petros was surprised to hear Savas *could* pull rank, let alone that he held it over Periodos.

He continued. "I don't know what's gotten into him. Overnight, it seems as though he's taken to throwing his weight around." Periodos frowned in shadow and whispered, "You're being fought for, for what that's worth."

The paedocast turned on his toe and made his way back down the prison hall. As he turned, Petros caught a flash of something strange. His right eye had been facing away during their conversation, but when Periodos turned, Petros saw mounded purple flesh, swollen and tender, forming around that eye. He'd been struck hard.

Into the Issurian deep went Periodos the Paedocast, his footfalls ringing loud and clear as he paced down the narrow hall.

And this too Petros pondered in his heart. He stood a long while, still as stone in the apse of the prison gate, staring intently at the tray held in his arms. A swell of sorrow and anxiety filled his breast. Suddenly, he clutched the tray and motioned as though to throw it at the barred gate in frustration. He held back and shuddered with a tremor that would shake most mountains.

I—I can't—can't possibly—what do I do? I told myself I would live . . . for Nami and Melia! But how could I live, knowing . . . ?

As Petros quarreled in his mind, he heard a sudden noise that may as well have been a sentence upon him, sounding the condemnation of his own spirit.

"Friend child, what was that noise?"

The abba's question was as innocent as a child's and as soft as a twittering bird at dawn. Petros hid in the apse of the doorway, clutching the tray of food in one hand and his breast in another, as though his lungs would collapse under the weight of his sinking heart.

"Nothing, abba. Just a rat."

"Who were you speaking to?"

Silence fell like a stone. "It was a talking rat, abba." The lie was such nonsense that Petros struck at his chest for having told it, let alone to this poor creature. However, the old man thought it was as natural an answer as any other.

"Ah! Well. Tell it good night from me."

Wistful slumber took the old man into a peaceful night, for an early darkness had stolen the sunset.

Shadows swirled in the cell. Bare snatches of sounding, crashing waves lifted up from the seashore, but all else was as quiet as the tomb. A sob broke the silence and then was shuttered up like a window before a storm.

Petros had been wrong. The food had a kind of flavor. The small slab of bread, the shriveled tomato, the stale cheese, and even the water: All tasted faintly of salt.

Weeping itself has a way of washing away bitterness. With it comes a swift, if troubled, sleep.

The darkness of nightmare and the shadow of waking life had merged. Petros did not know whether he was awake or asleep. But he thought he heard the faintest whisper of something—someone—whistling. Though Petros fell down again into the valley of his dark languor, another was awake and active.

The Chronicler was whistling, if only in breathy tones, to the patch of garden at his feet, clutching his chronicle about him. And the grass shone and grew.

Morning brought Petros back to life, but the Chronicler was already awake and as active as he could be, given his near-paralytic state. He seemed to be cupping his hands to the circle of grass about him and bringing them to his lips.

Petros shook his head to clear his vision, long curls of matted hair fluttering about his head. "Abba, what are you doing, there?"

The answer came in a kind of haggard, singsong voice, like hearing a distant bird intone in a rainstorm. *"Breakfast!"* Petros crawled closer and realized what the old man was doing. He was supping on the sparse morning dewdrops hanging delicately from each blade of grass.

Hours came and went, dragging Petros through the tortures of his own spirit. To deny the abba another meal would be murder, but he couldn't let himself die here. The daily meal would not be enough even for himself; in less than a year, he would be a wasted shell of rubber skin and ashen bone. Hadn't the Seafarer's Sign been a promise of deliverance? Yet, how could he possibly be delivered from such a place? Even the days were merely a less oppressive darkness, with night air thicker than a mist of steam. Why was he sent to suffer here for such a mere infringement of the law? Was the Kalitan's fishery really so important as to condemn a man, a solitary man without even the pleasure of a crowded prison, to this?

In the midst of the haze of time now enshrouding him, Petros heard the clang of metal on metal. It was Periodos again, clanging his gauntleted hand against the bars while clutching the day's scraps.

The paedocast was in direr appearance this time. Bagged eyes told the tale of a sleepless vigil. No sleep at all. Not that a restful night could ever be the norm here. The mass of swollen flesh around Periodos's right eye seemed to have doubled and shut the eye firm, but he spoke past it as though it didn't exist.

"Can't sleep. Something moves in the night. I think it's the prison—in the floor, in the walls, sometimes even the ceiling. Or Savas. He hums all day and night. Haven't seen him sleep, but he keeps disappearing to winds-know-where. Have you seen him? Has he come here at all?"

Petros shook his head. The tray was exchanged.

As Periodos left, he chimed in with a little snatch of some proverb lost to time and history: "Two leaves folded on the door, holding fruit in a secret store." And with that he was gone.

Petros looked over the tray of scant morsels. All looked the same at a mere glance. But wait. There. In the wide clay cup, beneath the water, shone two verdant leaves. He sipped down the water and pulled at the leaves' stems. Three spinach leaves; they were packed against something beneath them, which was also tightly packed to fill the wide bottom of the clay vessel. Petros pulled away the leaves and gasped.

It was a veritable cornucopia of olives and figs littering the bottom of the clay cup. By normal standards, it would constitute a decent lunch. But for the starved, it was extravagance.

Petros was stunned. What had Periodos done? Shaved more food stores from their catches—more than was allotted to this prisoner? Or from his own guard's rations . . . ? Snuck it below the spinach leaves and hid the evidence from Savas below a shallow pool of drinking water? Clever and, more importantly, kind. This was a feast. An absolute feast. And such a feast demanded company with whom to share it.

When he returned with the tray, the old abba was smiling but looked confusedly at the object in Petros's hands. Before he shared, Petros laid aside the tray and fell on his hands and knees before the old man, crying tears of joy and sorrow intermingled.

"Abba, forgive! I did something terrible to you!"

The Chronicler waved his hands in dismissal. Petros placed the tray in the old man's lap and exclaimed, "We share a feast tonight!" At first, the confusion wracked the abba's face. He simply couldn't believe, or remember how to identify, what was laid before him.

No radiance of sunrise or sunset, no jewel of the earth, no moon of heaven could be said to outshine his face: he with the moonsilver eyes in the moment of his euphoria. It would not do to tell of his ecstasy, his tears, his unspeakable sorrows all lifted up at once in sacrifice of praise and thanksgiving. No one can tell of it without failing in word, and the peace and joy beyond description must be felt by him alone. I cannot speak of it. All that can be said is that the abba, the Chronicler, with great light in his face, spoke his beatitude with full-throated ease:

"Bless you, friend child! Bless you! Thrice and forever bless you!" They feasted on what otherwise would have been a meager meal; feasted, laughed, cried, slept, and dreamed.

In the deep, unyielding night, a set of footsteps echoed in the tall, broad hall dividing the chambers of Tol Issul.

Savas had not slept since arriving on the island. The last he remembered of sleep was when he dozed off on his duty aboard the mistico. Now, that seemed like a world and an age away.

Even if he could sleep, he wouldn't desire it. Oppressive darkness had surprisingly little to do with that decision.

There was a voice. A voice in his head. Every hour it crescendoed very lightly, almost imperceptibly, like a throbbing buzz in the back of his skull. But it didn't resonate in his head. No, that would be relatively normal: a sign of fatigue, or of paranoia, or clenched teeth. No, this blasted voice didn't swim in his skull, but in his chest. Not his ears, but his heart swallowed the sound whole. It burned in his gut like an undigested rind of cheese that hadn't settled, causing terrible visions of wailing statues in his sleeping quarters.

The first night he'd tried to sleep, the voice became very loud the moment his doze settled. So he neither dozed nor settled. He didn't know what to do. Tell Periodos? The blasted paedocast would use that as an excuse to strip him of his leadership role. Not that he cared much for it, but the reason he took the post at all was to boost his rank for a job nobody else wanted. So what, then? Ignore the voice? Would it go away? Surely it had to.

So he walked. He walked all over that terrible castle, up every shadow-spun spire, down every night-woven hall. However, he avoided the prison chamber, as though it were hidden from his thoughts and distanced from his feet. Something kept him away.

The darkness of the tourmaline rock began to swim in his vision like black clouds sweeping through the night. He began to see colors in that darkness: deep blue at the ends of halls, simmering red at the fringe of his vision, white eyes reflecting off the diamond-polished rock. And every time he returned for some guard duty or another, Periodos reprimanded him with a sarcastic remark. Well, he'd shut the paedocast up good and well. Took the pommel of his sword and bust it into the right side of that sorry Helian's face. He didn't even protest. Just stood there and stared at him.

Savas would make captain yet. Rigor was what was needed. Good, solid discipline and authority. Then he'd bust in the face of any sorry sod who tried to talk quippy to him. He hated that. As though his intelligence were being questioned. His aptitude. His hygiene.

That night, after inspecting the prisoner's food tray—
he'd be damned if he'd let Periodos get a bleeding heart
and swipe *his* food to feed the prisoner more—he walked
to the rear of the atrium, a place he'd not yet been. There,
he discovered a network of long, tall tunnels leading down
and away from the main chamber. The shadows must have
been stronger here because he couldn't even see the
streaks of color at the hem of his sight. Just blackness. He
didn't bother walking slower because these halls didn't
hold anything to strike his knee against. They were all long
and tall and empty from wall to wall. It was infuriating.

Savas remembered the pendant he'd nipped from that
prisoner of his. He rummaged through his right pocket.
Nothing. Strange. His left pocket also was empty. Now,
he was sure he'd put it in his pants pocket. But he checked
his personal satchel to be sure. And as sure as midnight,
it wasn't there.

His anger boiled over and he was about to shout his
frustration, but at that moment his foot caught no floor
beneath him and he fell with a cry. It was a long, bruising
fall; each tumble brought a spasm of pain and anger.
Wherever he was falling, it wasn't a stairwell, but the floor
was hard and jagged all the same, and it kept inclining
downward to some nebulous chasm. Savas tried his best
to catch an edge or crevice in the rock, but his gauntleted
hand had lost all dexterity due to his sleepless fatigue.
Finally, he reached the end of his fall and rolled into a pile
on the dark ground: motionless, bruised, and groaning.

The pain was terrible but for some reason he felt a
strange calm come over him. He had thought immediately
of Periodos, how the paedocast had probably stolen his

pendant from under his nose at mealtime. But he didn't feel any anger. And the voice in his heart didn't bother him anymore. It wasn't soft and quiet, but it didn't scream at him. Instead, all he heard was a solid, steady *thruum* in the air. He couldn't even hear his own groaning or breath. Just the *thruum, thruum, thruum* droning in the air about him, like a colossal machine bleeding oil in the walls. Gradually, he realized the voice was no longer in his heart, but in the enigmatic darkness all around him. It was warm. He pulled the voice over him like a blanket and fell into a sleep that could last a thousand years.

And as he slept, the Thing whose voice had spoken to him from near and afar these last three nights crept upon him from the abyss. Long sinews and tubes of black rock wound their way about his motionless body, removing his armor, then struck a sharp edge into his side with venomous purpose: stabbing like a spit through a lamb. But Savas did not die, nor did he wake. He was lifted up into the air, albeit painlessly and without knowledge, like a puppet on a string. And the great *THRUUM* grew and pulsed like the beating heart of a titan. And Savas's body jutted with the pulse of its black blood coursing within and without him. The dark caved in and a crystalline wall sealed the poor host's doom, to be pulled and held on heartstring.

And in that same night, small wonders of flitting lights pulsed within the body of the old abba, sleeping and recovering from his long dearth of nourishment. He had subsisted on the drink of grass dew for ten years in that terrible place. As hard as it might seem to an onlooker, for him, it was not impossible. Patient calm and a winnowing wind had upheld him in his long trial. His musing whistle had grown the grasses and nourished the soil, and all because he had caught a stray grass seed floating on the wind outside his barred window. He had grown this seed, this shield against the darkness, with music and breath and long, tender care. And now, the same was being done to the old abba by the flitting lights of wind and fire that coursed in his blood, spurred by the food given him in tender care.

The night grew long and pulsed with the light of the three moons: Allia the Silver, Dalvino the Sapphire, and Uillo's crimson keep. By their collective shine, the island and all the ocean depths encircling it were illumined by august, festal porphyry.

A great commotion brought Petros out of his dream with a start. No middling morning sunlight had peeked in the window as yet. But the whole dark chamber now glowed with a faint purple sheen. Winnowind's Sea.

A cacophony of clanging metal and hurried footsteps came directly to Petros's ear around the corner of the door's awning. Shouting erupted.

"Stay still."

That was not the whisper-thin voice Petros remembered hearing. It was ringing, robust, like a cello string. He rose from his sleep-dead pile in a wedge of the chamber and looked in awe at the figure occupying the space where the abba had fallen asleep. He wore the same gray garb. Bright, moonsilver eyes stared out at the chamber door across the wide, black expanse. Those eyes were awaiting something.

But the infirm elder Petros had known was no longer there. Instead, a man neither young nor old but ageless as a river lay like a frozen waterfall in winter. His skin had gone from revenant white to swarthy bronze seemingly overnight, and the face was chiseled and scarred like fine tanning leather. He wore the same hair in the same fashion, but it was now dark as pitch instead of white, edged in dark brown with no sign of fray, and still the massive beard fell to his knees, neatly tucked in at the sash. In his left hand, he cradled his tome.

"Chronicler," Petros uttered.

This was the one unchanging name for the figure he now beheld in full. Somehow the old abba had shed the blight of years and put on reborn flesh.

A cry came from just outside the chamber. The bars of the portcullis rattled and shook. "Petros! By the winds, help me open the door!" It was Periodos, shaken to his core by some unknown fear. His eyes were bloodshot and his pupils dilated. Parts of his gold and silver armor were torn from their straps, and his crimson garb had been ripped in places. In his right hand he held the key to the cell door, and in his left, the moonstone pendant, Uillo's Eye, brightly gleaming in the midnight darkness. He tossed the gemstone to Petros, who caught it somehow in his dumbfounded haze, pocketing it by near-instant instinct.

Petros stood up and began to move for the door, but was struck motionless by the firm voice of the Chronicler. *"Stop, friend child. Stay still."*

It happened in a flurry beyond mere motion. It was as if the whole outer hall had warped, coiled itself like a serpent, and struck like a thousand glass shards. An ocean wave of black diamond cascaded down on Periodos and smothered him at the doorway. It fell and swirled around him, then parted to reveal the paedocast, cast in a black tourmaline shell. His horrified face was all Petros could see. He cried out in anguish but couldn't move for fear of the terrible Thing beyond, which now swayed and swirled like a sea in turmoil.

"Friend child, please step out of eyeshot of the door. It cannot get at us here."

Petros faltered as he stood up, still struck with terror.

Chronicler eased the man's fear with his temperate baritone. "It is near powerless at overcoming clean, tended earth. The Claw-heart of a Titan must first twist, burn, and break the earth to suit its black temper. Then it seeps into every crevice. Your friend will be all right; it takes centuries for the Claw to enter and maim a good heart."

A horrible noise boomed in the deepness of the prison-castle. Issurio itself groaned, then spoke in a tumultuous quake of sound.

In the end, NONE resist me.

It was as though a thousand small voices were screaming in a bacchanal of agony: accompaniment for one monstrous, world-shifting rumble.

Meanwhile, the Chronicler was singing and chanting, loud and strong, in counterpoint to the raving carnival of terrific, thundering noise.

Petros remained paralyzed in place. The swirling whirlpool of black rock outside the door slowed, stopped . . . and laughed. In an instant, a pillar of darkness shot forth through the bars of the cell door. There was no time for Petros to react, except to offer one more silent plea in his heart. But the blow he expected to come never did. Thunder crashed, an explosion boomed above and below, and Petros was thrown back.

A great, sharp blade of wind had shot into the pillar of darkness, widened itself and carved through the pillar's entire midsection, then blown furiously and with such force that the entire chamber filled with a gray gale. The two hewn blocks of the pillar of darkness had been thrust through the floor and ceiling, smashing into the foundational stonework, crashing below and sent flying above.

Petros only had time to realize that the Chronicler had run to him; suddenly, a swift whirlwind had enclosed itself around them. Then he felt a rush of intense motion outside the enclosure of galewinds. It was louder than a crash of thunder, swirling and undulating with pockets of furious airs. And all at once, everything stopped. The gray airs, flung out of their makeshift shell, spread to the prison hall, and swept out the windows. In their wake, the dark rock of the castle was no more, having been buffeted by the winds. Whatever this wind was, it removed any hint of that black ocean of rock.

Periodos, however, was still a prisoner in his statue's cell.

"Come, friend child. We have work to do." The Chronicler chanted a phrase in a language foreign to Petros, just as he had before the great winds descended and combated the black waves of Issurian rock. About his right hand, a pocket of silver airs twirled and formed a candelabrum of cloud. Seven fixtures in that candelabrum held small pockets of fast-swirling airs that seemed to burn as they flitted about in their small cones. The seven burning winds blew out a mist that shone with warm light. For the first time in what seemed an eternity, Petros could see the full glory of real light, undiminished by the Shadow-city's ominous presence.

They walked to Periodos. Petros took the moment to notice that the Chronicler was improbably tall, now that he did not lie infirm upon the ground, but he remained thin, his skin wound taut against his dense bones. The Chronicler stood and stared with pity at the poor frozen soul before them. He lifted his great book of chronicles in his left hand, knotted it into his sash, and let it hang from his left side. Passing his candelabrum of winds to his left hand, he extended his right and laid it upon the crest of the statue. Chronicler hummed to himself, intoning with few oscillations in a steady pitch. And Petros gasped to see a light spread down Periodos's body, slowly at first from the top of his head downward, then swiftly descending the rest of his body. It peeled and blew away the encasement of stone like fine ash. The Karitaruk stood there, completely entranced, eyes wide open as if he never expected to be released from his standing tomb.

"*Zephyr*," Petros whispered in awe.

All at once, Periodos wept great tears and embraced Petros like a brother. They were no longer guard and prisoner, but both brethren in newfound freedom.

Steadily, the three made their way through the winding arabesque of Tol Issul. The Chronicler seemed to know exactly where he needed to go, and the two onlookers followed in tight succession. All about them, wherever the warm mist of the candelabrum fell on the Issurian darkness, a great chattering of pained voices sprang up, fell away, and was silenced. The rock quivered and cracked, graying into an ashen heap that still held up the three travelers as they walked over it. Cleansing hall by hall like this, they finally came to the very rear of the atrium chamber where Savas had descended and finally fallen.

"Brother-sons, I must ask you to leave here. I will return to you shortly. All will be made right in due time." Though he said this in full confidence, Petros noted the Chronicler seemed to be breathless, as though he had run a great race and was near to finishing.

"But you—"

"LEAVE."

No response or rebuttal was offered. Petros would have to be addled to think he could convince such a being to change his mind. The Chronicler's face had hardened in firm resolution, but softened after he saw Petros's quiet nod of assent. He placed his right hand on both of them, one after the other—they flinched in worried recoil at first, as though they would be consumed in wind and flame. But the Chronicler only smiled.

With that, he began his swift, final descent.

Old memory returns to me, like terrible river water on a desert WASTE. Here is the Zephyr of great intent, whose body was BROKEN and is renewed. IDLE was my wait. LONG was the patient struggle. I CLAWED for you, hungry and needful for my own rebirth. And yet you come to me willingly, as a lamb to a SPIT. THIS one will not do.

Savas hung limply in the air, tossed on the giant's heartstring like a ragged doll. With his limp form in its steely grip, the heartstring withdrew into the shadows.

Time and PATIENCE I have had. Now I require reward—a BODY once more. My Claw-heart beats with THUNDEROUS quickening. Now, it harvests the black FRUITS of its sown seed. Step into the MAW of my heart's chamber. Be ENGORGED with my blood.

The Chronicler held his wind-torch aloft and looked to the heights of the tall chamber, humming all the while. All the walls pulsed and throbbed with fleshy blackness, molten black rock descending the sides like waterfalls of blood or oil.

In the middle of the chamber, however, was the cause of the inexorable *THRUUM* that had ensnared Savas. A great, black heart hung from the ceiling along its aortae. Manifold tentacles hung from the heights like perverse vaulting. In its center, above a raised dais and encased in a transparent ventricle, hung poor Savas, broken and still. The heart thudded and hummed and thudded again, quickly, repeatedly, like a sickly organ bound for a swift death.

"Tanis," came the Chronicler's thunderous baritone. "Titan of the Underworld Mount. You are known to many in Nüun. But they speak of you in tales told to children, frightening them to chores or sleep. You are remembered and you have life, bare and fleeting as it now appears to be. But the fear of you will not last, for your name is not written here"—he gestured to the book hanging from his left side—"in my chronicle. And it never shall be. Your dominion is *desolation*"—*THRUUM*—"your kingdom is *death*"—*THRUUM*—"your memory lives not in the light of star and cosmos, but in their dark shadow of *void*"—*THRUUM THRUUM*—"and there is your heart. Listen to it! Thudding in its self-wrought *sepulchre*."

THRUUM THRUUM THRUUM.

A cawing, screeching tumult rose as if a metal mountain were struggling to claw its way out of the depths of the earth, and in every direction, the pulsating flesh flung itself at the Chronicler in a maddened rage. But the Chronicler's resounding song emanated from his spirit, and with each line a force of wind and fire and light struck out like a shield to parry and rebuff the darkness, until . . .

> *"Ennis navaris, na passi numa,*
> *Kelli ne kavaa nevrosin;*
> *Evthrosis sam ani navis suma*
> *Ke anin palitev phrosin!"*

. . . with the final word, a spear of wind shone forth and was thrust into the Titan's heart. The feverish pitch of Tanis's cry rose and fell and was silent. The foul rock was turned to brittle, gray ash. The Chronicler stepped, breathless and staggering, to the dais where the heart had fallen backward, stone and silent as the grave, cracking in parts and drying into dust. On the dais, Savas's body had fallen, loosed from the heart's veins and fallen from its ventricle. The young man was sleeping peacefully, though his torso was pocked with wide, dark openings in the flesh. The Chronicler raised him up and turned to make the

long ascent back. The bleak foundations of Tol Issul began
to crumble and quake.

The sky was on fire. Something was wrong, for its
entire shape was small; encircled like an eye of flame in
the distant darkness. Sounding crashes and cries
reverberated in the deep night, as though the world were
falling away from the firmament and all the Zephyrim of
the Worldrender were weeping for Nüun. But the circlet
of flaming sky wasn't rising away. It was drawing nearer,
growing larger as the tumultuous noise subsided.

Savas could not comprehend this. His voice had
escaped him. Even the light of his eyes seemed to fail him.
It looked as though eternity were stretching toward
eternity—the sky, bounded in a circlet, bending down to
reach a hand of wind-tossed rosy cloud to the fallen
earth—and he feared it greatly. But the fear subsided as
his understanding grew.

He could feel . . . they were not arms. They were strong
and firm, but they felt more like the onrush of falling
waters or winds, concentrated into human form and
bearing him up. Up. He felt motion. The great jostles of
a tall human gait. Savas was being borne up by someone,
something.

He remembered the darkness, the horrid pulse of oily
blood running through him, the black fire and its terrible
heat; and over all, the overshadowing threat of a titanic
claw hovering above him, drawing its longest barb across
his chest as though to lacerate and spill him.

Savas could not move until he recalled that rendering
nail. He struggled to pull his right arm to his chest. He

used it to feel across his whole chest's surface, drawing across it to his side. There, in his right side: a gap. It was like the ocean Maws that swallow whole islands, descending sheer into the sea, but this gaping hole descended into him. Though he felt no blood rush from him, he dared not place his hand inside that fleshy chasm. Yet, he also felt . . .

It was closing. The wound was mending at its edges and glowed with a faint gray light. He drew his hand across it as the flesh sinewed together. He might have recoiled in disgust had he been able to look at it from an onlooker's perspective. Yet, the feeling was so intensely strange, and thrilling, and a steady stream of warm water issued forth from his eyes like a river that nourishes its people.

Raspy air drew itself from his mouth. "*H-h-h-o-o-w-w-w* . . ." came his tear-stricken voice. Had his body the strength to bear a sob in its chest, Savas would have convulsed with all the maddening joy welling within him. Instead, it spilled from his eyes. He could not hope to contain it, else it burst out of the waning wound in his side.

He looked to the figure carrying him. Garbed and cloaked in mute gray. A dark and tumbling beard. And eyes with the same color and light that flitted over his wound.

"Still, friend child. Be still."

Savas stopped moving but couldn't hold back his joyful cry anymore. It was more than he could take. He was alive. Alive! And there! Savas could see better now. The winds in the sky were descending to greet them. All the flaming night burst into morning light, and the darkness suddenly abated.

The man had gently risen from the atrium and out the gate of Tol Issul, bearing Savas's still body in both arms. The castle crashed around them. Its terrible chambers smote upon the seawater, descending to the ocean depth, and its twisting spires crumbled to dust and were tossed on the four winds. All the black rock of the island, all of Ilo Issurio's fell blood, was swept into the blazing morning sky, and a fiery dawn consumed it.

Savas held his arm over his eyes, for the dawning light was too strong and he needed to adjust. When he could finally open them, he saw Periodos and the prisoner, Petros, standing before him with utter amazement dancing in their eyes. Peri! Periodos! He had to tell him!

"A-n-a . . ." Savas barely managed to say. His voice cracked like the subtle crackling of wood fire. Again!

"A-n-a-f . . ." Blast his ragged lungs! Say it!

Periodos came to him, rested his hand upon the poor soul's brow, looked over his tattered scraps of red and brown garb, and finished the word for him.

"*Anaphora.*"

The Chronicler cast back his cloak's hood, stepped forward with ongoing purpose, and handed Savas to Periodos, who held him up under his arm. Periodos had discovered his legs anew.

The renewed abba, the Chronicler, went out to the island, to every corner of it, seeing the black dust rise and dissipate in the morning air. He went to every statue of that island, every person encased in the Issurian bloodstone. And upon every head he let fall his open palm. The rock fell away and the person was revealed.

An old fisherman in bonds.

"*Anaphora*," came Savas's ragged but full voice.

A prostitute and her progeny.

"*Anaphora!*"

An entire family. Men. Women. Children. Innocents. Condemned. One and all: prisoners no more.

"*ANAPHORA!*"

The day was long ahead of them but the newly created family of Issurian convicts had much to share with one another. Hours were passed telling seafaring tales, or narrating personal foibles, or relating old family stories. Each person was like an old relation to the other, lost to memory and newly found. None touched upon what brought them to the island, nor anything resulting from the Claw-heart of Tanis and his blood plague. Time beyond measure would be needed to heal those wounds completely.

The Chronicler took Petros, Savas, and Periodos aside as a bonfire was lit: a cask and crate of food had been discovered, salvaged from the shore rocks. The four of them would return for the feast, but questions needed answering, and no one else could bear the pain of reliving the Titan's curse.

"Tanis was so immense," the Chronicler related, "as indeed were all the Titans, that it took a twofold heart to engine his body. The heart you were trapped in, Savas, was but the second fold, an inner core. Tol Issul itself was the cavernous skeleton of his old heart, held in stasis by the second, which remained: alive, if only because of haughty pride. Although the body was cast to the sea long ago, the heart had not been dealt with, and so Tanis was in waiting for a host to renew himself; to build up a new body with his heart's blood."

Savas clutched at his side, which had been sinewed together completely. No damage had been done to his body, for it was a vessel that Tanis had prized. A sophomore offering to engorge with his own foul, sanguine fluids.

"Was I . . . was I weak? Did he choose me because I was weak?"

The Chronicler dropped to one knee and looked with stern sincerity directly into Savas's eyes. "Not weak. Weakness would have availed you. Your failing was something else, something you must discover now, within you, and tear from your very chest."

The question of what to do now still hung over the heads of everyone, but the Chronicler was not dismayed. He sat in quiet contemplation at the cliffside of an edifice of rock—good, earthy rock. Petros came to his side and sat down, looking out over the frothing waves and spirited gulls flying freely. "What do we do now? How do we get home?"

The Chronicler smiled and playfully tousled Petros's hair. "You? You have done enough! You saved me. You saved everyone here. It is I who ought to prepare the means of our leaving. And I can do it, but it will need a day of time and good rest." Petros looked at the Chronicler and saw how the aged lines of his decrepit form seemed to have returned somewhat. He was tired and worn from the exertion of his great winds.

A day passed and the island's inhabitants crowded

around the Chronicler, who had called them. He asked that they take hold of one another, and that as many of them take hold of him as well as they could. They all stood, feeling rather foolish at such a thing. The Chronicler looked up to the sky, as if to gauge something. To seek out some object on the wind. Or prepare himself, as though a great wave were coming. He intoned and chanted:

"Into this world, you gift us your wind,
The good and sustaining elixir;
Come and abide in me, all of my soul,
And spirit my heart far from here."

With a force like a cyclone, the whole party of people was surrounded with a circlet of gray and white cloud, thrust at a perilous speed by tumultuous winds that enclosed around them. An onrush of motion sounded outside the enclosure of galewinds. A crash of thunder broke, rippling and surging with blasts of furious gusts— and suddenly, the storm ceased.

The swirling sphere of winds died away and the group was left standing in a field unlike any they'd ever seen. Everywhere between the sky and their feet shone billowing waves of crimson grasses, tall and dense, swaying and undulating in a dance of slow passion. Furloughed valleys were pocked with denser blades of lavender, pricked with spots of pink and flowering with yellow and orange tassels. Atop hills of swaying grandeur stood a few trees of deep pomegranate, their branching foliage extending in a flat horizon at gradients along the twirling brown trunk. Off in the distance, beyond the sharp orange mist of leagues and before a pink and purpling sunset, great pillars of mountains, rounded at their tops and jutting sheer and straight from their roots, towered over pillowing blue clouds. And wherever the clay soil showed forth, it glowed with a faint, white-red aura.

"What . . . what marvel of the winds . . . ?" Petros could not help but smile and laugh in utter bewilderment. The smile gave way to consternation, and he asked, "Chronicler, where are we and by what power are we here?"

"Look to your pendant."

Petros rifled through his tan pants, then brought it forth. Rather than emit any beam or further red mist, it glowed with a white-red light, like the soil of this place but brighter and crystalline.

"Where do you think we are?"

Petros felt his knees quake and he fell to the ground, sitting and staring. He knew the answer. It was impossible. It was true. It was mad and brilliant and terrible all at once. "Uillo. We are standing on Uillo. The Third Moon."

"Indeed! And without a moment to spare." The Chronicler seemed rather animated at this, awhirl with excitement. It *was* exciting, but Petros was so totally overcome by everything that he didn't dare register a response. Off in the distance, some strange animal like a tall, long-necked lamb grazed upon ruby grasses. "But . . ." he began to ask, "But isn't the moon a desert waste? The gnosticists declared—"

"HA. This place is alive and it flourishes. See. Taste. This world is alive, and good. And you, my friend, will be likewise, as will everyone else here. I'll introduce you all to the Elledi! Oh such wonderful persons. Tall folk, good at fly fishing; bit pale, but love to lounge in the sun, go figure; very good at parties; can get too long-winded, but sharp with a turn of phrase . . ." And he went on like this for a while. It was strange how different the abba seemed now that he could finally move and talk without the looming threat of a monster, but through all that impish humor he still maintained wise acuity and childlike wonder.

Petros asked, "But why take us here and not home?" The Chronicler stopped talking, furrowed his brow, and frowned. "I had considered every possible plan to bring you all to safety, but . . ." A shadow passed over his eyes. "Nüun has been taken. It's no longer safe for any of you."

The words had no significance for Petros until he looked up into the fiery sky and saw something that stole his breath. His home, his world, Nüun. It was a shock to see it hanging in the sky rather than below his feet, surely. But even greater was the shock of seeing it . . . enclosed.

Blue oceans were muted and covered by some kind of fierce storm that encircled the whole world. Billows of tall, black clouds bustled around it like predatory lions rounding prey.

"That is why I came to your world, Petros." The Chronicler had never called him by name before, so Petros could do little other than stare at him in quiet consideration. "Ten years ago I came here. I am not one of the Zephyrim, as you thought. Yet they are similar to me, and their strength is my strength. But they are under siege."

"From whom? From what? Why could we never see these terrible storms?"

"The storms are as invisible to you as the spaces between worlds are to me. I pass across them like a pilgrim. But the deeper truths I see as though they were lit by a bright sun."

Petros was in a sudden panic. "Nami! Melia! My wife and child are there! And everyone else's families—"

"Will be brought here with haste. However, I must await the next anaphoral tide." And the Chronicler looked to the sky as he had done on Ilo Issurio, awaiting the great storm of winds. Petros looked to him and knew it must be some great power that came through like an ocean tide that swept them here to Uillo. "I am bound to help you all, for I fear this is somewhat my fault."

Petros laughed. "Your fault? How?"

The Chronicler laughed, but the laugh was not the throaty kind of jubilee that tousled his beard and erupted from his belly. It was a laugh edged in sorrow.

"I cannot say. For now, we will rest, and when the new day comes I will depart and bear all your loved ones here to your new home, though you must tell me where and how to find them."

Your new home. Suddenly, Petros was struck with a new fear, but also a great hope and even joy. He had lived through a similar time, when he'd finished with his travels into the whirling gales of the Windveil and the Worldrender on Nüun and planted himself alongside his family in a new, strange place. A place where they'd built for themselves a new peace. He looked to his pendant, and then to the distant mountains rising in pillars of flame. *Seafarer's Sign*.

"I'm coming with you." The words were effortless, natural, like the breath of the wind.

The Chronicler appraised his friend's great courage, but could not help closing his eyes in newfound sorrow.

"This is right and needful. Brother-son, Petros, you are needed for this final effort. But I wish it were not so. Would that none of this had come to pass under my wing."

"I am afraid," Petros said, eyeing the storms of Nüun. "Deathly afraid. But my land cries out—my people cry out—for release from this wailing storm, and from the hardness of terrible beings who have been formed by its foul wraith-winds. We can't hear their cry from such distances, but I feel it within me. I must go."

Petros looked to the distance in awe and readiness, as though he were absorbing the whole sight of Uillo and treasuring it in his soul. He imagined Nami barreling across the ruby-red grasses, kite in tow, smiling her toothy smile, and his winsome wife Melia making swift friends with a kind of tall, skeletal creature, white as bone but gentle as a doe.

The Elledi! He saw them in the distance, walking toward his friends and those rescued from the Titan. Some nervously bounded away, but Periodos and Savas walked forward eagerly to greet the tall creatures.

The Chronicler looked at him and smiled. "What are you doing?"

Petros pondered the question in his heart, then nodded to himself. "Remembering this."

Such treasures. Who had netted him such treasures? From what sea did they spring?

BLEEDING FROM COLD SLEEP
Peter Fehervari

In a universe filled with monsters, the soldiers of the Frontline are humanity's best defense. Vikram was one of them. Once. But when everything you've ever been taught is a lie, what is there left to fight for . . . ?

The witness was close to losing himself when the hunters finally caught up with him. Years of hard labor out on the ice and harder oblivion in the confines of his cabin had buried him deep in the lie of another life, where one routine bled into the next, bereft of any purpose save the stark imperatives of survival.

And yet, somewhere down below, he endured, sustained by his betrayal like a ghost coveting a stolen grave.

Waiting.

He couldn't have said *how* long he'd been waiting exactly. It was hard to keep track of time when his body refused to age and the days and nights were just different degrees of darkness and cold. His shadow could have told him, of course. She never lost track of anything, but there'd come a point where he stopped asking, then let the question slip away. It was easier to live a lie when you bought into it. Besides, when the time came, she would tell him the only thing that mattered.

"They are here," a voice whispered into the sleeper's ear, waking him from slumber and his deeper oblivion. He stared into the darkness above his bunk, breathing slowly as he shed the lie.

"How far?" he murmured through a wash of memories.

"Approaching from the town's southern edge," his shadow replied. There was no urgency in her liquid contralto whisper, but that meant nothing. There was never *anything* there. "They are moving slowly."

"Coming this way?"

"Indirectly. Their probable destination is The Huddle."

The town's center... That was good. They had his scent, but they weren't *sure* of anything yet. Probably looking for leads.

"How many?" he asked.

"Three, Vikram."

Vikram... Though he'd worn himself into the name it sounded strange now, yet also *right*, like every name his shadow had offered over the years, along with the stories behind them. It was like she drew them from a nebulous wellspring of possibilities within him—a string of lives he might have lived for real if he hadn't been dealt a pair of poisoned Aces. Every one was a loner drifting through the backwaters of human space, believing in nothing but the here-and-now.

His lives had grown more tenuous the farther out he
went, much like the planets they played out upon. He'd
begun his flight as Marko Sladek, a laborer with a knack
for heavy machinery, working his way across the outer-
world shipyards, then fled the Sol system as Harmon
Rashe, a prospector who could handle himself in a fight.
Later he'd become a hunter himself, tracking down
lawbreakers among the rowdy worlds of the Third Orbit,
but that drew too many eyes and he'd moved on quickly,
both from the identity and the region. He'd been too good
at the job. A natural, they said.

Now, a dozen nobodies later, he was Vikram Trager, a
trapper who could last longer out on the frozen tundra
than most folks who'd been born to it. True, there weren't
many of those yet. Iscarcha was still a fledgling colony,
barely into its third generation of settlers and only a
couple of orbits behind the Communion's stalled frontier.
He was running out of places to hide.

"Will you stay with me?" he asked the darkness. "If they
take me."

"Yes, Vikram."

Will you give a damn?

He dismissed the question. Trying to understand her
was a fool's game. She was what she was, which wasn't
anything remotely human. Maybe that's why she didn't
have a name. She'd dreamt up so many for him, yet never
offered one of her own, or answered when he asked.

"Keep watching them," he said.

"I will, Vikram."

Her expanded perception was another mystery. He
didn't know what its limits were, but it easily covered the

whole town. Her talk of a "diffuse consciousness" went over his head, like most of her explanations, but he was grateful for her talents. He'd be long dead without them. Then again, if she hadn't latched onto him he wouldn't be on the run, so who could really say.

It's all dust in the wind, the mason-priests of the Stone Hand preached. *Gone before you can grasp it.* That was a rare scrap of faith-talk that still rang true to him.

He rolled from his bunk and his shadow followed, a richer darkness in the murk of his cabin. The lights flickered on as he crossed to the wall-sink and splashed himself with water. Green eyes stared back from the mirror above, bright among the swarthy crags framing them. His hair hung past his shoulders in a graying black tangle that matched his beard. It was a hard face, weathered by worse things than the wind, but its eyes almost redeemed it. There was a sadness there that defied the harshness. Something still lived behind those eyes.

I'll keep the name, he decided, weighing up the familiar stranger. *Vikram . . .* It was more honest than the one he'd been reborn to.

It was dark outside, as it always was on this midwinter world, but the sky was cloudless and starlight washed the town, teasing an eerie viridian glow from its snow-swept streets. That was the strangest thing about Iscarcha—the green snow. Apparently it was infused with a bioluminescent fungus that thrived in the cold. Since it was cold *everywhere* the stuff was like the planet's skin— sagging and prone to shedding, as though wasted by age.

It could get under human skin too, staining it a sheen that looked reptilian. The settlers claimed the "winterskyn" was harmless, but Vikram didn't trust it. Space was full of traps. Some just took longer to spring than others.

"Every sky tells a different lie," he murmured in a rhythmic cant as he set out. "Quick or slow, they'll kill you just the same."

It was the opening verse of the Frontline's battle anthem, drummed into every Pioneer like a second heartbeat, underlining their whole reason for being. Despite everything, he still believed that verse. His hunters certainly would.

"Where are they?" he asked, glancing at the shape gliding over the snow beside him. Nothing showed through her. She was a skewed silhouette of himself cut from the void.

"Tithe's Rest, Vikram."

That made sense. The town's only saloon never shut its doors. The difference between day and night wasn't worth a damn here so most folks kept to their own time, working or resting when it suited them unless they were indentured to someone bigger. The whole town was a den of imagined liberty, bitter endeavor, and whatever precious little iniquities its citizens could dredge up, which mostly revolved around drinking, gambling, and whoring. None of the faiths had taken root here or likely ever would.

Vikram spat into the snow. No matter how things played out tonight he was done with Reliance. Calling the sprawl of prefab domes and cabins a *town* stretched the definition, but give it a few decades and it would swell up

like a tumor. Or fizzle right out. Personally he'd bet on
growth. Mankind was tenacious once it got its hooks into
a place.

Just ask the locals, he thought. The planet's indigenous
species were out on the streets in big numbers tonight,
their rangy green-furred bodies pressed against buildings
or under carts, coveting any scrap of shelter from the
wind. Some huddled in family groups, but most were
alone, their boneless arms coiled about their slender
torsos, as though mimicking the bond-collars around their
necks. A repellently humanlike eye blinked from the
center of each face, vast and mournful among a tangle of
tendrils, tracking him as he passed.

Slaves, Vikram judged, *like the rest of us, except they
know it.*

With its talons unsheathed an adult indigene was a
fearsome sight, hence the name assigned to the species—
the wendigo, a primal spirit that haunted frozen places.
The Frontline always picked fancy names for the aliens it
ran into, as well as its own forces. The practice gave its
endless war a sparkle that masked the bloody reality, at
least for those behind the frontier.

Most species lived up to their new names, but the
wendigo fell far short. They were herbivores on a rare
world without predators, seemingly incapable of anger, let
alone fighting. Those wicked-looking talons had evolved
to dig up icebound vegetation. The settlers' efforts to
provoke them into war had gone nowhere. Unsanctioned
culls still went on, but the natives were too useful on the
ice to exterminate.

Vikram avoided the searching eyes. He didn't trust

Iscarcha's spawn any more than its tainted snow. How long could it take to *learn* anger?

Turning a corner, he caught sight of Tithe's Rest at the street's end. The saloon was just an oversized dome fronted by a lopsided sign bawling its name in blue lights. Why make an effort when there was nowhere else to go?

"There are two hunters in the street, Vikram," his shadow cautioned. "One has entered the establishment."

Vikram nodded, but kept walking. He ought to be long gone by now or waiting in ambush somewhere, yet he couldn't bring himself to do either. His hunters hadn't got this close in years.

I need to see them, he realized, though he couldn't say why.

His hand reached for the pistol under his greatcoat when he spotted the pair outside the saloon. Restraining the impulse took effort, as though the hand didn't belong to him, which was true in a sense. It was a miracle of synthflesh and bionics, forged in the Frontline's biomantic vaults, along with most of his body. At some irredeemable level he still belonged to his makers. That's why they'd never let him go.

You live, die, and sell your corpse to the corps, went the saying, *then throw in your soul to seal the deal and keep on fightin' down below!*

He'd been in his early twenties when he was selected for the nascent Exo-Pioneer program, one among the magnificent seven thousand who'd made the cut from millions. Those lucky few would spearhead the conquest of space, pushing back the frontiers of Earth's new-forged Communion, but the odds against them were long.

There was life *everywhere*, most of it hostile, either through instinct or intent. From the lava plains of Mercury and the acid jungles of Venus to the abyssal oceans of Neptune and countless worlds beyond, Earth's explorers found monsters—ravenous, ruinous things with forms and abilities beyond measure. Even the gas giants were infested by horrors. Everything that crawled, swam, flew, or floated was predator or prey to something else, as the wendigo learned when human settlers arrived.

Mankind wasn't special. It had no right to rule, either God-given or biological, except the one it earned with blood, grit, and courage. To survive and prosper you had to *fight*.

The pride Vikram felt at being chosen remained vivid, branded into his psyche as permanently as the silver starburst icon riveted into his right temple, but the rest of his old life had faded. The memories lingered without substance, like phantom baggage carried from a meaningless dream, impossible to handle or discard.

Focus, Vikram chided himself, weighing up the puppets who'd come to reclaim him for their masters. The pair stood beside their razorsleighs some forty paces ahead, facing the saloon. Both were tall and powerfully built, with broad shoulders and unusually long arms. Gamma Paradigms then, like himself, but probably more refined. How many waves of would-be heroes had been forged then broken on the frontier since his own, each a little tougher than the last?

Thirty paces . . .

The pair wore the hooded white parkas and armored

leggings of local icebreakers. He couldn't tell whether they were male or female, but that was a minor distinction beside their more fundamental nature.

Twenty paces . . .

"You must decide, Vikram," his shadow prompted.

"Decide?" He halted.

"On your course of action."

"What do you suggest?"

This was met by silence, as such questions invariably were. His companion was forthcoming with factual information or practical advice, frequently of the life-saving kind, but never broader opinions. She was an observer and facilitator, not a guide. She'd made that clear from the start, but that never stopped him asking. He saw it as a ritual between them—a kind of flirtation even, though her reserve never wavered.

"If you linger they will see you, Vikram," she predicted calmly.

It was his turn to be silent. In that interval he realized he'd already made up his mind.

Enough.

Raising his hands, he called out to the hunters.

A smear of light was showing on the horizon when the razorsleighs sped out of town. Dawn was just another shade of gloom, barely bright enough to smother the starlight, but the prisoner gave it his full attention, knowing it might be his last. He'd watched a dozen suns rise over twice as many worlds, yet he'd never grown tired of them. Even his hard-wired distrust of *the other* couldn't stifle his awe at the variety of colors, textures, and patterns that painted different skies. His shadow had once tried explaining the science behind it all, but her account left him cold.

"You're missing the point," he'd protested.

"It is an astrophysical process. It has no purpose."

"Of *watching* them."

"Which is?"

He'd been at a loss to answer her. Perhaps his firstborn self, who'd harbored a spark of poetry in his soul, could have explained it. Something of that sensitivity had survived his rebirth, which was why he clung to it, afraid it would wither if he didn't exercise it.

"Being alive," he'd answered finally. It was the best he had, but he knew it wasn't nearly enough.

You should have picked an Aleph, he judged. *They'd have found the right words.*

The Alephs were the Frontline's elite paradigm. They were stronger, faster, and sharper than their kin, but that wasn't what set them apart. There was an uncanny magnetism about them, like they were plugged into something beyond the material world. Few recruits got a shot at the Aleph trials and most who did fell short and wound up as Betas, the Pioneers' junior officer class. There were only thirty-three Alephs in the first wave.

Probably a lot more now, Vikram guessed, returning his attention to the present. He was riding behind one of the hunters, his wrists cuffed to a sleigh's chassis. It looked like they were heading for the northern tundra, where the ice was hardest. Maybe they had a ship out there or planned on calling one in. Either way, there was nothing to do but wait. Oddly that didn't bother him. He felt detached from things—serene almost—as though his surrender had *freed* him.

So far things had gone about as well as could be expected. The hunters had taken his gun and run a scan for hidden weapons, but said nothing beyond curt commands. There hadn't even been a declaration of arrest.

The third hunter had turned up soon afterward. He or she—even up close he couldn't tell through their hoods and padded coats—was shorter, thinner, and lighter on its feet than the others. A Delta, he guessed. They were geared for support roles, with a psych profile that prioritized caution. The ones he'd fought alongside were dull to the bone, but they'd rounded out Orpheus Company's tactical capabilities nicely.

The thought of his former comrades dented Vikram's tranquillity. They'd probably been wiped out to the last man, woman, and robot by now, even if the company's name still staggered on, pumped up on fresh blood and dreams. Besides, that bond was broken past fixing. Any of the old guard would kill him on sight for his betrayal.

"Bitch," he murmured, dropping his gaze to the dark shape skimming the snow beside him. He still blamed her for that loss, with his heart if not his head.

"You acted out of necessity," his shadow whispered over the sleigh's roar, though its driver couldn't hear her. Her voice was only ever for him. That was fine by Vikram, but the way she *read* him rankled. She'd picked up the thread of his thoughts from that one halfhearted curse, as though she'd looked right into his head, but he suspected the truth was more humiliating.

I'm an open book to her.

A child's storybook—the plots of his mind so obvious she could predict the next page from a single sentence.

"They would have killed you," she added. "You know this."

"Sure." But was that true? Sometimes he wondered whether she'd been playing him from the start, rewriting his story as they went along, twisting it toward a payoff he'd never understand, let alone want.

And then he remembered what he'd seen.

"Argo Mace, Gamma-Two-Four-Five-One, First Wave," the Delta said, enunciating each word precisely. Her lips were as bloodless as her complexion. Cropped black hair framed her long face. "Confirm?"

"I don't go by that anymore," Vikram answered. After his rebirth he'd been delighted with the name. Now it sounded hackneyed, like all the Frontline's creations. They were a patchwork of mythology and martial history, probably slotted together by a machine to reflect each paradigm's character.

"I was born Mathias Rees," he added.

"Irrelevant. Confirm your forgeborn name."

If his stubbornness irritated his interrogator she hid it well. The same couldn't be said for her companions. One of the Gammas, a square-jawed woman with an ash-blond crew cut was frowning so hard her stony features looked set to crack. The other, a man with a head like a skin-wrapped sledgehammer, had closed his eyes, as though the sight of his prisoner might tip him into violence. His elaborately braided dreadlocks were at odds with his brutish appearance, not to mention Frontline etiquette.

There'd been no ship waiting at the hunters' camp, just a ring of silvery tents and a hulking snow crawler. The vehicle was local, but the tents were military-grade gear spiked with sensor arrays. His captors had herded him into the largest and cuffed him to the central pole, which felt unbreakable. Though it was past sunset there'd been no pause for rations or rest. None of them needed it. Even the Delta could go for days without water.

"How many waves has it been?" Vikram asked. "Since I've been gone."

"Name," his interrogator repeated.

"Vikram," his companion whispered. She was smeared across the canvas floor, mimicking his kneeling posture. Her darkness looked hungry in the glare of the tent's thermo-lanterns, but only to his eyes. To the others she was merely a shadow. "Is it your intention to provoke aggression?"

"No," Vikram muttered. "That would be stupid."

"It is protocol," the Delta replied dryly, assuming he'd spoken to her. "You will comply."

"It's *him*, Thetis," the female Gamma growled.

"Protocol requires—"

"To the hells with protocol! We're long past that."

I like her, Vikram decided. She'd probably end up being his executioner, but she was a straight-talker.

"Argo Mace, Gamma-Two-Four-Five-One," he said, addressing his fellow Gamma. "How many waves?"

"Eleven." She dropped to her haunches so she was level with his face. "That I know of."

"Are we winning?"

"Winning?" She laughed—a harsh, humorless bark. "Why would you care?"

"I'm built to. Got no choice in it."

"You *chose* to betray your company, Mace."

"I wasn't the first. Or the worst."

"There's worse than betraying your species?"

"Never have. Never will." Vikram expected a fierce rebuke, but it didn't come. She just kept staring at him, her expression unreadable. The moment stretched, but neither of them looked away.

"Why didn't you run?" the male Gamma asked, finally opening his eyes. There was no anger in them and his tone was mild. "You have been running for fifty-six years. Why stop now?"

Fifty-six? The number wasn't really unexpected, but hearing it aloud was sobering. Shaming.

"Mathias?" the man prompted then smiled at his prisoner's surprise. "Yes, I will use your firstborn name if you wish. I also prefer mine. It is Guillermo."

"Guillermo . . ." Vikram echoed, still thinking of those wasted years. How far had the cancer spread while he'd lost himself in one nowhere after another?

"I agree the name is incongruous with this form." Guillermo rapped his slablike chest. "But it is the one my mother gave me and I choose to honor her." His rumbling voice was softened by a singsong accent. "Moreover, the disparity amuses me, Mathias."

"Vikram . . . It's Vikram now."

"So be it. My sisters here still cleave to our makers' artifice." Guillermo indicated the Delta. "This is Thetis Ombra and—"

"Skaadi," the female Gamma hissed, sharpening the name into a threat. "Just Skaadi. I've junked the rest."

Vikram nodded, trying to mask his confusion. The Frontline's enforcers shouldn't be talking this way. Was this an act to soften him up?

"You *were* the first, Vikram," Guillermo said gently.

"The first what?"

"To wake up," Skaadi spat. "I'll give you that. But you're not so special, deserter."

"We are all deserters here, sister," Guillermo admonished. "All betrayers of our kin."

"No, we are not," a voice said behind Vikram, accompanied by a gust of freezing wind as the tent flap opened. "If you believe that you've lost the war before it's fought."

"I stand corrected, Captain." Guillermo bowed his head. "I spoke without care."

"I doubt you're capable of that, comrade," the unseen speaker said, "but let us agree you spoke in haste, from the heart." The voice was resonant and male, but its authority was tempered by sincerity—the voice of a leader who was also a faithful friend. Vikram recognized that precision-engineered alloy of qualities immediately. He'd know it even if he buried himself a hundred-lives deep across as many decades.

An Aleph.

Why hadn't his shadow warned him? She must have sensed another presence nearby, yet she'd said nothing.

"Yes, we are deserters, but never traitors," the newcomer continued. "It is the traitors we have betrayed." There was a perfectly timed pause. "That makes us *patriots*, comrades."

Buried emotions welled up inside Vikram, reeled in by the speech like treasures trawled from the depths—dignity, pride, conviction, and the purest, most precious of them all: hope.

We are for the light! the speech proclaimed, powered by something beyond words. *Join us!* It offered fellowship and redemption, yet Vikram resisted the call.

It's too much, he judged, staring at his captors' rapturous expressions. Even Thetis's sour face had lit up. *Too much like The Lie . . .*

"My name is Niemand," the Aleph said quietly, as though sharing a confidence. "It is neither the name of my birth or my rebirth, yet it is my true name. Do you understand?"

"No."

"Nor I . . . Not entirely, but I recognize truth when I find it." Niemand pulled the tent flap closed, stifling the wind. "Will you answer my comrade's question?"

"Argo Mace, Gamma—"

"I know who you are, pathfinder. Tell me why you surrendered."

Pathfinder? Vikram started to turn around then decided against it, though he couldn't say why. He felt an irrational certainty that Niemand had sensed his earlier rejection.

"I'm done running," he said.

"It took you long enough," Skaadi mocked. "You've been—" She fell silent, clearly obeying some unspoken signal, but Vikram answered her anyway.

"It was never about me. That's not why I ran, sister."

"I'm not your sister."

"But you are, Skaadi," Niemand demurred. "Our fellowship walks in his footsteps."

"How long have you been on my tail?" Vikram asked, stalling for time to think.

"We terminated the sanctioned hunter triad over two orbital years ago," Thetis answered. "Subsequently your pursuit has been one of our primary objectives."

"Why?"

"Because you have a story to tell," Niemand said. He was much closer now, though Vikram hadn't heard him approach. "I think it worth hearing."

And there it was—the opportunity Vikram had staked his life on, offered freely by a judge who might even be on his side. The best he'd hoped for was a chance to make a defiant confession—to get the truth out there and maybe *seed* it in someone who might actually use it. Why hold back now?

Vikram glanced at his shadow, seeking advice she'd never give. "Should've warned me," he mouthed silently. "About him."

"I did not perceive this one," she replied. "It was absent until it entered our immediate proximity. Even now it remains incoherent."

Absent? Vikram frowned. *Incoherent?* What the hells did that mean?

"I already know the color of your tale, pathfinder," the Aleph said. "So I shall begin for you." He placed a gloved hand on Vikram's shoulder. "There are worms at the world's heart, coiled at the seats of earthly power like a manifold tumor that has awoken to its own hunger and craves more. There may be many worms or only one that manifests as many, or perhaps myriad strands of the One True Wyrm, but it equates to the same misery. The parasites feed, grow, and spread in Mankind's wake, infesting new worlds through the blood, sweat, and fears of their hosts, leaving us enough to survive and occasionally even prosper, but only ever in service to the sickness we bear."

Vikram was staring straight ahead, his teeth gritted and his fists clenched. He realized he was nodding along to the tale. *Worms?* Yes, that was the right name for them. Why hadn't he found it himself?

"Our masters probably delight in cruelty, for that has been the most constant thread in human history," Niemand continued, "yet it is possible they imagine themselves equitable, benevolent even. Have they not driven Mankind to survive, strive, and conquer with a ferocity its foes cannot match? Would there be a union of faiths and nations without the invisible coils binding us to a common cause? Would we have seized the stars without their hunger to drive us?' Would we have endured at all?" Niemand's voice dropped to a whisper. "Perhaps worms are the gods we deserve."

"No," Vikram rasped. His eyes met Skaadi's and found a rage that mirrored his own. "No," he repeated, fiercely this time.

"No," Niemand agreed. "*Never*. We will raise our own gods—or better yet, do without them." The grip on Vikram's shoulder tightened. "So tell me, pathfinder, how did you wake up?"

There isn't much to tell, really. Not if Vikram leaves out his shadow. Without her his tale is full of holes, but he isn't ready to share that secret yet. She hasn't forbidden it, but she's warned there might be consequences. Does that mean she'd quit on him and latch onto someone else? No, he can't risk that. She makes no sense, but what does anymore? Besides, she's all he has left.

So he tells it without her.

He is Argo Mace again, back on Fort Io with the rest of Orpheus Company, or what's left of it. They've taken a beating on Mars nobody saw coming. All the real action is out in the Sixth Orbit, where the frontier is being hammered on multiple curves by Seti fleets. There's even talk of falling back to the Fifth Orbit, but that's got to be crap coz the Frontline *never* falls back. Anyway, once Orpheus is patched up they'll be shipping out there to do their part.

That can't come soon enough for Argo.

Things haven't been right with him since Mars. The vermin that swarmed out of the Red Planet's guts were the worst he's seen—a scuttling tide of maws and claws that sang sweetly as it chewed through everything in its path, leaking more filth as it came. It was the stuff of nightmares, but burning monsters is what Argo lives and expects to die for.

No, it's what came *after* that got to him.

Mars is the first planetary colony, wiped clean of hostiles centuries ago, right down to its shrivelled core, so what went wrong? How could an army of monsters come out of nowhere? Well, not exactly *nowhere*. The vermin crawled out of a pit under one of the Martian ruins. Thing is, that pit hadn't been there before. Nobody could say how it got there, but somebody had to go down and take a look. That somebody was the 3rd Platoon, along with Argo Mace.

Well, they didn't find any answers in the pit, but they did find the grave chamber. At the time Argo couldn't suss out why the Aleph in charge called it that coz there weren't nothing buried in there, but later he wondered how she'd *guessed*, and whether she knew more than she'd let on. He'd never met an Aleph he really trusted. Maybe that part of his wiring was busted.

Anyway, the chamber was what you'd call a *sphere*, like the inside of a giant crystal egg that'd cracked open and spilt its slime into the world above. The walls were still slick with vermin goo, but real sharp to the touch, like broken glass. There was a blue tinge to the white crystals that made Argo think of corpse-skin, but they glowed so bright it hurt his eyes to look at, even with his visor's shades maxed out. As the team rappelled through the chamber he noticed he didn't have a shadow. There was too much light coming from all sides, like the place was built—or grown?—to drown out the dark.

Weeks later, when Argo notices his shadow getting darker, he remembers that light and thinks maybe the place wasn't a grave after all, but a prison—or maybe both at once. Either way, *something* was in there and it's hitched a ride out with him.

A ghost, maybe...

Or is he just losing his shit? Nobody else can see the change in his shadow so it's gotta be in his head, right? Pioneers aren't meant to go void crazy like regular grunts do, but everyone knows it happens. That's why every company has Wardens to weed out the head-jobs before they turn thermo.

Let it go, Argo tells himself. It'll pass when he ships out and gets back to burnin' vermin. It's just the dead-time getting to him.

But as the wait on Io stretches he quits kidding himself. This is *real*. He can feel the ghost's presence all the time, even in his dreams.

"Why me?" he asks whenever nobody's around. "What you want from me?"

And eventually he gets an answer and discovers *it's* a *she*. There are no words at first, but messages bleed through, telling him there's nothing to worry about. She's just a visitor come to see what's going down with the galaxy . . . through his eyes . . . coz he's her *witness*.

Argo is psych-wired to distrust everything except the Frontline. He knows she can't be on the level. No alien ever is. He knows he should go talk to Pastor Gary or report himself to the Wardens—tell 'em he's been *compromised*, like what happened to the whole of Perseus Company when the Siren Sharks got into their heads on Neptune.

He knows all this, yet he waits. Maybe that's because he's started to notice *other* things around Io that don't feel right. Worse things than his shadow . . .

"You believe this chamber in the Martian abyss awoke you to the deception?" Niemand asked. "How exactly?"

"Can't rightly say," Vikram lied. "The light . . . It was so bright. Maybe it did something to my eyes. Changed 'em."

"The eyes are conduits for the worms," Niemand said, sounding strange—pained almost. "They are both the door and the key. Do you understand?"

"Yes," Vikram agreed, surprised he meant it, but not by

the anger that followed. "We've been seeing 'em all along, but they've made us blind inside."

He breathed deeply as he slipped back into Argo Mace again. That self felt like a child now, his thinking stunted by the worms' neural tinkering. They'd dazzled him with easy answers and robbed him of the words to frame the growing cracks in his world. Even now, all these years later, he hadn't entirely escaped those chains, but he'd come a long way. His shadow had woken him in more ways than one.

"Someone once said eyes are like windows," he murmured. "Windows into souls."

Argo remembers that line from his old life, when his head was full of fancy notions. He hasn't thought of it since his rebirth, but lately it keeps running through his mind, over and over, coz it's so damn *true*.

It's their eyes that give the worms away.

Argo never used that name for the deceivers, but now Vikram has it he can't remember them any other way. They're not *actual* worms, of course. The galaxy is full of worms, plenty of them killers, but these don't look like any sort he's run into before. No, it's not the way they look, but how they work—burrowing under the skin of things so they can hide and seek out more 'n' more coz there's a hunger in them that won't ever let up. But on the outside they look like people.

Mostly.

Once Argo notices them he starts picking up on small things that keep getting bigger until he can't *stop* seeing them, even if he tries.

There's something off about the way they wear their faces, like the skin's stretched so tight it's strangling the muscles beneath, making them play all the familiar tunes outta key. Every smile, sneer, grin, or grimace might be something else. Most of the time context makes up the shortfall and he can guess their expressions from the things they're saying or doing. That's important coz he doesn't want them to know *he* knows. If they find out it'll be the end of him. He can see that in their eyes, coz that's where the worms are closest to the surface.

Those eyes aren't black or milky white or anything like that. They don't glow or wriggle around on stalks like some he's burned on the frontier. Fact is they don't look wrong at all, but there ain't nothing right about the way they look *at you*. They're full of hunger and contempt for the blind, which is everybody except Argo Mace.

And his shadow, who sees everything.

Argo still isn't sure how he feels about the ghost, but having an ally in the game feels good, especially since she's so sharp. She never tells him what to do, but she'll pick apart whatever's on his mind when he asks and let him know how it'll go wrong, like his plan to kill a worm and take a look inside its skull.

"You can see them," she's warned, "but you are not impervious to them."

That means the bastards can still *play* him. That's their other trick: They can grab hold of your body in a heartbeat and run it like a robot—right into the ground if they're in the mood, which is often.

The worms *love* messing with the blind. Sometimes its terminal stuff, like making folks cut their own throats or go skin diving into the void, but mostly it's longer-lasting hurt they like—things that'll leave their victims torn up inside, like making 'em screw over a mate or act like head cases. He's seen good men turned into the animals then set free, leaving them believing the sin was always in them and there's no way back. The worms enjoy playing with their prey.

Prey? Yeah, that's about right, Argo reckons, coz wrecking lives is how they feed. He feels that in his gut. Killing might be part of it, but it's not the point. It's suffering that really gets them off.

But they're not stupid. From what he's seen they mostly feed on newbies from the regular troops or vets who're nearly over the hill anyway, spicing things up with tastier pickings from time to time, but they never ruin Pioneers. That's not because they *can't*—he's seen his comrades being played as easily as common folks—but the worms play nicer with them, like they don't want to break them.

At first Argo is stumped by this, but slowly the truth dawns on him. The worms want to win the war. There aren't many of them on Io, but most he's seen are high-ups in the Frontline. The fort's colonel is one, along with all his top flunkies. They've even got their hooks in Orpheus. Captain Ortega is clean, but both the company's Wardens are worms. Pastor Gary too. If that's how it is across the whole Communion the bastards are running *everything*.

The thought sickens Argo, but he's got bigger worries right now. He's not built for keeping secrets and pretending one thing's another. Without his shadow's help he'd have slipped up long ago, but she won't be enough. It's just dumb luck one of the worms hasn't tried to play him since he woke up. One look inside his head will give the game away.

"I've gotta get out, don't I?" he keeps asking his ally.

"If you want to live," she always answers.

They both know it, yet he keeps stalling. There's no way off Io without kicking up a storm, but that's not why he hesitates. No, it's the thought of throwing his world away that stops him. The Frontline is his life, even if it's a lie.

And then it's nearly too late.

As he's leaving the mess hall one night his wristcom buzzes. It's an order to come see Pastor Gary before lights-out. The preacher likes dropping one-to-one "spiritual catch-ups" on his flock so maybe it's nothing, but that doesn't matter. Argo can't be alone with one of them, staring right into its eyes and acting like everything's rosy, especially not Gary. He used to look up to the old man and his hellfire sermons. Was that all a lie too? Was there a worm under every church?

Rage flares up inside him, but he clamps down on it before it turns him stupid. Now's not the time for fire, but ice, though fire will be part of it. He's planned for this moment with his shadow.

"We're on," Argo tells her, heading for the docks. On the way he picks up his stash from an air vent—a pistol, a coilblaster, and a bandolier of grenades. He's been squirreling weapons away for weeks, filching them from others during drills so the flak wouldn't fall on him. The blaster caused a storm when it went missing, but he's glad to have it now. Armor would be even better. He mulls over cracking the armory to grab his Hammersuit, but that's not in the plan—too much heat too soon—so he presses on.

"You find what we need?" he asks.

"Yes, Argo," she replies. "I have identified three viable vessels."

"You sure I can fly one?" Like all Pioneers he's psych-wired to handle land vehicles, but wings are something else.

"With my guidance, Argo."

All too soon he's at the dockyard, on the edge of no return. He halts on a gantry above the sprawling steel expanse, sizing it up. The fort is well into its night cycle, but things never stop here and there's still a crowd. It's mainly regular troops and workers, but Argo counts two Pioneers among them, both Deltas. He'll have to take them out first. His skin crawls like it's rebelling against the betrayal, but he's been over this with his shadow. A ship can't be stolen by stealth. His only chance is to hit hard and fast, then be gone before the worms work out what's going on.

"What's your business here, Gamma?" someone demands behind him. "You don't—"

Argo slips his dagger free and lashes out as he turns, cutting so deeply he almost takes the guard's head off. There's another man behind the first, his mouth gawping with shock. Argo's hurled dagger slams between his jaws before he gets it together.

"Burn cold and smell the stars," the traitor growls, yanking a grenade from his bandolier and raising his blaster. It's the last time he'll utter Orpheus' motto aloud.

Then he amps up the killing cold inside and tunes out everything else. After that there's smoke, fire, and the bright crackle of killing current, along with the booms and screams they rip from the world.

It's just like being on the frontier, except this time he's the monster. He can see that on his victims' faces whenever he kills them up close, the regular troops and the dockworkers alike. Their terror pierces his combat fugue, skewering what's left of his loyalty. His creed is a lie. His war is a lie.

"I'm a lie!" he yells as he swings his coilblaster in a wide arc, lighting up a chain of charging guards. He knows he's running too hot, but with every kill it gets harder to rein in the rage. He's been holding onto it too long. Now it's loose it won't be muzzled.

Right at the tail end of his escape, with his chosen ship in sight, he almost surrenders to the madness. He's barrelling through a panicked mob when a figure staggers into his path. It's more a human-shaped tangle of fire than a man, but the heat hasn't popped its eyes yet. They glare at him from the charred husk of its face, brighter than the flaming halo around his head.

Too cold to burn . . .

One of them, Argo realizes as it reaches for him, not with its hands, but with the *will* powering those unholy eyes.

The psychic blow hits like a spiked hammer, making Argo stagger, but the wielder's pain bleeds through it, blunting its focus. That's what saves him. It hurts like all hells, but doesn't stun him. Blood spurts from his nose as the hammer splinters into a claw and clamps around his head, clawing at his thoughts wildly. *Desperately*. It's trying to rip his mind apart before its own burns up.

"No!" Argo bellows, throwing his fury into the denial as he rams a fist into the worm's charred face. His punch tears through skin, bone, brain, and *soul*, annihilating the malignant thing squirming at their core. It's the best kill he's ever made. He can smell its finality through the stench of seared meat. There's a purity to it he's never felt before.

I want more!

The exterminator grins, picturing himself striding through the fort with his coilblaster blazing, purging it of worms one by one. He'll burn down the whole damn place if he has to, along with every slave who stands in his way. It's the only way to be sure. The only—

"There are reinforcements approaching," his shadow observes. "Pioneers. Many of them."

Argo's rage recedes, cooled by her voice as much as her warning. He doesn't want her to think he's a savage, or worse, stupid. His head is pounding from the worm's attack. It feels like there's filth left inside, trying to beat its way out. The pain doesn't bother him, but the violation does.

That's why he has to live. Somebody has to get the truth out.

A glance at his wristcom tells him it's been under two minutes since the slaughter began. The alarms are blaring like tortured bots and sprinklers have kicked in everywhere, turning fire into steam.

"Did you get the cams?" he growls, glancing at the nearest monitor globe.

"I have impeded all signals in our vicinity."

Argo takes that as a yes. Hopefully that means nobody

knows what's going on yet, otherwise the fort's cannons will blow him outta space the moment he takes off. Anyway, it's outta his hands.

He staggers toward his escape ship. It's a compact one-man scout with enough grunt for short interplanetary jumps. With luck it'll get him as far as Neptune. After that . . . Well, he'll deal with *after* if he makes it that far. He's sure his shadow will come up with something.

"The rest don't matter," Vikram finished. "All I did was run."

"You survived, brother," Guillermo shook his head. "Few could have done that."

"How'd you fly a planet hopper?" Skaadi challenged. "I've never known a Gamma to do better than a skimmer."

"There are multiple improbabilities in the sequence of events as described," Thetis added. "Firstly—"

"I'm sharp," Vikram cut in. "And I got lucky." It was a thin answer and they all knew it, but he couldn't give them more. Besides, these three weren't important. There was only one judge that counted here and his silence was telling.

"The worms," Vikram said, tilting his head toward Nicmand. "Do you know what they are?" If he'd reached the end of his road he'd prefer to go out with some answers.

"I know they are *old*," Niemand replied. "They have walked beside humanity since its first steps into sentience. Perhaps long before that."

"They aliens?"

"Not as you imagine. Their claim on Earth is as valid as our own."

"Devils, then?" Vikram asked, not liking that possibility at all.

"There's no such thing, whatever the faiths may say." Niemand sounded amused. "You need not fear the hells, pathfinder."

"How'd you know? About them, I mean?"

"I have a prisoner. It is uncooperative, but I am persistent."

Vikram's hackles rose at the prospect. Was the worm nearby? How could something like that be contained safely?

"So you going to tell me your story now?" he asked, covering his revulsion.

"Yours is better." *Even if I don't believe it*, the Aleph's tone suggested. "And the time for stories has passed. It is imprudent for me to linger anywhere for long. I am also hunted." He stepped away. "Call in the Astaroth, Thetis."

"Did you get what you were after?" Vikram pressed.

"I was after the truth. And an edge." There was an implicit challenge in Niemand's reply. "Can you give me that?"

Vikram's eyes slipped to his companion.

"Yes," she answered. It was the first time she'd openly led their shared fate, even if she'd been casting it all along.

"Yes," the shadowed man echoed. "I'll be your edge." He rattled his cuffs. "Do I get to see who I'm fighting for?"

"You are fighting for yourself, Vikram Trager," Niemand countered. "Like all who have the eyes to see." The cuffs clicked open, seemingly of their own accord. "And those who see without them."

Vikram rose before turning, unwilling to face the Aleph

on his knees. The others were watching intently, as if this was a ritual of some kind. And perhaps it was. Despite his denial of the otherworldly, Niemand talked like a man who'd found one of God's true faces. Or maybe one of the Other's . . .

Screw it, Vikram decided, turning. *It's dust in—*

The Aleph had no eyes. His face was an echo of fallen glory, its flesh withered and deeply lined, like gray parchment scribbled with pain. Every drop of vitality had drained away into its hungry sockets. Staring into those pits Vikram understood where the Aleph kept his prisoner.

"I am also a first, pathfinder," Niemand said gravely, fixing his empty gaze on Vikram. "The first Pioneer our makers dared to seed with their stain. They cleave to the shadows, but they resent being *overshadowed.* Their envy was as inevitable as their folly." He smiled, melding sorrow and satisfaction into something inhuman. "That's why I am also the last. The Aleph and the Omega."

Vikram stiffened as the revenant reached out to grip his shoulders. "Will you stand with me, Vikram Trager?"

He's insane, Vikram realized. On the back of that revelation came another: *And maybe that's how it's got to be.*

Perhaps madness was the only way to wake the worlds before they were bled dry. Or was that just an easy way out? Another lie pretending at Truth? Or a truth that would turn on you the moment you bought into it?

What do I know?

He glanced at his shadow.

THE TEST
T.C. McCarthy

*When the world has fallen and the old times have come
again, who shall defend the realms of men if not the great
lords and kings of that far future time? But the world is
fallen, and what lords there are are petty, venal, and cruel.
Who shall protect the people? Who but God?*

A love for killing earned me a place at the front, next to
our father as one lance among hundreds, each topped
with a flapping pennant. My younger brother's horse
waited several rows behind us. His anger burned through
the back of my armor, augmenting the sun's afternoon
heat and focusing it into a single white spot that felt as if
it would melt through. He was a coward; this would have
been fine except that my brother *knew* he was no warrior
and over several years the knowledge had formed a pocket
of poison, a bubble lodged deep inside his abdomen that
had spread wisps of noxiousness to permanently
contaminate his soul. So although an army of raiders
waited on the field below us, behind me was a greater

enemy—one of flesh and blood that, if given a chance, would slip a dagger into my back.

Father spoke to the priest next to him. "These are standard raiders, yes?"

"Unknown, sire. We suspect the monks will not be needed and that these raiders are mongrels, untrained. Even their watch has not yet detected your army's presence and our strategists conclude their slaughter is almost guaranteed. But there is always the chance of dark arcana. If so, it will be hidden in the main tent—the longest one in camp center."

"I hope for dark arcana; *that* is the last test my eldest has to face, after all. Have your monks ready in case they are needed." He turned to look at me. "Are you drunk, boy?"

"No."

"Did you bring your whore with you, Camden?"

"Sire, how would I do that?"

My father laughed and then spoke loudly enough for everyone to hear. "It appears that God *does* work miracles. Today my son is sober, and has opted to join us for his final test—that of combat against magic—rather than take his day at the brothels."

I closed my eyes while the men around us laughed. The heads of great houses had gathered around my father and me, on all sides, their horses snorting and pawing hard ground in anticipation of our attack, their instincts so honed that even such mindless beasts sensed that bloodshed was to come. I opened my eyes again. The first rays of a rising sun glinted off the tips of our lances, but still no sound came from the camp below, its occupants likely sleeping off the previous night's drinking. My father hated his villagers. But they were *his* and that meant nobody but he could touch them. Soon the raiders would feel his vengeance in a pitiless wave, one that would soak the fields in blood. Some of the raiders would fight and might even wound or kill the nobles and I would be there smiling as those who had just laughed at me expired under my approving grin.

It was easy to hate these men—*nobles*. The word no longer held meaning. At least the raiders had reasons for their actions: They needed to eat and so came down from the eastern mountains to steal crops, at the same time stealing women so they could procreate. Nobles had no such excuse for their self-serving actions, for the rape and slaughter of their own people, and they did these things any time it suited them or the king.

"There," my father said. "Smoke from one of their tents. This filth begins to stir."

"Shall we charge, sire?" one of the men asked.

"The deep winter approaches. Soon these fields will be encased in ice and snow, and the raiders will be confined to the eastern mountains."

"Yes, my king."

"Then we must move quickly. *Charge.*"

The same man raised his fist, after which trumpets erupted in calls up and down the line, the signal for the horses to advance. We moved off the ridge. Our horses picked their way down the steep slope, never breaking the line, their training so ingrained as to have converted to instinct, while behind them came the king's foot soldiers. Rocks and pockets of brush broke up their formations but the men soon reformed so that they resembled a living organism, an amoeba-like thing that crept across the landscape. Sprinkled within their ranks were our monks, their black robes flapping in the wind. Several of them carried rounded packs on their backs, a kind of ovoid tortoiseshell contraption that connected to rods the monks cradled in both arms via thick black hoses. At the rods' ends, blue flames sputtered and hissed.

"The word of God," said Robert, who rode at my right. He was my personal arms-man and bodyguard.

"Indeed. I have not seen it used."

"It is a sight to behold. Only to be loosed upon the darkest of arcana."

"Have you seen the dark arts used before?" I asked.

"In war?"

"Anywhere."

"When you were still swaddled. I was sixteen and it was my first battle at your father's side. The farthest eastern villages had all been wiped clean and at first we thought it was raiders; we were wrong."

"What was it?"

"Monstrous creatures. Insect-like in appearance, massive things that stood as high as your knee and who emerged from cracks in the ground by the thousands, their high-pitched whines intense enough to split a man's head open, after which they sucked the blood and internal organs out through the neck. Without the priesthood and *their* arcana, we would have all been lost."

"And where are they now—these creatures?"

"A monk told me that they emerge only once every fifty years; a seasonal enemy, thank God."

"Robert, was there dark arcana in the old times—before the deep winters?"

"Who knows, boy? And why would it matter, since the darkness is with us now and there's no going back in time?"

"Indeed."

The cavalry line reached the slope's bottom and we trotted before shifting to a canter, the iron-shod hooves thundering across the plain and sending tremors up my legs. A chorus of clinking mail overwhelmed everything. Armor draped off my shoulders in a weight that made me feel protected and exhausted at the same time, a shirt of tightly interwoven metal links that—no matter how well oiled—always went light red with rust. Once we'd reached a point about a hundred yards from the outer ring of raider tents, our force broke into its final gallop and closed the distance.

Still, nothing emerged from the tents. By now the raiders must have heard the horses and should have sent up the alarm, but everything ahead of us remained calm.

"Something isn't right!" Robert yelled.

The king held up a closed fist. At his signal the horns sounded again and we drew to a halt, just inside the outer encampment, so that a number of scouts could drop their lances and jump from horses with swords drawn; they moved to the closest tents and threw them open. One of them sprinted to my father, arriving almost breathless.

"Empty, sire."

"What?"

"The outer tents, my king; they're empty. The sleeping pallets are occupied by straw dummies—not a raider to be found."

"What in God's name does that mean? Bring me the priest."

"The foot soldiers will be here momentarily, Sire," said one of the nobles.

My father glared at him. "Not soon enough. You will ride back to them and lend the priest your mount." When the man had gone, he turned to me. "Tell me, son: where are we?"

"We are in the far reaches of Easonton, sire. Near the foothills of the White Range."

"Correct. And where is the Lady Elder?"

"I have not seen her this day, m'lord."

"Have you seen any from her house?"

I glanced around the field, lifting my helmet visor for a better view of the pennants and standards. "No, m'lord. I see none from House Elder."

"And what do you suppose that means?"

My brother had snuck forward, where he wormed his horse amongst the front ranks and between me and my father. He answered while I was still in thought.

"It is cowardice, m'lord. A clear indication that the lady and House Elder cannot be counted on when needed."

The king ignored my brother and gestured at me with his raised lance. "You. You're the eldest; what do *you* say?"

"This could be a trap. House Elder was always a close ally to the former king and the lady may have set this up to kill us while her forces remain safe. My guess would be that they provided an excuse of why they could not be here with you, m'lord—perhaps Lady Elder claims to face another threat?"

"You are correct. Lady Elder sent word yesterday of a

raider threat at Easonton's southern border—one that required her personal attention and all her men at arms. The question is: Where is the trap?" He glanced at my brother. "And you are an almost *total* moron. Get back to your ranks."

The pounding of hooves sounded behind us but I didn't bother to turn and look, knowing it was the priest. A moment later he arrived. The man jumped from his mount and knelt before my father before rising back to his feet with great effort, using his staff to augment the movement, betrayed by the decaying knees of an old man.

"Move your men into place, priest. We may need them."

"Why, sire?"

"Do you not smell it? Or feel it?"

"No, your majesty. I sense nothing."

"This is dark arcana, priest; get your monks in place, *now*."

Without warning a roar erupted, an ear-splitting scream that made my horse rear in terror, throwing me through the air to land flat on my back. The wind had been knocked out of me. For what felt like hours, I struggled to breathe against the weight of my chain mail at the same time I moved to my hands and knees to see panic unfold. Horses sprinted in every direction, some of them without their riders and noses and eyes flared wide. The fear had to come from a spell, I decided, a kind of invisible mist that emanated from hell-born creatures that once more roared and screamed.

The long tent in the center of camp had been at least a hundred yards from us, and wasn't visible because of the

rows and rows of smaller tents that encircled it. Its poles
flew into the air, flapping upward toward the sky. They
trailed canvas behind them like a kind of solid smoke and
the site hypnotized me at first, my mind incapable of
understanding what could have flung massive wooden
shafts in such a high arc. They crashed to the ground out
of sight.

"*Protect the king!*" Robert shouted, bringing me back
to my senses. My father and Robert had also been
unhorsed along with several noblemen who now formed
a line between the king and camp's center.

I moved into the line next to Robert. "What is this
magic?"

"I know not, my prince." He gestured to the ground
near my feet. "Take up that lance. We will form a pike
wall."

"This is madness. I can feel the spell, Robert, a fear
that rides on air in a miasma. Where are our priests?"

"They will come, lord." Robert's helmet had no
faceplate and his cheeks went bone white. "*Stand fast and
hold this line! It comes!*"

I turned to look in the same direction as Robert. Tents
in the distance flew in either direction, launched upward
by whatever it was that now bore down on us, its screams
coming from multiple locations. *There is more than one.*
From behind came the panicked shouting of what
remained of our army, trying to reassemble and form
ranks, but the terror had scattered them in every
direction—too far now to come to our aid quickly. We
were alone. Only ten men stood between my father and
the monsters now bearing down, and my arms trembled

with a sense of doubt and uncertainty, my muscles having already decided that our adversary was invincible. And my brother was nowhere to be seen.

The old priest took a position in front of us. He lifted his staff and moved bony hands over the shaft in a series of precise movements, after which it clicked and swung apart in sections to rejoin into a three-foot-long contraption of wood and steel. When he'd finished, the priest raised it, pressing the wooden section against his shoulder and lowering his cheek to peer down its length.

"The word of God is absolute," the priest said, barely loud enough for me to hear.

My father drew his sword and placed his hand on my shoulder for just a moment. "To think that I now have to trust my life to you: a drunkard and brothel rat. God truly despises me."

"It comes!" the priest shouted.

The closest row of tents flew apart, torn into pieces by three creatures that charged us, atop them bearded raiders whose faces had been painted in brilliant red stripes. I froze, horrified. The creatures had been formed through an unholy marriage of snake and mountain lion, so that they slithered forward on a python section more than five feet in diameter, at the same time a giant, catlike front pushed off the ground with two clawed paws; one bore down on me, its face four feet across with jaws peppered by thick fangs. Without warning the priest's staff barked. The noise startled everyone, its loud explosions reminding me of small cracks of thunder that made me flinch at first, and I watched flame erupt from one end.

The closest raider clutched his chest, which had

exploded in a burst of blood, and it occurred to me that the priest's weapon must have been a kind of bow—its arrows invisible and holy. *The word of God.* Now the man aimed his weapon at the creature, its face spurting jets of blood with each hit the priest scored until the monster roared in pain and collapsed onto the ground, spilling its rider into the grass near Robert's feet. One moment the priest had been fighting, the next he was gone. The right-most creature had lunged toward him and snapped the man in half, before turning its attention on the pikes, using a massive paw to swipe at them.

"What are these monsters?" I asked.

"This is your first encounter of arcana," Robert hissed. "Do not fear. These creatures are like grizzers—mindless in their thirst for blood, but not intelligent like you or me. God is with us."

"God just let his man die!"

The monster on my left knocked lances out of the way with one swipe, then charged forward; with its other paw it swiped at the noblemen beside me and flung them through the air. One of them screamed. The thing's claws had raked the man's sides and broke through his mail so that as he flew, his innards spilled out to trail streamers of intestines and blood. Now it looked at me. The raider shouted a war cry and raised his axe at the same time his monstrous steed swung at my lance. I lowered it, dodging the blow, and then charged. Part of me wondered how my feet had found any ability to move, much less move forward, because the fear had become so intense that I lost all sensation in my extremities. Somehow I screamed in rage and thrust the lance as hard as I could; it speared the creature in the mouth. Carried by its own forward momentum, the cat-snake moved forward and the wood flexed, pushing me back until I dropped the lance's base to wedge it against a rock. The steel tip broke through the creature's head and it fell to the ground, dead.

The raider dove from the dead monster's back, slamming into me and pinning me to the dirt. He raised his axe. Time slowed and the odor of the man made me feel nauseous, the smell of sweat mixed with rotting meat making my eyes water while I struggled to draw my sword, which had pinned beneath me. This was the end, I thought. The raider's axe started its arc downward and would soon impact against my helmet, its hard steel capable of splitting through and then cleaving my skull. But the blow never came. A moment later my father lifted me to my feet and then pulled his sword from the raider's neck.

"Dammit, boy, you should have been ready for that. What has Robert been teaching you? Always keep your sword free and clear."

"Where is the last monster?" I asked.

"Look and see. The Church has finally arrived, and they brought a pillar of fire."

I drew my sword, using it to prop myself up on my knees, and looked. A line of priests had arrived. These were the ones who resembled turtles and now instead of sputtering with a small blue flame, the priests' rods erupted in cones of fire. They spat flame with a hiss at the final creature, which now roared in agony as it turned and fled, fully engulfed in flame. But the raider stood before them, untouched. He raised his axe and shouted before one of the priests aimed his rod at the man, spraying him with orange and red fire, not stopping until the raider collapsed, twitching on the ground in death spasms.

"What magic is this?" I asked.

"It is not magic, my prince," Robert said. "It is the will of god. *And the enemies of God will burn in eternal flame.*"

"A pillar of fire by night," my father said. He nodded, a grim expression on his face. "God be praised for such a magnificent display. He is truly all powerful, is he not, Robert?"

Robert was about to answer when he instead motioned to me with his chin; I turned to look where he'd gestured. My father now faced my brother, whose face had gone red from tear tracks and whose armor was bright—spotless from having not been touched during the entire engagement. He sobbed now, and wiped his nose against a mailed sleeve.

My father slapped him. The blow knocked my brother's helmet off, his face only partially hidden now by a mail hood.

"*You ran!*" my father bellowed.

"My horse bolted. It took me forever to regain control."

"That's not what my scouts say. They say you left with both spurs kicked into your horse as if late to a wedding feast."

"Your scouts lie."

Now my father struck the other side of his face; his metal gauntlet split my brother's cheeks so that blood streamed down to his chin. "The only things worse than cowardice are the lies that come with it. Get out of my sight. Go ride with the grave diggers and saddle boys."

As soon as my brother left, Robert and several surviving nobles gathered around my father, their expressions dark with worry.

"Your majesty," Robert said. "This was an assassination attempt. It was clearly not a standard raid, and the precision with which these barbarians charged in an effort to get to you tells us everything we need to know."

A nearby nobleman nodded. "Your arms-man is correct, highness. These creatures were sent for you alone, this entire encampment a ruse."

"Do you think me a moron?" My father paced before them, his sword bared and its tip dragging in dirt. "House Elder dares to use the dark arts against me—against the Church."

"Father, you cannot openly accuse House Elder of this," I said.

"*Why not*, boy?"

"They are not here. There is nothing concrete linking them to the attempt, and of all the houses, Elder is the most powerful. They have allies—houses who remember the old king and who we can assume were in league with them."

"And," my father said, "what do *you* think we should do?"

"Plan. There is always a way to deal with traitors, even ones so well positioned."

The king gestured to Robert, who stepped closer and bowed his head. "Robert, this boy is to stop his drunkenness and whoring. Do you understand me?"

"Yes, highness."

"And Camden." The king grabbed my mail shirt in a single fist, almost lifting me from my feet. "You are my eldest. But the high families will only tolerate so much from their king and they will never accept a lecherous puppy like you as being the legitimate heir. If you can fix yourself, then you will be king after me. And God help us all when that happens."

The nobles grinned and chuckled, some of them cheering and raising their swords. "God help us all," one repeated.

My father let go and pushed me away, where I stumbled over the body of a raider and fell flat on my back. Robert lifted me. But I felt nothing, the joy of what my father had said coursing through my veins and making everything feel weightless. Together we joined ranks with the others, all of whom had begun marching homeward, following in the direction of our horses, who by now were most likely halfway to their stables. Mud that had worked itself into my mail soon caked and dried, falling out in clumps as we marched, but the ground underfoot was still wet and soggy from rain the previous day. Before long, my boots sunk three inches into muck, trodden and re-worked by the men before me.

"You passed the test of dark arcana," Robert said. "So the king will make you his heir."

"My brother will hate me for it."

"Your brother hates you already, m'lord. It is the way of noble families."

"I don't know if I want to be king."

"Really?" Robert laughed. "This is clear to even the most idiotic of those around you since the way you drink

and whore is legendary—even among the king's arms-
men. But your father is right, Cam."

"About what?"

"You *are* made of the stuff that a king needs."

The sloping mountainside was a godsend at first, its
upward trail free of mud so the ground didn't paw at me
and slow my progress. Soon, though, the effort of climbing
with added weight of mail and sword made my legs burn.
To be the king. I'd never thought much about being heir
to the white throne and what I hadn't told Robert was that
I hated my father just as much as my brother; my dreams
had always been ones of getting away from the noble
houses—of having my own life. I looked back at the grave
diggers, now far below us. They struggled with the bodies
of noblemen who'd died when the monsters attacked, and
among them I spied the shiny mail of my brother. He
glanced up. Even from that far away I sensed the hatred
with which he looked at me.

"Fine," I said—grabbing Robert's shoulder when I
slipped. "I'll do it."

"Do what?" he asked.

"Be king. But don't expect me to stop whoring and
drinking; those are the only things that make this life
bearable. I'll just have to do a better job hiding it."

"How old are you, Cam?"

"Sixteen last month."

"You're too young to be so jaded."

"Nonsense," I said. "I learned it from you."

Robert clapped me on the back and laughed. "Then
there's hope after all."

QUEEN AMID ASHES
Christopher Ruocchio

For hundreds of years, the crusade against the alien Cielcin has gone on unending. The invaders have left devastation in their wake, razing entire planets, kidnapping billions. Unto this, Hadrian Marlowe, the man destined to end it all, the man they say cannot be killed. Newly made a knight of the Empire, his first true battle won, Hadrian is about to learn again that nothing is simple, and that the battle for justice and truth is a long and hideous thing. . . .

✢ ✢ ✢

CHAPTER 1
THE SUN IS HIGH . . .

The red light of battle still raked the sky as the wreck of inhuman ships turned to cinders upon the upper airs. Each streak of light—like the mark of a claw—left its smoldering wound upon the heavens as vessels burned and fell. They had never seen us coming. Ten years the Cielcin had besieged Thagura. Ten years they had hounded its millions, hunted them for sport, gathered them into camps, into ships for transport to the fleet that hung in orbit like a school of vampires and sucked the blood of the world.

We had traveled as fast as we could, but the space between stars is vast, and even the fastest dromonds of our fleet are not fast enough to bridge such distances. The locals had put up a fight, the *ruins* said that much. We had reports of survivors in the hinterlands, of towns gone underground, retreating into tunnels and caves Thagura's first settlers had dwelt in before mankind brought air to that desert world. But of the capital? Of the city of Pseldona—Pseldona of the Hundred Gates, Pseldona of the Many Towers, Pseldona of the Rock?

Only the Rock remained. The Rock, and the broken bones of a few towers torn down and torched from orbit.

"'Tis an evil place, Hadrian," Valka said, coming to my side. The winged shadows of our fliers cut the rusted soil like knives, made darker by the great burning of the fleet in orbit.

Unrolled like a carpet beneath us, the ruined city yawned: a black stain on that red world, its tumbled towers and white streets charred with plasma fire, the silicates fused to glass. The settlers had built her high upon knees of the Rock, terrace upon terrace, so that once her silver fountains and white halls rose above the desert sands. Brightly painted she once had been—the queen of the cities of Thagura—her houses blue and gold and white, her banners snapping in the desert air, and everywhere brimming green with date palms and olive groves.

No more.

I shook my head. "No," I said, "evil has been done here."

Would that I might have seen her in her flower, before the enemy came.

"Where's our man?" asked Pallino, who had volunteered to captain my guard for this journey to the surface. Unlike Valka and myself, he had donned his helmet, the faceless ivory casque of an Imperial legionnaire, and carried his energy-lance in the crook of his right arm, its bladed head swaying as he moved, leaving the double column of our escort behind him. "Shouldn't he be here?"

Again I shook my head. "They'll have seen us descend," I said, and pointed up the ruined path toward the Rock itself, to where the remains of the baroness's palace moldered like the worn teeth of a fallen jaw. "Malyan's people said they would make contact near the crag."

"'Tis a miracle there's anyone left alive at all," said Valka, sweeping golden eyes over what remained of Pseldona.

It was her first time seeing anything of the terrors the enemy left in their wake. She had not come to the surface with me on Rustam, had not seen the black scar of the old city stretched for miles across the face of that far world, nor seen the squalor of the ship-city the survivors had built for themselves.

"But there are," I said, as bracingly as I could manage. "You heard the transmission! The baroness is alive, and saved some of her people." I hooked a thumb through my shield-belt, reassured myself that the hilt of my sword hung proper in its clasp. It would not do to dwell on what was lost. We were victorious! Our fleet—and our new flagship, the *Tamerlane*—had broken theirs in less than a day. Thagura was free, and though there was pain and loss and tears of grief, there would soon be tears of joy, and song, and hope as man rebuilded. And a new city would rise from the ashes of the old, and in time all that would remain of this destruction would be the tale of man's endurance.

Clapping Pallino on the shoulder, I said, "Let's move!" And raising my voice, I addressed the men of my guard. "Eyes forward, lads! Let's make a proper show for the baroness!"

As one, my guard shifted their lances, the ceramic bayonets flashing in the red light of Thagura's star. Gone were the red ceramics of the old uniform, the black tunics and blocky, foreign style. My Red Company had been transformed. What had begun as a mercenary outfit half my life before had been transmuted into an Imperial force. The brand with which the Emperor had anointed me his knight still seemed to rest upon my shoulder, its touch upon my brow like that of one of the seraphim of old—all flame.

I was a knight of the Empire, no longer a rebel, no longer just a boy. Nearly half my life I had quested for Vorgossos and peace. I had found Vorgossos only.

The Rock loomed above us. A great red dome of the living stone that towered thousands of feet above the sands of the Tagurine Erg. The Rock and the palace that crowned it had served House Malyan for generations, and though the palace was gone, the Rock remained, and the faces carved upon it. Thagura had been settled thousands of years before, and the nobiles who ruled over it had carved their likenesses a thousand feet high into the face the Rock itself. The relief images of Baron Aram Malyan and his son, Vahan, stood holding up the rim of the acropolis, their muscled bodies supporting the palace their family called home.

I had seen them as our fliers circled to land, but the sight of them still had not quite sunk in.

I had already traveled far in my forty years, had plumbed the depths of Vorgossos and knelt before Caesar himself in the Georgian Chapel of the Peronine Palace on Forum, but there is no shortage of wonders in creation, and the twin colossi carved into the face of the Rock were mighty indeed. How many hands had labored there, and for how many decades?

Still they had not fallen, though the palace above them was dust.

"Oro, sound the horn!" I called to the herald as we mounted the steps to the plaza that stretched beneath the feet of the colossi. Shattered masonry lay all around, and the lesser statues in the dry fountain lay broken. Old blood stained the tiles, and everywhere the signs of old violence glowed white hot for those with eyes to read.

The herald sounded his clarion, and the bright noise of that trumpet echoed and died on the breeze. There was nothing. No one.

"Black planet!" Pallino cursed, "It's quiet."

"There's nothing left," Valka agreed, and drew close beside me. "There aren't even birds, do you see?"

She was right. We might have stood upon the surface of an airless, desert moon. A tall banner—a hundred feet high—swayed from one iron pillar at the corner of the square. White with three blue lions, the banner of House Malyan. All the world was still.

"Oro, again," I said.

Again the trumpet sounded.

Bang!

A bolt of violet light struck the tiles of the square not a dozen feet from where I stood, and the trumpet blast died at once, choked off. My men reacted at once, swinging their lances from their parade holds to readiness as they crouched and searched for targets. I stepped forward, one hand slipping to the hilt of my unkindled sword, and shifted to place myself between Valka and the enemy.

"Hold your fire!" I shouted, and raised a hand.

It was the bolt of an energy-lance that had struck the tiles. The Cielcin did not use such lances, preferring to fight with scimitar and claw and the flying snakes that chewed men's flesh and slavered blood as they flew from target to target.

"Show yourselves!" I called. "We are men like you!"

"If your herald blasts his horn again we'll shoot him dead!" came a rough voice from the roof of the crumbled building that lined the far side of the square. "There may still be Pale about!"

Both hands raised then and visible, I stepped forward, black cloak snapping about my armored shoulders. "Look above you, friend! The battle is done!" I gestured—not unlike the colossi graven above us all—until I felt as though I held the burning heavens above me. "I am Lord Hadrian Marlowe, Knight-Victorian of the Empire. We have a gift for the baroness."

"A gift?" the man repeated.

"I come to give her back her world!" I shouted. "Were you not told? The siege is lifted! I say again: the battle is done!"

In the silence that followed, Pallino muttered, "Bit slow, aren't they?"

A man stepped out from the shadow of a second-story arch. He wore a dun greatcoat over his scratched white armor, but his bald head was bare, and though he wore a plasma rifle on a strap over one shoulder, he raised his hands to mirror mine. "Her ladyship said . . . but I did not dare believe!" The relief in his tone had an almost physical weight. "Ten years . . . Is it really over?"

"I have orders from the Emperor and Lord Hauptmann to bring the baroness to Marinus!" I said. "She must give her account to the Strategos, that we may determine what may be done to restore your world."

The man shook his head, though whether in negation or disbelief I could not say. He rested one hand on the wall beside him, sagged as a man who has relieved himself of a terrible weight. Presently he shook himself. "Stand down, you men!" he said. From the ruined buildings all around, I felt more than heard the shifting of boots and swish of cloaks as men relaxed. My own men did likewise, settling back to rest.

A moment later, the bald captain emerged from the shadows of the building, tails of his coat flapping on the wind. Half a dozen men filtered out behind him, sans order, each man's expression more hollow-eyed and hangdog than the last. The captain saluted, fist to breast as he bowed slightly. "I can't believe it."

"Were you not sent to greet us?"

"We were, aye, but still . . ." His eyes flickered to Valka at my side, and I knew how out of place she must look, a Tavrosi witch, golden-eyed and tattooed, the shoulders of her red jacket black-feathered and strange. "Ten years, lordship. You're sure they've gone?"

I was growing tired of the man's disbelief. "What's your name, soldier?"

Coming back to himself, the fellow saluted again, fixed his eyes on a point over my shoulder. "Maro, sir. Vahan Maro. Captain of the lady's guard . . ." At this he glanced around, taking in the haggard collection at his back. "What's left of it."

Vahan, I thought, glancing up at the colossus on the left, *like the old baron.*

I extended my hand. Maro looked at me a moment, surprised to find a lord of the Imperium so offering his hand like a common soldier. He took it only apprehensively. "Good to meet you, Captain," I said, and nodded in a way that said we should proceed. "I am Hadrian Marlowe, as I say. This is my . . ." I stumbled, about to say the word *paramour* as I turned to gesture at Valka, and while it was so, I was not sure how she would take the label, and so said, ". . .*companion.* Valka Onderra of the Tavrosi."

The man's eyes widened. "A witch?"

"A doctor," she said icily, using the Tavrosi word. *Vechsrei.*

I translated for the perplexed captain, and waved him forward. "Lead the way, Maro."

They kept looking at the sky. I have never forgotten

that. Stopping every dozen steps to glance at the clouds and the heavens where the enemy's ruined fleet fell burning like so many prayer lanterns lit and let fly. Maro and his men led us toward the foot of the Aram's colossus, where I spied the ruin of the huge lifts that ran up behind the statues to the top of the Rock. We did not climb up, but instead circled the inselberg and descended down a paved street where the barracks of the city guard stood carved into the foundations of the Rock on our left. The invaders had carved the round symbols of their speech in the stones with claws and the points of knives. Windows stood smashed, doors staved in.

"Lower city's worse," Maro said. "They didn't burn up here by the Rock. They firebombed the whole city once it was clear they'd-got all they were getting from it."

"What of the rest of the planet?" Valka asked, hurrying along beside me.

Maro shook his head, but did not break stride. "We know they hit the other cities. Aramsa, Tagur, Port Reach, but we lost contact early on. The Cielcin tore down the satellite grid, and the hardlines were all cut in the bombing. We had the QET—that's how we got to you—but we couldn't raise anyone else on the planet. We could be all there is."

Pallino cursed.

Raising a hand for quiet, I said, "There were forty million people on Thagura by the last census. They can't all be gone."

The captain shrugged. Up ahead on the left, the squarish shapes of the barracks buildings retreated farther into the overhang of red stone above, creating narrow

streets that pierced the rock and led up and down narrow
steps to hidden chambers within the lonely mountain. The
heavy metal door of some hangar or motor pool stood shut
and scarred, and farther along the path, I saw the thin
shape of spears hammered into the earth at irregular
intervals. Green banners—tattered and faded—flapped
there tall and thin. I could not read the alien signs painted
on them, but I knew the skulls that decorated their points
were those of men.

The tired captain stopped before one narrow opening
and turned back. "I know, lordship—and by Earth, I pray
you're right. But ten years is a long time. It may be some
of the miners and the desert folk got away, or some of the
lesser lords survived in other bunkers, but the cities?" He
shook his head, then gestured down the passage. "It's this
way."

The great lords of the Imperium had been digging
tunnels since the days of the God Emperor. The dangers
of inter-house warfare were never zero, and shielded or
no, the great palaces and estates of the various barons,
counts, dukes, and marquises were ever targets for orbital
bombardment, whatever the Great Charter and the
formal rules of war may say. There was hardly a palace
beneath any of the Sollan Empire's half a billion suns that
did not possess something like the bunkers in which
Gadar Malyan and her court found themselves. Some
planets and castles possessed only the most rudimentary
of bolt-holes—sufficient to sustain a lesser lord, his family,
and a scarce dozen or more retainers—while others
boasted a complex warren of tunnels from which a planet's
resistance might be directed. Still others were the palaces

themselves, whole halls and galleries themselves all resided in darkness below the earth.

They were relics of an older time, when man battled man for honor and for gain. How prescient that need had been, and how fortunate. In preparing to battle ourselves, we had prepared for the invaders, for the Cielcin to sweep in from galactic north and lay waste to our many worlds.

Valka and I turned down the narrow way. Three of Maro's men hurried on ahead, head-lamps illuminating the path as they reached the top of a winding stair that angled down. At the bottom, a pair of men in tan cloaks like Maro's greeted us with curt nods, and from the way they saluted Maro I guessed they'd been left to hold the garret. The room itself was dark, and from what little I saw I guessed it had been an intake chamber of the sort one finds in the offices of urban prefects under every sun. It was not hard to imagine criminals dragged off the streets of Pseldona, hauled in to explain themselves to a prefect before being dragged down to lockup. I spied reinforced glass on the inner doors, and empty lockers— the doors twisted and strewn about the place—where once the effects of detainees were kept.

"The entrance to the bunker is through the dungeons?" I asked, somewhat surprised.

"No," Maro answered. "Through the castellan's offices. Through here." He gestured, then turned back to his men. "Tilcho, Garan, you two stay here until my signal. It's quiet out there, but that doesn't mean we haven't been followed."

"Aye, sir."

Once we passed through the intake chamber, we

followed Maro's men along the ruined hall. It seemed there was nowhere the xenobites had not gotten, for here too were signs of looting and more rude graffiti.

When we hurried down another three levels by a spiral flight of stairs, Maro asked, "Is it true, lordship? What they say of you?"

I had passed Maro then, and flinched as though the man had rammed a dagger between my shoulder blades. Had the story reached even here?

Is it true you can't be killed?

Valka's golden eyes—artificial as they were, confections of metal and glass—glowed at me in the dimness, her face opened in concern. She had been there, had seen me die, had screamed as the inhuman Prince Aranata's blade struck off my head. As had Pallino and a number of my guard. The story had begun to get out, of how I had simply *appeared* again, alive. Of how I had saved Valka and my people from the prince at the last moment.

Had the story reached so far already? Whispered from soldier to soldier as the legions traveled between the stars? *No blade can cut the Devil down.*

But Maro did not ask the dreadful question, instead he said, "Did you really kill one of their princes in single combat? The Cielcin, I mean."

I felt my shoulders relax, and smiled. Valka smiled too and turned away. "Don't believe everything you hear, Captain," I said, smiling after her and glancing to Pallino, who had fought by my side. "I had help."

"But you did kill one?"

"Aranata Otiolo," I said, thoughts running back to that monstrous prince. Nearly eight feet tall and thin as Death, but broad-shouldered, with arms that reached its knees and horns long as daggers above its broad, white face. "Yes."

The men about us whispered in surprise and admiration. In all the centuries of war between our two kinds, I was the first—the very first—to kill one of their princes face-to-face. Titus Hauptmann, Cassian Powers— the great heroes of the early Crusade—these had killed princes by the dozen, whole blood-clans, but they had done so with the fire of their guns, with atomics and armadas to outgun the sun itself for firepower. I alone had met such a lord of demons sword for sword.

I had lost.

And lived only because *they* had brought me back. The Quiet. The ancient beings whose ghosts I first encountered in the ruins on Emesh. They had handed me back my life, and I didn't even know why.

"My lord?" Maro's voice brought me back to the moment. "Through here."

The castellan's desk had been overturned, lay broken on the moldering carpet. A portrait of His Imperial Radiance, the Emperor William XXIII, hung slashed on one wall. Still I recognized the green eyes and fiery red hair of the man who had knighted me. The same portrait hung in duplicate in ten billion offices on a hundred million worlds. Torn books littered the ground, and smashed bits of quartz that had once held all manner of data.

One of Maro's men circled the perimeter of the room, admiring the destruction. He made a warding gesture with both hands, first and last fingers extended to ward off evil. "Black planet, they got close."

"But they didn't find the door," Maro said, unslinging his rifle. He pounded the butt of the weapon on the floor once, twice, three times. "Ciprian! Open the gate!"

A deep *click* resounded through the low, stone room, and an instant later the floor began to shake, and a terrible grinding filled the air and set my teeth on edge. A slit opened in the floor beneath where the desk had been, and two of Maro's men hurried to fold back the rug to keep it from sagging into the fresh opening. Yellow sconces flickered to life, and a dirt-faced boy in ill-fitting white armor peered up at us from the bottom of the stairs.

"Is *he* the knight?" the boy asked, eyes wide as he looked at me.

"He is," I said.

"You've come to save us!" he exclaimed. I guessed he must be Ciprian. "And the lady?"

I nodded, and looked to Maro.

The captain extended a hand. "After you."

CHAPTER 2
THE BARONESS
⚜

Thus I bring you, Reader, through that hidden gate. Many times I would enter the underworld in our long war, and many times come to some catacomb, some deep-delved place dark and dank and stinking of desperation and unwashed men.

Many times.

But Thagura was the first. Though I had fought before—on Vorgossos, on Emesh—I had never come to so formal a theater of war. Our fight against Aranata beyond Vorgossos had not been planned; and on Emesh the enemy had surprised us, falling like fire from the sky. The Emperor had anointed me, created me as a knight, and though I chafed in my new station, I wore it proudly as I could. Thagura would anoint me again, a second baptism greater than the first. How many times would I stand in so dark a tunnel in the decades to come? On how many worlds?

I can name them all now, though as I followed the unwashed Ciprian I still believed I might count my battles on my fingers. I still hoped for peace, though I no longer knew how to achieve it. The boy who dreamed of peace on Delos long ago was dead, indeed, and though I bore his name and blood alike, I was not him. With every threshold we cross we become someone new, for every place is new, and every hour, and with every moment we are changed.

We may not step in the same river twice, nor with the same feet.

And I had stepped into the last redoubt of House Malyan upon Thagura, and doing so became *a hero*. The gallant rescuer, though it had been Captain Otavia Corvo and my officers who broke the siege in orbit, and not *Lord Hadrian Marlowe*. Gone was the boy—I say again—and in his place there strode a knight, young and tall and clad in black: Black of hair and cloak, his knife-edged face so pale it seemed to glow in the dimness, his witch-companion at his side.

"They're here!" I heard a hoarse whisper, and saw a haggard face peer out from a side passage.

"Is it really over?" an old woman in the pale smock of a nurse appeared in another passage.

More faces flowered from doors left and right. Dark shadows showed beneath every eye, and nearly all had a gray pallor that spoke of want of sun. To judge young Ciprian by his age, I wondered if he had ever known the sun—or if he had, I wondered if he remembered it.

"Everybody stand clear!" Captain Maro proclaimed, joining me at the bottom of the steps. "He's for the baroness!" Then he turned aside and spoke from the corner of his mouth. "Just the servants, lordship. My lady awaits in her chambers. This way!"

But before I could go another three paces, a young woman broke from one of the side passages and fell to her knees before Valka and me. She seized my ankle and kissed my polished boot. "Lord!" she said, looking up with shining eyes. "Earth bless and keep you, lord! Is it done? Are we free at last?"

At a sign from Maro, two of the Malyan soldiers seized the woman roughly and spurred her back whence she had come. "Get back!" said one.

"Hadrian!" Valka's hand settled on my arm.

"Stand down, you men!" I exclaimed. "Leave her!"

The soldiers let her stumble against the wall, where she slid once more to her knees.

Maro moved to my side. "They were ordered not to speak to you, lordship."

Taking him to mean this order was intended as a courtesy for me, I raised a hand. "It's all right." The woman peered up at me, one dark eye luminous through curtains of unwashed yellow hair.

"Lordship," Maro said, "the baroness is waiting!"

Valka's shadow moved on the wall as she shifted at my side, not speaking. Ignoring the captain, I went to the woman and dropped to one knee beside her. "Are you all right?"

She nodded. I tried to smile, knowing the expression was cold comfort when played across my satyr's face. Brushing my black hair back, I said, "It's almost over. The enemy is gone." I touched her shoulder, and standing once more raised my voice so the gathered servants might all hear me, I said, "We have driven the Pale back into the Dark! Their worldships have retreated, and their lesser vessels are burning now all across your skies!"

It was as if some dam broke, as if some taut, invisible cord were cut and loosed the breath from so many tortured lungs. The woman broke down and buried her face in her hands, her shoulders heaving.

"Lordship!" Something in Maro's voice cracked as he took half a step toward me. I should have marked it then, and wondered, or felt the tension in his men, the way they bristled as the crowd clapped and cried aloud in joy and disbelief, but it was lost in the moment, as I turned from the serving girl and ducked my head.

"Lead on."

There was a guard posted at the door to the baroness's chambers: four men in the colors of House Malyan, their faces hid behind plates of blue ceramic. They stood aside as Maro approached, and the door behind them rolled aside, disappearing into a slot in the wall, rolling on huge gear teeth to admit us.

"Your men will wait here," said Maro, gesturing to a side chamber.

"They will *not*," Pallino said, stepping forward.

Addressing Pallino directly, Captain Maro said, "The baroness has ordered that this will be a private audience." Pallino did not move. He might have been a statue, a suit of armor on display. Captain Maro blinked. "But you may accompany your master."

Amusement flickered at the corner of Valka's eyes.

Gone at once were the drab walls of painted stone, the floors of plain concrete. Gone were the ducts and stripes of wire mold bracketed to the arched ceiling. Gone were the open metal doors and unwashed faces. Tavrosi carpets lay thick on the floors before us, and the walls were minutely tiled. A dozen mosaicists had labored many months to decorate the walls with mandala designs in shades of blue and white and violet, with here and there a spark of red glass bright as gems.

A flight of stairs as ornately tiled descended beneath an oiled balustrade to a level below, and the reflected light of glowspheres dancing on water flowed up to meet us, catching on the tiles. So beautiful it was—and such a contrast—that my breath caught.

Hand steadying his weapon on its sling, Maro hurried down the stairs. I followed him, boots ringing as we descended into the central chamber, where a long, narrow pool of clear water stretched beneath marble caryatids whose crowns upheld the rock above.

"What the hell is this doing here?" Valka asked from

my side, hissing the words in her native Panthai so as not to be understood.

I could only shake my head. What compulsion had so seized the lords of House Malyan that they had felt the need to place a thing in their underground shelter? Gold and porphyry gleamed at the base of the caryatids that supported the vaulted ceiling, and more mosaics—these showing the great Heroes of our Imperial past—decorated the vaults. I recognized an image of Prince Cyrus the Golden with his great sword and gilded mail, and one of Simeon clothed in red and seated on a stone.

Maro led us around the right of the great pool and up a short flight of steps to a balcony overlooking the water.

"This is him?" a rich voice wafted from a divan to greet us. "Enough, Ravi! Our hero is here!"

That the woman who rose from her cushioned seat was of the highest Imperial blood no man could deny. The porphyrogeneticists of the High College who had sculpted her for her parents from conception had lavished all their art upon her, for she was perfect as any of the statues that upheld the roof of that grotto—and almost as naked. Her eyes were twin chips of black jade, and her hair was like a cascade of fresh ink—dark even as my own. She sat up, arranging the translucent silks that draped her like faint shadows of evening, hardly concealing the creamy flesh beneath.

Perched then on the edge of her divan, the baroness extended one glittering hand. Lapis enamel coated each taloned nail, and the diamonds on each finger I felt must weigh on her. I stood a moment, stunned by the display and our circumstances. Of all the ways she might have greeted us . . . this?

Remembering himself a fraction too late, the woman's cupbearer—a nobile boy of perhaps sixteen standard years—cleared his throat and said, "You stand before Her Excellency, the Lady Gadar Berhane Amtarra-Vaha Malyan VII, Baroness of Thagura, Archon of Pseldona Prefecture, and Lady of the Rock."

I swept my gaze over the cupbearer. He was bare chested, and wore only a white cloth bound about his waist. Unable to keep a faint frown from my lips, I went to one knee. Taking the offered hand, I knelt and kissed the baroness's signet ring. "Lady Malyan, I've come to give you back your world."

Gadar Malyan withdrew her glittering appendage. She smelled of salt, and I guessed that she had been swimming in anticipation of our arrival. Standing, I drew back to a level with Valka and Pallino.

The baroness smiled lazily, staring up at me. "Hadrian Marlowe. I expected you would be taller!" Her tongue curled as she grinned. "It is an honor to meet you! We are gratified to learn the Emperor has sent his best *at last*!"

"The honor is mine, my lady," I said, and fixed my eyes—as was the military custom—on a point over the lady's shoulder. "The Emperor will be relieved to know that you survived."

"Certainly he will," she said, her grin freezing on that marble sculpture of a face, eyes gone hard as glass. "That no doubt is why he has left us to languish under the alien boot for so long. *The sun is high, and the Emperor is far away,* they say. But I thought Thagura counted for more in the Imperial books than this."

I frowned at her. It was an old Mandari proverb she quoted at me, from an age when that people had emperors of their own, but she used it wrongly.

"I beg my lady's pardon," I said, and bowed my head, letting my confusion go. "We came as swiftly as we were able. We were at Monmara when we received our orders from the Solar Throne."

"The Throne itself?" She brightened. "The Emperor himself ordered you to come?"

"Yes, my lady," I said, eyes flickering to her face and away. A bead of water—or was it sweat?—was tracing its line down her white neck, and where it ran I glanced dutifully away from. The order had in truth come from from the Imperial Council, from the War Minister, Lord Bourbon, and the Director of Legion Intelligence. But let her believe as she liked. If believing the order had come direct from Caesar softened her disposition, that was just as well. "I have orders to bring you to Marinus to meet with Lord Hauptmann and the Viceroy. They wish a full report of what has transpired here."

Gadar Malyan's perfect lips twisted, but settled on a smile. "I will be able to tell my tale in person? To plead for my people?" She almost rose from the divan. "Are we to go now?"

"Not at once," I said. "The Cielcin have been driven from orbit, but it may not yet be perfectly safe to move you. I wanted to ensure that you were safe and to put my men at your disposal. I have brought half a hundred of my men to help keep you safe until we are certain the system is secure."

"And yourself?" she asked. "You are staying?"

Hooking my thumbs through my belt, I answered her. "I would hear what happened."

"Yes, yes you must!" she said, her lazy smile returning. "Send your servants away, my lord. We haven't much, but we shall make you as comfortable as we may. Will you not sit? Ravi! The wine!" She waved one bangled arm at a chair beside her divan.

I moved to accept her invitation, swept my cloak aside, but seeing there was no other chair near at hand for Valka, I asked if one might be brought.

Malyan's face turned downward. "Are you not going to dismiss your servants?"

"I'm not his servant," Valka snapped, angling her chin.

Eager to head off any incident, I raised my hands. "Lady Malyan, may I introduce Valka Onderra Vhad Edda. My companion."

"Your companion?" Malyan's eyes flickered from Valka's face to mine. "Your concubine?"

"His paramour," Valka corrected, using the very word I'd avoided with Captain Maro. I caught myself blinking at Valka in surprise. She had spent much of the years since Vorgossos in cryonic fugue, and though I had aged five years since she first had kissed me aboard the ship of Kharn Sagara, she had scarcely counted one, and so her admission surprised me, so cautious had she been to give our entanglements a name.

"Paramour, really?" Gadar Malyan reclined against the rest of the divan, breasts heaving beneath the gauzy shadow she wore as she accepted a goblet from her serving boy. Speaking round the rim of the glass, she inquired, "There's a wife, then? I had not heard."

Why were we talking about *me*? I looked from Valka to the baroness, back to Valka as she replied, finding her tongue before I could: "I am all."

"I'm sure you are, dear," Malyan said, black eyes taking Valka in. "I'm sure you are."

Before Valka could conjure a reply, the boy Ravi approached with a chair from farther down the way and set it beside my own, so that Valka and I faced the lady as she reclined, raising her goblet for the boy to charge. He did so dutifully, and it was only as he did so that I marked the hollow quality and glassiness beneath the charcoal that rimmed his eyes. Like everyone in the vaults beneath the Malyans' Rock—everyone except the baroness, it seemed—the boy was exhausted body and spirit. When he had finished with his mistress's cup, he poured for Valka and myself before drawing back, his shoulders hunched.

"He is such a good boy," the baroness said wistfully, gazing at her servant. "The last of his house, I daresay. His father, Lord Vyasa, was my archon down in Aramsa."

Turning to look at the boy, I found his eyes were on me, hard as glass. "I am sorry," I said, and to the baroness too I added, "We'd have come sooner if we could."

"I know," she said, and lifted the goblet to her lips. "But it *is* over, yes?"

"Yes," I agreed, and tasted the wine. It was Kandarene, and red as arterial blood. No wine of Earth was ever so bright and violent a color. "Will you tell us what happened?"

The baroness set her goblet aside. "What is there to tell?" she said, adjusting the drape of her garment. "They overwhelmed us. They were in orbit before our deep system satellites flagged them. My captains told me the surveillance grid was ill-maintained."

"Your man Maro said as much," Valka said, eliciting a terse expression on the lady's face.

"Did he?" Malyan asked, chewing her tongue. "Maro is very good. Very thorough." She drummed her fingers against the bowl of her goblet. "But my fleet never stood a chance. The Cielcin outnumbered us five to one, I'm told—ship-for-ship—and their flagship! You can scarce imagine! There are moons about our outer planets that were smaller. We were fortunate Thagura does not have much by way of seas! We might have drowned, you know?"

Lady Gadar Malyan shifted where she sat, leaned forward to place her glass on the table between us in such a way that her shift fell open. She caught my eye in the fraction of a second my attention slipped, and smiled. Her own eyes flitted to Valka as she covered herself and sat up. "They besieged Pseldona that same day. Dropped . . . half a hundred landing towers on my city. Mother Earth alone knows how many of my people they made off with. My men were overmatched."

"Is that when they burned the city?" I asked.

"Oh no! That . . ." She caught herself. "*They* burned it later. Their prince—Muzugara, I think his name was— sent a herald to order my surrender. I refused, of course. I can't imagine my capture would have done much to dissuade his men from sacking my world."

My fingers tightened on the goblet they held. *Our swords shall play the orator for us.*

When I had gone into the tunnels beneath Emesh to first confront our enemy, I had done so in the hope that I might reconcile our two kinds. As a boy on Delos, I had dreamed of traveling the stars, of seeing man's dominion, and of meeting the xenobites that dwelt beyond and beneath us. Not just the Cielcin, but the Irchtani, the Cavaraad, the Umandh, and all the rest. I imagined that the war that plagued mankind and the Cielcin both was all a misunderstanding, that surely we could be made to coexist. That it was only human greed and human cruelty that kept us apart.

I was half right.

We are no angels, we men. But the Cielcin?

Too well I remembered the screams as Aranata and its men tore our captured crewmates limb from limb and feasted. When I closed my eyes to blot out Gadar Malyan's failed and obvious attempt at seduction, I saw instead white, inhuman faces raised to watch me, red and smeared with gore.

Five years since Vorgossos. Five years and the nightmares had never quite stopped.

Aranata's blade flashed at my neck.

Darkness.

"You're quite right," I told the lady. "There is no reasoning with them."

When I opened my eyes, I found the baroness watching me with one eyebrow arched. "My fleet was lost. Every ship in orbit—nigh on every ship I had—was destroyed within the first month. Archon Vyasa and the lesser lords launched what resistance they could. Perhaps the exsul houses on the edge of the system came to our assistance, I don't rightly know."

"Perhaps they fled," Valka said.

The baroness dismissed this with a gesture, neither denying nor allowing this. "We lost our satellites after the first sack of the city. Muzugara's ships used them for target practice. For a time we communicated via the old hardlines, but those went out in the second year. We had the telegraph, only none of the in-system numbers answered. Not Vyasa, not Acre, not the exsuls. What could we do but wait?"

"Waiting seems to have suited you quite well." Valka's tongue cut the air like a razor, like highmatter.

I flashed a glare at her, but she didn't seem to notice. Her eyes were on the baroness, who leaned back in surprise. "Perhaps you should consider a wife, my lord," she said to me, ignoring Valka as one might a barking dog. I felt my own blood boil. "Your woman speaks above her station."

If Gadar Malyan expected me to apologize for Valka, she was fated for disappointment. "She's Tavrosi," I said, an explanation—not an excuse.

"She is most uncouth," Malyan said. "Though perhaps such wild blood has its merits."

"That is quite enough, Baroness," I said. The woman was palatine, and of higher rank than I, but I was a knight of the Royal Victorian Order, one of the Emperor's own, and her liberator. "So the Cielcin firebombed the city?"

Malyan blinked, fetched her goblet, for a moment uncomprehending. "I . . . yes. In the second year. They took out the bastille sooner, and the palace, of course. A few other targets, but they spent their time harvesting the population. I gave orders to evacuate to the countryside as soon as they arrived, but I don't know what good it did."

"To the countryside?" I echoed. "To the desert, you mean?"

Malyan shrugged. "That is what countryside we have on Thagura."

I clenched my jaw. Too many of the great lords of the Empire I have known have thought too little for the men and women in their charge. Only Caesar himself ever seemed to care, and perhaps a few, precious others. I never understood them, these men and women—like my own father—who viewed mankind not as man, as men and women, but as ants, as numbers on a balance sheet.

Pallino spared me the trouble of responding, for he hurried back up the steps whither he'd departed, boots ringing off the vaults above and the bare forms of the caryatids supporting them. "Had!" he said, forgetting formality in his haste. "Word from Corvo! They've pacified high orbit, but there's evidence the Pale dug in near the pole! Corvo says there's camps. Miles of camps!"

"Prisoner of war camps?" Valka asked, rising to her feet.

I felt my blood run cold despite the heat and the damp beside the pool. I had seen holographs taken at Cielcin war camps before, but only still images. The longhouses—tents, really—and the ill, starved people crowded into pens. The bodies and human refuse piling about the ankles of the living. Pestilence, famine, and death. I did not want to go, and knew I must.

My chiliarch nodded behind his faceless mask. "Most like. She's launched an attack group to take the camps. They'll be there in three hours."

"Can we join them?" I asked, rising as well. "Is there time?"

"I thought you were staying!" the baroness objected. "Am I not to go with you?"

It was the boy who once had dreamed of peace that moved me. If my men took Cielcin prisoners, I might speak with them. If I could speak with them, I might find a way at peace, might repeat what I had done on Emesh— might use our prisoners to barter with Muzugara, *somehow*. If I could turn even one of their clans to our cause, it would be progress and *proof* that things could change, that the Crusade which had for four centuries racked the galaxy might end at last.

Drawing my cloak about my shoulders, I said, "Plans have changed, my lady. The enemy is still on your world. Pseldona may be safe, but I would not risk your safety. You must stay here until the security of your planet may be guaranteed." To the room at large I said, "I will leave my guard with you, my lady. For your protection. Valka, Pallino." I gestured, and without waiting to be dismissed, hurried to the steps.

"You're not thinking of leaving *me* here, are you?" Pallino asked when we had returned to the hall. Maro had remained behind a moment in the wake of my sudden departure, no doubt consoling his lady for the rudeness of her rescuer.

Fearing we might be overheard, I took Pallino by the

arm and leaned in. "There's something amiss here, Pallino. The baroness is far too cavalier for a woman who lost her entire world."

"Ten years ago," Pallino said. "And being trapped down here so long's enough to drive anyone a bit mad."

"She was trying to seduce you," Valka said, appearing between us. "You saw how she reacted to *me*."

"Is she that desperate?" I could hear the wry grin in Pallino's voice, and flashed him a look. It was not the time.

I could only shake my head. "Possibly she thinks her family is done for. With Thagura ruined, maybe she thinks throwing herself at me will save her. I don't know. She could just be putting on a brave face, but circumstances have been so dire here for so long . . . I want you and the men to hold here and keep order. There's bound to be a bit of unrest now these people know the end has come."

"I don't like it, Had. Sending you alone." Pallino placed an arm on my shoulder.

"I'll take the shuttle and link up with Corvo's attack group. Did her message say who had the command? Crim?"

"Aye."

CHAPTER 3
THE SATANIC MILL
⚜

Fires were already burning by the time our shuttle landed on the ice beyond the perimeter of the camps. So far to the north, the sun would not rise for years—so long were Thagura's seasons—and the angry red of the broken Cielcin towers like a forest of malformed trees set the glaciers to gleaming like molten glass.

I had donned my helmet, and so could not smell the burning as the ramp lowered and I hurried down flanked by the two guards I'd allowed Pallino to send with Valka and myself from Pseldona. The unseen energy-curtain of my shield muffled sounds, but still the roar of engines overhead and the blast of weapons shamed any natural thunder I had ever heard.

Our frigate lay ahead, parked on the snows like some quiescent beetle beneath shields of its own. A small fleet of troop landers nestled about it, their holds emptied, snow trampled flat or melted away where our legions had passed. Through the smoke and swirling snow, I could make out the shapes of the rear guard dug in about the ramps with artillery gleaming at the ready.

"By damn, 'tis cold!" Valka swore. "We couldn't have docked with the frigate direct?" She alone of the four of us was not armored, and the cloak she'd taken from the shuttle was hardly enough to keep out the cold.

"Not landed, ma'am," said Oro, the senior of the two guards and the man who'd served as herald on our arrival. "She's a *Roc,* that one. The holds are all along the ventral hull."

"It isn't far!" I said, wrapping an arm and my own cloak about her.

The four of us hurried across the snow. I had to resist the temptation to duck as lightercraft winged overhead. It would have done for the men to see the Halfmortal crouching like some backbench logothete afraid of fire. As we drew near the *Roc*, a trio of men hurried forward from an auxiliary ramp to greet us. Two were legionnaires in red and white, their faces hid. The other was a lieutenant in the blacks of a naval officer, one of the new men the Emperor had assigned me when he'd elevated me to the station of knighthood. She wore a white, fur-lined cloak over her greatcoat and held her matching red beret to her head to keep it from being blown off by the wind.

"It's Bressia, isn't it?" I said, relying on my suit's amplification to boost my voice over the wind. I did not shout.

"Yes, my lord!" the lieutenant replied. "Lieutenant Commander Garone asked me to bring you to him! This way!"

No sooner had the words escaped her lips than a flash of violet light split the polar night like a wedge, and overhead a line of our Sparrowhawk fliers tore toward the camp. One of the Cielcin siege towers—standing like the rockets of uttermost antiquity—had been trying to rise. The roaring we had all been shouting over was the distant fury of ignition as its great engines blazed. The Sparrowhawks' beam weapon had found their mark, and for an instant I stood transfixed upon the snows as that dark tower fell back to ground amidst a nimbus of golden fire fretted red about the edges.

Bressia escorted us up the ramp and through the hold to the bridge, where Karim Garone had taken up command of the assault. Like most of my high officers, Crim had been a mercenary before casting his lot in with my Red Company. A Norman of Jaddian descent, he had spurned the blacks and silvers of the Imperial naval uniform and retained the braided dolman and bright tunic and trousers that were his custom. Even on the bridge of the *Roc,* he wore his shield-belt with its white ceramic saber and a bandoleer that glittered with knives.

His dark face brightened as Valka and I appeared, and he looked up through a holograph map of the field of battle.

"You made it, boss," he said, straightening. "We've crippled what fleet they had. Bombed the landing field."

I returned the commander's lazy salute, ignored the momentary stiffness and quietude of the lesser officers in the command post. Many of them had never seen me before. Thagura was our first mission under the Imperial banner, and while the senior staff was composed of *my* people, the Normans who had fought for me at Vorgossos, the bulk of our personnel were Imperial levies, men and women assigned me by the Emperor when he gifted me the *Tamerlane.* Almost I felt their eyes crawling over me, examining every line of my face and of the black *lorica* and sculpted black armor that had been another gift from the Emperor.

"I saw your work," I said.

Crim smiled. "Small good escape would have done them. Those siege towers aren't warp-capable. If they'd gotten to orbit, they'd have had nowhere to go."

Still I felt eyes on me, and glanced round at the junior men at their duty stations. In the brief silence I heard one whisper, "Halfmortal."

I flashed a glare in his direction, and he turned

hurriedly back to his work. Approaching Crim by the central podium where the map gleamed, I said, "What of the camps?"

"Petros took his chiliad around to the east," Crim said, and pointed, highlighting where the Cielcin had erected a palisade of overlapping plates. Guard towers—more landed rockets, I deemed—stood at intervals along the wall. "Sword Flight's hammering the towers."

"When did you engage?" Valka asked, coming to my side.

Crim answered, "Three minutes past two, ship time." I checked my wrist-terminal. That was nearly half an hour before.

"Gravitometers are showing huge pits bored into the ice beneath several of the buildings." The commander gestured at a number of red highlighted cylinders thrust deep into the glacier.

I heard Valka's frown in her voice. "Geothermal sinks?"

"Maybe?" Crim replied. "If they are, they're not lighting up on thermal imaging. Might be shielded."

"Or something else entirely," I said darkly, glancing from the projection to the thin stripe of window that ran along the forward wall of the bridge. Smoke rose in a mighty wave from the burning camp, and the firelight flooded through that horizontal slash of a window like blood from an open wound. "Are there captives?"

Crim followed my gaze. "I'm not sure. That's why Sword Flight's sticking to the towers. Dascalu and Ulpio took their chiliads straight forward, toward the south wall. Here." Again he pointed, highlighting the alien palisade directly between the landed fleet and the camp proper.

"They're to keep the Pale from breaking through and taking a run at us. Petros is there—on the east as I said. One of the groups will get through. If there's anyone still alive, we'll find them." He met my eye, and his face hardened until it seemed as stone as Aram's colossus. "How was the city?"

"Gone," I said. "The Pale blasted it from orbit. Atomics, maybe. Plasma. I'm not sure."

"Noyn jitat." Crim exhaled. "Earth rot their bones."

Valka gripped the rail of the console podium. "Perhaps there are survivors."

"We can hope!" Crim said, and wheeled round to stride up the central aisle toward the window and the spot where the helmsman's and navigator's stations stood, one hand on the hilt of his sword. "M. Irber! What of those towers?"

A dark-haired ensign at one of the tactical displays raised his voice in reply. "Just need a little more pressure and time, sir. There are seven on the eastern perimeter still firing. Sword Flight's swinging round."

Drumming his fingers against the hilt of his sword, Crim said, "Righteous."

"Fifth Chiliad's pinned down on the ice, though," Irber continued. "Towers Twelve and Thirteen have clear lines of fire on their approach."

"Raise First Sword," Crim said, turning to join Irber by his console. "Order his wing to concentrate fire on those towers. I want Petros to have a clear line against those walls."

Valka leaned toward me and asked, "First Sword?"

"The aquilarii," I said, meaning the fliers. When we were but mercenaries in the Norman Expanse, we had

had no air force of our own, no lighters. Though Valka had
been a ship's captain in her youth, that had been for the
Tavros Orbital Guard, and their ways were not our own.
"Their wing leader."

While Irber relayed his orders to the wing commander,
I brushed past the holograph podium and stalked toward
the window. Another flash of violet light cracked the sky
and bled its color on all creation.

My first *real* battle.

Not my first brush with violence. That had come in the
streets of Meidua when I was young. Nor was it my first
encounter with Death. She had visited my father's house
when I was just a boy, had taken my grandmother from
me. For an instant, my eyes reflected in the smoky
alumglass seemed to become her eyes, preserved forever
in the blue fluid of the canopic jar I'd carried to our
necropolis in her funeral train. And I had known war, had
ventured beneath Emesh and into the bowels of
Vorgossos—and into the howling Dark that awaits us all.

But I was a knight then, and at forty *finally* a man,
though by rights my ephebeia ought to have happened half
my life before. Before I had led of necessity, led because I
alone possessed the *pothos,* the *vision:* my *dream* of peace.
But that was—quite literally—another life. That dream
had died with Aranata's prisoners of war, and with me. On
Thagura and after, I led because I needed to. I had a duty,
and a purpose, and a mystery to solve.

Understanding why the Quiet had restored my life
required that I serve the Emperor, for I knew the
Emperor possessed knowledge of that ancient race, and
that he alone might command his magi to illuminate me.

And I fought because it was right, or so I told myself, consoling myself while the screams of Aranata's prisoners resounded in the vaults of my mind.

"Are you all right?"

Valka had come up beside me, was peering up into my face with her luminous yellow eyes. How strange it was— even then—to see softness on a face so long hardened and sharp as glass. We had not begun our acquaintance well. She had thought me simple, a barbarian, and despised me for it, as she had despised the Empire I called home. After so many years of coldness and disdain, seeing concern on her hard but lovely face was like returning for the first time to a place in spring that one has only ever known in winter.

"I'm fine," I said, responding in her own tongue so we might not be overheard. "I've never really commanded an army before."

"'Tis not so!" she said, smoothing the cloak over my shoulders. "You led the charge from the *Schiavona*. You saved all those people."

I took her cold hand in my gloved one. "That was different."

"'Twas not."

"I didn't have a choice, then. I didn't have time to think about it."

One corner of her mouth lifted in wry bemusement. "And now you have the time for thinking you are not so sure?"

A short laugh escaped me, and I looked round to see what eyes were on us. There were none. The helmsman's station and the navigator's were both empty with the ship grounded as it was. Another flash of violet cut the night, and the distant thunder boiled as the earth shook and Irber shouted, "That's Tower Twelve!"

When I did not reply, she turned me fully to face her and leaned against the console. "These people's lives are in my hands, Valka," I said. "This *planet* is in my hands."

"'Tis what you wanted, is it not?" she arched an eyebrow. "A purpose?"

What man is a man who wants less?

Or more.

She glared up at me, eyes truly glass, bright as crystal. Reaching out, I took her hand. "I wanted peace."

"And if you can't have it?"

I found I could no longer look her in the eye. I could not say what I was thinking. The words would not gel. Perhaps I had no words at all then. I have them now. There will always be peace. It is only a question of when. War is energy, and energy runs down. The universe returns to rest, and whether that rest comes without any conflict or *after* it is another matter entirely.

"We will have peace," I said, and stooped to kiss her. She did not shy away.

I did not say, *One way or another.*

Smoke rose from the field like a swarm of locusts, like a shoal of black fish writhing before the diver. Crim and Valka had both objected when I announced my intentions to join our chiliads in the camp: Crim because his commandant should not risk his life in what still an active war zone, and Valka because I ordered her to stay behind.

"We have no armor for you!" I told her, though armor

might perhaps be found aboard the frigate. In truth I could not risk her. Valka had been a soldier once—of a sort. But she had been a ship's officer, and known only one battle—and that had been brief. What was more, but for our ill-fated adventure on Vorgossos, she had never known personal combat, never fought an enemy she could see. She had no experience leading men and fighting tooth and claw, blade-to-blade with the enemies of man.

The camp towers were like guttering torches staked about the camp. To our left—where the snowdrifts piled high against the palisade—one had fallen entirely, and the blue lightning of ruined circuitry spat in the frozen air.

Our shadows danced tall and shapeless on the red snows ahead as we hurried forward, cast by the great lamps on our landers. Crim had ordered thirty hoplites for my escort, and not far ahead a full century—mixed light and shielded infantry—hurried toward the shattered gates. The violet crash of hydrogen plasma and silent flash of beam weapons resounded ahead with the mingled cries of human and inhuman voices. The men around me might have been living statues, faceless and precise in their movement, communicating on direct bands or my brisk signs. Above us, the knife-shapes of Sparrowhawk fliers with their single, solitary wings circled slowly now, floodlights shaming the great burning all around.

I might have been alone in all that movement—the only true person on Thagura—were it not for the screaming, for the occasional noise on the comm line.

"Up ahead! On the right!"

"—get a clear line on the target!"

"Form up, men! Form up!"

"Th—think the bastards fired on some of their own ships!"

"You seeing this?"

"The walls! Earth and Emperor! The walls!"

This last came from one of the men in my guard. We'd come to just within a stone's throw of the palisade then, the heads of our shadows just tickling the base of the metal wall. The alien structure had been erected without any intention of permanence, though it might have stood for years. It was fashioned of great interlinked sheaves of metal-like leaves—like the scales of some unholy terror—each crowned with a row of spikes perhaps a cubit high.

What I had taken at first for misshapen deposits of snow at the base of each snapped then into focus.

"They're heads!" cried one man behind me.

"Mother deliver us," another said.

I have seen men beheaded. Hanged. Whipped. Put up in stocks before the halls of justice on a dozen Imperial worlds. I have seen the corpses of rebels hanged, seen criminals branded. I know man is no angel. But the faces leering down at us had been savaged. Cheeks flapped, torn open to the ear, eyes were missing or else hung by slender cords. Scalps were torn or torn away entirely, and every face bore the mark of teeth and talon.

It was the contrast, I decided much later. It was the contrast that was the thing. The will that had set so many heads upon that wall and raised that wall in the first place was like our own. It had taken intelligence to build the camp and the rockets that encircled it, an understanding of nature's laws. But it was an animal's savagery that had done the rest, and worse . . . for the blood was frozen and dried.

They had not done this thing to frighten *us*, had not intended any statement, any warning. They had done this for themselves, and only for themselves.

This black thought hounded me as we reached the level of the ruined gate and passed beneath the watchless gaze of that broken humanity. One of the Sparrowhawks slewed overhead, drifting on its repulsors, its gunner picking targets from the camp ahead with admirable precision.

"Dead ahead!" cried the decurion on point before me. "Fire! Fire!"

I saw what he had seen an instant later. One of the longhouses stood dead ahead, and indeed five of them converged on a yard just within the gate like the spokes of a wheel. The doors of the foremost longhouse stood open, and lit by the fires that blazed within, a dozen warriors stood tall and thin and terrible as Death herself. Taller than any man they were, but narrower in the shoulder and longer of limb, like shadows themselves stretched by the light of dying sun. In the red light of war, they gray-slick armor might have been green, but their pale faces—white as chalk, as bone—shone terribly even at this distance. Even as we drew near, one among leaped toward our men who'd gone before and laid into them with its scimitar tall as a man. The milk blade flashed, crashed through the shields of two hoplites—left, right— for there is no shield which man has made sensitive enough to turn back the meager energies of a sword blow.

Two men fell dying, and the beast that slew them fell

an instant later as a dozen plasma rounds struck its face and chest. My own chest tightened as the memories of war came flooding back, but I clamped down on my fast-galloping heart, clenched my unkindled blade in my fist.

Where that first warrior fell, two more leaped into place, each wielding not the milky blades of their kind, but whips like braided cords of silver, which they uncoiled and—whirling above their heads—let fly.

"Snakes!" cried one of the men about me in warning.

The silver whips writhed through the air between our party and theirs fast as any arrow, rolling on repulsors. I squeezed the twin triggers of my blade and raised the weapon in reflexive guard as they slithered in among us, swimming through the air chest high. The blade shone blue-white as distant stars amidst the angry reds of all that burning, and the exotic material rippled as the liquid metal blade shaped and reshaped itself with every motion.

"Hadrian!" Valka's voice sounded in my ear from where I'd left her on the *Roc*'s bridge. "Hadrian, what's happening?"

"Nahute!" I said, drawing my blade high. They were machines, the weapon of a Cielcin berserker, flying snakes whose steel and diamond maws clamped, lamprey-like, to their prey and drilled into them, seeking the heat of a man's body and center mass. How many men have I seen chewed and hollowed out by such weapons? How many thousand?

Our shields would buy us time, and indeed I saw the first drone strike straight for one hoplite's face and rebound as his energy-curtain repelled the shot, but they would snake among us, would worm their way in slowly, through the shield, and do their lethal harm. Fast as they were and slim, they were tricky targets for any man with lance or plasma burner, and they were then among us.

My men were too close. I could not strike at the drones without carving through them, and nothing save adamant and highmatter itself could stop that highmatter blade. One man screamed as one of the *nahute* pierced his shield and found a gap in his armor. Red blood smoked in the freezing air as his suit's integrity failed.

"Spread out!" I shouted, waving my sword above my head. "Spread out and fire on the Cielcin! Fire on the Cielcin!"

The men all moved to obey me, and the xenobites pouring from the longhouse ahead began falling, but not before many threw *nahute* of their own. The drones flashed among us, and leaping aside I struck one in half with my blade while above, the torch-beam of one of the Sparrowhawks passed overhead, so that the snows of the yard—trampled gray by so much traffic—shone hard-edged in every detail. Shots rained down from above as the belly-gunner picked his targets.

Beside me, another man fell screaming, wrestling with one of the serpent-drones as it bored into his side. I ran to him, seized the tail of the horror as it wriggled in deeper. The dying man looked up at me, and from the angle of his blank visor I knew he was staring straight into my eyes. Though I pulled, I knew I could not get the snake free, and the poor bastard went limp an instant later.

When he was gone, the drone slid out easily, but before its spiral maw could turn to strike at me, I slashed it clean in half.

The skirmish had ended without my notice. The bodies of men and xenobites littered the yard or else lay piled by the doors of the burning longhouse. Shaking the blood from my hydrophobic cape, I straightened beside the body of the dead man and—blade still burning cold in my fist—stumped to that open portal.

Safe in my suit, I had no fear for air, and on account of the fires there was sufficient light to see what lay within.

The bodies to which I guessed the heads belonged hung skinned and bound by their ankles, their blood left to drain through a kind of grate laid upon the floor. There must have been hundreds of them in that longhouse alone, each hanging like some hideous fruit. Many had their arms missing, and so little resembled men or women at all, but those who did hung down from on high, trailing like a forest of kelp from the floor of some grasping sea.

I turned away as quickly as I could, and was glad of my mask and helmet to hide the sickness and horror in my face. Still sensing that something was amiss with me, one of my decurions came and put a hand on my shoulder. Voice amplified by the speakers in his suit, he asked, "My lord? Are you all right?"

I wanted to vomit, but found the words instead. "This isn't a camp," I said, choking. I had known intellectually, had known all my life, that the Cielcin devoured the flesh of men, had seen the frenzy fall on Aranata's prisoners aboard the *Demiurge*. But to see so many lives ended, so many human persons treated with such systematic industry . . . it was a horror unlike anything I had faced, more terrible even than the Brethren who dwelt beneath the waters of Vorgossos.

"This isn't a camp," I said again, more strongly. "It's a slaughterhouse."

CHAPTER 4
DEATH BY WATER
⚜

As much as my instincts demanded that I let the fires burn, I could not do so. An examination would need to be made of the camp, holographs and phototypes recorded, samples collected for study. Despite four hundred years of war, there was much—too much—of the enemy we did not understand. Though I speak their tongue and though I'd set out to understand them and make peace, there was too much I did not understand.

Such horrors as that camp there are in human history, but they are only shadows. Imitations of the deeper horrors and depredations of the Pale. The Cielcin have no compassion. I know that now, though I then hoped it might prove otherwise. If they extend mercy, it is because they require something still of those shown mercy. If they surrender, it is ever with the thought of revenge. Often I have wondered if they may truly be called evil, for a tiger—as I have said—is only hungry when it hunts and slaughters man.

When I doubt, I return to that camp.

The heads on the walls had been placed facing *inward*, peering down at the survivors laboring in that living hell. The lips of many had been cut away, or torn by inhuman fangs, so that they smiled on the men and women below. The whole palisade was a cruel mockery, a vicious jape and reminder that those within its bounds were never going home. And when I think of this, my doubts within vanish like mist before the sun.

Evil *is*.

The tiger is not cruel, nor the tidal wave. The meteor is blind and the solar flare heedless as it burns. Men are cruel—and beasts sometimes, yes—but they are men. And the Cielcin are Cielcin. What peace is there to brook between predator and prey?

"My lord?" inquired a rough voice over the comms. I recognized the voice of Dascalu, one of my new chiliarchs. An instant later his name and ident code flickered in one corner of my suit's entoptics.

I was standing in the middle of the yard just inside the ruined gate, snow and smoke roiling all about me. Above, a trio of our *Ibis* shuttles circled, repulsors gleaming blue against the polar dark. Fire retardant fell like rain from nozzles in their underside, and slowly the conflagration began to ebb.

"My lord?" Dascalu's voice intruded again. "My lord, you should see this!"

Shaken from some dissociated reverie, I at first mistook Dascalu for one of the men around me, and said in reply, "No one should see this."

There were still intermittent sounds of fighting in the middle distance as our troops encountered a new knot of the enemy barricaded in some outbuilding or in the tunnels we were just starting to find beneath the ice. A staccato burst of gunfire sounded just then, as if to punctuate my reply.

"What's that, my lord?" asked the decurion next to me.

Realizing my mistake, I shook my head, keyed the comm response. "What is it, chiliarch?"

Dascalu's response came after the barest hesitation. "We're in the southmost of those domes along the western wall of the complex. We've found . . . well, I don't know what we've found. Some kind of monument?"

"Monument?" I echoed the word. "What do you mean?"

"That's what it looks like. Petros said I should call it in."

An image appeared in one corner of my display. I studied it a move, stomach turning over. "I'll be right there," I said. "Forward your images to Dr. Onderra at the command post." Turning to the men of my guard, I gestured that they should follow and began crossing the yard. The men had piled the bodies of the enemy in a great mound in the center of the yard formed by the five slaughterhouses, and the few dozen of our dead had been laid in neat rows along one side. Moving toward the domes—which were visible just over the flat roofs of the longhouses—I switched comm channels, broadcasting to all battle groups. "What news of survivors?"

"Negative, my lord," came Petros's reply.

"Nothing yet," said Dascalu.

"No sign," replied Ulpio.

We passed between two of the slaughterhouses and turned right, following a path of compacted snow past what I guessed was the intake for the longhouse in question. My mind sketched the images of men and women in rags herded barefoot and bloody through the shutters then closed.

"Holy Mother Earth, have you ever seen such an awful place?" one of the men at my back muttered, voice flattened by his suit.

I could only shake my head.

The camp was not large, covered perhaps a dozen hectares, perhaps two. The palisade with its row of ruined heads encircled the thing entire, buttressed by the then blasted or fallen shapes of the siege towers. The gate by which we'd entered—the gate nearest the slaughter-houses—had been nearest the broader landing field, whence more of the alien landing craft now smoldered, the first casualty of our assault. Later reports would funnel in of similar camps, all of them clustered in the north polar region where the sun then little shone, for the Cielcin were creatures of the subterrane, reared in caverns beneath the skin of their homeworld, and their eyes little loved the light.

Beyond the far end of the longhouses, a series of squat towers marched. These were the lower segments of siege rockets, I realized, pods dropped by the xenobites to serve as housing units for the xenobites themselves, for the slaves and slave-soldiers of Prince Muzugara whose job it was to tend the prisoners and administer the camp itself.

"Why couldn't they build somewhere warmer?" one of the men muttered, trying not to be overheard by me. "Thagura's half desert, ain't it?"

"Cold's got to be hell on the prisoners," another man agreed.

"They aren't prisoners," I said. "They're food. Did you not see the bodies?"

The men went deadly quiet behind me. My brother

Crispin's voice resounded in my ears, his old question. *Is it true the Cielcin are cannibals?*

Cannibals they were, and worse. Anthropophagi.

"Enough talk," I said, voice dark and flat through my suit speakers. I turned to face the men, who—deadly quiet—went deathly still. "This is not a camp. Do you understand? It is a *ranch*. This camp is meant to dress provisions for the Cielcin fleet. When I said it is a slaughterhouse, I meant it is an *abattoir*. The Thaguran population was brought here, *processed*, and shipped to the Cielcin fleet. That is why they have been here for these ten years." I shook my head. "We will not find many survivors. Hundreds, perhaps thousands on all this world."

The men made no reply, but shifted awkwardly where they stood. One ducked his head.

I turned away.

Half a dozen domes, each some five hundred feet in diameter, stood along the western wall of the camp complex. Snow covered each of them, but here and there that shroud lay cracked, broken by the ridges in the dark material beneath it. I felt certain that these were built of the same interleaving plates as the outer palisade, a light and quick construction designed to provide rapid protection from the snow and wind. Thagura was warmer than Earth of old had been, but still the ceaseless winters of that frozen north froze deep enough to kill in hours.

More inhuman bodies littered the approach to the low slit of an entrance, and more of our men stood armed and vigilant along the path. The snow there was trampled black by so much foot traffic, and a broad, shallow sort of gully ran down to the rim of the dome, where a sort of tunnel led beneath the dome itself and inside.

What doors there might have been were gone, blasted to shrapnel by the breaching charges my men had used to get inside. Picking my way over the tangled limbs that clogged the descent, I passed under the shadow of the arch. The walls to either side were carved from the polar ice and studded with bits of alien electronica whose functions I could only guess at. Ribbed cables ran along the walls and across the floor. The tunnel turned sharply right, following the curvature of the dome overhead. The few lights that yet functioned were red and dim as dying suns, and my suit's entoptics boosted the image projected on my eyes to compensate, contrast sharpening until the hall seemed a simulacrum of itself; unreal.

Seeing how cramped the confines were, I turned to my men. "Decurion, you and your men with me. The others will wait here and guard the entrance." I did not wait for his reply.

Catching sight of me in my black mask and armor, one of the legionnaires in the hall thumped his compatriot, and the two stood straighter. A third hurried forward. "Lord Marlowe, the chiliarch sent me to retrieve you."

"Where is he?" I asked.

"Just inside," the man said, saluting a little late. "This way."

Turning, he led us past more stationed men and over more bodies, following the icy corridor along its gentle curve. The hall slanted steadily down, deeper into the ice, and I felt certain the air must be bitter cold. Half a dozen men waited at an inner door below, and stepped aside at my approach.

The image I had seen briefly on my mask's display greeted me at the bottom of the stairs. We had come out beneath the black metal of the dome, and from beneath its structure it revealed itself like the petals of some venomous flower, black and razor-edged. The apex must have been two hundred feet above our heads, and all about us the native ice rose twice the height of a man to where the spiked foundation posts of the dome rested in the planet's surface.

The Cielcin had melted a space for themselves beneath the dome and I spied a number of side passages that led to further tunnels, doubtless connecting to the other domes that lined the western edge of the camp. About the walls were stacked barrels wrought of some gray cousin of plastic and heavy crates marked with alien runes. Dead ahead, in the center of the room, a steep-sided pit—like a well—opened in the icy floor; great chains, hung from cranes bracketed to the dome above, descended into the shaft. I might have wondered at their purpose had I not been distracted by the horror erected along the wall opposite.

"Holy Mother Earth, deliver us," hissed I, who did not pray.

Skulls lined the wall opposite, set in a broad arc that must have circled a full third of the circumference of that chamber beneath the dome. Each was polished clean of flesh and shone in the low light. Inhuman hands had set them there, and stacked them high and neatly, rank upon rank, their hollow eyes staring down at me, asking, *accusing*.

What took you so long?

Each had been nailed to the ice wall of the chamber, pinned through the back of the head. The sculpture—for sculpture it surely was—rose two dozen heads high in the center, where a central column, undulating, rose from the ranks massed about the base. These rose like a wave of skulls above the tide, like a serpent standing, ready to strike.

For the second time that day, I thought I might wretch, and shut fast my eyes against the sheer *number* of them. There must have been thousands.

"My lord!" A familiar voice startled me from my horror, and opening my eyes I found the chiliarch, Dascalu, hurrying toward me. "We called as soon as we were sure the dome was secure." He gestured at the wall of bones. "What is it?"

I could only shake my head.

I had never seen anything like it before, not on Emesh, not on Vorgossos. Ice crunched under my feet as I circled the pit toward the effigy. Beneath my mask, my mouth hung open. I felt increasingly sure that I was looking at some crude impression of a snake. The Cielcin had placed each skull with care, with reverence, with malefic intent. Curling tendrils snaked from the central column like arms, coiled across the surface of the ice, each wrought from femurs and tibias and the long bones of arms.

For what felt then the hundredth time that day, I thought I might be sick.

"I don't know," I said at last, when Dascalu asked again.

How little I knew of the enemy then. A knight I might have been, and cloaked in Imperial favor, but I was a boy of forty little years, and for all my reputation, I was ignorant as all children are. When I had left Delos, I imagined peace. I had not imagined places like that camp, or horrors like that grim effigy. I would see such sculptures many times, on many worlds.

They never got easier to see.

"They piled what looks like spoils from the people here," the chiliarch said, gesturing to a pile of rags and various oddments high as a man that lay mounded between the arms of the macabre display. "But that isn't all." He pointed—as I knew he must—at the pit. Dascalu shook his head. "My lord, I . . ."

I raised a hand to quiet him. I didn't need to hear.

Black water waited at the bottom of the pit, its surface disturbed by the movement of something unseen within it. The Cielcin had melted a shaft down into the glacier—it must have been twenty feet to the dark surface.

"Is there a light?" I asked.

"Torch!" Dascalu shouted, casting about.

One of the men at hand produced a glowsphere about the size of a grapefruit and passed it to the chiliarch, who handed it with deference to me. Without comment, I pulled the tab. The thing vibrated and flared in my hand, and a cold, white light fierce and several times brighter than the alien lamps filled the domed chamber. Not engaging the lamp's repulsor, I let it fall. The light vanished down the shaft, hit the surface with a distant *splash*.

The waters churned as things pale and eel-like swam away from the light. The glowsphere sank like a fallen star, illuminating the waters.

Those waters were not black at all, but *red*.

"Those things aren't native, are they?" Dascalu asked.

"I'm not sure," I told him, studying the monsters. Each was about as long as a man's arm, and milk-white. "Valka?"

Her voice sounded in my ear. "I'll look."

But I didn't need her answer. I knew. They were Cielcin creatures, some species of fishlike organism brought from the circle of some dark star.

"What are they for?" the chiliarch asked.

The glowsphere had reached the bottom of the shaft then, had settled on the bottom. Its white light had colored pink from the waters below. How deep those waters were was hard to say. It might have been half a hundred feet. That redness was clue enough, but I knew what I would find at the bottom, and sure enough, there they were.

More bones lay mounded at the base of that shaft, stripped as clean as the ones mounted to the wall.

I drew back, overtook by a vision of men and women crowded into this place and forced into the waters a dozen at a time. Had they been living when their Cielcin captors fed them to their worms? Or were these the castoffs? The men and women not fit for the slaughterhouses or for a life in chains aboard Muzugara's ships?

"We'll need to get a science team in here," I said. "Radio Captain Corvo and the rest as soon as you're sure the compound is secure. Ask for Varro and his best."

I heard Dascalu salute, but did not turn to look at him.

"Would that we'd come sooner," I said to no one in particular.

"'Twas no way we could have done," Valka said into my ear. "We came as swiftly as we were able."

I bit my lip. "I know," I said, and wrapped my fingers around one of the frosted chains that ran down into the horrid pit.

Dascalu had not left my side, and I found him peering down with me. Presently he ventured a question. "How many do you think there are down there?"

"We have no idea how deep it goes," I said, eyes moving back to the serpentine icon wrought of human bones. "And all these must have been down there, once." A terrible thought occurred to me, and I asked, "Is it the same with the other domes?"

Dascalu's silence confirmed my deepest fears.

"But why?" I asked, shaking my head. "Have you ever heard of anything like this?"

"No, my lord," the man replied, glad to have a less weighty question to answer.

I thought I knew them. The thought kept rebounding in my head. *I thought I knew them.* Since I had been a boy, learning their inhuman tongue at Tor Gibson's knee, I had dreamed of traveling among the xenobites, among the pale Cielcin who wander the stars in ships like homeless moons. I had read everything in our limited collection there was to read on their culture, their biology. What little we men knew we knew from war. From the hulks that littered our star systems or broke upon our shores when their raids had come and gone. Though our two kinds had warred for centuries, there was much—so much—we had yet to learn. But for a few symbols, their written language was still a mystery, and though we knew their weapons and their warships, understood their tactics, much of their culture, their literature, their art, remained obscure. I might have been one of our Empire's foremost authorities on the enemy, but I knew too little.

We all did, in those days.

"Look out!" A shout shocked me back into my body, and turning I saw a hulking, black shape leap into the central chamber from a side passage, its white sword flashing in the misty air. Two men fell before it, weapons discharging, punching holes in the surrounding ice. One shot grazed a conduit, and power sparked and died, plunging all the low, red lamps the xenobites had fixed to the walls into stygian black. Only the distant shine of the glowsphere at the bottom of the pit lit the chamber, and by its glow I saw another trio of Cielcin cut their way into the room. One tackled an armored centurion to the ground, pinning his arms like an aggressive lover as it lowered its fangy jaws to tear out the man's throat.

Conscious of the pit at my back, I darted to one side, circling right to hit the intruders from the side. I ignored Valka's questions ringing in my ears and snapped my sword from its magnetic hasp. Dascalu had moved to follow me, and the few of my guard who had stayed with me scrambled to adjust their bearings.

One of the Cielcin hurled its *nahute* toward us, and my men fired at it before the chiliarch roared. "Bayonets! Bayonets, hold your fire!" That stray shot had, after all, destroyed the dome's lights. A second *nahute* flew at us, and its owner chased after it, sword drawn to strike at the men before me. My guardsman raised his energy-lance to parry the alien scimitar, and he twisted, struck the monster with the butt of that lance.

The Cielcin staggered against the wall, huge black eyes

glaring. With its sword it battered the man's lance aside
and slashed at his neck even as the *nahute* drone impacted
the man's shield, disorienting him. The soldier fell like a
toppled tower, head striking the ice wall. Not realizing he
was already fallen, the *nahute* found a chink in his armor
and burrowed its way in.

The xenobite's eyes found mine and, blade dripping, it
advanced on me. *"Tuka yukajjimn!"* it barked in its rough
tongue. *"Tuka eja-ayan!"*

You are vermin! It said. *You are nothing!*

"Nothing?" I echoed, repeating the word. *"Eja-ayan?*
You have lost! Surrender!"

In answer, the tall xenobite bounded toward me,
raising its sword. I raised my own, fingers squeezing the
triggers to kindle the liquid metal blade. The highmatter
fountained from the hilt, pentaquark nuclei locking into
place. The Cielcin blade descended, met mine without
resistance. The alien blade sheared clean in half, and the
part that should have struck my head clattered against my
shoulder. For an instant, the xenobite stood clutching its
stump of a sword, black eyes confused. I guessed it had
never seen highmatter before, did not know it was dead.

My own blade rose and fell, bit into the monster's
shoulder and slid clean through from collarbone to the
opposite hip. The creature fell in two pieces, and I
stepped into the space it had occupied a moment before,
bloodless weapon gleaming in my fist. The two behind it
stumbled back, adjusting to this new development. One
launched its *nahute* at me, while the other uncoiled its
drone and cracked it like the whip it so resembled.

Reflex made me draw back, recoiling even as Dascalu

and the hoplite at my side moved forward, lances aimed
at the small knot of survivors who had burst into the room.
I held the right flank by the wall, with Dascalu at my left
and more of the men hemming them in. There was
shouting and a tight burst of plasma fire—despite the
chiliarch's orders—as the men at my left slew the *nahute*
the enemy had let fly.

"Where did they come from?" the decurion asked.

"I don't know!" Dascalu answered. "We swept the
dome! I swear it!"

Our men had encircled the remaining Cielcin then.
They had nowhere to go but back along the side passage
whence they'd come. Thus cornered, trapped on Thagura,
their ships burned, their fleet fled to the outer Dark, they
had nothing but to give up their lives.

"No matter!" I shouted.

There were seven of them left. Seven against the sons
of man. Seven against Earth.

The fighting stilled then, if only for a moment as either
side measured the other. The Cielcin were all taller than
us, slim and crowned with horn. The tallest among
them—an officer of some kind—must have been eight
feet high. The lesser berserkers wore versions of the gray-
green armor the warriors above had worn. If the cold
bothered them, they gave no sign, each crouching,
adjusting their posture, daring us to attack.

The fighting would be over in instants if we could be
sure of our aim, but I understood Dascalu's caution. We
outnumbered the Pale at least three-to-one in the
chamber, and more men were not far. We had only to
summon reinforcements.

"Take them alive if you can!" I said, surprising the men about me.

"Sir?"

"You heard me!" I said, then barked a word to the xenobites. *"Svassaa!"*

Surrender!

"Surrender?" the officer echoed. "There is no surrender!"

"You will die here!" I replied, wary of the discomfort the inhuman words coming from my lips placed in the hearts of the men about me, but I had studied their tongue since I was a boy, and though no man may speak it properly, I spoke it as well then as any man could.

The officer held its *nahute* limp in one hand. "We are dead already! Our prince is gone!"

"He abandoned you!" I agreed, adjusting my guard. "But surrender and I will permit you to die honorably. You may take your own lives, so that you did not die at the hands of us *yukajjimn."*

The thought seemed to tempt the xenobite for a moment. The officer hesitated, hands slackening on its weapons. Its round, black eyes searched for some evidence of my eyes in the black sculpted mask that hid them. It did not find them. "Those are not our orders."

"Damn your orders!" I said, and said again, *"Svassaa!"*

The officer flinched—a curiously human motion. "We are Cielcin," it said. "Cielcin obey."

"Your prince does not!" I replied. "He commands! And he is gone."

Still the officer hesitated, and only then did I mark the wound on one temple above the narrow hole that served it for an ear. Ichor dark as ink ran down the far side of its face. Sensing that I had knocked it back a step, I continued, "You have the command of these." I gestured with my sword at the others. "Are you not now their prince? Do you not now command?"

"*Dunyasu!*" one of the others roared. "The worm speaks blasphemy! Mutiny against our master!"

"I have a shot!" interjected one of Dascalu's lancers.

"*Dunyasu!*" another of the lesser warriors agreed. "Don't listen to it, Emasu! It lies like all its kind!"

"I have a shot!" the lancer shouted again.

The underlings chose for us. The two who had cried out *dunyasu*—*abomination*—leaped forward like gargoyles from the buttresses of a chantry. I jumped aside as one bowled into Dascalu, knocking the chiliarch from his feet. The violet flash of an energy beam felled one of the others, and in the next instant I saw the officer, Emasu, fall as invisible light scorched its shoulder.

I cursed, and ran my sword through a swung *nahute* as one of the warriors whirled the serpent-drone over its head. Another cut stole the legs from under the demon, and it fell, blood smoking where it met the ice. My own bootheels crunched, and I slipped as a third stroke took the head from the downed creature. My knee struck the ground, and I groaned as Valka hissed a sympathetic word in my ear.

The fighting was done as I stood, reduced to a blurring of slow movement on the ground as the dying died. Dascalu had emerged victorious, clutched a bloody knife in his off hand as he staggered back to his feet.

"Give that to me!" I ordered him, and the chiliarch did

not argue. I snatched the bodkin from him, held it reversed, with the blade flat against my arm.

Unkindling my sword, I went to the wounded officer, and seizing it by its horn forced it to look into my masked face.

"You are dying," I said flatly, voice amplified by my suit. "You may yet die well. Answer me: What is this place? What is it for?"

Emasu blinked up at me, nictitating membranes flicking vertically across its eyes. Confusion? Surprise? *"Paqami wo,"* it said. *We must eat.*

The thought of men hanging skinned and headless in neat rows flared whitely in my chest, and straightening I released the demon's horn and pressed the heel of my boot against its wounded shoulder. Emasu winced, and before it could move I pointed the emitter end of my unkindled blade in its face. "The pit!" I said, leaning my weight onto my foot. "The statue! Explain!"

Emasu's eyes went to the sculpture of bones, the many-armed serpent rising along the interior of the dome, almost to the metal leaves that formed the roof over our heads. *"Miudanar!"* it said. "The Dreamer!"

"Your god?" I asked. I had never seen any of the Cielcin gods rendered in art before. Had never seen any art from them save the round glyphs—like clusters of bubbles—that passed for calligraphy among their kind.

In answer, the officer groaned. "His is the time before time, and the time after it."

Emasu hissed as my heel dug into its wound. "You killed my people to make an idol?"

"Veih!" the officer said. "No! These were the scraps.

The leavings, and those who could not work, or would not serve to nurse our young."

Behind my mask, I blinked. "Your young?" But I shook my head. It didn't matter. I held Dascalu's knife up for the officer to see. My meaning clear, I pressed, "Are there survivors? More of my kind?"

Emasu eyed the blade with emotions I could not name. Longing, perhaps? Disgust? Relief? "We could not kill you all. Belowground. There are pens." It jerked its head back the way it had come, down the side passage that had been sealed before the assault. "We waste nothing. Even your kind has its purpose!"

I pressed harder, and the officer cried out in pain. I didn't care. The hollow eyes of so many thousands glared down at me—I hoped—in gratitude and belated triumph. "You wasted plenty when you torched the city. How many millions died that day?"

"We didn't burn the city! That was you!" Emasu tried to sit up, and snarling I stomped it back into its place, making the men about me fumble anxiously with their lances. "We would have sucked it dry if we could. Taken our fill and fled! But our fleet was starving! We could not leave without our fill, and your kind breeds but slowly! We could not replace what you took from us that day!"

Emasu's words rattled me to the bone, and I *did* stagger back then, reeling as I turned my back. "They didn't burn the city," I said numbly, speaking so the other men would understand. The full horror of what it was saying—that they had forced the human captives to breed more food, that they required us to help *nurse* their young—was lost for me in that moment beneath the

weight of this *other* revelation. "They didn't burn the city,"
I said again.

Malyan did.

I thought of the devastation we'd seen in Pseldona,
the ruins of the city stretching for miles across the shelf
above the desert, blackened, sand burned to glass. If
what the monster said was true, it was not the xenobites
who had wrought that devastation, but the very woman
whose duty and sacred charge it had been to defend that
city with her life.

"My lord, look out!" Dascalu exclaimed, raising his
lance to fire.

Whirling, I found Emasu half-risen to its feet, claws
extending from its six-fingered hands like so many knives,
teeth bared and black with blood. It never found its footing.
Before it could stand, a dozen men discharged energy
beams into its body, sending up faint coils of white smoke
in the dim air. Dead, the officer teetered a moment and fell
back where it had lain a moment before. Disgusted, I raised
Dascalu's knife and hurled it into the body. To my surprise,
the blade stuck in the xenobite's throat.

A sudden need for air overcame me, and I clawed at
my helmet. The casque broke apart and folded away into
the neck flange of my armor, and tugging at the elastic coif
that bound my hair I sank to my knees before the pit,
gasping at the frigid, stinking air. It was worse—far
worse—than the sterile closeness of the helmet had been.
When Dascalu approached and put a hand on my
shoulder to check if I was all right, I seized it and glared
into his visored face. "It said there were survivors down
below," I said. "Find them, and bring them to the ships."

"Yes, my lord." Dascalu turned to go.

I did not release his arm. "Dascalu."

"Yes, my lord?"

"Do not let the survivors see . . . any of this."

"Yes, my lord."

CHAPTER 5
THE SURVIVORS
⚜

"I wish you'd have let me go with you," Valka said.

We were alone for the moment in the command frigate's ready room, a spartan chamber in the usual Imperial gloss-black, brass accents worked into the walls and about the imitation window that showed the smoldering ruins of the camp. I could just make out the domes, snow-frosted, in the distance, black against the blacker sky.

Seated in the high-backed chair at the head of the ellipsoid table, I glanced at her. "I know. But you weren't kitted for it. It's cold out there."

"'Twould have been time for me to find a suit if you'd but waited," she countered. "'Twas no need for you to rush into the heat of things."

"It wouldn't have been right for me to sit here safe on the ship while the men seized the fortress," I said in reply.

Valka held my gaze a moment, silence stony.

"I have a duty to my men," I said, spreading my hands defensively.

"You have a duty to *lead* your men," she riposted. "Do your knights not lead from ships such as this?"

Her golden eyes had started boring holes in my face, and I turned to look back at the ember-lit camp through the false window. "I am not those men," I said. "I don't have the head for strategy. That's for Crim. And it isn't right that they should risk their lives while I stay safe on the bridge."

The smile in Valka's voice shone through. "Hadrian, you really were born ten thousand years too late."

"Twenty thousand," I countered, taking her point.

Before she could respond, the door opened, and the chiliarchs, Dascalu and Petros, entered the chamber. Both men had removed their helmets, and their red-and-ivory armor still bore the grime and damage of battle. Both saluted in unison, raising gauntleted hands, but it was Petros who spoke. "My lord, we've brought our wounded and those of the survivors most in need of care to the ships, but it'll be another ten hours before the *Tamerlane* is in position to drop shuttles enough to carry the survivors all out of here."

"Ten hours," I chewed the figure like something sour. "How many are there?"

"More than ten thousand for certain, possibly so many as fifteen."

"Fifteen . . ." I rubbed my eyes. It was a staggering figure, perhaps more than we could transport south in a single journey, perhaps more than we could adequately provision and care for if Thagura was truly as devastated as it seemed to be. But to be all that remained—if they were all that remained—of forty million? "So few . . ." My tongue felt swollen in my mouth. "Do we have the provisions we need to bring them south?" Pseldona was gone completely, but there was a chance that one of the lesser cities had enough infrastructure in place to help sustain so many.

Petros shook his head. "That's a question for the captain. We can bring them south, but all the bromos protein on the *Tamerlane* won't feed so many for more than a year or two. They'll have to get to planting."

Half-turning to Valka, whose perfect memory would ensure the task did not go undone, I said, "We'll need to telegraph Nessus. Tell them to send a seed ship. These poor people won't survive without offworld aid." The sick feeling that had not left me since the doors of the slaughterhouse opened only intensified. There would be more death on Thagura in the years to come as the survivors worked to decide just what life after the invasion would mean. "And I'll want the aquilarii to scout the countryside. All wings. I want the message broadcast to every corner of the planet, I want to know where any and survivors might be. If there's so much as a fishing village intact that can take refugees, they must."

Petros nodded, turned his dark gaze on his associate. "We think we found the people you were looking for. Survivors from the city. Took a measure of doing. Once it got out we were looking for those who survived the sack all manner of folk lined up."

"But you think you found people who were really there?" I asked.

"Not many, and they aren't well," Dascalu put in. "Pseldona was rocked in the first weeks of the invasion.

The poor bastards have been in the camps all this time. Pale used them for workers."

A shadow passed over Petros's face at the words, and I had to remind myself that the chiliarch's own home had been devastated by a Cielcin horde. He knew what it was like to live under alien occupation, to see people taken and used, to see others turn against their fellow man for an extra few months of life. "Collaborators, most like," he said. "Take what they say with caution, my lord."

I held the chiliarch's eye for a solitary moment. It was a trick I'd learned from my father. Say nothing, let the other man chastise himself. Prudent as his advice was, he should not have offered it without my asking.

Realizing his error, Petros looked down. "We can bring them to you at your convenience."

"Please," I said. "Send them in."

There were nineteen. Nineteen men who had survived the ten years since Pseldona burned. Most of the other survivors had come not from the primary cities, from Aramsa, Tagur, Port Reach, and the rest, but from the lesser cities and townships that dotted the planet in the wetter, temperate zones above the ergs that dominated the equatorial regions.

They were all men, not a woman among them. My men had forced them to scrub in the sonic showers aboard the command ship, and each had been given a standard-issue single-suit of unmarked black to wear. Many were missing ears or fingers from so long in the polar night, and though nearly all were darker skinned from generations in the deserts that girdled the world, there was a sallowness in their complexion that spoke to years without light. Thagura's seasons were long, its orbit slow, and so in all the years the Cielcin had spent sucking the blood and life from the planet, the long nights and short days so far north had not even begun to reverse.

They shuffled through the door, each emaciated and skull-faced, pale eyes bulging at the sight of Valka and myself and at the faceless men of my guard. Several sat at the table without being ordered to do so, and I did not reprimand them for it. These men had lived in hell, and needed no more from me. I could then scarce imagine the horrors they had known, and that failure of imagination held my tongue for several long instants while the poor men waited for me to speak.

I do not have to imagine now, for I have lived as they lived, and for longer.

Had I then known, I would have spoken sooner, for the sound of any kind word would have been like drops of rain in a desert. "Gentlemen," I said after another long moment passed, "I am sorry."

No one spoke, and how could they? What were my words measured against the breadth of their suffering? Had I the panacea of the ancient alchemists to hand, it would not have served them. The marks of talon and lash—and those of teeth—could be seen upon their hands and faces, but I sensed the deeper wounds lay in their souls. There was a hollowness in every face, a cadaverous light in their eyes, as those the lamps of the chamber illuminated nothing within.

My words were nothing.

And yet I knew I must speak, and so opened my

mouth. "My men tell me you come from Pseldona. Is that so?"

A couple nods, but mostly vacant stares greeted me.

"I am sorry," I said again, and found my own eyes sliding to the polished black glass of the table between us. "That is a very long time."

"My family!" one of the men burst out, dark eyes meeting mine. "My lord, do you know them? Lorna and Emin? Are they alive?"

There was a desperate hope in his eyes, one I'd no choice but to snuff out. "No, no I don't know."

The man crumpled into his seat, and the instant he did so every other man began in the same vein, shouting one over the other for news of his family, his children, his parents, his wife or lover. They shouted until the hard walls rang with the rough sorrow of their voices. I felt the tears rise in me, and shut my eyes to stem their flow.

I raised a hand, and only steadily did quiet fall back into place. Confusion, hope, despair . . . all hung in the air like incense. "We only just freed the camp," I said. "It will take time to learn who all we have. My men tell me there are thousands. It may be that some of your people have survived, but I don't know. I don't know yet."

The new silence deepened, and almost I could see the dark cloud settling on every heart. But I had to know, had to ask, and so proceeded. "There is something I want to know, something I was hoping you all might be able to confirm for me." Not a one of them would meet my eye, their hopes all crushed or forwarded as they dreamed of hurrying through the other survivors themselves, scrambling for any sign or symbol of those they'd lost.

"During our attack on the camp, I interrogated one of the enemy. An officer, I think it was."

"You spoke to them?" one of the men asked, shaken from his torpor. His pale eyes shimmered as he looked at me, horror plain in his face. "With those demons?"

Valka placed a hand on my shoulder, quiet support. The man sketched the sign of the sun before extending his first and final fingers in the ancient warding gesture against evil. Others did the same. I was well used to my familiarity with the xenobites' tongue frightening people, nobiles and plebes alike, but in that room it was something different. The mere admission that I *could* treat with the enemy placed their stamp on me, like a burning brand on my forehead, and the knowledge of that brand terrified, as though the captives had not escaped at all, as though I were half-Cielcin myself.

But I would not lie, for lying has never ordered the world, or made it better. "I did," I said, and felt the temperature drop about me. "And it told me something I think only you gentlemen can confirm. It told me that they were not behind the bombing of Pseldona. It told me that *our* forces—the Lady Malyan's forces, that is—were the ones who destroyed the city."

I could still hardly get the words out. The mere thought was more sickening than the camp itself. Why would Gadar Malyan do such a thing? I thought back to my meeting with the baroness. She had planned to seduce me, that much was clear. Had she hoped to distract me? To play the ingenue, to place the blame on Vahan Maro— or on some other officer now dead? Or was she really that simple? Really the vapid and sensual debutante she'd presented? I couldn't be sure, but there was a sour taste in my mouth, edging more bitter with each instant I reflected on our meeting.

"It ain't true!" said an earless man by the door. "Her ladyship would never do such a thing. She's ruled us since my grand-da's day, and her family's kept Thagura since the beginning! Four thousand years!"

"Aye!" said another man, his left eye and the whole side of his face wound in fresh bandages. "The lady would never. Seen her, I have! Like Mother Earth herself. It was her engineers what brought the water down from the north and saved my village."

"Your village?" Valka interjected. "Are you not from the city?"

The man stammered, looked down, as if shamed by her question. "That was when I was a lad, 'fore I come to Pseldona."

We were all quiet then. For my part, I could not quite tell if the man was lying or no, but I supposed it didn't really matter. Surely one of the nineteen was from the city itself. I would punish the men for lying. In retrospect, I should not have offered a boon to anyone with information. I knew that generosity was likely to bring forth liars, and I should not have been surprised to find one or two had slipped by Petros and Dascalu's net.

The vehemence with which these men defended their lord surprised me, though. My father had never encouraged such loyalty from his people, but then my father had been a different sort of ruler, inspiring fear, not love.

Hadrian, name for me the Eight Forms of Obedience. Gibson's words floated back to me.

Obedience out of love for the person of the hierarch, I thought, imagining these peasants seeing the statuesque Malyan from afar. Genetically perfected by the magi of the High College, she was a goddess to them. How could they not love her?

I ran a hand back over my hair, pushing the dark fall from my face. How long had it been since the medtechs had taken me out of fugue? I glanced at my wrist-terminal. Not quite three days. Ye gods, I was tired. Had I slept? There would be too little sleep in the days ahead. I would need what I could get on the flight back to the city.

"There weren't no raid sirens," a voice interjected.

Looking up, I could not at once identify which of the men had spoken, but after a second or two those around him gave way, carving out an empty space between them and the speaker. Thinking back to Petros, to his contempt for these survivors, I wondered if just that behavior had been a part of how these men had survived for so long, and felt a shred of my chiliarch's contempt.

The man who had spoken was old, though perhaps it was only his torment that so aged him. The tip of his nose was gone, and one ear, and claw marks marred the side of his neck.

"I'm sorry?" I said.

"There weren't no raid sirens, *my lord,*" he said, taking my question for anger at his failure to use the proper honorific. A felt a pang of guilt. "Remember it plain as, I do. I worked down in the greenhouses. Out on the edge of the erg. Lord Aram—the first baron, I mean—he had raid sirens built all through the city. All up in the rocks, like, so as folks would know to shelter if Extras or some other house come raiding in from the Dark."

"It sounded!" another man interjected.

"When the attack first came," the old man said, "aye. And the second time. When the Pale come and raid the city proper, by Blue Square and all. But they didn't sound that next day."

The man who'd interjected, a flat-nosed fellow bald as an egg, interjected again, "You've gone and lost it, man!"

"I have not, Lodi! It's you who don't remember!" The old man looked around at me. "I'd not lie to a nobile, my lord. Not for anything. On my honor!" Obviously nervous, he scratched at the ruin of his nose.

Eager to head off any interruptions from the man called Lodi, I asked. "What's your name, sir?"

"Siva, my lord. If it please you." If the man had had a hat he might have wrung it in his hands.

"Tell us what you were going to say," Valka said, and something softened in the freedmen, as though it were a relief in itself to hear a woman's voice. I wondered again that there were no women among them.

The man Siva let his hand fall from his frostbitten nose. "We were sheltering, sheltering in place as ordered. There weren't no proper bunkers down on the sands, but there was the old bio station out by Sharkey's Point. That's where we were when the bombs dropped. Lucian—he were in the Legions once—said they weren't no atomics, but I don't know the difference. Bright as twenty suns they was. Blinded a couple of us. Didn't stand a chance when *they* came circling back. Figured it was *them* what done it, but there was no sirens, I'd swear by Earth's bones, my lord, begging your pardon."

"I think he's right," said a younger man from the back. Scarred as he was, the man's accent betrayed a greater polish than that of the others. "I was in the city. In one of the public shelters. I don't remember sirens that day. And they didn't come until later. Months later. We had to open the vault when the water went bad. That's when they found us."

I glanced up at Valka.

"They said the sensor grid was decimated in the first attack," she said, speaking Panthai so as not to be understood.

I nodded, remembering, and replied in kind, "It doesn't take a satellite grid to know a fleet's incoming. Warning might have come later, but not at all?"

Our use of the Tavrosi language seemed to perplex all but the man with the urbane accent, and I returned my attention to them. "There is a very real possibility that your lady ordered the bombing of Pseldona," I said, as measured as I could manage. To my surprise, the men did not burst out in objections this time. "What her motivations might have been, I cannot say. Perhaps she had bad intelligence in her bunker. Perhaps she thought destroying the city would discourage the Cielcin from raiding in it. I don't know . . ." I tapped one of the magnetic hasps that held my white Imperial cloak in place over my armor. "I am a servant of the Emperor, and no other man. If she has done this thing, I must know of it. His Radiance must know of it. And I will find out."

"Shouldn't you be worried about *them*?" asked a man

from the rear, hard-eyed and obviously half-blind. "Not pointing fingers at her ladyship?"

"She brought water to our village!" the man who was *not* from the city blurted out again. "When I was a lad. Folks were dying they were, and she saved us!"

A third man cried out, "The Pale are still out there!"

His words set the other men to shouting: "They took my Ari, they did! Killed her in front of me. Put her head on the wall!"

"And my Lorna! And my boy, my poor boy . . ."

"It's them you ought to deal with!"

Eyes shut again, I forced the words out sharp as I could make them, though my voice shook. "The Cielcin have been driven from your system. Their fleet is gone."

The man called Lodi shook his head. "They'll be back, then. The minute you're gone, they'll be back. They'll not leave so easily. They know we're here."

Unable to keep quiet any longer, Valka exclaimed, "The Cielcin have done all the harm they can to Thagura! They'll move on to some fresh target. 'Twas only desperation that kept them here. They were underprovisioned for another journey."

"It may be they'll have to eat one another before they reach wherever they're going," I said, thinking back to my conversation with Aranata Otiolo—before it killed me. That prince's people were starving too, suffering from so long a time in space, with so little food, so little protection from the radiation that bathed the Dark between the stars. I had pitied the Cielcin at the time, but my capacity to pity them had worn through. Like old shoes I'd walked too many miles in.

My words seemed to perversely comfort the men. Looking around, I said, "The Cielcin will not return here. Not in your lifetimes . . ." Nineteen pairs of eyes—mostly pairs—looked back at me with bruised hope. "You will all be taken south as soon as possible. We are scouting for a place to move you and the other survivors. My men will see to it that each of you receives a wine ration before you return to your tents. Tell the others their suffering is at an end." I waved a hand to indicate they were dismissed.

The men shifted where they stood; some turned, others rose unsteadily from their chairs.

One coughed, and the younger man with the scars and the city accent asked, "What is your name, my lord?"

I glanced up at Valka, hesitating in the knowledge that these men would return to the refugee tents we'd ordered erected on the ice. They would share the news of this meeting with the others as they shared or hoarded the wine rations we gave them—each according to his nature. It felt strange to take credit for their freedom. I had not won the battle in orbit, though I had briefly confronted Muzugara over the holograph. That victory belonged to Otavia Corvo, to Bastien Durand and the other ship's officers. I had been only an accessory, a part of the audience. Nor had I smashed the camp and freed the prisoners, though I had done my best to stand in the thick of it alongside my men. That victory belonged to Crim, to Dascalu, Petros, and Ulpio and the other chiliarchs, to the wing commander of the aquilarii.

Valka spoke first, addressing the men. "This is Lord Hadrian Marlowe."

Looking back, that moment stands out to me, not

because it was the first such moment, though in a sense it was—the men whom I'd saved at Vorgossos were my own, and knew me—but because it was in another sense the last. There was no recognition of that name in the faces of the men, no opening of eyes and mouth, no reverent whisper of *the Halfmortal*. I was only a man to them, as I had not been to my own people aboard the *Demiurge*. I would not be a man much longer.

I had just become a name, and names are seeds whence heroes grow.

The city man bowed deeply. "Lord Marlowe. I am called Antin. Thank you. I . . . Thank you."

Several of the others bowed, or bowed their heads.

"Thank you, Antin," I said, awkwardly, felt Valka's hand once more upon my shoulder. The old man who had first spoken of the raid sirens had reached the door, and I said, "M. Siva, would you please stay?"

The old greenhouse laborer froze. Head bobbing, he turned back, frostbitten hands over his heart. "Yes, lordship."

Antin was the last to go. He lingered on the threshold a moment, looked back at me one last time, and I knew that he would be the one to take his tale to the others, the thousands who waited in the tents. His story—not mine—would be told to the survivors of Thagura and spread like a virus. In a generation, there would be songs and tales of how Hadrian Marlowe alone stole into the camp and freed uncounted thousands. How with his own hands he tore the gates asunder and stormed in while his men set fire to the alien ships. I might have smiled if the thought were not so discomforting.

I did not want to be a hero. That was not my dream.

"M. Siva," I said when the door hissed shut at last. "I'm sorry to keep you, but I must know. Were you holding anything back for fear of the others?"

The old man shook his head, but did not raise his eyes.

"M. Siva, I must know." Still the old man did not speak. "I will not bribe you," I said, "but if you know something, I *must* know it." Valka moved and seated herself at my right hand, placed a hand on the table near to the old fellow, comforting as best she could. "Was it the baroness's forces that bombed the city?"

Siva screwed shut his eyes, and I realized in the next instant that he was shaking. Valka reached out and took his wrist. "'Tis all right," she said. "No one will know you told us."

The laborer bit his lip, shook his head furiously, but he said, "It wasn't *them*." He sucked in a deep, rattling breath. "There were no warning. No sirens. No bells. It were the third day. *The third day*, didn't even give us a week to fight back. I'd gone out with the basket to raid the greenhouses—they hadn't smashed them yet, hadn't bothered with the outskirts. The others as could had taken all the skiffs, the groundcars . . . emptied the bloody motor pool. We was trapped. Couldn't run if we wanted to, and anyway, Pseldona was home. I thought it was them when I first see 'em flying in. They came out of the sky, down from orbit. But the Pale landed those towers. They wanted people. Wanted them alive. Breeding stock, I reckon. Those as can. They ranch us, you know?"

I nodded barely as Siva cracked his watering eyes. "I do."

The old man shuddered, snot bubbling from his ruined nose. I had no kerchief to offer him, and looking round I spied no box in the conference room. Siva continued, "And the things they do to the others . . . the ones that ain't fit to eat. The ones they can't breed . . ."

"What about the bombing, M. Siva?" Valka asked, gently as she could. "What about the towers?"

"They weren't no towers," the old man said. "My Uncle Raji, he was in the ODF, used to fix jump ships. Lighters. Used to take me with him. I know my ships, lordship, I do." The tears had come again, and again Siva shook his head, moved his hands to shield his eyes.

"You're sure?" I asked, feeling dread like cold iron clamp round my heart and twist my guts in its fist. "You're sure they were human ships."

"They were old *Manta-III*s, I'd bet my life on it. All these years . . . I still don't know why. Why would they do it? Why would they rain fire on us?" He let his hands fall, eyes shining. "They were supposed to keep us safe."

"They were," I agreed, and placed my own hands on the table. "Thank you, M. Siva." I looked round again, hoping to find some junior officer or adjutant, but we three were all alone. "Valka, can you go find one of Crim's lieutenants? Any of them will do. I want M. Siva taken to the *Tamerlane* and treated."

She stood, understanding my intentions without having to ask. Siva had been very brave to speak. After all he'd been through, I had just asked him to speak against the landed ruler of his world. He would not be safe on it anymore. The others would know he had spoken to me, and if the baroness were indeed guilty of the mass murder

Siva had accused her of, then those loyal and devoted to the baroness would never forgive him, nor would the baroness herself. He would never find peace on Thagura, not anywhere. He would have to come with us.

"I'll wait with him," I said, and did my best to smile, hollow though the expression was.

CHAPTER 6
OF FLIES AND SPIDERS

❖

Pseldona again.

The blackened city stretched away beneath us, a desolation of twisted metal and pale ash. When first we'd swept over that ruin, I'd felt myself sick at heart, thinking of the horrors of the Cielcin, the horrors of our too-long war. That second time, I saw it with new eyes. I spied the greenhouses as we approached, shattered but still standing on the sands below the inselberg crowned by the ruined palace. Peering back, I saw the shapes of the other ships of escort, each carrying half a hundred men. Crim and Bressia and the high officers had remained behind to coordinate relief and mop up any remaining Cielcin at the polar camp. Varro's science team would want to perform forensic work as much as possible, and when that was done, I'd left orders for the site to be annihilated with antimatter charges. Wiped from the map.

No part of it should remain.

"She has to pay," Valka said from the seat across from

me in our private language, peering down at Malyan's devastation.

"If she truly is guilty," I agree.

"Truly?" she glared at me with hard eyes. "Do you doubt it?"

I shook my head. "She must answer for what she's done," I said, casting about the chamber, counting the helmeted heads of my guard. Not a one of them understood Tavrosi Panthai, but I still wished we had no audience for this. It would not do for my men to see us argue, and so I kept my tone as neutral as I could. "If she's guilty, she must go to Marinus. She may face the strategos and Imperial justice."

"Imperial justice?" Valka echoed me again. "Please. She is one of your palatines. She will be ferreted to some prison planet. She won't even have to live her sentence. Your Emperor will put her on ice for a century. Two. Only to have her thawed out again and sold to some Perseid count for her genome. She won't suffer a day in her life."

The venom in her tone shocked me. We had been so long apart—her in fugue while I mingled with the Imperial court—that I had forgotten the intensity of her hatred for our way of life, and of our nobility in particular. She carved some exception for me in her heart, and I supposed that I had thought it a sign that she had tempered in time. Evidently I was wrong, who could not say that she was.

"You may be right," I said at last.

"I *am* right," she said, crossing her arms over her crash harness. She peered back out the window between us. "How many people do you think were in the city?"

I didn't answer her at once. It was a question we could have answered. I knew there had been forty million on the planet itself, making Thagura far and away one of the largest fiefdoms in the Norman Expanse. But in the city itself? It could have been as many as ten million, or as little as two. Much of the planet's population was spread across the temperate zones, where the planet's rare water was more common.

How many of them yet remained was hard to say. It would not be until Malyan's people—or whoever replaced them—were able to import relief forces and conduct a new census that we would be able to fully appreciate the cost of the invasion . . . and of the baroness's reply. I know the answer now. That census was done, years after I departed, conducted by Sir Albert Trask, the man made Imperial proconsul on Thagura after the invasion.

Two hundred and twenty three million people remained on the planet, barely more than half . . . and there were eight million people in the city when it burned. Eight million people gone in a day. In an instant.

"It doesn't matter," I said at last. It didn't really. "Too many."

"The woman should die for this," Valka said.

Her words tore my attention away from the city beneath us. We had passed back into the shadow of the great Rock, and Vahan's colossus peered in at us. "If she's guilty," I agreed—or thought I did.

"She is guilty," Valka asserted.

Resting my head in my hands, I pressed the heels of my thumbs into my eyes. I had barely slept on the flight down from the pole, and it had taken medication to get me there. The sight I'd seen through the doors of the abbatoir would not leave me, nor the mute accusation in the eyes of the heads on the wall. I almost yearned for cryonic fugue again, to sleep between the stars. Half-dead, at least, I'd sleep.

"It hardly matters who wins this damned war," Valka muttered, her bitterness like acid on her tongue. "We're as bad as they are."

"We're not," I said, reflexively.

Golden eyes found mine. "How can you say that, even now?"

Perhaps you ask yourself that very question, Reader. Perhaps you sit there and whisper to your pages, asking if I am not the *Sun Eater*? Asking if it was not I who burned the fleet at Gododdin, and set fire to that whole world? It was. In the annals of history's greatest killers, Gadar Malyan merits but a chapter, a heading.

I have written several books. I take no joy in it. What I did, I did for all mankind. What Malyan did, she did only for herself. Judge me if you will, but read on, and know that I have asked these questions too, and asked them of myself—and not only myself.

How many years have we added to our wars? How much higher have we piled the corpses, how much deeper are the rivers of blood because of us? Because of our failings? At every turn, with every step, I have found the horrors of the enemy met with horrors of our own. It was us who shot first at Vorgossos, breaking the fragile—and indeed, impossible—dream of peace. It was us who tortured our prisoners on Emesh, was us who fired first at Cressgard and started the war, whatever the official records may say.

We are no angels—nor am I—but neither are we the Cielcin.

"We don't eat *them*," I said in answer.

When at last we landed and returned along the path Maro led us down to the dungeon and the office of the castellan, it was with another hundred men. The other soldiers—a full chiliad—waited in their ships in a line above the descent to the lower levels and the hidden gate. A new sun was rising over lost Pseldona as we went down, and the dorsal fins of our shuttles rose like black sails against the blushing sky, a solitary line like a row of funeral monuments. Much of the people in Malyan's bunker were only servants—courtiers like the cupbearer, Ravi Vyasa, not soldiers. We must have outnumbered the baroness's guards ten-to-one.

Valka had not liked being left behind a second time, but when I had explained my plan to her, she relented. It would not be easy to extract the woman from her hole without bloodshed, and indeed I half-expected to find the baroness locked in her paradise, and had ordered a plasma bore and breaching team be deployed from the *Tamerlane* at the earliest opportunity.

So much nearer the equator, the wreck of the battle still smoldered in the skies, its traces visible in the tongues and streaks of acrid black staining the heavens. But where before the effect was strangely beautiful, I could then only think of the smoke of thuribles in Chantry, the scents of frankincense, benzoin, and myrrh.

But Maro's guards did not resist us when we returned. Quite the contrary. We were ushered back down the hidden stair and along the corridors below to the inner door, where Pallino and the men of my guard I'd left behind remained with Maro's men. Between them they had swept the path clean of onlookers.

My lictor greeted me as I rounded the last corner, my helmet again firmly in place. He and my men saluted—Maro's, too—and waited for me to speak. "Is the baroness still inside?" I asked.

Pallino must have blinked, judging by the pause and the faint shift of his head. "Yes, my lord. Her and her captain. Some others. They had word of your return."

I had not ordered word be sent, but I supposed they had yet some access to the surface, some lookouts in bolt-holes throughout the ruined city, and some way of running messages through other doors and tunnels. I paused for only a moment, wondering if I should have sent word, if my silence implied cause for alarm on the baroness's part. Had I erred?

If I had, it was too late to change. For the plan to work, I needed Malyan to trust me. To come willingly. I had no wish to fight with Captain Maro or his men, or to make a charnel house of the bunker to rival the polar camp. If she was innocent, no harm would be done, and if she was not innocent, then it was better to win the battle before it even began.

"Survivors?" Pallino asked.

"Yes," I answered him. "Not so many as I hoped. But the planet is ours. I spoke with Corvo on the flight back. She's telegraphed the news to Marinus." Conscious of the native audience, I added, "It is a pity the worldship got away. We might have had another of their princes."

Pallino drew aside, fell into step as I approached the door to the paradise. "We may yet, lad," he said, a bit of the old myrmidon friendliness creeping through. "They might not have gone far. If we wounded their ship, maybe they wash up in local space."

I clapped the fellow on the shoulder, indicating by that gesture that it was time to move on. He was right: If Prince Muzugara's worldship had been damaged, there was always the chance we might hunt it down, but that was a problem for another day.

The baroness awaited.

Discreetly as I could, I tapped the chiliarch twice on the shoulder with my fist before pointing at my eyes, making the gesture casual as could be. Pallino and I had been myrmidons in the coliseum together when I was *outcaste,* before I had regained my station. It was an old signal, one of many, one not used by the legions standard, but the sort of thing we relied on in the ring, fighting shoulder to shoulder in ranks, most unlike the shielded hoplites and dragoons of the Imperial service.

Pallino caught the signal plain enough and drew back. *Be ready for action.* There was no time to explain, and always the chance that any subvocal suit communication might be intercepted and overheard. Like as not, the baroness had neither the means nor the personnel for such intelligence work, certainly not there below ground, but it never hurt to be cautious. I had a hundred and fifty men in the bunker. The baroness had perhaps a hundred, but they knew the territory, they had the door controls. We were in *her* net, and in her power, if she would but use it.

Apparently unawares, the guards opened the gates to the paradise and ushered us inside.

Captain Maro was halfway up the grand staircase from the pool in the grotto below when we stepped over the threshold, and it took every ounce of my scholiast-trained control not to flinch for my shield catch.

But he raised a hand in greeting. "Lord Marlowe! What news from the north?"

Hooking my thumbs through my belt, I stopped with feet apart, white cape hanging from my elbows. "The camp is liberated, Captain Maro. We've saved several thousand of your people. My people are as we speak preparing to relocate them south. There is a settlement near Iudha Oasis apparently unspoiled. My comms officer was in contact with the archon. They are able to take refugees."

Maro touched his brow, heart, and lips, raised his fingers in the sign of the sun. "Mother Earth and God Emperor bless us," he said. "The archon, did you say? The archon of Iudha? Lady Sirvar?"

The name sounded familiar, and I allowed a short nod.

A smile bright and terribly joyous broke across the bald man's rough face. "O Mother!" The captain put a hand to his brow. "Sirvar Donauri! So the country survived? Thagura is not lost after all!"

It is lost to the dead, I thought, but did not say. Gesturing to my guards, I said, "I am here for your mistress, Captain. We were interrupted before, but Thagura is hers again for true, and needs must that she accompany me to Marinus."

That much had not changed. I thought of Valka's words on the flight down, and wondered what I must say to Titus Hauptmann and the Imperial Viceroy if I failed to bring the baroness to them. I was a knight of the Royal Victorian Order, one of the Emperor's own, and my victory of Aranata Otiolo had won me a great deal of latitude, but to execute a baroness of the Blood Palatine without trial, without Inquisition, without anything but my own judgment would be an overreach. I would suffer for it, and yet Valka was right. Gadar Malyan would find no justice on Marinus, and what she did find would be no justice for her victims.

If they are her victims, whispered a little voice within me.

"To Marinus?" Maro repeated, evidently having forgotten that those had always been my orders. "Is that . . . really necessary? My Lord Marlowe, Thagura has suffered. My lady wishes to remain here. To see to the reconstruction, the future of her people!"

"She did not wish so when I spoke to her before," I said. Gadar Malyan had all but thrown herself at the possibility of travel offworld.

Vahan Maro nodded, but did not step aside. "My lady has been long in thought. It is nine years to Marinus. Even if we were to go and return at once, that would be nearly two decades she would be away from her world, from her people. She must not go! She is needed here! If she must give her report to the viceroy, let it be by telegraph."

"There will be time for this discussion before we depart," I said, taking one measured step down the stair. "We would not set sail today at any rate. Stand aside, Captain. I would discuss these matters with your lady."

Maro hesitated only a second before stepping aside with a muttered, "Yes, of course." He and the two fusiliers who'd hurried up behind him fell into step just before Pallino and myself. We left the bulk of my guard at the base of those stairs—Maro had been too late to keep two dozen men from descending with me—and proceeded as we had done before around the pool.

The baroness was not where we had last seen her, on the garden terrace overlooking the pool. Maro led us along the marble walkway beneath the nude caryatids, past a pair of round doors in that terrace to a broader door at the far end. The chamber within featured a dining table of pink petrified wood and carpets two inches deep. So lush were the appointments and so deep the silence there that I felt an absurd need for quiet myself, as though I were a rude child again in my father's house. But I caught my reflection in the smoky mirror glass opposite. Where had that rude child gone? In his place a black devil stood armored in Roman fashion, his sculpted armor and serene face mask drinking the light, his white cloak seeming to shimmer in the jewel-light of crystal lamps.

Maro led us through the chamber to a narrow hall that ran along the back wall of the dining chamber and teed off it in the center. We turned down this branch to an armored door at the end—I marked the garret to the right where half a dozen Malyan troopers languored, on-duty but bored. They peered out at me as I passed, curious to see the newcomer.

The captain pressed the door panel, and said, "It's Maro, ma'am. I've brought him."

The panel glowed blue and chimed as the door slid open.

Gadar Malyan sat in a tufted, high-backed chair beside a dormant holograph well, her young companion Ravi not far off. Like any good palatine nobile, she had not seated herself with her back to the door—even a door she controlled. Her hand was on the wood-faced panel built into the chair that had opened the door. She had abandoned her diaphanous robe in favor of a form-fitting gown of Malyan azure. She had pinned up her inky cascade of hair, and the pins that held it glittered silver in the low light.

With a pang and thrill of horror, I realized who she reminded me of. The paracoita Kharn Sagara had sent to me on Vorgossos, the one who had forced herself on me. It was her coloring, the dark hair and pale skin, and the full feminine excess of her figure, nearly spilling from her too-tight dress. She arched an eyebrow, and I reminded myself that the threat here was the same. "Lord Marlowe!" She placed her cigarette and its long-stemmed holder on a stand above a crystal ash tray at her elbow. "I feared you would not return!"

"There was never any chance of that, ladyship," I said, putting a hand to my heart in soft salute. "The matter at the pole has been seen to. Thagura is *truly* yours once again."

Gadar Malyan mirrored my gesture, one hand flitting to her heart. "For this you have my gratitude. Will you not remove your helmet, my lord? Ravi, the wine!"

I felt a strong urge to refuse, to order her to come with me at once. But I had to play matters carefully. I had to make her feel secure enough to leave her crypt. And so I raised a hand and keyed the release that opened my helmet like a flower. The segments of the casque broke apart and tucked themselves into the collar. I tapped to loosen the elastic hood and pulled it down, doing my best to smile. "We mustn't stay long," I said, and explained that we had found survivors in the polar camp and meant to relocate them to Iudha in the south. "Your people here should be brought south as well. Pseldona is a ruin. If Thagura is to be rebuilt, it will not be from here."

"Not until relief may be brought from offworld," the baroness said, brightening as Ravi returned with the wine service. "*Will* relief be brought from offworld?"

"Eventually," I said, moving to examine a painting on one darkly paneled wall. It showed a team of farmers toiling at their crop, dressed in the homespuns of Sollan peasants. One man wielded a great hand-scythe, blade raised against the sky, while in the distance the huge gray towers of a drydock glimmered about the half-build shape of a starship. There were no such fields on Thagura, and I wondered from whence that canvas came. Upon it, the great contradiction of Imperial society glowed in greens and browns and silver: the plebeians at their primitive toil—or so Valka would have it—while we nobiles and soldiers sailed the stars in apparent glory.

What I would not have given then to trade places with the man wielding the scythe. Scion of the Empire I might have been, but as a boy I'd shared Valka's sympathies, her fury at our castes, our hierarchy. Her sense of the injustice of it all. But even in those early days, even in my youth, I had long worn the chains of duty. Of station. That painting was a celebration of our way of life, of the peasant farmer and of the spacefarers who protected him. For it was for them, and for mankind itself that the Empire was ordered. For what is mankind if not the lowest? If not the ordinary women whom we knights and nobiles are born to serve and to defend?

Beneath my white Imperial cloak, I clenched my fists, thinking of the spider in her chair.

"Lord Marlowe?" Gadar Malyan asked. "Will you not sit a while?"

"I . . ." I turned, eyeing Pallino where he and Maro waiting by the door. The chiliarch adjusted his posture, stood a fraction straighter. "Yes, sorry. I was admiring your painting."

Malyan smiled very prettily. "Ah! Do you like it? It's one of Duri's pastorals. My grandmother was a bit of a collector. She furnished most of this place. We had a genuine Rudas in the palace, but I suppose it is gone now, lost with everything else." She accepted a goblet from her page, and gestured at the lesser armchair positioned at an angle from her own. "It is a pity, my lord, that we could not have met under better circumstances. I feel we have very much in common."

The boy, Ravi, put a glass into my hands as I sat— pausing only so long as it took to brush my cape to one side. "Is that so?"

"Do you not see it?" she asked, putting a hand to her coiffure. "We favor, you and I. A matched set."

I did not point out that where her eyes were black as jet, mine were violet. It would not do to antagonize her. "As you say."

Gadar Malyan lifted the wine to her lips. It was a different vintage from the one we'd shared days earlier, black as her eyes. "I observe," she began with careful grace, "that your paramour is not with you on this occasion. Does that mean you have reconsidered my offer?"

I blinked at her. "You made no offer."

"But I did! You are such a man, my lord. Oblivious, the lot of you!" She laughed, directed its music toward Ravi, who smiled stiffly. "My marriage offer, Lord Marlowe!"

Again, I blinked at her. Not in surprise, not precisely, but in shock at her plain boldness. I had suspected—and Valka had smelt it light-years away—that the baroness had intended to seduce me. I should have guessed that seduction would go so far as marriage, but I was still unused to my restored place among the palatinate. I had spent more than fifteen years—my entire adult life—outcaste and stripped of rank and inheritance by my father. I had spent those fifteen years as nobody, devoid of status and social worth, and did not expect to find a palatine baroness throw herself on me. On Emesh, Count Balian Mataro had attempted to secure me as a breeding stud for his family line, for he was a distant cousin of the Emperor, but Malyan had no way of knowing that.

"Don't go all silent on me!" she said, brows contracting. "It is only natural, after all! Thagura must rebuild. I am unwed. You are a knight with no holdings, and my hero! What a story it would be."

Something of my hesitation must have shown in my face, for she reached out and gripped my wrist. "You needn't say yes at once. You are a Royal Knight, and have your duties, I know. But think on it." A long-nailed finger traced the full curve of one breast. "You needn't dismiss your girl, either. I am unworried about competition."

That sent a charge through me, and it took all my composure not to jerk my hand away, to smile my crooked smile and say, "My *girl* might feel differently."

"Does it matter?" she asked, innocent as anything. "She is a tribesman of the Tavrosi clans. You are I are the descendants of kings." She angled her chin as she leaned back, releasing my wrist to take another sip of the black wine. "Perhaps we may discuss arrangements aboard your ship. We have . . . time before you must go, do we not?"

That gave me the foothold I needed to reply. "Before *we* must go, my lady. Have you forgotten? I am ordered to bring you to Marinus to keep you safe. Thagura will not be stable for some time, and the viceroy and first strategos both wish to learn what happened here, and to provide you with an opportunity to coordinate relief efforts with them."

"But I cannot go!" she argued. "I cannot abandon my people, now most of all!"

Rage is blindness, said the part of me that spoke in my old tutor's voice. A muscle twitched in my jaw. Was she serious? Or only afraid of the consequences of putting herself in my power? She meant to manipulate me, that much was clear. Her offering of herself—now and later— could be nothing else. I hid my irritation behind a sip of the black wine, and it was only after I'd swallowed some that I feared for poison. Too late. But nothing happened, and I broke the brittle silence, saying, "You can do more good for them on Marinus. The Wong-Hopper Consortium has offices on Marinus. You'll need to procure construction crews, housing, agricultural equipment. This you cannot do here. Your satellite is gone. You have no connection to the wider galaxy. The datanet. Nothing."

This seemed to sway her, and her proud shoulders slumped. "I have a planet," she said. "If Iudha is unspoiled, as you say, we have have what we need to rebuild."

"You do not," I said. "You have no military power, no officers. Nearly all your administration was lost in the battle here." Her head began to droop as she listened to me, and she cradled her goblet in jeweled talons. "Has it occurred to you you may need to *reconquer* this planet, my lady?"

Her head jolted up, and she narrowed her eyes at me, head moving side to side. "What?"

"You misunderstand your situation," I said pointedly, and leaning forward set the wine cup—barely touched—on the table between us. I took a deep breath. "The Thagura you knew is gone. Your power is gone. If I were to leave you here, what is to stop anyone, *anyone* from removing you from what remains of your office? Your captain here?"

I heard rather than saw Maro advance on reflex, but he said nothing.

"You will die here, ladyship," I said, flatly as I was able. "Your cause is not hopeless, but it is hopeless here. Now." I stood, and extended a hand for her to take. "You must have connections. Relatives offworld."

She looked up at me, and for the first time I saw through the veil of coquettish denial she had woven about herself. Her full lips compressed, and there was a glassiness in her eyes I had not seen before. Almost I pitied her, for even if she was guilty of the horrors the Cielcin and survivors alike accused her of committing, she was too a victim. She had lost her world, her home, and everything.

But a bit of Valka's cruelty—and the old Marlowe family fire—flashed in me, and I said, "And you may wish to reserve your generosity. Save it for a man with more."

She had no words for that, but understanding her position at last, rose and took my hand.

CHAPTER 7
JUSTICE

⚜

The crushing silence greeted us with the sunlight. No birds in the skies of Thagura, nor any grass to stir. The very air was still in the alley and on the street that circled the Rock.

"Do you have her?" Valka asked, words conveyed through the conduction patch behind my ear.

"We do," I answered shortly, looking back over my shoulder. The baroness looked utterly out of place in her azure gown and intricately styled hair, as if she were from some other world and not the desert ruin about us— which in a sense she was. Vahan Maro stayed dutifully by her side, face grim. I sensed that he had been behind her sudden desire to remain on the planet, and he was not happy about the way things were developing. Had he pointed out that she was putting herself entirely at our mercy? Had he conspired with her in the bombing? Had it even been his idea?

But I smiled, and pointed around the bend to the stairs and up the wall to where the black line of our shuttles waited. Another of our *Roc*-class landing frigates had arrived from orbit while we were underground, and crouched on the stone above us. "We've not far to go! The frigate will take you and your retinue direct to the *Tamerlane*. She's in low orbit now, straight up! Do you see?" I moved my hand, gesturing to the fuzzy, black knife-shape where it scudded across the pale sky. At more than a dozen miles long, the ship appeared the size of an arrowhead at its height of several hundred miles, and its ion engines gleamed dully in the daylight like a fogbound star.

Gadar Malyan advanced, Ravi at her side with a sunshade held over the both of them. The baroness squinted through small, dark glasses, shrinking from the light. "I see!" she said, casting about nervously like her men. I had to remind myself that she had lived ten years underground, lived in fear of the sky and of the creatures dwelling in it. That experience had surely activated some primitive part of her biology that remembered being small and scurrying in fear of birds. "When will the others be able to make the move to Iudha?"

Falling into step beside her while Pallino led the way, I answered, "Within the week. We will remain in-system long enough to ensure the survivors at the camp and here relocate safely. My people have been in contact with Archon Donauri there. She will join us aboard the *Tamerlane* before long. We will take counsel before we return to Marinus." I winced inwardly at the words leaving my mouth. They were half-lies. Lady Sirvar Donauri *was* expected to join us aboard the *Tamerlane,* but there would be no counsel. Not with the baroness.

Sensing a shadow at my back, I turned, found Captain Maro close behind, ever watchful. His dragoons stayed about us, a line to either side of the baroness and myself, and behind there marched a ragged assortment of the baroness's surviving court, those retainers she deemed too important to be separated from her person. She believed they would accompany her to Marinus—and they might yet. They were to be, in truth, witnesses against her. I could not decide if the baroness were canny enough to surround herself with know-nothings, or foolish enough to keep any confidants close.

We would know soon enough.

We hadn't far to go. My men waited above, ready to surround our column at my mark.

I performed a quick head count. Baroness Malyan had perhaps half a hundred dragoons in her personal guard, and less than half that number in her train. My own men outnumbered her two-to-one, but that was still close enough that a desperate man like Vahan Maro might risk shielded combat if the chips came down.

"What manner of ship is she, Lord Marlowe?" inquired one of the courtiers, a portly man with an absurdly painted face. "Your vessel?"

"She's one of the *Eriels*," I said in answer, turning to face forward again and resume my pace beside Lady Malyan.

The courtier whistled appreciatively. "Red Star didn't make very many of those, did they!"

"Seventeen," I said. "My lord is quite correct." Taking Gadar by the arm, I leaned beneath the damasked sunshade. "Too expensive, you understand. She was a gift from the Emperor from my services."

The baroness put her arm in mine. "How many crewmen?"

"Crewmen? About five thousand, full out. But there are ninety thousand men aboard, mostly legionnaires on ice." We had reached the stair by then, the once smooth and polished stone chipped and scarred by the fighting that had come so near the palace. Above and left we would find the square where we first met Captain Maro and the survivors, and beyond that the crumbled road down from the Rock to the shelf where Pseldona lay in ashes.

Not far.

Gadar Malyan's fingers tightened, and leaning in she said, "Then could you not be my army?"

"I have my duties, ladyship," I said, "Even were I to take up on your generous offer."

"Please," she hissed, and leaning close breathed. "Help me take back my world. You can have me tonight if you would but do this thing."

I did not turn to look at her, but neither did I drop her arm—though every thought of Valka screamed for me to do so. Let her think that I pondered her words as we climbed. We were nearly to the top. "My lady, you dishonor yourself. And me."

She flinched, and drew her arm away.

"We will sail for Marinus," I said.

She did not speak again as we crossed the ruined plaza

and exited by the arch to the slope leading back down toward the city. There the pavement cracked and the withered stumps of olive trees rose blackened and gnarled to either side of what had once been a mighty avenue. Our frigate and the line of shuttles waited just below, and I felt my heart beat faster in my chest. We were nearly there. The *Tamerlane* had passed almost to the horizon, its dark shape hurrying about its low orbit. We'd have a few hours before it circumnavigated the globe and was ready for rendezvous.

Time enough, and none at all.

At a sign, my herald sounded his clarion, signaling to the watch below that we had come back. I saw a sentinel on the ramp of the frigate vanish inside, saw Pallino put a hand to his earpiece. He was far enough ahead now that he would not be overheard as Valka or the lieutenant in command of the frigate explained what must be done.

"Are we for the frigate?" asked Captain Maro.

"Yes," I said, "she'll take the lot of you." We passed the nearest of the personnel shuttles, and I marked the shuttered ramps, knew that behind each fifty men waited, ready to encircle us.

"So many ships!" remarked the fat lord who has asked after the *Tamerlane*. "You do travel in style, Lord Marlowe!"

"Indeed, Master Pardo!" I said, remembering the fellow's name in a flash. He'd introduced himself as we were preparing to leave the bunkers. He'd been a senior logothete working for the Malyan treasury before the war. "The baroness's security and yours are of the utmost importance!"

A woman beside Pardo chimed in. "Sweet Mother Earth! I forgot what wind feels like!"

A breeze had chosen that moment to blow up and rake the escarpment, carrying with it the bitter alkalines of the desert and ash. I felt its dry fingers in my hair, and stopped a moment, transfixed by something that should not have been there. There, at the base of one of the ruined olives, stood a solitary spot of green. A lonely blade of grass, its seed blown there and deposited by just such a wind as blew through our company, bent toward us.

Life had not ended. Not here, not anywhere.

The men manning the shuttle controls chose that moment to drop the ramps. The baroness had gone on ahead of me, ushered along by her court and Pallino's men, and had reached the base of the frigate's ramp. Men in the ivory plate and red tunics of the Imperial Legions came spilling out, lances flaming and ready as they rushed to encircle the Malyan loyalists. The dragoons scrambled to alertness, hoisting plasma rifles beneath their dun cloaks, drawing in around the baroness and her people.

It was a miracle no one fired, though many swore and I heard Maro's voice lifted in an oath to blacken the clouds. But it was the fat man, Pardo, who found his wits first. "What is the meaning of this?" he bellowed, looking all round for me. "Lord Marlowe, what is going on?"

My men all stood still as chess pieces, bayonets aimed, muzzles threatening. I had to push through their ranks to reach the front, where a small no-man's-land separated the Malyan island from the sea of red and white about it, clicking my shield into place as I went. The static charge of it prickled my brow, and the small hairs of my neck stood on end. More troopers awaited in the hold of the landed *Roc,* and a junior officer in blacks with the red beret and long coat stood among them, his sidearm drawn.

Baroness Malyan said nothing. Her eyes were utterly unreadable behind her dark glasses. But she did not act confused. She stood poised as any of my men, not uncomprehending—or so it seemed to me. When I examine my memories of my short time on Thagura, it is to that moment I turn first. I knew then and there that she was guilty. An innocent woman would have shown fear, would have acted lost, overwhelmed. But then and there—for just an instant—I saw the iron in her spine. A moment of defiance and resignation known to many a cornered king throughout the long and bloody march of mankind across the centuries and countless worlds.

"Gadar Malyan, Baroness of Thagura, you are charged with high treason and genocide against the people of Thagura. Surrender, and order your men to stand down, and no harm need come to you or anyone."

She did not, but stood there like a woman weighing her chances. Presently she removed her glasses, eyes shining and narrowed against the light of the sun. "Genocide!" she echoed, forcing incredulity into every syllable. "You cannot think I did this! You saw them, did you not? You broke their fleet!" She pointed at the sky. "You said you found survivors at their camp! *Their* camp! You think *I* did this?"

The various courtiers were starting to raise their hands, bunching together to put as much distance between them and the long knives. Maro's men—shielded to the last— kept their rifles level at their shoulders. The captain himself glared at me with eyes like blue fire.

"We are the *victims*, Lord Marlowe! I am the victim!" Gadar beat her chest. "I am Thagura, and Thagura burned!"

"Order your men to put down their arms!" I said again, not negotiating.

"Rogue!" she hissed, cheeks flaring as she spat the word. "You...you cannot do this! I am Baroness of Thagura. This is *my* world! My world!" She jabbed a finger at the ground. "Maro! Kill this man!"

The captain's eyes scanned the crowd, taking in the ranks of Red Company legionnaires encircling his charges and his dragoons. He did not fire, but neither did he lower his weapon. "Maro! Anyone!" the baroness shrilled.

I raised a hand, reminding my people of the need for calm. On the ramp to the frigate, Valka appeared beside the black-clad officer. She caught my eye, but did not speak. Gadar Malyan was the chaotic eye in the center of a storm of utter stillness. "Are you mad?" she asked, jabbing a finger at me. "Arresting a palatine lord on her own world! There'll be hell to pay when we reach Marinus, Marlowe, mark my words! You *dare* talk of treason! *This* is treason!"

"Order your men to lay down their arms, Lady Malyan. Thagura has seen enough of violence."

"Put your guns down, all of you!" cried a senior man near Pardo.

Maro and his troopers did not move. Neither did mine. *Stalemate.*

"For Earth's sake, ladyship!" exclaimed one of the other women, dropping to her knees.

Malyan's eyes were wide and black as hell, twin spots of

ink in broad whiteness. Her nostrils flared, and again she ran the tally, gaze sweeping over her men and mine. One strand of coiling dark hair had come loose from its place and flowed, disheveled, down the side of her perfect face.

"Please," I said, hands spread on the air before me, as a man placates a wild thing. "Stand your men down."

Her lips trembled, and shook—though whether it was from rage or fear or grief none but she could say. Her shoulders drooped until she seemed some rag-stuffed effigy propped on a staff. "Lower your weapons," she breathed, voice barely more than a whisper.

Maro and the nearest of her dragoons complied, rifles dropping. One tossed his to the ground, put his hands on his head. When the others did not move as quickly, the baroness shrilled, "I said lower your weapons, you damn fools!"

Relief played in me, and played out on the faces of the courtiers encircled and on that of Valka and the junior officer. My men did not lower their own lances, but advanced to collect the weapons from the dragoons as they followed the lead of the first man, placing hands on heads and dropping to their knees.

The lieutenant descended the ramp, black coat flapping like wings, and said, "Bind the soldiers and take their weapons."

Pallino relayed the order more loudly, "Double quick, you dogs!"

I crossed the no-man's-land to face Gadar Malyan, who looked up to face me. "I know you ordered your own city burned," I said, and as she opened her mouth, added, "Don't deny it."

She shut her mouth. Was she defeated? Or only afraid?

My gaze flickered to where Valka waited in the *Roc*'s hold. I hoped what we were doing was right. It felt like justice, but what is justice? Only a statue in Chantry, her eyes blinded, a balance in her hands. Thus the cynics would have it. But I am no cynic. That what is right and just is often difficult to see and more difficult to know does not mean there is nothing just or right in creation, only that we are ourselves inadequate in its pursuit.

"You could have been *baron*," Malyan said, black eyes filling with tears. It was *almost* a confession, and I think she realized it, for she continued. "This insult will not stand, *my lord*. The viceroy will hear of your treachery."

"The viceroy?" I said, and shook my head. "My lady, I serve the Emperor himself, and like the viceroy, *the Emperor is far away*."

That snatch of the old Mandari proverb struck her as I intended. Her eyes widened, and she realized the folly in her words. The viceroy was on Marinus, and she would not come to Marinus except through me. *I* was the reigning power on Thagura, not her. I advanced until I was within the reach of her arms. She was almost so tall as me, tall as all palatines were tall, but her posture broke again, and she shrank back. "You and your court will be detained aboard the *Tamerlane* until we have reached our decision." Turning my head, I regarded Captain Maro where he stood not far from his mistress's side. "Your men will be placed in our brig under guard. No harm shall befall any of your people. By the Blood Imperial, I swear it."

She spat at my feet. "What good are your words?"

"Take her away," I said, and stepped back, gesturing

that my men might approach and bind her. I brushed past to mount the ramp to the hold.

Then several things happened at once. A bluish light bathed the ramp before me, accompanied by a humming drone. The men behind me cursed. One of the courtiers—a woman—screamed, and Valka shouted, "Hadrian! Look out!"

I knew that blue, the color of watered moonlight, and knew as well that constant humming. I twisted aside, pivoting around my right foot like a hinge before leaping back to avoid the slash of Vahan Maro's highmatter blade. The weapon sang through the air, exotic matter rippling like the surface of a pool. The tip whistled past mere microns from my chest. The blow would have severed me clean in half, the blade cutting without resistance.

Time slowed around us, and the fire in Maro's eyes shone cold as distant stars. His jaw was set, and the iron in his heart and hand was a thing terrible to behold. He was a dead man, and he knew it. He only hoped to make me join him in death, in the mad hope that my absence might spare his lady her fate. Wasting no time, Vahan Maro lunged, thrusting out with the blade none of us had known he had. Twisting aside, I snapped my own sword free of its hasp and squeezed the triggers. Liquid metal flowed to its proper state, the blade crystallizing in a flash to parry Maro's thrust. The captain recovered speedily, drawing back his sword to aim a cut at my head.

I let him throw it, stepped in with my own parry to stop the captain's blow from carving me in twain. For a moment, we met each other strength for strength, met each other eye to eye. I held my sword in both hands, the blade nearly perpendicular to Maro's own. We stayed there only an instant, each of us mapping the manifold possibilities of the next instant, each anticipating each.

One instant ended, another began.

I arrived in it half a step ahead of my opponent. Before he could move, I brushed his blade down and to one side, and before he could respond I slid in and punched him square in the nose with both hands still on my hilt to stagger him, to stop any remise that might have claimed my life or limb. Maro stumbled back, tried to recover.

Too late.

The highmatter encountered no obstacle as it bit into Maro's shoulder, nor any as the blade passed through heart and lung and liver before exiting the other side.

Stunned silence filled the air above the ashen city. No birds sang, and all the men and women seemed not to breathe. The whole thing had happened in less time than it takes to write about it. In seconds. Maro knew he was dead before he fell. You could see it in his eyes, in the soft *oh* his lips made, hardly to be heard. Then his head and right shoulder and the arm with it slid along the fault line and fell. His body fell a moment later, and the stones ran red at my feet.

Gadar Malyan cursed and turned away, shading her eyes. Several of the court women screamed, and Pardo belted an oath. I unkindled my blade and stepped back. Still no one moved. My own troops stood around shocked, realizing each in his time how close I had come to death, and realizing—too—that they had been no use in the critical moment.

Stowing the hilt of my sword back in its hasp, I said,

"Take the body away and bury it. Make a cairn if you must." Two of the men nodded. Knowing I must, I stepped over Vahan Maro, taking my cape in one fist to keep it from falling in his blood, and returned to Gadar Malyan, who turned red-eyed to face me. "Those were your orders he died on," I said. "Tell your men I'll tolerate no more heroics from them."

She shook as she glared at me, and so I took her place, shouting, "Every last one of you, on your knees!"

One by one at first, then five by five, they knelt at last. Two hoplites approached with manacles for the lady then, but I raised a hand to stay them. "That won't be necessary anymore, soldier. She's done all the harm she can." The men both stopped, and seeing the pain and fury in Malyan's eyes, I said, "A courtesy for the lady."

CHAPTER 8
THE HANGED MAN
⚜

It was cold aboard the *Tamerlane,* as it is almost always cold in space. Two days had passed since Lady Malyan's arrest, and still I had hardly slept. The thought of this interview filled me with a sickness and numb dread that forbade sleep. I had meant to speak to the baroness the day before, but could not bring myself to do it, and so she had waited in the unused cabin I had ordered should serve for her cell.

Two legionnaires in masks and full armor stood guard

by the door, each armed only with ceramic blades, for lances and plasma burners were not permitted on ship except at high alert. "Has she given you any trouble?" I asked them, facing the trapezoidal door.

"No, my lord," said the senior of the two men. "Quiet as a lamb. Nothing on camera either, or so Lieutenant Bressia says. She's had watch."

I nodded. "Well, let me in, soldier."

"Aye, sir," the fellow answered, tilting his head. "Shall one of us go in with you? She isn't chained, per your orders."

"That won't be necessary," I said. "She is no danger to me."

"Very good, sir." The man saluted and turned to key the door.

It slid smoothly upward, revealing a small and comfortable cabin of the sort usually set aside for the senior lieutenants, perhaps a dozen feet deep and a little narrower, with the bed built in along the far wall and a notch to the left to fit the sonic shower pod and small commode. There was no decoration, nothing to soften to spartan nature of the polished black metal. The room had been unoccupied before, untouched since the *Tamerlane* was put into my charge. There weren't even scuff marks and the usual signs of human occupation. It was pristine.

The baroness lay on the bed, and turned to look at me as I entered, peering out from her hair. That once magnificent style snarled about her lovely face, a disordered chaos, and from the drawn look in her face and the redness in her eyes I knew she had been crying, knew she had hardly slept.

The door slid shut behind me. Not wishing to give her

the first word and the opportunity to direct our conversation, I said, "There were survivors from Pseldona at the camp."

She sat up then, lips pressed together, but said nothing.

"They must have been taken in that first assault, or so I told myself. Ten years they endured in Cielcin hands. Mother Earth knows what they saw, what they had to do to survive . . ." I let my words trail off, let them hang like smoke upon the air.

Still Malyan said nothing. I hooked my thumbs through my belt. I was not armored, wore only the belted black tunic, dark flared trousers, and polished high boots that were my custom, militaristic but not military. My sword hung from my shield-belt, a comforting weight. I chewed my tongue. "Can you imagine? Of course you can't. You haven't *seen* what they are. The Cielcin, I mean." I hung my head, studied the polished black metal of the floor between our feet. They had given Malyan a soldier's burgundy fatigues to wear, but no shoes, and her painted feet stuck out from the rough leggings like that blade of grass from Thagura's desolation. "I used to think they were like us. Monsters, yes, but monsters such as we. Monsters I could understand—thought I could understand. After all these years, I'm not sure I understand them any better, but I'm sure I understand us less." I held her gaze. When still she said nothing, I continued. "There were *millions* in your city, my lady."

"You think I don't know that?" Her silence broke like glass, but I marked the delay, the second's hesitation, the second's *contemplation. Calculation.*

She *was* guarding her words.

"These survivors!" I spoke as if she had not, raising my voice to override her. "Told an interesting tale. Perhaps you know it." Then I found I could hold her gaze no more, and turned to one side, paced to the nearby wall and back to the other. At that second wall I stopped, turned my head away. "You see, I was wrong. They were *not* captured in the initial sack—before the burning. At least, not all of them were. They were taken *later,* after the city was destroyed." I paused to study the baroness's face. Her red eyes were utterly unreadable, her face a study of exhaustion and grief. "Do you know what they told me?"

Still nothing.

"They told me that it was human ships that bombed the city. Your city." I pointed right between her eyes. "Your ships."

"My ships?" the baroness said, again pausing to find her words. "I . . . don't understand."

"Don't you?" I asked. "That wasn't all they said. They told me the raid sirens did not sound. That they had no warning. There had been warnings of the earlier raids. But none that day. I asked myself how that could be?"

The baroness sniffed, snarled, "You killed the only man who could still have answered that question days ago."

"Do not hide behind your captain, ladyship," I said. "You were the one holding his leash. It was your words that caused his death. Your orders." Sensing that I'd pushed too hard on a raw nerve, I drew back a step to put more distance between us, straightened. "You *are* Thagura, you told me. Or are you telling me your own military went rogue?"

She blinked up at me. It was her only defense. She

must have known that. I fancied I could see the gears turning in her head. But she knew as I that had that been her move, the time to make it was days ago, on our first meeting.

Still, she had to try. Looking at some spot on the wall beside my elbow, she said, "I know nothing of war. That was the province of my captains."

"You have played the damsel well, and tried to conceal much by pretending that you are only a woman," I said. "But I do not believe it. Of you, or any woman." I returned to the center of the room and faced her square on. "Eight million people, Gadar Malyan. How many of them died by your word?"

"They took so many!" she said, gripping the edge of her bed until the mattress squeaked in the confined space. "So many in the first days!"

"That may be so," I said. "But that is not an answer an innocent woman would give."

She seemed to deflate then, to collapse entire, like a fleet of sails tangled on the solar winds. She knew I was right, knew there was no sense in deception. She stayed that way a long time, and I left her alone with her secret thoughts, not speaking. Her black hair hid her face, and seated on the edge of the bed, she appeared shriveled, shrunken by the weight of her life.

"How long did you wait?" I asked at last. "A week? Two?"

Nothing. Again.

"Why did you do it?" I asked. "Why give the order?"

She shook her head, knowing she had already betrayed herself.

"Tell me, Lady Malyan," I said, putting my hands behind my back. I tried to sound kind.

One reddened black eye glowered up at me through hair dark as my own. "We lost our fleet. We had nothing. No defenses. And the Emperor was *far away*." She started shaking, clenched her fists upon her knees. "I had to act."

"And so you massacred your own people?"

"You would rather they end up enslaved to the Cielcin?" She looked me fully in the face then. There was no light in those jet chips she called eyes, none but the reflection of fires only she could see. "We were alone! Defenseless! Without any starships to reply!"

I had to walk away, turned to face the wall, ears pricking for any movement from the baroness, but there was none. *"The sun is high, and the Emperor is far away,"* I parroted, shading my eyes. "You said that before. It's an old Mandari proverb, but it doesn't mean what you think. It doesn't grant you latitude and a long leash. It's a lament. A lament that the Emperor is not nearer his subjects, and better able to defend them from the likes of *you*." For has it not been the case in every age that the greatest ally of the common man has ever been the emperor? The king and his laws against the nobility who ever believes itself above them?

Malyan scoffed. "You think you're the only lettered man in the galaxy?" She tossed her raven hair. "I have done *nothing* that others have not done before me, that you would not have done in my place. You know well as I that when the barbarians come calling, you burn your fields to deprive them of food and *pray* they pass on."

My mouth hung open an instant, and for one of the

vanishingly few times in my life, I—the son of a poet and
student of the scholiasts' tradition—was truly speechless.
Valka's words whispered at my shoulder. *We're as bad as
they are.* Every cell and synapse wanted to argue with her,
but I could never argue with her. Not to her satisfaction.

We're as bad as they are.

At length I found my tongue. "Men," I managed, "are
not *wheat*."

She held my gaze and did not look away. After another
silence, she said, "You're wrong." I opened my mouth both
in stunned amazement and to shout, but she plowed
ahead, saying, "I have seen what they are. The Cielcin. I
know what they're capable of." From the way her voice
shook—the audible pathos of it—I knew this, at least, was
truth. "They came to my world to *feast*, Lord Marlowe.
To carry off my people! Even the children!" Again her
shoulders shook, and those red-black eyes fixed on some
indeterminate point on the wall behind me. "So do not
talk to me of *them*. I did what I had to to try and stop
them."

"You thought . . ."

But she was not finished, and the fire in her flared hot
as any corona. "I thought to deprive them of . . . of fodder."

"You fool," I said, quietly as I could. "You did not
deprive them of a feast, you deprived your people of *hope*.
The Cielcin travel between the stars for centuries. They
don't freeze themselves as we do. They eat what they can
raise on their ships; or their slaves; or each other, if they
have to. And they *would* have had to. They were starving
when they arrived." For a third time, I turned my back.
"The ironic thing is, if you had done nothing, they might

have had their fill and left sooner. You gave them no choice. Pseldona was their best option; a fifth of the planet lived in that city."

"And I ask you again," she said, "ought I to have let them be eaten?"

"So you committed genocide from an abundance of mercy, is that it?" I snarled, unable to bite back my retort a third time. "Spare me, Lady Malyan! You were afraid! You're still afraid! It's written on your face, plain as anything. You thought that if you burned the city, they might spare you. You and your little court underground." My hand moved to my sword hilt, fingers squeaking on the wine Jaddian leather. "Do you deny it?"

She must have seen the gesture, for she fell silent as a stone. I took my hand away, turned once more to face her.

Baroness Gadar Malyan had drawn her knees to her chin like a child, and hugged herself, unblinking. In a voice pressed flat and dry as flowers between the pages of a folio, she whispered, "What is to become of me, then? On Marinus?"

I shook my head. Valka was right. On Marinus, the viceroy and Lord Hauptmann might find her guilty, but like as not they would sentence her a term on some prison colony, to Belusha or Pagus Minor. It wasn't right, nor could it be made right. Once, I might have balked at the thought of doing what I knew I must, but those who balk at justice and shudder at its retributive nature are fools— as all young men are. Justice, by its very nature, must be retributive. Punishment must follow crime, and cannot precede it. Criminals cannot be brought to justice before their crimes, because before their crimes they are not criminals. Man becomes monstrous by his actions, though the monster dwells in all our hearts, as it dwells in mine.

None of us is born evil.

"You cannot go to Marinus," I said shortly, knowing what must be done. "We will return to Thagura . . ." I tarried then, tarried because I did not want to say what I must, but I ought to have gone on. For hope, bright and terrible hope, blossomed in the condemned woman, and her eyes cleared for an instant. For just an instant. I shut my own. "You shall die on your own world."

Silence then. Total and absolute.

"I see," she said, and to my astonishment, she did not argue. She did not grovel. She did not beg. She let her knees fall, feet back on the cold, metal floor, and sat square and still. She did not even blink. "I see," she said again, and nodded. Tears shone in her eyes but did not fall. "How?"

"You are palatine," I said in answer. "You'll be beheaded, in the old way."

That answer made the reality more real, and her stunned expression shattered. Her eyes found me then in all the emptiness she perceived, and sharpened to twin points of black. "Who are you to judge me? You are no magister! No praetor of the Chantry!"

I studied her face once more, seeing not the eugenic beauty there, but the stains beneath her eyes, the hollowness in her unpainted cheeks, the pain and horror and care. Earlier I spoke of the plebes, of the survivors from the camp, of all they must have suffered and had to do to survive. Survival makes animals of us all, as it had made one of her.

Animals.

Monsters.

"I am Thagura," I said at last, not really thinking. *And a servant of the Emperor,* I thought. She inhaled sharply, as if slapped, and I amended, "I am all Thagura has."

"Mother Earth rot your bones, Lord Marlowe," she hissed, and spat again between us. "You'll sit here one day. Right here. For just such a sin as mine." She slapped the bed beside her. "I pray you lose everything, too. Your world, your people, that little witch who's wrapped you round her finger. Everything. And I pray you have as self-righteous a judge."

I might have struck her then, and it would have felt like righteousness. But I knew that it was not. She was beaten, and having no venom left to sting, still bit. Having no reply or comfort for her, I could only smile. But it was the broken, crooked smile of House Marlowe, and no comfort at all.

My fist was raised to bang upon the door by the time she called out, "Lord Marlowe!"

I froze. "What?"

"How did you know? Know that the Cielcin were starving?"

So simple a question at the end of so much talk. I struggled not to laugh, and pounded on the bulkhead all the same. The door slid smoothly up and open an instant later, and the two guards peered in through blank masks. "I asked them," I said shortly. "They told me."

Gadar Malyan *almost* snorted. "And you believed them?"

There was nothing left to say.

CHAPTER 9
. . . AND THE EMPEROR IS FAR AWAY

⚜

Dry as Thagura was, there were but few clouds in her sky. Perhaps a week had passed since my meeting with the baroness in her cell, during which time I had met with Lady Donauri, the archon of Iudha who had survived the siege. It had taken much to convince her of the truth: even the baroness's confession to me seemed not to convince her, and there had been such love for Gadar Malyan before. But Thagura was not the same world it had been—would never be the same again, though new life would grow and rebuild.

You can never step in the same river twice, nor upon the same planet. Time, Ever-Fleeting—as I have often reflected—flows in but one direction, and it is not *back.*

At length, Donauri agreed to rule on Thagura in our absence, pending the arrival of Imperial troops from Marinus or elsewhere. Unto her would be given the survivors of Malyan's court, and unto her would fall the decision of what to do with them. Let her sift the lambs from the goats, let her determine who else was guilty, and how. I had a different destiny, would have to answer to Imperial command on Marinus in my time. Standing in the ruined square, I told myself that would not matter, that what I had done was just . . .

. . . and that what I must do there—that day, in that square—must be just, too.

My own men filled the plaza, formed ranks about its perimeter, lances or rifles held at rest. Faceless as they were, I felt myself almost alone in the universe. Two dozen of my officers stood in a line at my left, black-clad in their bridge coats, red berets bent over the left. Crim stood chief among them, wearing his black coat like a cape over his bright Jaddian dolman with its belt of throwing knives. Seeing me watching him, he gave a tight nod.

Valka stood to one side of the crowd, protected by my men. She did not see me looking, but looked herself back to where the shuttle carrying the baroness circled in its final descent. Seeing it, the gathered Thagurans—survivors from the camp, Siva among them; men and women up from Iudha; and some of the courtiers who had endured in Malyan's bunker. These seemed even more remote to me than the faceless soldiery, almost members of another species.

My men had toiled the previous night to erect something like a scaffold. Thagura had little wood, and so they'd lashed a number of supply crates together to make a kind of stage in the center of the plaza. Their black faces gleamed dully in the colorless light, and I could feel the faint heat of them through my boots. The day was warm, was likely to grow warmer, and dressed in my tunic and trousers—without my armor's cooling suite—I experienced Thagura as never before. Dry and hot, the air leeched the moisture from my face, and the wind snapped at my hair.

"Not long now," Pallino said, speaking from my shoulder. "Bressia says they've landed."

I raised a hand for quiet. I did not trust myself to speak.

I had killed before, in battle and in duels, but I had never once performed an execution. Though I had spent the night contemplating the possibility of my own death in the morning, I had never been made to pause and ruminate upon the death of another. Almost I wished to trade places with the baroness. She at least would not have to live with the consequences of what she had done.

The old systems of democracy and parliament only allowed the cowards to hide. My father's words floated at me from childhood, from another world. Those old systems had killed bloodlessly, painlessly, by bureaucracy, as the kings of the Golden Age killed by the servants. I knew I could not, and touched the hilt of sword where it waited, to reassure myself that it was still there.

At the entrance to the square, Oro sounded his trumpet, a deceptively bright and airy sound. Three long notes he sounded. Three to mark the arrival of the baroness and her escort.

Oro fell silent as my guards brought her forth. They *had* shackled her for the occasion, and she wore still the burgundy fatigues—without emblem or device—of a common soldier. But her hair was clean again and brushed over one shoulder, running like spilled ink, and her eyes— as dark—were fixed on some point beyond human seeing, somewhere on the Rock above, where the graven images of her ancestors looked down and shouldered the shattered legacy of their house.

We have to show the people we are people, not some abstraction. It was like Father stood beside me, a hand on my shoulder. How I'd hated him then. How I understand him now, as I had tried to teach the baroness.

It is by the sword we rule.

It was by the sword I ruled Thagura then, if only for one more day, would be by the sword that Sirvar Donauri must rule the survivors in Iudha and retake her world, as I had taken it from the Cielcin. It would be a long campaign, but there was order at the end, order and life again. And peace, if not the peace I'd sought as a boy.

Which ancient god was it who said he brought not peace, but the sword?

Is it not oft true that peace comes only after the sword is drawn and bloodied?

So it has been for me.

An eerie silence played over the square as bright-haired Lieutenant Bressia led Gadar Malyan to the platform on which Pallino and stood. No true silence, for a murmur of dry words floated on the air, carried by the stiff breeze. Though my men all were silent, the Thagurans shifted and whispered, elbowing one another, jostling that each might get a better look at his lord.

"My lady!" one cried aloud, and turning I saw a hand upraised. "Lady Malyan!"

"Lady Malyan!" another shouted, drawing her gaze, too.

"Is it true?" A woman's voice rose up. "Is it true what they say?"

The baroness did not answer, but turned her face away.

At a sign from one of the officers, Oro sounded his horn once more, a brief flurry of notes calling for the attention of all gathered. Fresh silence fell, and turning from the baroness, I raised my voice to be sure all gathered might hear. "In the name of His Imperial

Radiance, William XXIII of the Aventine House, Firstborn Son of Earth, I, Hadrian of the House Marlowe-Victorian, a Royal Knight and Servant of our Honorable Caesar, have declared that for the high crimes of genocide and of treason against sacred humanity, the Lady Gadar Malyan VII, Baroness of Thagura and Archon of Pseldona Prefecture, shall die this day by the sword."

The words belonged to some other man, were spoken in some other voice. A voice that sounded so very like my father's. If I try, I can almost hear it now, can remember the flat echoes rebounding from the crumbling facades of the buildings all around, can feel the uneasy shifting of the crowd.

As in antiquity, the firing squad and the noose were common ways to die and so tradition demanded that all palatines die by beheading. That same tradition—codified in the Chantry's Index of law—specified that the sword should be not highmatter, but polished zircon, a white ceramic blade lighter than water and sharp almost as highmatter itself. I met a student of the law once who told me that the Chantry Synod had decreed it so because highmatter required no skill to cut, and the death of any great lord should be a ritual undertaken with the utmost care. The carnifex should have been a cathar of the Chantry, a man trained in the arts of death.

But there were no such students in the throng.

"Is it true?" a new voice called out, and I could not find the speaker.

"It isn't right!" another shouted. "You are a knight, and she a lady! By what right do you judge her?"

"By this!" I called in answer, snapping the hilt of my

sword free from my belt. I raised the Jaddian weapon high for all to see. "And by her own words! She has confessed her crimes! It was by her command that this city and its millions burned! She sought to save herself, in the hope that by burning Pseldona, she might encourage the enemy to move on! It did not work, and even if it had, it would not have worked for the millions dead here."

The strength of my words seemed to still their objections a moment, and so I pressed on. I did not anticipate a riot, but I needed to keep control of the crowd, and so I moved to the edge of the makeshift platform, sword unkindled in my hand. The wind tousled my hair and my cape and pulled at the red aiguillettes pinned at my shoulder. "The Cielcin are gone. I pray they will not return. But Thagura is yours, is *ours,* is man's once more! You must rebuild your world, but you cannot do so under the command of this!" I pointed at the silent Baroness. "Eight million people lived in this city. *Four million people,* and she killed them."

So many. So few when measured against the billions my own actions would one day claim.

So very few.

"The sun is high," I almost murmured, and turned to look at Gadar Malyan, "and the Emperor is far away. But I am his servant, and in his name I will not leave this world in the hands of its greatest criminal. My Red Company sails tomorrow, and your world will pass into the stewardship of Lady Donauri, who has safeguarded many among you for so long already." I gestured to the archon— an older woman with hair like spun steel and a face like old porcelain—who stood impassively. I had shown her

Malyan's confession, and she had believed. "We will not return, but the Emperor's justice—which I do here today—*has* returned."

"Is it true, my lady?" a familiar voice cried out then, breaking the stiff silence that followed my pronouncement. "Say it is not true!"

Gadar Malyan bowed her head and did not speak, though we had not gagged her. Turning, I signaled that she should be brought forward to the emptied munitions box my men had erected to form a block. I faced her then, the baroness bracketed by her two guards. Those black eyes found my face and iced over.

"We have no chanter on our ship," I said, "no priest. But I will have my men light the prayer lanterns for you, ladyship."

Her lips curled. "You pretend to care about my soul? Another courtesy for a lady?"

"Yes," I said. I did not then and do not now believe the Chantry's teachings, but I was not without succor for her in those final moments. "It does not end here, you know?"

"What?"

"There is . . . more. After."

Malyan only blinked at me. Those were early days, and the story of Hadrian the Halfmortal had not yet spread across the galaxy. She did not know it, did not know that I had died and come again. "What are you talking about?"

"Death is not the end, my lady," I said, and found as I spoke the words that I could not explain them. It was as though my tongue would not obey. And so I swallowed, recalling for myself the Howling Dark beyond death, the warmth and light I'd felt as I journeyed down toward the hidden light at the end. I could not share it with her. It was not mine to share. At length I found my rebel tongue again, and gesturing to the block, I said, "Kneel."

She did not, not at once, but raised her chin, defiant.

I circled round to the side of the makeshift block, giving the nod that brought one of my guardsmen's lances into the back of her knee. She fell gracelessly to the platform. I caught her wince as her knees took the impact, and the lashed crates beneath us shook. She raised her head, faced her people behind the lines of my men. "What I did," she cried aloud, "I did for Thagura!"

"What you did, you did for yourself," I said flatly, and kindled my sword.

The blade shone pale and very fine in the colorless light of that foreign star, too beautiful to be what she was. I raised her then, gesturing with the weapon. "Bow your head."

The baroness turned to look up at me, eyes hard and wild. "You'll lose everything, too," she said. "One day. You'll have to choose as I did, and when you do, you'll see." She nodded and turned her head away, eyes sliding shut. "I did what I thought was right. You'll do the same, and then you'll be *right here* with me." She squared her shoulders.

Often I have found that god puts truth in the mouths of our enemies, for their words are the only ones we ever truly heed.

"It will be cleaner," I said, not rising to the bait, "if you bow your head."

"Earth and Emperor damn you," she said, and bent her neck.

I stood over her, my shadow falling across her and the block as the crossing of a moon blackens the sun. I can say at least I did not hesitate with the eyes of so many on me. I raised my sword and—doing so—blackened her sky forever.

ABOUT THE AUTHORS

TIM AKERS was born in deeply rural North Carolina, the only son of a theologian, and the last in a long line of telephony princes, tourist trap barons, and gruff Scottish bankers. He moved to Chicago for college and stayed to pursue his lifelong passion for apocalyptic winters and traffic. He lives with his incredibly patient wife, and a nearly unmanageable collection of plastic miniatures.

SUSAN R. MATTHEWS was raised in a military family and spent her younger years living around the globe in a myriad of places including Germany, both coasts of the U.S., and India. Often cut off from television and other media, she read voraciously. Her first encounters with science fiction came via classics such as *I, Robot* and *Stranger in a Strange Land*. Matthews's debut novel, *An Exchange of Hostages*—the first entry in her critically acclaimed Under Jurisdiction series—was nominated for the Philip K. Dick Award. Matthews was also a finalist for the John W. Campbell Award for best new writer. Matthews lives in Seattle with her wife, Maggie, and two delightful dogs. She is a veteran of the U.S. Army, where she served as operations and security officer of a combat support hospital. She is also an avid ham radio operator.

D.J. ("Dave") BUTLER grew up in swamps, deserts,

and mountains. After messing around for years with the practice of law, he finally got serious and turned to his lifelong passion of storytelling. He now writes adventure stories for readers of all ages, plays guitar, and spends as much time as he can with his family. He is the author of *City of the Saints*, *Rock Band Fights Evil*, *Space Eldritch*, and *Crecheling* from WordFire Press, and *Witchy Eye*, *Witchy Winter* and *Witchy Kingdom* from Baen Books. Read more about Dave and his writing at *http://davidjohnbutler.com*, and follow him on Twitter: @davidjohnbutler.

Amazon bestselling author **L.J. HACHMEISTER** writes and fights—although she tries not to do them at the same time. L.J. is a world champion stick-fighter, a black belt in Doce Pares Eskrima and Taekwondo, and a purple belt in Brazilian jiu jitsu, but maintains that no opponent is as daunting as the last 30 percent of a manuscript. L.J. is a cross-genre author under the umbrella of science fiction/fantasy. Her Cuban roots and LGBTQA+ ties greatly impact her writing, as well as her career as a registered nurse. However, her love for rescuing puppies and working with other animal charity organizations drives her passion to succeed as an author so she can continue to give to animals in need. L.J. is an avid sponsor of Lifeline Puppy Rescue. Connect with L.J. at *www.triorion.com*.

JODY LYNN NYE lists her main career activity as "spoiling cats." When not engaged upon this worthy occupation, she writes fantasy and science fiction books and short stories.

At science fiction conventions over the last thirty or so years, Jody has taught in numerous writing workshops and participated on hundreds of panels covering the subjects of writing and being published. In 2016, Jody joined the judging staff of the Writers of the Future contest, the world's largest science fiction and fantasy writing contest for new authors. Jody lives in the northwest suburbs of Atlanta with her husband, Bill Fawcett—a writer, game designer, military historian, and book packager—and three feline overlords: Athena, Minx, and Marmalade.

JESSICA CLUESS is the author of the young adult fantasy trilogy Kingdom on Fire and the House of Dragons duology. A graduate of Northwestern University and the Clarion Writers Workshop, she lives in Los Angeles.

SIMON R. GREEN has spent most of his life in the small country town of Bradford-on-Avon, the last Celtic town to fall to the invading Saxons in 504 AD. He has committed series several times, including Deathstalker, Nightside, Secret Histories, Ghost Finders, the Ishmael Jones mysteries, and the Gideon Sable caper novels. All told, he has written seventy novels, two collections of short stories, and one film, *Judas Ghost*. He has also worked as an actor, journalist, shop assistant, and bicycle repair mechanic. He once wrestled a ghost. Yes, really.

R.R. VIRDI is a two-time Dragon Award finalist and a Nebula Award finalist. He is the author of two urban fantasy series: The Grave Report, and The Books of Winter. One of his short stories was part of a collection of artists' works to go to the moon aboard the Astrobotic Peregrine Lunar Lander in 2021. Should the writing gig not work out, he aims to follow his backup plan and become a dancing shark for a Katy Perry music video.

ANTHONY MARTEZI is a blessed husband, newly minted father, and the great-grandson of four immigrant families from Greece, Turkey, and Lithuania. He obtained his degree in Creative Writing, with a minor in Classics, from North Carolina State University. When not traipsing about Tennessee's Great Smoky Mountains or North Carolina's Blue Ridge and coastal region with his adventurous wife, he enjoys swimming, playing viola decently, painting poorly, and chanting at church. Very unfortunately, he also is a Pittsburgh Pirates fan until death's sweet embrace takes him.

PETER FEHERVARI is a freelance television editor who dabbles in writing whenever the sullen spectres of reality and sanity misalign to permit such madness. By fate or fortune, if indeed there is a difference, he has served as a scribe for the Black Library for over a decade, carving out an eclectic—some might say heretical—niche in the *Warhammer 40K* mythos. His stories, informally known as The Dark Coil, include four novels and a dozen shorts that are reputedly grimmer, darker, and stranger than most tales of that war-torn dystopia. He wouldn't have it any other way, even if it consigns him to the shadows, where only the lost linger to listen. "Bleeding from Cold Sleep" is his first foray beyond the walls of the Black Library. As within, so without.

T.C. McCARTHY is an award-winning and critically acclaimed Southern author whose short fiction has appeared in *Per Contra: The International Journal of the Arts, Literature and Ideas*, *Story Quarterly*, and *Nature*. His debut science fiction trilogy, *Germline*, *Exogene*, and *Chimera*, was released in 2011 and 2012 to critical acclaim. In addition to being an author, T.C. is a PhD scientist, a Fulbright Fellow, and a Howard Hughes Biomedical Research Scholar who served as a weapons expert in the CIA during Operations Enduring Freedom and Iraqi Freedom. He has neither been fired on nor fired a shot in anger, but is a recognized expert in future warfare who has been invited multiple times by USSOCOM to speak on the topic of future warfare.

CHRISTOPHER RUOCCHIO is the award-winning author of The Sun Eater, a space opera fantasy series, and the former Junior Editor at Baen Books, where he edited several anthologies. His work has also appeared in Marvel Comics. He is a graduate of North Carolina State University, where he studied English Rhetoric and the Classics. Christopher has been writing since he was eight and sold his first novel, *Empire of Silence*, at twenty-two. His books have appeared in five languages. Christopher lives in Raleigh, North Carolina, with his wife, Jenna.

Christopher Ruocchio
Editor Par Excellence

"... spectacular space battles and alien contacts ... themes of military ethics, the uses of artificial intelligence, and the limits of the capacity of the human mind. ... it is the human interactions and decisions that ultimately drive the stories. ... will appeal to fans of military and hard science fiction and any readers fascinated by the possibilities of space travel." —*Booklist* on *Star Destroyers*

Sword & Planet
TPB: 987-1-9821-9214-3 • $16.00 US / $22.00 CAN – Coming Summer 2022!
Science fiction? Fantasy? Swords *and* blasters? Is it too much to ask for it all? Here are stories not where magic is science, but *with* magic and science. Enjoy original tales from Tim Akers, Jessica Cluess, L.J. Hachmeister, and more.

Edited with Tony Daniel
Star Destroyers
TPB: 978-1-4814-8309-4 • $16.00 US / $22.00 CAN
MM: 978-1-9821-2414-4 • $7.99 US / $10.99 CAN
In space, size matters! Boomers. Ships of the Line. Star Destroyers. The bigger the ship, the better the bang. Big, bold, and edge-of-your-seat original space opera and military science fiction from David Drake, Sharon Lee & Steve Miller, Michael Z. Williamson, and many more.

World Breakers
TPB: 978-1-9821-2551-6 • $16.00 US / $22.00 CAN
MM: 978-1-9821-9206-8 • $8.99 US / $11.99 CAN
Brute force. Intransigent defiance. Adamantine will. These are the hallmarks of the AI tank. But are we humans worthy of the extraordinary instruments of war that we have created? Original stories of world breakers and world makers from David Weber, Larry Correia, Wen Spencer, and more.

Edited with Hank Davis
Space Pioneers
MM: 987-1-9821-9230-3 • $7.99 US / $10.99 CAN
Your future is in space! Enjoy stories from classic and contemporary masters that explore the wide-open frontier that awaits humanity when we take to the stars. Explore with David Drake, Sarah A. Hoyt, Theodore Sturgeon, and more.

Overruled
TPB: 978-1-9821-2450-2 • $16.00 US / $22.00 CAN
MM: 978-1-9821-9206-8 • $8.99 US / $11.99 CAN

Order in the court! A new anthology of classic science fiction stories that explores what the future of jurisprudence might well be like, with thrilling, hilarious, and downright entertaining results! With stories by Robert A. Heinlein, Larry Correia, Clifford D. Simak, Sarah A. Hoyt, and more.

Cosmic Corsairs
TPB: 978-1-9821-2478-6 • $16.00 US / $22.00 CAN
MM: 978-1-9821-2569-1 • $8.99 US / $11.99 CAN

Space pirates: the phrase conjures up rousing tales of adventure, derring-do, and brave heroes battling the scurvy vermin of the galaxy. Join an award-winning crew featuring Robert Silverberg, Elisabeth Bear and Sarah Monette, Larry Niven and more, and set sail—er, thrusters—for a universe of freebooting adventure!

Time Troopers
TPB: 978-1-9821-2603-2 • $16.00 US / $22.00 CAN

Battlezone: Eternity. Once, military actions were entirely two-dimensional, confined to the surface of land and sea, but then submarines and aircraft added a third dimension, vastly extended by spaceflight. Now a fourth dimension has become possible. With the introduction of time travel, a battle that was once a decisive victory may be refought. Classic stories by Robert Silverberg, Poul Anderson, Fritz Leiber, and more.

Edited with Sean CW Korsgaard
Worlds Long Lost
TPB: 978-1-9821-9230-3 • $16.00 US / $22.00 CAN – Coming Fall 2022!

The world is older and more alien than we can ever understand. We are not alone, and the farther we push into the universe, the more obvious it becomes. These stories explore the ruins of lost civilizations, solve ancient mysteries . . . and awaken horrors from beyond the dawn of time. Featuring original stories by Orson Scott Card, Griffin Barber, Adam Oyebanji, and more.

Available in bookstores everywhere.
Or order ebooks online at www.baen.com.